A TINY UPWARD SHOVE

A TINY UPWARD SHOVE

MELISSA CHADBURN

Farrar, Straus and Giroux ❦ New York

Farrar, Straus and Giroux
120 Broadway, New York 10271

Printed in the United States of America
First edition, 2022

Library of Congress Cataloging-in-Publication Data
Names: Chadburn, Melissa, 1976– author.
Title: A tiny upward shove / Melissa Chadburn.
Description: First edition. | New York : Farrar, Straus and Giroux, 2022.
Identifiers: LCCN 2021053954 | ISBN 9780374277758 (hardcover)
Subjects: LCSH: Victims of crimes—Fiction. | Pickton, Robert William—Fiction. | LCGFT: Biographical fiction. | Novels.
Classification: LCC PS3603.H325 T56 2022 | DDC 813/.6—dc23/eng/20211105
LC record available at https://lccn.loc.gov/2021053954

Designed by Abby Kagan

www.fsgbooks.com
www.twitter.com/fsgbooks • www.facebook.com/fsgbooks

10 9 8 7 6 5 4 3 2 1

For Jaimie,
my king,
my queen,
my lion,
my familiar

A TINY UPWARD SHOVE

TINIKLING—DOUBLE DUTCH FILIPINX STYLE

Don't believe anyone who tells you that death comes quick and painless. That's bullshit. Dying hurts like fuck-all everything; you can feel all the pains, the hurts, the joys, the cries of all the world. There's no numbing dope, no dick wows, no kitty kitty yum yum, just a floodlight on all the world's needs. Death is a dump. You see it all: kids, parents, teachers, the rats under the street that run through the sewers, suck suck squeak squeak, the pigeons that shit everywhere, the throwaways nobody else wants, the thugs, the queers, the hoes, the junkies, the brats, the fuck-ups, the killers. Let me get this straight, the way I'm telling you any of this: I'm Aswang. And I know about the slow agonies of death because this body belonged to one of the throwaways—an eighteen-year-old girl named Marina—who wound up murdered on a pig farm in a place called Port Coquitlam.

Before I finished the tinikling, before I jumped into her body, before Marina found Willie on the corner of Main and Hastings, before the track marks on the insides of her knees and elbows, she lived a cleaner life. Before the late-night diner trips, where she saw, before falling into sleep, her mother's face (a face took up with large dark eyes reflecting the suspicion of others), she still hoped to be a pure spirit. Marina used to be twelve; she used to live in a group home named for trees. Five in a cottage, out in the Valley, she had the bottom bunk, and Alex on top—too close to the popcorn ceiling plastered with CK One ads torn out of fashion magazines. She used to look into people's dining rooms as she walked down the street. She put herself at one of those tables, with roasted chicken and vegetables picked from a garden, not mashed potatoes poured, flakey, out of a box, like her ma used to make, not Carnation powdered milk mixed with water (though she did like to pick out the congealed lumps and feel them separate like pudding on her tongue). She used to do graffiti on government-issued desks, waiting for her name to be called. Marina used to stand around with teenage boys on the street corner, waiting for the light to change. She used to hitch rides through the Valley and give strange men hand jobs for twenty bucks. Marina used to worry about gonorrhea and feel like she was the worst piece of living pakshet. And before all that, Marina used to be five. She used to lie on her tummy, a thumb plunked in her mouth, index finger curled around her nose, and sometimes Mutya would come in and rub her back and tell her a story of a time long long before. Marina used to leave a small music box outside in the rain, hoping to attract fairies. She used to practice kissing girls on the back of her hand or her own shoulder just to see what her skin tasted like. She used to get all squirmy and thrilled watching whodunits with her ma. She used to long for the ordinary.

She used to live with just Ma, and they might've been poor, but they had a good time. Their homemade games were sometimes

Reena running out to the garage behind the apartment building and picking up the water hose. She'd learned how to spray the water so it swooshed up toward the sky and back down like her own private waterfall. Then she ran around the apartment shouting bam be bi bo bu. A pillowcase, her white wings, tied around her neck. Her childlike chatter so candid and fresh, and right then, she figured she was the luckiest girl alive.

This man who strangled Marina was a pakshet trick who didn't know how to be a trick—always fell in love with the wrong girl. Pure PoCo trash, drove around Vancouver in his van loaded with possibilities. To him, women like Marina were nothing but a reminder of all his failings.

There in that room, leaning above her, his closed smile turned into a full-on cheese. There were his rotted teeth, his puffy gray gums. And for a split moment, for the final time in her throwaway life, she felt her mithiin. That exquisite pain of Want. Desire. But Want is for the living, and by that dark barely morning hour, Marina was already near dead.

As he throttled her, she felt her own muffled sounds push into the part of her that had been sleeping, cut off a long time ago. Her screams clung to that hollowed-out part, to her guts, to the trailer walls, then zipped along the hot gas of the cosmos as the dark stone sky settled over the farm.

The moment she was dying, Marina prayed. First, she prayed an invocation. Something she'd heard her lola say over and over again. *Let light stream forth into the minds of men. Let love stream forth into the hearts of men. Let purpose guide the little wills of men. Let the Plan of Love and Light work out. And may it seal the door where evil dwells.*

She thought of her lola's cool hands on her burning forehead when she was stuck home sick.

Mounted on the wall above them was the head of a golden horse. Marina stared deep into the dark nostrils of the horse. Her murderer straddled her on top of the bed, his hands clasped around her neck. The face he showed her, the face that was breathing hard, placed no more than a foot from her own, was stuck in a tight grin. The face of an oink-oink baboy. The pigs he farmed. Both of them drenched in the toxic effect of all the sorrow coursing from his hands to her neck. From her neck to his hands.

The smudges of smoke on the walls, the dark corners of the ceiling. A wisp of spider's web in the corner. Of the nostril. Of the head. Of the horse.

Her lola's prayer wasn't working. Lola belonged to a generation of obedience and atonement; Marina's was a generation of don't-give-a-fucks. So she made a special kind of prayer: Marina imagined hipon wrapped in taro leaves, stewed in chilés and coconut milk. She imagined a small loaf of sticky rice with mango. Flyswatters, brown rubber discs used to open jars, large wooden utensils hanging from a kitchen wall, bamboo mats painted with anthuriums. The mats that she slept on in her lola's ranch house in Seaside, California. She thought of Alex, the love of her life, and her perfect eyeliner, how it made her look elegant, like the flawless face of a calculating wife.

This prayer didn't work either, if working means saving her from death. But the prayer did work, if working means turning her into me, into something powerful, into Aswang. The truth in the prayer summons the aswang first by bringing up her ancestral bloodline. And then the key, to tying me to her? Unfinished business. Marina was murdered midquest. She chanted this mantra in her mind over and over, pulling me out of the ether and down into her body. Merging with the powers that carry me across time into generations of her family. The words spread out around her, invaded her ears, her mouth, until the sound of her scream became me.

A parade of poplar fluff floats by, silent and weightless as air. The light weaves its way through the branches, makes the shape of a small bird, then an owl, then a crane, and then comes apart again. The trees against the dark sky look like veins.

Marina fell through the crack between the world you know and the worlds you do not know. Then it became my turn to tinikling. I dove in, skimmed across the bottom surface, the moon making a diamond-shaped pattern that danced across the floor, I pushed up and permeated Marina's howl. The noise of our scream so thick in what were newly my ears that I couldn't even hear it. The scream started in my stomach, and then rose up to my chest, throat, banged against my teeth, the trees, and tops of buildings. It grew louder and flew into the atmosphere. It grew and grew and grew, the intensity bursting like a dark shrill rainbow. Other cries joined mine—an orchestra of screams—until I no longer felt like a dying person. I was beside a plane in the sky. The moon above, then vultures, then sky. It felt like erupting from a safe, dark place into the unknown. Leaving a matinee, the anonymous dark comfort of the sinehan on a summer afternoon, unclasping a lola's hand at the gates of school, the cloth book offered by the social worker at the county hospital being torn away. Booted out of a mother's womb—the source of nourishment and life, buhay, a soft string of molecules, the final small cord that keeps you tethered and rooted to the only other world you knew. The scraping on my now skin, like a thousand angry gnats.

I passed through the doorway and stepped into Marina's life.

The body of a woman Marina saw a half a dozen times walking the ho-track had been thrown across what was formerly Marina's back, now mine, facedown, the woman's head resting on my shoulder. Another woman's body was across my legs, her breast pushing into my feet—I felt someone's thick Tootsie Roll nipple against my toes. Worms sliding beside my cheeks, my mouth, my legs, my hair. Darkness closed around us; nearby, I heard pig snorts.

This was the pig trough, where Willie stored the bodies, fed them off to the pigs before he took the final remains to the Waste Redux, a plant that sorts through and repurposes waste. Animal parts ground up, moved into deep fat fryers and cooked until the grease could be separated. The mud on the ground below us was rich and cold. I slithered out from between the bodies. I crouched low—careful not to disturb a nearby gang of pigs, the largest one in a deep sleep, looking as if she were running a race, rocking back and forth, spewing out barking farting um-otot noises. I crawled my way into the forest that emerged behind Willie's house.

At first, it seemed I was surrounded by fireflies; tiny lights danced in and around my face. Then I had that sketchy masamang feeling of being watched, and the sky darkened. The dancing lights took on the shapes of women. The forest next to Willie's farm in PoCo filled with them, all around me, a kutra of spirits, not just his women but all of the women who have gone missing, throwaway women, murdered women. I recognized one of them—a junkie whose face was plastered all around the WISH Drop-In Centre. There, her junkie face looked wet and warbling like a poached egg, and now here her face was fresh like one of those ladies on a soap commercial. She looked at me before she closed her winter-colored eyes, and she was so palaisip, so wistful; to look at her made me feel like I swallowed all the broken windows.

The faces of these women, these spirits turned to trees, their hands to leaves, their arms to branches. And it's here in this too-late time, where, as trees grow all janky and twisted—we aswang know—they aren't destroyed by grief but are made special by it. It's the *story* they tell.

I see the inside of the body, mind, and spirit of the woman who was once called Marina. I am filled with visions of joy and beauty, happiness, a piece of throbbing thunderous music like the sea, growing louder and louder and louder. Something bounced up and down and flitted against my insides. I did not recognize it, though it reminded me of many sensations I have stopped feeling. That constant achy itch to use drugs, the desire to eat or pee or sleep. I do not feel these. But this sensation in my belly creates an aggravating hunger, a tiny ringing noise, Popsicles on front teeth, nails on chalkboards, then blossoms into something all-consuming, a torn Achilles' tendon, maggots in ears, a traveling itch—a Need. I thought of every small thing, everything this body had experienced, felt, smelled, everything Marina might be hungry for. But none of them appealed. Then a glimmer. I need to close my jaw around his neck. I need to sink my teeth into his skin. I need to taste that raunchy yellow man who killed Marina. I can think of nothing more than filling my belly with his cowering body, to swallow all the parts of him, his toes, his feet, his thighs, his dwindling dingle dangle buto. This is not a hunger Marina ever felt. I am not Marina Salles anymore, no Blackapina foster girl. I am Aswang. And this is a hunger only we vengeful feel.

Pulsing through the trees, I heard their voices: Anita killed by Willie's bare hands; Jordan strangled with a belt around her neck;

and Elaine, her final breath on a slaughtering hook. Together they whispered plots and plans. *You could get him in his sleep. You could get him on the road. You could pluck off his toenails, carve off his eyelids, make him watch, make him cry, make him beg. You could get him on the farm, with the pigs, with his brother, with the motorcycle guys, with a hammer, with a knife, with a needle, an infected needle, left to always wonder. Getimgetimgetim*, a schoolyard chant, pushing me on all sides.

I turned and looked back to the farm, to where we all came from. I saw a pile of missing women's parts. What Willie thinks is Marina's hand, some other throwaway's black fingernails, muddied cuticles, the putrid smell of rot, the hair, the flesh, then meat, then bone. The flow of blood, our blood, the missing women, thickened, oozing down the sides of trees, a vicious sap.

THE LOLAS

I hear an echo from Lola Virgie's kitchen . . . Lola sitting at a doily-covered table, marmalade on her cheek, holding court with all the other lolas. They appear like twelve girls dressed in white, with crowns of flowers, their hair in curls, their faces bright. They seem like little genies of light. Across the table, they clutch pan de sals like the bright blue ribbons tied to the Virgin's cart. Atop the table are colored glass jars of various local fruit preserves. On the patio outside the window, chicks peep, hens cluck, pigs grunt. We are in the middling place, the stranger, the foreigner, the friend, the enemy, the Filipino, the Spaniard, the pauper, the rich man, their place of prayer, where there's still the possibility, where they can merge happy and satisfied.

All the lolas have a different story about the aswang. Jasmine's lola, like most grandmothers, connects it all back to The Man. She said when The Man first came to the Philippines, he did not know what to make of the independence of a Filipina woman. He didn't understand that she could take several lovers or none. That she could be the provider in the household. That she had all the healing powers. She said the story of the aswang starts with a woman who feels a strong passion, usually for a pakshet man, and who is brokenhearted. This passion is like Hudas. God knows Hudas does not pay. The pain is so strong it actually tears her in two: the lower half of her body on the ground, her torso and head free to float about and ravage the city.

Ligaya's lola said the aswang was half pig, half woman. She could be hiding in any living thing—able to read a child's thoughts, live in the bodies of animals, the shapeshifter, steal away your spirit at night. An aswang is all things, she used to say. Her people are from the western side of the Visayan province of Panay, where if you ask children what an aswang looks like, they will twist and quake and wrench themselves into strange positions as they walk. They are imitating a brown-skinned man, with bones poking against his skin, and hollowed cheeks, who once wobbled about nearby. He had a disease that makes men twist and turn with uncontrollable fits. The only time his muscles relaxed was when he was sleeping. The only time he felt relief was in his dreams.

Nelly's lola said to beware of older women who live alone. She herself was an older woman who lived alone. She said if a woman has a large mole or keeps too much to herself, she is likely aswang. Basically, any woman who was having too much fun without the responsibility of other people, especially if she was luka-luka, occasionally her eyes rolling every which wild way.

Marina's lola told a story of fraternal twins, a beautiful young girl and a strong boy, who were living with their auntie in a village where all the farm animals were being hunted by the aswang. The villagers knew it was just a matter of time before the aswang would get hungry enough to eat the little children. Especially a young girl as maganda as the sister; Lola warned pretty girls are always in danger. Whenever someone called Marina maganda, a smile on their face, their voice pitched up in admiration, stroking her curls, she'd hear the echo of this story. The boy disobeyed the aunt and snuck away from home so he could hunt the aswang. The boy knew he should watch out for the aswang coming disguised as a large rat, where he would see his own reflection upside down in the rat's eyes. One day he did find that rat and stabbed it in the leg with his ginunting sword and ran home. The next morning, their auntie appeared in the kitchen, and a slip of her robe revealed a bloodied mangled arm.

Kitoy's lola reported the aswang was an old woman, and then other times, they thought she looked like a big boar with the back shiny like a June bug. Victor's lola reported that the aswang appeared as a perfect young child, cheeks sticky with sweet milk, to lure the other children.

The only one who got it right was the espiritista.

There are three ways to become an aswang.

The first is with fertilized eggs: You hold a fertilized egg against your belly and tie it in place with a cloth. After the new moon, the chicken from the egg will pass into your stomach. There's some stuff you have to do with the eggshell beforehand, make a powder out of it, and mix it with coconut oil and chicken shit. If the timing is right, you can also take two fertilized eggs to the cemetery after Good Friday. Gaze directly at the full moon, place an egg under your armpit, and mumble some top secret words three times.

The second way to become aswang is by transmission. For transmission, a person who is of aswang lineage must be willing to give up their immortality, by granting it to another. This is usually by way of some kind of sexy time; while kissing, the person who has the aswang spirit breathes it into the other.

The third way is heredity. Once the aswang has entered a family line, she can be passed on through heredity for seven generations.

The aswang is only activated within a lineage when someone has died with unfinished business. Maybe she has to avenge the death of another, maybe she has yet to complete some mission, a gift that she has that she was not yet able to share with others. In order to stay aswang, she must eat the flesh of another. In order to detach from that family line and move on, she must complete the duties of aswang—she must finish what the mortal host began, yet it cannot be anything she began, it must be her most *pressing thing, the thing most heavy on her heart.*

This is my final round in this pakshet place. My last tour with the women in this family. Seven generations of duty, love, and magic.

MARIA LOBO

In the Beginning was Maria Lobo. I arrived to the women in this family in 1742. The Philippines was all hiss and screech, fighting and praying, and the muffled screams of women in bushes. Men pushing their weight on them. *Saving them,* they said. Over and over again. Until Hail Mary became the call of rape. Hail Mary Full of Grace. It was a cry for help and then a mantra and then a chant to transport you somewhere else.

Smoke and too much hot sun and people who were all terribly dry-tongued and hunger and death and all the usual diseases brought over by ship to the small island. Maria Lobo, Marina's great-great-great-great-great-great-lola. Maria lived there in a small hut, ignoring her children, saying snappy hurtful things.

Since San Pascual did not give her parents the boy they had requested, she was given the name Maria Lobo in honor of the Virgin and Lobo, a wolf-spirit that was circling their little house—a small nest among a cover of thatch, tile, zinc, and palm—on the dark morning of her birth.

Maria Lobo was everyone's darling and grew up on smiles and

sweets pressed into her palm. Even the friars fussed when she was dressed in white for religious processions. Banana leaves, fixed to the back of her dress like silver wings, jasmine flowers woven into her hair. They loved her even though she cackled at times like a wildling . . . bam be bi bo bu. She'd run off at the friar's extended hand, rather than kiss it.

You could still see ranks of prisoners tramping along the streets of Manila. Heads shaved, they walked in tattered clothes, their legs wrapped in chains, rags tied around their joints to protect them from abrasions. Their dark faces would never see peace. Maria Lobo smiled as they passed, and they lit up for the moment. She had this kind of effect, a flash of pink among the moody trees at sunrise.

She found love and married, yet she and her husband were so poor, so strangled with need and want. They argued like a couple meaning to have sex, but then put it off for another day. She found a job helping an ugly mangled man who was rumored to be an aswang. Everyone knew exactly how to find his house, surrounded by an orchard and gardens. For Maria, everything served as a sign: a tree, tamarind, its sparse foliage, a coconut palm with nuts like Astarte, the goddess of fertility. The man was overrun with wild twitches, the evil spirits tickling him. He'd thunder and growl. His voice edged with curiosity then sarcasm then outrage. Anyone near would look away in desperation, their rescue was off on the horizon somewhere. They called him MRP—most rich property owner. A kind of demigod. Virtuous and eloquent, cultured, because of his home, his servants, he was said to have a different nature from everyone else. People felt he'd brought God to earth. That God knew who he ate and whose blood he drank and, more importantly, who he let live. People warned he was only hiring help to satisfy his hunger for human flesh, livers, and phlegm. Viscera. This was true. He himself was undying but on one condition. To remain aswang, he had to eat human flesh to stay alive.

Maria Lobo sat before him. Outside his house the land halved by a river, like a monstrous glass serpent. When she interviewed for the job, she was wearing something very modest. A thin dress. He struck fear into the hearts of men, because of his deep voice, his low-set eyes, and the way he laughed. But with Lobo, he had been soft; he appeared like a cat. She did the most endearing thing. Before he could even ask—she took a small rough cloth, wet it in lukewarm water, and wiped the dry spittle from his face, and furthermore, she pushed his bangs out of his eyes and tucked them behind his ears. She looked at him there in the eyes and smiled as if she had done this every day of her life. Maawa ka. Mercy. His face smoothed with the expression of someone who was choosing to die. He pulled her close, then closer. The MRP breathed the spell into her—his mouth on hers, his tongue searching. He was giving her the gift of eternity. Upon feeling this death moving into her, Maria screamed into the sky, howled at the moon, the weight in her heart fell to her stomach, her toes, the sound a deafening loudness, her eyes darkened with blood. Aswang. She was afraid, and yet there was something else here, a power she'd never felt before. Kalayaan. But not any kind of freedom, a freedom from caring about the judgment of others. Agency. With this agency came the loss of all she had before, the doting adoration, the way people loved her. Like they loved a doll. This was the transmission. The scream invaded her ears, her mouth, spread out around her, until the sound became me. Then she thought of food, a baboy barbecued in a pit, an apple in its mouth, turning until its skin is taut and succulent, juice bursting out its pores. Piña and lechon, and sticky rice with mango, she chanted this mantra in her mind over and over, building up a wall of words to protect her from the outer sound of her scream.

In her eyes he saw it, a flash into her past, with her hungry children and her desperate husband. A flash into her future, Maria returning to her province a wealthy woman. Even greater, she was confident. Maria, at home with her family; she threw her cigarillo out in the yard, came in, and, as she undressed, stood boldly in front of her husband. He turned his face away, shy in her presence. She'd grown muscular from the transmission, from the caretaking, taller even. She slid between the sheets on the bed, and then because everyone was still so excited for her to be back home, they kept talking. There were little blips of laughter and outside the sounds of dogs, and finally, the room fell silent, and Maria blew out the lamp. A hundred good nights were whispered. And their life couldn't have been more perfect, and her husband couldn't have held her more tightly or closely, and she breathed into his neck, and soon there were kisses, and then he was there inside of her, and she quaked on top of him like there had been no lean years.

Eventually, Maria Lobo had to flee from her home, afraid she would eat her beloved children or her beloved husband. The tsismis multiplied like winter monsoons. People talked about the time she spent with the MRP and knew she must be aswang. Her wild hair, her beady eyes. She cursed in three languages. Hijo de puta. Puki mo. Putang ina mo. Shitfucker. Mother. Whore. Coño. She was cast out and alone and hungry, and her hunger for human flesh accompanied by the intrusion of the colonizers had burned in her the impossibility of her own death. She had no destination; she just wandered, looking for nothing but other women to save. She responded to their screams, their calls, their Hail Mary mantras, and at some bend in the river, she had come across a church that was being built, and there she figured with all of her hunger, there would be men for her to eat. Horrible men, killing men, proselytizing men. The man who gave her this power never taught her how to live in the blank space between dreams and consciousness, magic and life. She could not bring herself to eat a man.

Instead of people there on the road, in front of her was a big brown bloated boar. She thought maybe she could eat this boar. She could swoop down on it, and maybe the boar's meat would gratify her. She was able to pierce the skin of the baboy and drag it to the corner, alone, and even though she killed it, it wasn't a strong enough spirit to keep her alive. Wasn't a pakshet man. In these villages, spirits shimmered among the live creatures, balanced and held by time and land.

A bright stripe flew across the dirt and over the nipa huts. Thunder rumbled so loud that they said God was writing his name with fire in the sky. It was All Saints' Eve, and here divine justice was sewn into the earth.

Her sons were seven and eight. They were trying to find sleep in their nipa hut. Their small bodies soaked in sweat. Their shirts, their shorts, crumpled at the foot of the bed. Ever since Maria Lobo left, they hated it at home without her. The food their tatay prepared for them tasted like burnt soil. And it was never enough. Why did she leave? What did they do to deserve this? Her older son drew two tropical ibons with enormous wings on the walls of the nipa hut—one for him, the other for his brother. From where she was perched, Maria Lobo closed her eyes, and there she could see the eagles her son drew. She could hear the blood glutting her sons' veins, and the hunger eating their bellies.

At dawn, Maria Lobo was wandering; jumping from nipa hut to nipa hut, she could hear the wind. She tried to find direction, tried to grasp the message in the air. A black bat flew ahead to guide her to her natural death. Either she would eat the pakshet men or she would die. In the end, she knew she was too softhearted to indulge her appetite for man. She knew she had bodily strength and control. She would not pay the price, lose all her good. The moon barely moved. By a sliver of light, she saw the darkness pulling shadows into itself, setting up magnetic whorls. Soon it would suck into her, a wind to replace the yin and yang of my aswang spirit. And there was a sound like a winter mountain air, dark pink skies—the sound

Maria made when she left this earth, a sound so high-pitched it could drive you crazy. Don't you hear it sometimes? You think it's in the wires, but it's here in the air in front of you. Lobo died, and so I remained with her family for the next six generations.

A century later, Lorenza, the wife of Jose, Maria Lobo's great-grandson, was dying. Jose worked as a laborer at the Cavite arsenal. Day in and day out soldering and hammering artillery. The governor at the time, Rafael Izquierdo, clutched tightly to his power. The engineers and laborers were exempt from paying taxes. Even though they spent their time building ammunition, it hadn't felt like war for many years.

In dim church basements, the laborers and priests began to share their concerns. Some confessed they were being forced to work overtime. Others said they overheard Izquierdo was threatening to tax them, they heard about it from their wives who went to swap at the market. They whispered and signaled plans in the workplace. After several nights of meeting—it would soon be time.

There in the basements of churches, Jose saw the shadows of his comrades, the soft ways they adjusted themselves on their seats, their muscled bodies, their tired eyes. The Seventh Infantrymen joined them, pledged their allegiance. They agreed to a takeover if Izquierdo dared tax them. Between devising plans of mutiny they brought up memories, little private gifts, slowly removed from that far back place they'd been stored. They bonded, hung their heads, grasped hands, and prayed together at the end of each meeting. Their hands made pale by forgoing meals to feed their families.

January 20, 1872, the bell rang at the end of the day, they all lined up to receive their pay, laborers, dark with soot, hands calloused, feet tender and bloated from standing. Jose and the others discovered their envelopes were thin. They were taxed not only the regular tax but a falla was applied, the fine for failing to work forced overtime. The night had come.

In January the Philippines is hot—never falls below seventy-three degrees. This night was hotter than most, forty infantry soldiers and twenty men from the artillery, including Jose, stormed Fort San Felipe, they fired cannons to let the world know they were mad as hell. They felt brave and bold and like men who were ready to tear the world apart. When they lifted the horn to their mouths and beckoned the Seventh Infantrymen to join them, there was no response. Jose felt his toes, sweating on the rock below his feet; the other men hot with sweat and angst had tied their shirts around their waists, their muscled backs, their once-tanned bodies, at once proud now overcome with fear and intimidation. The infantry soldiers began to arrive but their bayonets were raised in the air ready to attack. They'd turned, or perhaps had always been, against them. Jose and ten others ran to bolt the gates. The following morning, they were taken to prison. A week later, January 28, Jose, along with the other mutineers, was sentenced to death.

I tell you this story now so you understand what kind of blood you are dealing with. Marina's people are trudging people; they've got nothing to lose. They have all the time in the world and they just keep on pushing. This was the second time I entered this family, Jose's wife, Lorenza, distraught by his untimely death, tired, starving, forced to do the things of the day, feed their sons, wash their clothes. She could not even think of another night lying down to rest alone. No arm around her. Jose was the reward. The payoff, her husband holding her, the moon above, the dreams cloaked around them, nothing but possibility awaiting.

Upon hearing of his death Loy Loy screamed into the sky, howled at the moon, the weight in her heart fell to her stomach, her toes, the sound a deafening loudness, her eyes darkened with blood. Then she too thought of food, a thick mechado, big cubes of marinated beef, browned garlic, tangy fish sauce, rustic root vegetables, carrots, and potatoes nutty and warm, she chanted this mantra in her mind over and over, building up a wall of words to protect her from the outer sound of her scream. True, she was already dying, a slow fever brought on by the blankets from the friars, the books from the friars, the words and greed and harshness that killed her husband. The words spread out around her, invaded her ears, her mouth, until the sound became me. Here I could avenge her husband's death. Yet, like Maria Lobo, she feared she'd eat her sons to feed this ravenous malicious hunger. A hundred years of resentments boiling inside of her, flittering up and down in her belly.

And now a third time. Seven generations removed from Maria Lobo. Here I am in 1994 with eighteen-year-old Marina Salles. My first instinct after the tinikling—the painful dance from my world to hers—to go to where the hot pulse of energy is in Marina, revenge. A loud thump of electric beats in her heart—*kill the pakshet man, kill the pakshet man*—hammers hard at her soul. Yet if I pay close attention—I sense another tense beneath this, a counterbalance.

Two forces rule the universe, light and gravity—this riot in her spirit is weighing her down—the gravity to murder the murderer. If I seek further still—shake the branches in her soul—the fruit will fall. Around the bend I sense the light—like fairy dust dancing in the shadows—her quest. Maawa ka.

When I passed through the infinite thickness of time, that light force was pulling me forward. Strands of love and desire. Want is for the living. There is no question—what she wanted in that moment before her death was greater than this hunger to murder Willie.

I snuck into that pakshet's mobile home. I crept in the front door, by this time the sun had risen, I was crouched in the closet in the entranceway. I held my breath. There were footsteps in the kitchen, bare feet on the crumbly kitchen floor. I heard noises outside too, motorcycles, from across the road—the hiss of wind through the windows and vents in the floor. Our heart was loud. I steadied myself, held my breath. He took another step.

I guessed he was in the middle of the living room by now. The living room was facing the door, and on the other side of the closet was the kitchen. Willie was maybe sitting down and settling in to watch television. Maybe it wasn't even Willie. Maybe it was another girl from the Eastside. I wished I could shut up our breathing, our heartbeat.

Another step. Certain and heavy. The footsteps shifted in the direction of the closet. As he came closer, I could see the bottoms of blue jeans, the dirty bare feet, long jagged nails, maysakit yellow-white skin. I held my hand over my mouth, preparing to headbutt him with all my force should he open the closet door. He paused, and it seemed as if he looked directly at me—his gray-blue eyes. My legs were getting tired, and I accidentally shifted my weight from my right leg to my left leg. I think the coats rustled; they seemed loud. He bent down and wiggled into his shoes. He opened the door to the outside; I felt the air whoosh in. Heard him step down from the mobile home. I stayed there still in the closet listening hard for more footsteps. There were none.

An hour later, still hiding in the pakshet's mobile home, when it sounded as if the coast was clear, I slowly crept my way out of the closet into the living room. I walked low, crouched below the line of the window so no one would see me. The sun was coming up, and it glinted off the metal of Marina's inhaler beside the couch. The room was open, with no place to hide or duck. The kitchen had cupboards below the sink, but I wasn't sure I could squat down in time to tuck in there. I crept by the door but heard voices outside.

I strained to hear if they were coming or going. There was a back door to the mobile home. I could creep down the hall toward that exit. My legs were weak from standing still in the closet. I went down on my hands and knees and crawled toward the door. There was an overflowing ashtray at the foot of the couch; as the room grew brighter, I could see all the basura underneath, a couple of bottle caps, chips, pen tops.

The back door was at the end of the hallway, about forty feet away. There was a bathroom along the side of the hall. The door was closed. The back door had a slatted window with a small thin curtain hanging on it. I could see shadows flashed onto the hallway. I turned around to go back toward the front door and heard a loud crash from the bathroom.

I ran to the kitchen, still crouched low below the windows. I figured I could find a kutsilyo in there if I needed it. Even if it was dull, it was sharp enough to cut his pakshet baboy breakfast. Standing in front of the cabinet, our heart felt like a caterpillar slumbering in its cocoon. One of her memories from the previous night—she'd gone to that bathroom, sat on the toilet, and heard the same crash. There was a shower caddy, the little clear plastic suctions worn thin.

THIS IS YOUR WIFE

In 1958, Marina's lola, nineteen years old, came from the Philippines. The Philippines was and is part of something the banks refer to as the LDC—least developed countries—a little brown tropical country, sprinkled with religious fanatics, stalks of sugar like magic wands picked for five cents an hour sold for three dollars a box. Lola comes from recycled forty-ounce bottles of beer and shit and cigarettes smoked backward (the lit end in your mouth), and cassava, and ube, pickled duck fetus, and piss, and mahjong, gambling lots of gambling, and child sex workers (boys and girls). Untold numbers of pretty pretty boys.

Our people are lightbulb crunchers, bed-of-nails walkers, fire-eaters. Every day is a circus in our jungles, alive with naked intent. By the time Lola came to the States, she would be happy at any swap meet, all of us hollowed out like empty mango shells. Lola Virgie's kitchen floors were brown-and-white-diamond-checkered and lined with ants, every top drawer filled with little boxes of broken chalk for killing ants and roaches. She had big rubber flyswatters. She rested unplated sandwiches on the arms of chairs, and always had an open saucer with half-melted butter on the kitchen table, a block of Velveeta cheese in the freezer, an open rice cooker bubbling on the counter. She ate with her teeth floating in a glass of water next to her at the dinner table. Lola was short and toggled around like that bottle-cap game turumpo, broad shouldered, broad butt, big bosomy sofa of a woman—the shadow of her previous more graceful self lagging behind. She maintained perfectly manicured fingernails and was beyond denying that she was no longer thin and had never been rich.

Lola was strict and angry and never lacked for many grave reasons as to why Marina should act right. If Marina stayed out playing too late after dark, she'd call her in, warning, Don't let aswang get you. Part of Marina thought this was all just an excuse to get her to behave like the little girl she wanted her to be. But part of Marina was spooked.

She saw an aswang once in a storybook; her skin was green, her eyes long slits, her hair thick and black, and she was flying on top of a house, holding a baby perched upon a rooftop. Marina drew the aswang, paying close attention to her skeletal wings and her long flowy hair. Like my hair, Marina used to say, stroking it softly.

Hindi, Lola said, not at all. Nothing like your hair.

One day while Marina was giving Lola eyedrops for her cataracts, Lola told her how she met Lolo. Up until then, Lola mostly spoke about marriage in proverbs. She'd suck her teeth, and when Ma was struggling with patience in dating, Lola'd say, Even though the procession is long, it will still end up in church. Or if a woman on a daytime talk show was complaining about her sly man, Lola'd lecture out to her, It is hard to wake someone pretending to be asleep. She was slick with the smell of jackfruit and Oil of Olay, still trying to slide back to all her womanly needs that were flushed away by the needs of her too-soft children and her greedy husband. Lolo always wore his clothes pressed, a sharp crease down the center of his pants legs. You'd never guess that he'd sometimes throw Lola smack into the fridge, her face hitting the door handle. Or that she, every morning, dropped a pinch of ground-up ant chalk in his coffee.

The night Lola met Lolo, he was sitting in a café eating a supper of sticky rice with kare-kare. It was such a still night that the land seemed to lie open, like a woman ready to give up her puri. Lola knew when she saw him that he was not from her province. A place where the people were so poor she could not love them. The only person who could really afford to love them was O'Lord, and she surely was not O'Lord. Their love would pull her down like swamp mud. But this man she thought she could love. She was short and delicate, and her easy movements are what caught the eye of the man who gestured for her to come join him at his table. He looked kind and trusting, maybe even naïve.

She didn't know, though, that his mother was a mangkukulam. The bad kind of mangkukulam. The kind who pretend to be a doctor. His mother did not even know how to read books, but she took the money from the good people of the island of Panay in exchange for exorcisms or spiritual investigations. She would tell people if they suffered from demonic possessions or were blessed with fallen angels, forever-sweet angels not fake sweet like in the way a child is sweet when she wants something.

Lolo was an only child in a remote village at whose outer edge the Pacific surged and pounded. His mother worked from her small office at the back of the house, people coming from all over seeking remedies for broken hearts, and bad sex lives, and pains in their chest, and strange rashes. Marina's grandpa was a well-behaved boy, clever in class. He had his motley crew of friends and no enemies.

Eventually, he left school and shipped off to the army where bully boys and mild ones alike prepared for the same timid adulthood—full with hard edges but still delighted by the fresh fruit between women's legs. Lolo taught Lola about faith; she thought of Faith as a girl who's oddly pretty and always makes people wonder whether or not she's really ugly.

Then that night in the café at age twenty-eight, on his first leave from the army, he looked up from the veranda and saw Lola and her hair and her pale skin and her determined eyes and her little brush of mocha freckles across her nose and cheeks, and he thought, *Well, who is this?*

He heard a voice, a woman's voice, as sure as his drill sergeant. *This is your wife*, she said.

The two stayed up late into the night walking and talking, and then finally, at the end of the evening, he pulled her close and kissed her. His tongue thrust between her lips, and reality was a wet, thick thing alive in her mouth. The darting and wrestling of tongues, the heavy breathing, it seemed to her something that dogs might do.

Not long after that kiss she had nothing in this world but her two hands, her six children, and her crazy love for that man. He was a tyrant in the home, demanding order in the foods served, the time the foods were served, the clothes washed and starched and ironed, the creases that needed to be kept, the beds made. She even bleached and ironed the children's shoelaces, all of them hanging from the line in perfect single-file salute. Their home became cold and corporal. Lolo bopping between husband and father. He once even tried to spank Lola, put her over his knee; it felt awkward, like wearing a big hat. He seemed never to remember that night of love. Lola was persistent in finding her way back, flinging herself at him, like a bug at a flame.

After he came home to the Philippines from the military, where he'd sustained many injuries—bits of bullet on the surface of his skin—he sought help from his mother. She had him wear a belt of anting-anting around his waist. Oh, darling, no worries. It's magic, he explained to Lola. A bullet is nothing. These hollow seeds guarantee a peaceful death.

Ay! Sus! Death? Lola was shaking her fists at him.

I just need to make sure that I drink some fresh monkey's blood, and I'll be like new.

Lola went hunting for a monkey. On the way, she went to see her mother-in-law. Lola hovered in the doorway and watched her.

A small woman with a shrunken face. She had dark leathery skin that hung loose from her joints and bones. She was seeing a customer. He had a flesh wound on his hand; she'd wrapped it with a poultice of leaves and flies' eggs.

The man looked at her with the sad desperation of a hound dog as he walked out.

Lola burst into the room shouting, That man is going to lose his hand.

Her mother-in-law sucked her teeth. No—these wounds never infect because the fly eggs hatch and eat off the rot.

Lola winced as she noticed the room smelled strongly of spoiled flesh. Lola tried to breathe through her mouth. The stench putrid. She ran to the window and swallowed air from the outside.

You should be ashamed of yourself. You're killing them.

Really? What do you know? And how do you think I made a living to support us all these years? Who do you think paid for your husband to grow and be such a strong man?

Lola walked straight up to the woman and smacked her hard across the face. I'll tell you who did this, who paid for my husband

and my family; any hope we had, any way we could leave this wretched island, was not because of you but because of the U.S. Army. Tito Sam!

After a decade of marriage, they moved to California. By then, Lola concluded that love was mostly wanting something you supposedly already had. *No, don't say you love me because I want you to say it, say it because you want to say it.*

It was two decades into their marriage when Grandpa came to Lola in their little green house in Seaside. She was tired of him by then, tired of his continued dependence on his mother. She asked herself one, two, five, ten times a day, *When did I die? Why is God punishing me? Was I so cruel in my past life to deserve this?*

Sometimes, she'd joke that maybe he wasn't even really injured in the first place, just stuck on a bad acid trip from the LSD the CIA put in the Pasig River back home. Maybe she wasn't even really her and he wasn't him.

I have a pain. I need to see my mother back home, he said.

A pain? A pain? What kind of pain?

In my chest.

A pain like heart disease or a pain from your cholesterol or diabetes? Don't you know this is not something for your mother? Don't you know that drink she gave you made of horns and alcohol for libog did not do anything?

Years ago, when things had been distant between them, he had requested a special tonic that was supposed to make a man powerful in sexual matters.

Don't you know that people lose their hands and legs after seeing her?

It's true too that there is nothing more seductive to a man than a heated woman. So Grandpa took her in his arms and kissed her with his tongue and made love to her until his heart gave out completely. There may have been a time when Lola was too modest to tell this story, and while it's true Filipinos do have a lot of pride, we are far from stoic. We are never ashamed of our agonies. In fact, we broadcast them—each conversation a carnival of agonies.

I imagined what I would see if I had Willie's heart. I imagined holding it inside our body, slippery and soft, like concrete that hasn't set. I imagined the warmth of it. I closed my eyes, and then the sensations of all the things that disappeared from the night before came back to me. I have to fish for each memory, drag them up one by one, careful not to pull it all to the surface too quickly.

I can sense all the subtle, intimate things about plants and beasts, water, clouds, stars . . . I can feel the approach of wind, or a snowstorm, hours before it arrives—it's all there, imprinted in the brittle leaves, the halting pulse of the waters, the erosion in the wood planks of their cabins and park benches. On Willie's farm, a pig gave birth, and I felt it in Marina's guts. I felt it when miles away, on Vancouver's Downtown Eastside, a prostitute miscarried. In fact, on that night, in a small thatch where a Filipino cockfighter lived, fourteen eggs hatched below a hen. Fourteen blind little ogres who were gonna be legends in the sabongs. Men squatting to cock level, cigarettes stuck to their lower lips, cheering, hoping, praying, swearing. That night, they were merely needy little ogres squeaking up at their mama with their minuscule little tongues.

NOVENA

At a Filipino wake, the spirits of the dead walk amid the living, touching the food. A thumb in the pan, a petting of the mango. Titas in the kitchen talking smack. The spirits hang close to catch the tsismis: Who copied her recipe for biko? Who showed up with a black eye? Who sings like a hurt cat at the piano? Who cheats at mahjong? Where are those pearl earrings she was christened with? Madrinas in the living room playing a piano singing from that deep raw place. Singing like she can build the bridge from their place to mine. A hot-food buffet against the wall. White crocheted doilies beneath lit sternos. For Marina's lolo, his short thick soriso fingers poked at the things he loved, a sweet macaroni salad, fried egg rolls, banana leaves stuffed with rice and meat.

Filipinos know the spirits are among us. Yes, the pinay women know how to mourn. First, sitting up, saying the rosary, then sitting down in the church pew, then standing tall again. Then the crying, the screaming, huddled by the body of the dead. The pinay bend and quake over the dead. We hire mourners, experts at the performance of grief, their howls echo in the church and are heard all through the streets. These cries, at the right shrill pitch, forge a sling to carry off the spirit of the dead. From our pews in the church, the pinay keep our eyes fastened to the body, watch the body, make sure his spirit stays intact.

We know our dead may not be ready to leave. We perform rituals to keep the spirit from following us home. The body of the dead is carried in headfirst. The feet face the door, so they can take off easily. Men light their cigarillos by the gate at the cemetery so the smoke annoys the spirit and keeps them away. Once the wake is over, every guest takes a separate route, somewhere other than home first, to confuse the spirit so they can't latch on and follow. The guests scatter out into the city like marbles.

Several hours after the wake, we reconvene at the home of the deceased for the novena. The oldest living matriarch in the family remains at the entrance of the home to ward off bad spirits. Nine days of praying the rosary and partying. This is a time of food and mahjong, karaoke, piano playing, glossy brown noodles and bright red strips of pork, chicken adobo, rice, and all sorts of sweet gooey coconut things, thick stews. On the fourth day after death, the spirit of the dead returns. The spirit walks around the singing room and coos in the ears of nieces and eventually makes their way to their old bed. Then finally on the ninth day they can enter the pearly gates of heaven, sending the spirit to its final good sleepy night night.

I can't be free from the Salles women and complete my seventh-generation haunt unless I make the right move here. Like any good guest at a party, I need to learn the wants and needs of my host.

A quick procession of memories waltzes through her mind. Like when she and Ma first moved to Los Angeles. The air hot and still. Shit on a shingle—white gravy with ground beef spread over toasted Wonder Bread. That time at the grocery store when the clerk declined Mutya's check and she shut the whole store down with nothing but her knockoff handbag, her angry eyes, and her mouth.

All those times, Marina knew better than to answer back. Swallowed her words.

Then later, after Ma tucked her in bed and smoothed the hair off her forehead and kissed her cheeks and then stooped low and gobbled at her arm, threatening, I'm gonna eat you up, poopee face! Ah! What curly curly hair! Maganda! Can I have it?

No, Marina squealed, you have your own already.

But this one, look at the curl—so pretty—like a question mark. And Mutya held Marina's curls up against her forehead.

Okay, okay, that one's yours anyway. I took it from you.

Mutya would forget about the curl and dive back into her arm. If she did bite her, she'd discover Marina likely tasted like chicken adobo and tears.

Marina's body, her lineage, had been a battleground, the ways violence hailed upon our ancestors. I felt the carousel of lolas there from my place in the pakshet mobile home. I could see them there eating halo-halo, some of them dressed casually for the first time since their deaths, overalls, jeans, T-shirts. In Marina's mind, Lola Virgie had on tap shoes. She always loved Fred Astaire. She clicked them around to get Marina's attention. Thrilla in Manila! her favorite chant. Three months before Marina was born, the third and final boxing match between Muhammad Ali and Joe Frazier was held in the Araneta Coliseum in Quezon City. Significant only because that was the birthplace of Marina's ma, Mutya.

But also, it was ranked as one of the best matches in boxing's history, as Muhammad Ali declared before the match, A killa and a thrilla and a chilla when I get that gorilla in Manila. The only time one hundred million viewers across the world set their eyes steady on the Philippines. Lola Virgie chanted Ali's mantra throughout Mutya's labor, a killa and a thrilla and a chilla. She did not know what it meant but loved the sound of it. When stuck on hold or at a cross light, she'd silently chant to herself, A killa and a thrilla and a chilla.

The ground outside the pakshet's mobile home—wet and covered with leaves, the sky a thick fog. Willie and his brother, Elder, stood talking over by the barn.

Elder at least a foot taller than Willie, scuffing his boots against the dirt, antsy, half turned toward Willie's van, asked, Why don't we just head over to that tittie joint in town and get some breakfast? And we can talk there.

Willie unable to look Elder in the eye ever. Well, I gotta hit up the Waste Redux and drop off.

I felt the pakshet's rancid remorse and desire like water on a hot oil fire. He was heading back to the Downtown Eastside for another girl. I remembered, from the night before—there was a boar on the property. The Machine, he called her. She had to be six hundred pounds. That big face, flat and angry. Hair on her chin. That baboy was out for blood.

MAPLE LEAF TRUCK

Willie was born Robert, Robbie as a toddler, and then almost always Willie. He had an elder sister, Laura, and a younger brother, Elder. Willie plopped right in the middle—a year between each going up the line. His siblings were a lot better looking than he was. His sister was much prettier than their mother, if only for the kindness in her eyes. Their mother, Mary Margaret Pickton, had eyes dull with cruelty, that only flickered at moments of deep hate. Eyes on a girl make a big difference that way.

Laura and Elder did not, for the most part, have much to do with Willie. Although it's true that when they got older, Elder did go into business with him.

There were times when they were kids that Elder played with him, even if he did make Willie take all the dumb, boring roles in games. Like if Elder got to be the robber, Willie had to be the detective. He would ask his brother questions like, Where were you on the night of the first? And Elder would get shifty until he couldn't stand it anymore, and he'd explode with his hands in the shapes of guns and jump out of the room, making fast *bang-bang* noises. It was the best part to play, and Willie never got to play it. Instead, Willie was shot, sometimes early on in the game, and was left to play dead for hours afterward. A miserable thing to have to be still on the ground, listening as Elder got to make the sound of hot ammunition.

Willie heard all his life he was a *difficult birth*—an umbilical cord wrapped around his neck. Meg always secretly wondered if that was why it took him a while to figure things out, and his speech was so hard to understand—a thud of heavily tongued sounds. Her body could be to blame. The rough terrain. Later he'd get notes sent home that said this set him back in school and kept him from having very many friends. People warned Mother all the time about how slow he was, but nobody said, You think you're helping by putting this kind of terror in him, but really you're building a pakshet man, you're building a ticking time bomb of a person. Nobody knew.

Willie did not have any of the things other boys his age had. He never had the same clothes other boys wore. His clothes were all hand-me-downs, sometimes from his sister and sometimes even from his brother, although he was younger than him.

What they did have, though, was a small general store in town beside the Lougheed Highway. Sometimes kids his age would come in, and he'd try to win their favor by slipping them gifts of hot dogs or candy.

He'd been set back in special classes but his memory . . . woooweeee. Willie Pickton can tell you in perfect detail about a day when he was only two. He lived in a chicken coop. It was a thatched hut, small and wooden, and rimmed with chicken wire. He, his brother, and his sister shared a twin bed on a metal frame that folded in two and could be tucked away during the day. He, being the smallest, slept curled up at their feet on the bottom. He can tell you about how, at just two years old, he was sent to lift a floorboard under their little coop bed to get cold water from a spring that ran down below.

Ordinarily, his father, Mr. Perrish Pickton, was a quiet-mannered man. He began his days at the first touch of light, clanging buckets of hay and milk. Willie's brother, Elder, usually got up around that time too. They'd linger along the property of pigs and a couple of calves and some chickens until Willie's mom, Mary Margaret, padded her way into the kitchen to make breakfast. Willie's mother always looked irritated, even when she was just thinking, even when she was just waking up. Like a naked mole rat. She was perhaps the final sure choice in Perrish Pickton's lousy life. She'd met Perrish in a coffee shop. He shot in across from her on a bright yellow bench seat and plopped a warm slice of apple pie with a mound of whipped cream right in front of her face and said, Eat up, sweetie, we're going to celebrate. And she shot back a question of a look and he said sure as day, We're gonna get married someday. She was much younger than him. Sixteen years younger. This all seemed like a hoot to her but entertaining enough so that with not much more persistence, he soon had his way.

She had been hiding from her parents in the diner. If her mom was at home, she considered Meg a nuisance, and if her mom wasn't at home, she was in the hospital visiting her father. Meg had so wished her father would hurry up and die already. All those Sunday hospital visits, the putrid sterile smell, the contagion of grief or illness, or both. The saucy bland foods required little to no chewing, canned meats and applesauce, making it comfortable and easy for teeth to be removed and floating in glasses everywhere. There was no surface free of dentures. She knew her father loved ribs, loved meats; he loved chewing things.

For this reason alone, she wanted him to be put out of his misery. This was also a reason for her to marry this man. To escape the ghost life that awaited her most Sundays.

Mary's morning routine was accompanied by her bodily agitated barks and wheezes. She'd stretch her two big fists to the center of her back and push in until she heard her spine crack. She shuffled into her slippers and made the family breakfast out of whatever Father plunked in the center of the table in a bucket. That's how they called each other, Mother and Father. Most often eggs, though sometimes it was just bread and lard, and Willie does not remember a day in his upbringing without bacon. He used to dream his hands turned into hooves and he was released from all his schoolwork. No more school. Just bucking and wheezing and squealing.

Willie might also tell you glad and proud about a day when he was six years old, sitting in his dad's Maple Leaf truck. The sun was still up. The truck's seats were lumpy, and some wires were poking into his side, so he scooched over to the driver's side. Father was in the house, letting the engine warm up. Some pigs, about ten or so, were squealing in the back of the truck, their hooves clicking and bouncing against the flatbed. Willie will even tell you that he remembers thinking the pigs knew where they were headed. He'd woken up that morning thinking, *Bessie*.

Bessie was a prize sow. A fat sow who had three droves of piglets. Bessie with her smile and her soft adoring eyes. Willie cared for Bessie, hugged her and put water on her, and snuck her handfuls of his own dinner food. One of his first words was *Bethie*. Willie just knew that Bessie was the one sow who would make them rich. He dreamt that he was going to get a thousand dollars for her. He dreamt he was going to be famous for Bessie. Traipsing her around a ring of cowboys. His chest out, shoulders back, a rope tied around Bessie's neck. Bessie just as proud—her snout pointed to the heavens. Willie was excited to make an impression on everyone, but he most wanted to impress Mother, even if she wouldn't be there.

But every year, two months after the pigs' showing and depending on whether or not they placed, the sows were slaughtered. Part of him wished the pigs would just hurry up and be slaughtered. Not so they could be rich but to put the pigs out of their misery because every moment longer, every grunt and shuffle and snort, was an invitation for him to love them more. Because under all the bathing and feeding and hair brushing and those days when you doll up a sow and prance her around a ring, a kid who grows up on a farm knows the animals he is raising are food. Willie was gonna drive his prize Bessie to the show; his thick brain had no room to wait, no patience for Father. Sitting in the driver's side, Willie stretched out—moved the handle on the top of the steering wheel to drive and pressed on the gas like he'd seen Father do. And *VROOOOOOOMMMMM* the truck sputtered back in reverse and smashed right into a tree.

Perrish Pickton was a master farmer in the town. He was in good health, reserved, strict. Maybe the reason Willie remembers this incident so well was because of the beating he got afterward. His father liked to teach him lessons in a quiet sort of way. But the loss of the Maple Leaf, which was quite a collector's item, along with the loss of the pigs that they were going to take off and slaughter proper, this was all enough for his dad to erupt into a thwacking maniac. Perrish Pickton grabbed a wooden spoon, he took the spoon and bam bammed little Willie's arm with it. Willie was dazed. He smirked. This was not the right response. Perrish threw down the spoon and began hitting Willie with his closed fist. Just when he thought he was tired or he'd hit his son enough, he'd remember about his truck or all the money they'd lost on those pigs and he'd get a second wind. A third wind. A tenth. Then Willie lay bombed-out in the lot, mixed into the jumble of broken pigs and truck parts and gravel and false hope of slaughter money.

When Willie was around eight, his brother, Elder, was experimenting with language; when they'd play their robber games, he'd shoot off into the air and holler out fiery words like Whore! And Fuck this shit! Willie didn't know all that he meant, just that this was the big blast of the game now. One night he came in after dark from doing his chores. If the lights were on in the kitchen, he could see Father sitting there at the table with a drink in his hand and Mother cleaning dishes. But one time, she walked by and Father reached up and grabbed her on her waist. She stood still. Like it was her duty. His hands made their way around her butt. As he rubbed and rubbed, she got stiff. She didn't like it—her *body* said she didn't like it—but she stood there still.

Willie ran into the pigpen. He bent down low at his waist. At first, it stank. He sucked it all in with his nose. All the shit and mud and pig sweat. All that pink skin and pink hairs and black hairs and spots, and there was the all-brown pig and those with the spots. She doesn't like it. She doesn't like it. She doesn't like it. He screamed it three times. His cheeks brushing past the bodies of the pigs, their wet noses slobbering on his face. He went straight to the middle. They made a racket oinking and coughing and squealing and their faces against his, he even felt teeth on his butt, but they weren't fighting him; they were just trying to make room. They were screaming about what he was screaming about. She doesn't like it! they said with him, and drowned him out, and he slept there with them. That was the night they made him king. The moment they made him king was when he made it to the middle, and he stood up tall and threw off his shirt and screamed, She doesn't like it, and she does it anyway. WHORE! FUCK THIS SHIT! And they all went quiet and looked at him, and it was like they had an understanding from that moment on they were gonna fuck this shit.

People have always teased Willie about being slow, but he never had much schooling. The last day he went to school, he had a complaint from his teacher about his grooming. It was the smell all the kids used to tease him about. They said he smelled like a pig or the poop, and it was because he liked to stay out there with 'em pigs, and he spoke to them all the time in their special oink language. But also, he hates the shower. The firm beat and feel of the shower. He likes to soak his skin deep into the water but keep his head dry. Gotta have the eyes dry so he can see for any sharp objects.

One day he walked into the kitchen when it was still light out, and the windows were clouded with steam from Mother's hot water, and she was standing there washing dishes. This was shortly after his father, Perrish, had been dead. Elder and Laura were off working in the store, and Meg and Willie were already steady in a bleak routine. He slowly handed her a note. She snatched it from him.

What's it say? she asked.

I dunno. He said that 'cause it was the truth.

Ya don't know what it say?

Nah, ma'am. 'Cause he remembered to call her ma'am, and he looked around, and there was no real sharp object is what he was looking for, and he only saw that there was maybe some kitchen knives.

It says you smell like shit is what it says.

Sorry, ma'am.

Yes, you sure are. Now, why don't you clean up and stop smelling like all the damn pigs?

Yes, ma'am.

Get yourself undressed and get ready for a bath now!

He still looked around to see what he was gonna get hit with 'cause he knew something was coming, he could see her face and cheeks trembling like they do when she's about to boil. He started to try to take down his pants, but they got stuck around his ankles.

Ah, you dumb shit, you're supposed to take your shoes off first!

When he stood up, she had a big pot filled with boiling water, and she threw it on his penis. His whole body a scalding color red. He yelped and curled up into a ball. She grabbed her broom from the corner and started thwacking him with it.

Hey, if you wanna smell like a pig, I'll thwack you into the bathroom like a pig.

He couldn't help but pee on the floor there.

What is that, piggy? You gonna make a mess of my kitchen, piggy?

No, ma'am. Her cheeks were really shaking now. He was scared, and he peeked over the counter at the knife. Her eyes caught his—she followed his gaze over to the counter. He tried to look away. Too late. She grabbed the knife. He scrambled to his feet and ran toward the bathroom. She chased after him. She had him in her grips when he fell. He scooted back on his butt. She held the knife to his cheek.

You get your bum up and get yourself clean and never come home with another note again, or it's the last one you'll get, you hear?

There were glazed yellow fly strips studded and plump with fly bodies out by where Elder and Willie were talking, enough yellow ribbons to obstruct their view. Day-weary pigeons grazed past Elder, then a fly buzzed in front of his face just as he clapped his hands.

Willie must've gotten out of breakfast at the strip joint because a short while later, I heard his heavy, slow steps go in a different direction, while Elder slammed shut the truck door and started the engine to warm her up. I stayed listening in that hall closet, felt the reverberations drilling against our heart.

The truck peeled out backward and then onto the Lougheed Highway. He cranked up some heavy metal as he drove, he took a corner sharply. The same trees Marina saw from the night before whizzed overhead. Some of them still laced with the spirits of lost women, their schoolyard chant bleating with the cries of getimgetimgetimgetim.

A murmuration of starlings above, eerie and maganda, set off by a change in season, an attempt to flee their prey. Swooping and intricately coordinated, like Lola's fingers passing along her rosary. Hail Mary Full of Grace. Like soldiers, dancers, a swarm of soccer players—they moved together.

THE PLASTIC PALACE

The year 1982 was a time of cruel plastic runners that protected the carpets. The sharp tips that were supposed to meld into the floor often flipped back and wound up driven into Marina's knees. Ma and Marina called Lola's house the Plastic Palace. A cool salty breeze swooshed over the Monterey Peninsula, sand dunes for miles, the town smelling like sea animals, ice plants, with a sardine cannery off in the distance. Fewer than ten miles away, a forest blanketed with redwoods. Every day was a day for sand in the shoes. Seaports were Marina's six-year-old heart's delight—the crowded Edgewater Carousel, ship-clogged, fish, and sewage-scented cities.

This is where they lived with Marina's lola. It was in this house in Seaside and at that time when each of Lola's kisses tasted like a funeral: Jean Naté, tears, and Mary Kay lipsticks. Maybe it was her handkerchiefs, and her rosary beads clutched tightly in her palm. Or the painting of Lola and Lolo in the living room—their eyes dark wet pearls, their hands clasped like they knew one of them was due to die the next day. The house had a smell of burning charcoal and soured fish. There were paintings on the walls, one of Maria

Lobo, her hair with jasmine flowers. In the hallway, there sat a small velvet picture of a young boy with wings, riding boots, a sash belt, and a feathered hat. If Marina moved past the paintings, she felt their eyes track her movements. Her favorite painting was of a cluster of boys—little brown skeletons with paper lanterns of various shapes and colors, suspended from the end of bamboo poles and decorated to each boy's desire. She liked the colors against the tropical backdrop, and when it rained outside, she imagined the small lanterns swaying toward the sky. She felt the painting was most alive in a storm. When she was younger, barely able to reach it, she'd run to the painting and kiss it when the sky turned gray. She gently brushed all the little backs of the little boys, hoping to keep them warm. On All Saints' Eve, Lola covered the windows and mirrors with flags and multicolored damasks; the whole place burst with the smells of bibingka baking and explosions of music. Marina never thought it strange, this small house by the sea; it'd taken her much longer, growing older and moving away, to realize every home wasn't like the one on Harcourt Ave.

It was there she was suspended between the harshness of life and the strange festival of death. Lola visited her espiritista twice a week every week. Occasionally, she took Reena with her. They walked the alley behind Lola's house. One house had a German shepherd that jumped out of nowhere—its long face launched over the gate barking at them. Lola cussed at the dog, Ay nako! Stupid lunchmeat bastard! She walked ahead with her handbag thumping against her polyester pants. Always a different handbag to match her different pants. Filled with gum and Kleenex and three types of reading glasses. Marina knew when Lola wanted to walk fast because she put on a pair of canvas tennis shoes over her knee-high nylon stockings.

Marina carried her own purse, a metal Wonder Woman lunch box with a skinny blue handle. In an attempt to appear important, she stuffed it with marbles, a couple of sticks of gum, and Kleenex too. Lola told Marina stories of how misbehavior would lead to her demise.

Sometimes Marina got impatient, and she'd interrupt—Is this the one about the time the roaches crawled in your ears at night? Or about the time you heard babies crying in the well in your little village? Is this the one about the time Lolo's spirit got angry and made a bunch of knives fly around the kitchen like darts? Is this about how I am the prettiest one? Is this about the aswang?

As they stepped into the street, Be careful! We will get runned over by a car. And then you and I will have broken legs, Lola Virgie warned.

Then can I have a wheelchair? asked Marina.

No, you will be a handicapped. No wheelchair.

No wheelchair?

Wheelchairs are a thousand dollars. Do you know how much is a thousand dollars?

No.

A car is a thousand dollars.

But it's not even the size of a whole car.

Yes, but the parts are from somewhere special. And I myself have arthritis, so I cannot push a wheelchair. Someday you will have to push me in the wheelchair.

I'll push you in the wheelchair, Lola! Even if I'm in one too. I'll build special muscles so I can push you.

If you want to build special muscles, then you need to eat your dinner.

I do eat my dinners.

Even your vegetables.

The house was pink with a wooden placard—gold letters that spelled out ESPIRITISTA, bordered with etchings of big-lashed green and blue eyes. On the way, Marina asked Lola what an espiritista was, and she said that there were four types of espiritistas: (1) experimental, (2) inconsistent, (3) true, and (4) excited. She said the only ones Filipinos could go to were the true spiritists, the Catholic spiritists chosen by God to perform healing miracles. They were selected to be mediums and give messages from the dead to the living. They went to see the espiritista so Lola could communicate with Lolo, sometimes looking for lost items.

Plug-in heaters glowed all along the hallway. The espiritista was named Alma. Alma loved the smell and buzzy light of the heaters. All visitors had to stand outside on a small woven rug and take off their shoes before entering. The house had lots of draped velvets and cats and candles. A very glitzy fire hazard. The overhead lights were never switched on, but every surface twinkled with a vintage lamp or candle. There was a corner with lots of candles and a large black porcelain doll. Some crosses and busts of deities. The room had the smell of wet cats and cooking meat. All the candles let off the conflicting scents of those perfume samples in magazines that Ma would rub all over her wrists before a date or job interview. Marina loved going there with Lola. Ma used to tell her a story of special fairy dust she could get to make her toys come to life, and this seemed like the type of place she could get such a thing. Plus, when Lola was there, it seemed the only time she wasn't anxious. She would sit and pray and lose track of time.

Inside the house, Lola and Marina sat next to each other on a sofa and waited. Marina's first time there, as she sat staring at the varicose cracks in the wall, a dark lace curtain flickered, and then a black cat appeared out of nowhere and jumped on her lap, and her belly button felt as if it dived all the way into her body and pushed against the soles of her feet. Something prodded her spine. She nearly died from the fear.

A cardboard sign was taped to the wall, it read KAPAG HANDA KA NA SA AMIN! TAO PO!

As far as Marina could tell, the sign meant, When you are ready call out Tao po!

Tao po! Lola hollered when she heard Alma tottering out from behind some curtains.

Later, Marina asked if this meant, Hey, is anyone there?

Hindi, Marina, it means *human* here, Lola corrected.

She was Marina only when Lola was serious and Reen or Reena the rest of the time. Lola continued, Filipinos always must declare themselves human to separate them from aswang.

But what if you were aswang? asked Marina.

Alma appeared in her bright flowered muumuu, a colorful fabric wrapped around her head, gold-bangled arms. She had a birthmark on her face, dark brown on her right cheek. Marina tried not to stare at it when she spoke.

If an aswang came to see me, I would make her wait until after the new moon to walk through the door, Alma answered. It was as if Alma could see inside Marina's mind. She knew all her private and sometimes very bad thoughts.

Before the new moon, she is only half aswang; if she kills before the new moon, she becomes full aswang, and she can live forever. I will not see a half aswang looking for a fresh kill.

What if—

If she does not kill before the new moon, she is no longer aswang and loses her powers. She becomes like any other spirit with unfinished business. Useless, desperate. This is why your lola is here today to make sure the spirit of your lolo is doing well and not stuck in the Place of Wanting. Want is for the living.

How do you get unstuck? Lola threw Marina a sharp look and gave her hand a squeeze. Marina knew these visits cost Lola money and she didn't want to waste any of the precious time, the money that Lola prayed for and cried over and clipped coupons for and lit candles about. But she wanted to know where everyone went.

It depends. If an aswang finishes her unfinished business, she does not need to go to the Place of Wanting; she gets to be a pure spirit and rest for eternity, Alma explained.

Lola smacked her two hands in front of Marina's face before she could say anything more. Enough! No more questions!

Did she feel a sense of dread, or have any idea of what might happen to her one day? Did the espiritista sense me buried deep in the Salles bloodline? Of course not. Instead, Marina held on tight to Lola's hands. The whole magic of it clenched around the girl who sang songs and told stories and left treats out in the rain for the fairies, who in the afternoons, while her mother was out, closed her eyes and stroked Lola's paintings of little kids in nipa huts and touched the tela woven into time.

Alma gestured them to a round table. They sat quietly as she closed her eyes and spoke very fast. She was a big woman and wore no bra. Marina could make out her body's silhouette when she sat down and tucked the muumuu in close to all the rolls of her stomach. And sometimes she leaned over, and Marina could see straight down the center. Marina tried very hard to clear her mind when she went to visit because she was afraid Alma could hear what she was thinking. When Alma was ready, she'd lift the table on her side from beneath, presumably with her knees, and start saying all the letters of the alphabet. Every now and again, when she got to a letter, a loud knock sound came through. Marina did not know how she was making that sound because both of her hands were on the table. All she knew was that when Alma got up from the table, the heat from her body drew her muumuu close.

Later Lola told her it was Grandpa knocking. He knocked any time Alma reached a letter he liked so he could spell out the answers to all of Lola's questions. Lola's main concern was that Grandpa was a pure spirit. There are five different levels of good spirits. There is the top level—a pure spirit—then high spirits are second class, then wise spirits are third class, learned spirits fourth class, and the final fifth class of spirits are benevolent spirits.

Alma explained, Pure spirits have passed up through all the levels of progress and freed themselves from any impurities of want. They are the highest level of perfection and, therefore, do not have to go through any more trials or tribulations. You need to continue to visit him if you do not want your husband to come back as a beetle or a cockroach.

What level is he now?

He is a good spirit. A very good spirit. He is the wise spirit.

Lola made a disgruntled noise and then looked as if she would start crying. Her lip was trembling like a saucer on a table when a truck drives by.

Áte, please, please don't worry. Just continue to say the rosary every night and come and see me twice a week. His position will elevate with your good deeds.

Marina almost mentioned that Lola called the dog a lunchmeat bastard on their way over but then thought the better of it because she did not want Grandpa to be a cockroach.

Elder had reached the Downtown Eastside—a bitter, weather-beaten place. This is a place where the rich kids—Hoons, they are called—come when they want to see the poorest postal code in the country. You've never seen people so wretched, as if this country existed in one of those snow globes and you tipped it at one end and all of its shit-grunt-desperate people slid to the other end.

He drove past the Carnegie Library. The library has a message board, a place where people write pleas, notes, and signs about missing women. Only one of the flyers advertised a reward: the photo under the word MISSING, *a startled-looking young white girl, and below the photo the word* REWARD *and dollar signs. No specific amount mentioned.*

Beyond the library, a pay phone stands at the border between Eastside and Chinatown. Elder turned a corner past Blood Alley, the alley where the cops come and bring on some kind of shock to their system—a way to zap the junkies out of their sleep, guys sit around and play music for money. The day Marina died, she passed those guys playing music in the alley and thought for a brief moment about staying there—maybe stopping and drifting off to other happier places in her mind. Maybe if she'd done that she wouldn't have been killed.

GOLDIE

Wasn't till after Mother died that Willie got himself some freedom: a curvy tall shiny baby-blue Ford pickup. It rattled and whistled and then made a smooth *vroom* sound, but then it sputtered out. Willie knew it was time to take her apart.

Take-a-paw. He smooshed it aloud like one round word. A cigarette dangling out his mouth, he stood ankle-deep in mud. The whole front of the farm property was trucks and beat-up cars and mostly Fords. Willie had a passion for this ever since he drove his dad's Maple Leaf truck into the tree. If this was something to get your underwear in a mandy about, then this was something to get interested in, was how he saw it.

It was a Friday—which meant he spent the day separating out all the copper, aluminum, and brass. He'd heard that in America they had Japanese trucks with platinum catalytic converters that you could pop easy off the bottom. Boy, how he wished he had that option. It got so cold in Coquitlam—most of these cars were junk cars, people don't like to keep nice cars in the snow, and they end up rusting. He made it his job, his life, his mission to mine 'em for parts. Except Saturday mornings—set aside for auctions—haggling over chickens, rabbit, geese, llamas, cattle, and, of course, pigs.

He loved standing at the auctioneer's block. He'd show up late—let all the expensive livestock get auctioned off. The place smelled like shit, and sometimes a Chinook blazed past, setting his nose hairs on fire. He didn't often bid much because he always picked out the worst-looking animal—the blind cow, the piglet with sores. He saw a couple little thin-skinned puckered nude butts bubbled out before him right then. Abscesses thin and dark and bright with blood like the bloated bodies of ticks.

It was perfect. It was what he came for. Sometimes he'd wind up with an animal that was too big to slit its throat. Oh, to slit their throats, that was the best. Their tall trusting bodies looking off into the opposite direction, Willie'd mount them, plant his muddy-booted feet on both sides, hold the animal's head up toward its ultimate destination, and at the slightest onset of a shriek of deceit he'd quickly slide his hook from left to right from behind the ear and deep and fast through all the layers of skin. The animal would kick and scream then give in. Just as *there* as they were, with one brief prayer and swipe of a hook, they were gone. He was giving them a great gift. The gift of eternal rest. So many other farmers dismembered their animals while they were still half alive. Shrieking and squealing in agony. Not Willie—what he gave them was bright white light—no pain, no suffering. Willie would never do such a thing, some of them so sensitive it seemed their skin flickered and twitched just by the change in the wind. He'd press against them firm enough to steady their nerves.

Sometimes they were too big for that, and Willie'd instead crouch down, cover their eyes, and place a nail gun at their temple. The eyes was an important part. The eyes said too much all the time, asking, searching—he hated to see their trust turn to betrayal. He tried to drown out all the guilt and shame and the piercing look of those eyes. *Thump thump thump*; he squeezed the trigger three times. A nail in the head. A nail next to a nail next to a nail. He learned early on he had to move the gun to the temple and the neck. Too often, the nail hit the other nail or hit bone, and the animal made a big mess of noise. The squealing and crying and thumping were there, and it was loud.

Willie tended to the scraps of animal bone the same way he tended to the leftover car parts. Meticulous, and careful, with everything but his appearance—unafraid to get himself dirty. He quickly did away with all the animals—except one. A palomino filly he called Goldie. She was his favorite, his love, and one day he found her in the barn with a broken leg, screaming crying screaming. He was going to release her from her painful suffering. Release her from the shame of this earth, her weakness exposed. He quickly placed a set of quilted blinders on Goldie's eyes and took the nail gun—*bam*—right on the carotid artery—*bam bam bam bam bam*—he needed to drown her out. Hail Mawy Hail Mawy . . . he repeated the prayers in his thick, wearied tongue. The last good bit of grace he gave her in this life.

Now Goldie's head is perched alert on the wall in his bedroom. Nothing else in the room but the palomino head, stains on the floor and on the mattress, no sheets or blankets. The folks in town complained of his stench whenever he came through. The people who stopped by the store, the motorcycle gang across the street, and even some of the loopy kids who rode in his van held their noses and made yuck yuck noises. He was a gamey man. His pungent arrival loomed before him in every room. He liked the power in that—how he could smack people without even touching them.

Elder Pickton pulled into a parking space. There on the corner was a huddle of men throwing dice, and one kid on a bike. You can always tell the dealers and hustlers because they are the ones with bikes—some folks leaning up against the wall. People slept sitting up. Other guys warbled around on limbs, legs and arms amputated from infections. People stuffing their faces, shoving food into mouths without teeth. Even all the way back up the Lougheed Highway, back rummaging through the pakshet mobile home, I could see exactly where he was. Two doors down from the Astoria, Marina's SRO. The sleepy neon of the hotel's sign flashed all night outside Marina's window. Watching everyone come in and out of the place was like watching a moth club itself on a hot lightbulb. Everyone fizzing out by the time the sun began to rise. Then another nagging feeling came over me—Willie. I could sense Willie was on the hunt, I could smell it on him, I only had so much time before he'd return with another girl.

A TINY UPWARD SHOVE

Growing up, Marina assumed her dad had kicked rocks like all the other dads. Deadbeat is what they called it. Later she learned the nitty-gritty. Once upon a time, her ma awoke three years into their marriage, terrified of her mundane life. What triggered it exactly? Was it the laying out of his clothes every night before bed, or brewing the same old pot of coffee every morning, or taking out the trash every Tuesday at the same time—the same damn head nod to the neighbor, living in the same style home as everyone else?

Marina's dad was in the service. Mutya met him when she was in high school and Lolo was stationed on a military base called Fort Ord. She was eager to leave. Throughout her childhood, Lolo locked her in the closet and said she would be nothing. Mutya stood in lineup against the wall with her siblings to be inspected every morning. Their father came by and pointed to Mutya's wrinkled skirt or her scuffed shoes and ordered her to make penance, say a rosary, scrub a toilet.

Initially, it was the brave impossibility of their marriage—him Black and her Filipina—that left Mutya so worked up. When he was traveling in China, Marina's father was so exotic, people chased after him in the street and on buses and yelled out the names of famous basketball stars. But then came that morning when Mutya realized she had left one suffocating life with a half ton of rules for another. She wanted a different kind of life for herself, one without a ceiling, without walls. An unpredictable life. But she didn't know how to find that life. She fled back home to Lola's, baby Marina in tow. The Plastic Palace.

And then it was 1982, Marina would tell her lola how all the young spunky girls on television who looked nothing like her were beautiful. Lola patted her on the head. Reenie, you're more maganda than those stupid silly girls. The house next door was the same as theirs, but the debris and furniture on the lawn made Lola forbid Reena from talking to the neighbor kids. The neighbor kids, six, nine, and eight, they left their toys out. Carefree with everything, it seemed. They trusted that there would always be more the next day, more running, more playing, more wind, more time, more words to yell at the sky.

A little girl with shiny cheeks would wave and sing hello to Marina, and Lola would call her inside.

If you play with them, you will get lice, and if you get lice, I will have to shave your head, because your hair is not like theirs.

Just another small way to be shamed. Lola nagged Marina to tie her hair back, pin it away from her face, wear it up in a bun, braid it, cover it with a scarf, a hat, or a veil, straighten it, cut it all off. The torturous rollers and grease and heat were her punishment. So much of her childhood was sitting erect in front of the mirror while Lola pulled and straightened and greased. Marina clutched a spray that made an empty promise of No More Tears, *praying praying*

praying she would use more of it. She didn't want to ask her because she didn't want to get in any more trouble for being half Black. Marina could hear children laughing and playing in the street. Her heart was battling over the physical grief of the grooming of her hair (pulled back so tight her eyes seemed to be lifted two inches higher on her forehead), the need to be polite and well-mannered to maintain her status as Lola's favorite grandchild (there were others, but they never came to visit), the deep desire to go out and play with the other kids, and ultimately—*ultimately*—to unclasp the large purple plastic balls and rubber band that acted like a vise on her childhood. A dillybobber, she called it. There exists a picture of Marina smiling with all her teeth, her cheeks up by her ears, her hair in perfectly neat Shirley Temple curls, not a hair out of place, a pale pink dress, pristine white tights, and gleaming patent leather Mary Janes with taps on the soles, as if her immaculate precision would save all the world.

Most of these days ran together. These were the rice days. Mutya off at college and Marina at home and running errands with Lola. Each morning there was a full rice cooker, and by night it would be half empty: rice and butter and salt and pepper. For breakfast, there was Spam and a runny yellow egg all over her rice. Lola was all about eating—pig parts, canned meat, rice, salt, eggs.

Meanwhile, Ma drank two cups of coffee every morning and ate nothing else the rest of the day. She weighed ninety-eight pounds, slight but not to the point of meekness—she had no rings on her bony fingers. Lola walked around with hunched skinny shoulders, the rest of her thick body bouldering through the house on peasant legs. One day, Lola caught Marina staring at her and she snapped, What? Are you ashamed of me?

Marina paused, thought about how to answer honestly, then replied, No, Lola, I'm scared of you.

Which was the right way to answer because Lola smacked her

hands together in glee then jabbed the air in front of her with her little tight fists and chanted, A killa and a thrilla and a chilla.

In the summertime of the rice days, when they didn't have much to do, Lola and Reen dressed up and drove around the corner to the Kmart for a cherry Slush Puppie. Inside the Kmart, hit with the burst of air from above, Reen felt like she could be made better by all the sweaters and faux fur coats or jeans and bedding owned by one of Charlie's Angels, the brunette Marina secretly wanted for a mom. They could put it all on layaway. Lola pointed to a couple of ladies and said, Look, see how all trashy people look the same? Reen looked around; she saw that most of the people in the store did look the same. Something she couldn't explain: round, happy, sexless, like balls of blank Play-Doh. Marina did not know what Lola meant by *trashy people*, but then Lola bowed her arms out around her sides and puffed air into her cheeks and loudly whispered what-was-not-a-whisper-at-all, Fat.

Mortified, Marina looked the other way. Lola clarified, Where I grew up, trashy people could not be fat. I think it is what's in the food here—the Chrysler.

She meant *mercury*. Marina pictured little broken bits of car in all American food.

At the Plastic Palace, they did not revere animals in the same way as most Americans. Marina once brought a dog home, and as soon as she turned her back, Lola shooed it out the front door. Marina reached down and grabbed a handful of dirt and ate it. The cold dirt soothed.

Weekends were for Ma and Reen. Sometimes Ma took her to a

small Japanese restaurant called Itchi Riki, where they sat kneeling on a tatami, always served by the same pigtailed waitress. Ma was patient in showing her how to use chopsticks. Afterward, they'd go feed horses at the stables by the Peninsula, the smell of the sea nearby, the horses themselves hanging half out over the gates. Ma and Reen rode a bus to the Safeway and picked out giant orange carrots. Marina took such time with these things, but when faced with the actual mouth and teeth of the beasts, she shied away and urged Ma to do the feeding. Ma was not much better than her when it came to the fear of big animals. She stood steady with a flat palm, a quarter of a carrot on top, but once the horse's lips grazed her hand, Ma giggled and swooped her parts all back on their side of the gate.

When it was raining, they would duck into the bookstore in town, grab a book off the shelves, plop right there on the floor, and read the whole thing. Even if they didn't have any money, Ma told her to pick a book—any book—and she'd buy it for her. It was always one for Ma and one for Reen. Except when Reen couldn't pick just one. Then Ma'd look at her pleading eyes and smile and put her book on the shelf and let Reen grab two.

On days like that, when they had no money, they'd also go and dance with the Hare Krishnas who twirled on town sidewalks and off near the beach. When the dances were done, the Krishnas gave them an elaborate vegetarian feast complete with hunks of sticky-sweet baklava.

And then Mike entered their lives. Marina was messing around in Lola's garage, and Ma came home, and she called for her—all giggles—and her face smiling up to the sky in wonderment. Like a kid who just discovered cake.

Reen! Reen! Did you see that? Did you see him? Marina ran into the house, and there was Ma in the living room, running around the couch.

Marina jumped in the game. Ma saw her, looking for confirmation. Marina jumped up and down with her.

She had no idea what Ma was talking about—who this *him* was—but she looked like they were on a game show—the host hollered out, Merna Salles, come on down! And she put one hand over her mouth in shock and surprise, then ran toward the stage, arms flailing in the air. The answer to her question was YES. It was always YES.

He's perfect. He's just perfect! She went tearing through the small house, hollering about him, about this perfect *Him* that she met in class, and how funny He was, and oh so handsome, and yeah, He lives here right on the beach. Can you believe it?

Lola walked in right then. What? What? she asked, half smiling half agitated.

Oh, Ma. His name is Mike!

Lola thought this meant her daughter was getting married. You saw it when her face brightened. Marina had no idea how old Lola was just then, but she seemed to be both one hundred and five and a half years old.

It was at this same time that a girl Marina's age moved in across the street. Jessie was her name, and she spotted Marina first. She was wearing a tight white turtleneck with tigers on it and burgundy corduroys. Her father wrote her name on everything with a Sharpie so no one would steal them—but like Marina, all her clothes were junk clothes so nobody would be caught anywhere near them.

Reen was just coming back from the library.

What are you?

What do you mean—?

Like where are you from? Are you Mexican?

No. I'm Black and Filipino.

You don't look like it.

What does that mean?

Well, Black girls walk like this—and she sauntered—and Filipinos walk like this—and she strutted making little flouncy hands.

So how do white people walk?

Like you.

But I thought you thought I was Mexican.

Well, you look Mexican, but you walk white.

That's the stupidest thing I ever heard.

Yeah, you're right. I just made it up.

That spring Jessie and she were desperate for air and fast-beating hearts. They ran circles in her backyard practicing for the Olympics. They'd race each other around and around, using different trees as markers. Five laps was the most they could do, and then they'd fall on their backs, giggling and puffing out air and holding the stitch in their sides.

One evening when Marina was sitting at the kitchen table tracing the lace doily squished under the plastic table cover, she heard Ma come home from school. Marina heard her heels tapping on the front porch and realized that, for the first time that year, the kitchen window was open. Marina screamed out in happiness: The window is open! Ma shushed her. She was so incredibly beautiful, and she did not approve of Marina screaming or acting too much out of order in Lola's house.

Ma was hooking her coat on the outstretched arms of the coatrack. Gosh, I couldn't breathe in this big-ass coat on that crowded bus.

Why don't you get a summer coat? Lola asked, and came in with the giant JCPenney's catalog. She kept a stack of them by her bed even though she never bought anything.

They sat down beside each other, flipping through the pages. Look at that one, Mama.

It was strange hearing Mutya call Lola that. Strange to imagine her as someone else's daughter. Even stranger to imagine Lola having a baby or doing anything so . . . so *naked*. To young Marina, mamas and lolas fell out of the sky, parents neatly and miraculously did something like hug to have kids, and then the men would slide off, leaving the tough stuff for the mamas and lolas.

That's way too much money to spend on a summer coat. Fifty dollars? Are you kidding me?

You see, this is why I never like to look at catalogs with you. You have no idea how much things cost, said Ma.

I can make two coats for that price.

Two ugly coats.

This is why you cannot keep a man. You're too finicky, said Lola.

Mama! Ma glared at Lola and then over at Marina as if to say that these words were not right to say in front of her. There was never any mentioning of her father allowed.

Everything Marina knew of her life before Lola, Ma whispered to her as she went to sleep. A white frame house with a big red mailbox. Snow flurries in the winter. A fireplace, and earmuffs, and days of Ma and her together. Marina on her lap clutching her body while she watched daytime soap operas, all the fingers of one hand in her mouth, the other drawing circles on Ma's cheek (a hand full of her hair back and forth across her nose). She gave Reen these memories to help her sleep. They rested in the back of her mind like baby blankets.

Lola grew less casual. She used hot rollers for her hair and wore dark clothes and donned her canvas sneakers less and less. She began driving to the espiritista in her marshmallow-yellow T-Bird. Scarf on head, lipstick lined in dark pencil. She believed older women should wear hosiery every day. I am not a young woman anymore, she declared. On her dresser, where she kept her face powder and coral lipsticks in their shiny gold cases, was a small vintage wooden mule spray-painted gold and hammered to a coconut shell. It was a plaque that read BINIBINI NG GABI, Beauty of the Night; it was her award from a beauty pageant held at the Stillwell Hall soldiers' club on Filipino night.

She spoke to Marina about the spirit world. It's important that you're good in this life so you can secure your place as a good spirit. You do not want to come back as a spider.

Or a cockroach!

Lola sucked her teeth in agreement. She kept that warning for all of Marina's chores around the house. You better clean up in here. You do not want to come back as a cockroach.

Yes, Lola, I know. I know.

Marina, clean up your toys!

This didn't take much. Her toys consisted of two McDonald's Happy Meal vehicles, a plastic piggy bank Lola got for her from the Savings and Loan, almost the entire series of the Baby-Sitters Club books, and a princess diary with all of her secret thoughts written in a special language she had developed before she learned how to spell.

As the days grew warmer, Lola and Ma and Reen sat on the front porch and watched all the people in the neighborhood come and go, Ma with a book and a highlighter in her lap, Lola with some needlework, and Reen with the JCPenney's catalog. Sometimes the phone rang, and when the call was for Ma, Lola would holler out for Ma in a voice already hiked up in judgment.

There is an advantage to sharing a bedroom wall with grown-ups. You hear things, but that can also be a disadvantage. After Marina was supposed to have gone to bed, she could hear Ma talking to Lola about men she met. Ma talked about the men she wanted to date, the ones who wanted to date her. Lola might offer a suggestion here and there, almost always rebuffed with an Ewwww, no, Mama—over my dead body.

Lola would often bring up ways to conserve Ma's propriety. The hours it was decent to date, flirting, canceling, how to play hard to get, ways to excuse herself from the table, the appropriate age difference. According to Lola, Ma ought to date a man at least ten years older.

Mama, I don't know why you are telling me all this. I know how to behave on a date. Then Lola began to speak with Ma in Tagalog—which signaled that their conversation was heading in a more complex direction, a matter for grown-ups. Marina was only able to pick up every third word or so.

Lola had a rule. No one could leave the house with anyone who was too lazy to come to the door and knock. The first time Mike came by to pick up Ma, he sat in his little blue car and honked. Ma jumped and ran for the door. Lola hollered, Don't you dare!

Slowly, Ma eased her hand off the doorknob and walked back to join Marina on the couch. She had on tight jeans and a loose silky shirt. The collar slid off her shoulders, and Lola leaned over and adjusted it. Ma tapped her feet restlessly against the plastic floor runner. He rang the doorbell. She jumped up to answer it, but Lola beat her to it. There he was. Mike.

A blond surfer guy. The dreamy kind. He was tan and short and moved in slow motion. Everything about him small and slow. He looked at Ma, beamed his flashy teeth, and said, It's a beautiful day! Carpe diem, shall we?

Marina was standing between them. Both Marina's and Lola's hands extended. Mike didn't know it was customary to greet Lola with a manang, hold her hand up to his forehead. Mike didn't see either of them. Didn't hear Marina either as she said, I'm Marina! just as the door closed.

They stood with empty hands. A shutter closing over Marina's heart. Lola in her pants and shirt. She had taken off her apron and wasn't even wearing a muumuu for this. She looked nice for this. She had her teeth in. He didn't even say hi. Instead, he put the key in the ignition of his stupid BMW and patted the door just as he drove off, like giddyup.

For the next couple of months, Ma was never home because she was always with Mike. She collected M&M wrappers to commemorate their love. The wrappers posted up on the fridge with magnets and even more wrappers neatly folded in a shoebox beside her bed. Night after night, Marina saw her come home from night school at eight p.m., tired from a full day of both work and school, and thirty minutes later, she would erupt from the bathroom, ready to greet her date, her face alight with a bright smile. They'd go on dates four times a week. Lola cleaned, and Marina spent time entertaining herself by writing fake stuff on the typewriter. Lola had bought this typewriter when Grandpa was away in the military. First, it was to write him, and then after he died, she had to master the thing so she could get a good job being a secretary. Ma sometimes brought Marina back treats from her date to make it up to her. Stuff she'd picked up at the 7-Eleven. She opened a package of marshmallow-covered Snoballs, broke off a chunk, and brought it to Marina's lips. Marina swallowed the stale cake. She hated Snoballs, the pink marshmallow stuff, would have preferred a Ding Dong, but she didn't tell her that.

Around this time Ma promised Marina she'd take her to the Edgewater Carousel. A fun old-timey place, where she could get a fountain soda. On the way, Ma stopped at the bank to grab some money. Marina begged her not to stop. But she did, and inside, the thing that always happened, happened. There in the quiet carpeted building, Marina could hear Ma arguing with the teller, pointing at a small receipt. She snatched Marina's hand and dragged her back to the car. She drove back to Lola's house, Mutya yelling at traffic and banks and presidents and how everything was against them. They didn't go anywhere.

Ma's anger was rarer than Lola's, but sharper. She knew how to find Marina's tender spots. To pinch Marina's neck, lobe, waist, where the skin was thinnest, to withhold what Marina cherished most.

More than anything else in the world, Marina wanted to be successful when she grew up. She did not want to come home tired and then have to fix her hair and go on dates. Jessie, across the street, wanted to be a doctor.

Marina lacked a father, and Jessie lacked a mother, and they often looked at each other, wondering which of the two got the shorter end of the stick. Mutya was not cool in the way Jessie's dad was. Mutya was always so secretive and cautious, but Jessie's dad told Jessie all about her background and stuff like that. When he and Jessie's mom met, and what she was like, and he smoked cigarettes, and sometimes Jessie would pretend she was smoking a cigarette too. When Jessie's dad was home, he'd muck around in the garage at night and play old country songs he called "honkers." Marina tried to think what it would be like to be Jessie, a little girl raised alone by her dad.

You're luckier than me, Jessie said, as if she were reading her mind.

Why? I miss my dad too.

Yes, but there's just too many ways to miss your mother. There's like a hundred thousand ways.

Besides, Jessie's mother was dead, so really, there was no way for her to see her again. That's what made Marina think of the espiritista.

Why don't we talk to your mom the way Alma talks to my grandpa?

We need some scarves, said Jessie.

They made a plan for a special spell, and the plan lit up their minds and wrapped its tentacles around their little hearts like boomshakalaka. They were hit upside the head with a Filipino magic stick.

They covered her dad's folding poker table with a bunch of Lola's scarves. They dimmed the lights and sat opposite each other. Marina closed her eyes and began humming a tune and murmuring a bunch of letters like she'd seen Alma do. Then slowly, one end of the poker table began to rise.

You're doing that, Jessie said.

Marina wasn't doing it. Her hairs on her arms lifted, and her armpits prickled. She opened one eye and whispered, Am not . . . now close your eyes, or you'll break the spell. Marina repeated the sounds of the alphabet, and on the letter M there was a knock, on the letter O another knock, finally M again a knock. Marina opened her eyes, and they stared at each other. A staring contest sort of stare.

Mom? Jessie asked. Again, Marina gurgled a bunch of letters, forgetting that on the table, they had pasted the words *yes* and *no* in the center. A wave came over her. A strong one. Her arm flew across the table and smacked hard on the yes circle.

Jessie and Marina looked shocked at one another. Marina jumped up and screamed and turned on the lights. Was it wonderful news? Was it horrible news? It was just news, but it was enough to make them fear the space between the world they were in and the world they were trying to contact.

I'm sorry, we have to stop. I don't want to come back a roach, Marina explained.

Jessie, who was normally full of thoughts, tormented by all sorts of ideas, seemed relieved that Marina was the one to break the spell.

It's cool.

Really, you're cool with it? I don't want to mess this up for you but I hate roaches. Are you scared?

Marina pushed once more, hoping that Jessie would admit she was the one who was scared.

I'm not scared, are *you* scared?

Marina decided to change the subject to the next best thing. The other thing that consumed all their time—their problems.

Do you think one day I will be popular?

Umm, it's hard to tell. How popular?

Like famous?

Well, you're only famous if it's your destiny.

What's destiny?

Your life is decided when you're a baby.

Saints can escape it. Saints can escape anything.

Marina's real problem that she didn't want to share with Jessie is that she thought Jessie was much better looking than her. She thought she was so beautiful and Marina could not bear it. Sometimes after running laps in her yard, Jessie looked to her like she'd been rubbed with honey. Now that it was getting nearer to summer, her skin took on a golden tone. Most of the time, Marina did everything she asked and was careful not to displease her. Marina just knew when the summer was over and school started up again and they were going to have other friends, Jessie might not want to have anything to do with her. They would be going into the first grade, which she thought of as a big big deal. That is to say, Marina tried her best in their time together to make sure Jessie fell in love with her. But Jessie sometimes acted like the ladies on the soap operas. Marina saw this transformation happening one day when they were playing inside. It seemed out of nowhere, Jessie took a phone book and threw it at her and told her, Call a cab, why dontcha?

Neither of them knew exactly what it meant, but it sounded badass.

Still it hurt Marina's feelings. The phone book missed her by several feet.

Shocked, she asked, Are you kicking me out?

Yeah! Go on! Get outta here! Call a cab, why dontcha!

Jessie seemed like one of those dolls, you pull a string in the back and it talks, but this doll said the same thing over and over again.

Lola kept military food tucked away in her garage. Dark green cans that named some sort of food like PORK RIBS BONELESS or CORNED BEEF HASH. Some of them were airtight packages that said MRE across the top, which stood for Meal Ready to Eat. Marina liked to look at them. One day when she was in the garage checking them out, she passed the water heater, and one of those pretty neon birds like the ones that were set loose from the pet store up the street was stuck in the drain valve. Its tail and wingtips peeked out. She squatted below it. Her butt against the hard cold floor. She stuck her finger out like a ledge and said, Step up. Step up.

The bird didn't move. It just made strange whirring noises. Its neck pumping and whizzing. Its chest taut and smooth like peeled garlic. Its skinny clawed feet just dangling there. She placed her finger below the bird's feet, and they pedaled against the skin on her hand, and she hesitated. She tried to cajole it with words, Here, birdie birdie . . . come here.

Ma was getting ready to take her to the beach. Mike had invited her along. Mike Mike Mike. Everything Mike. Like Ma would sometimes turn up her shirt collars because she said that was the way Mike did it. Marina thought she looked like an aviator. Ma never missed a chance to say something about Mike. When they ordered food, if Marina ordered something spicy, Ma'd say, Mike hates spicy. Sometimes she'd change her order at the last minute, then cover her mouth like she was telling her a secret and whisper, Gosh, if I was with Mike right now, he would've just about had it. They'd been dating for months, and by the way she spoke, Marina could tell she wanted to marry him. After a couple of dates, she always wanted to get married. She and Lola stayed up nights talking about big weddings. She wanted a big long love life with him. But then she'd look at Marina, anxious like she was being haunted.

Mutya came into the garage. Reen, you ready? Her mascara made her eyelids look heavy, like one of those flappers on the edge of sleep. She sounded irritated. She was fine in her purple island dress. A small wraparound with a bamboo print across her chest and over her shoulder. She wore espadrilles and her hair in a tight dark braid. Her hair was the blackest black. Marina sat on the floor beside the heater. Mutya's voice came as a surprise. For a moment Marina tried to absorb the idea that it was just the two of them in the garage. It seemed so long ago that they were alone. Ma sat there twinkling like a gerbil covered in glitter.

Ma, look, she's stuck.

Ma sighed, took irritated steps down the stairs, and went over to the heater. Reen, forget it. It won't come out.

Why?

It doesn't want to. This is the water heater. It's warm in there.

I want her to come out! Marina cried. Her face scrunched up. Her finger extended so the bird could step on it.

Ma sighed and grabbed the bird around its tail feathers. The bird's garlic-clove chest pushing against the pipe. Its little bird heart on overdrive. Ma tried to pull it down. Marina watched. Focused. Shut her eyes. Nothing. Nothing. The grabbable parts of the bird were stuck tight and Ma couldn't get a good grip on it. The bird was squawking like crazy. It tried to move its wings, but it was trapped in the shape of a missile.

Well, there's only one more way to go if you can't go down.

Ma made her hand into a small fist and gave the bird a tight sock to its feet. The bird shoved up into the fat drum part of the heater. There was a snap—a crunching of bones. The bird fell onto the floor. Its leg snapped off. It fell on its side with a bent wing. It fluttered around in quick, loud circles. Then it stopped.

Now clean that up, and let's get going. Mike is going to be here any second.

Marina looked into the bird's dark, glassy eyes. It looked like a statue.

What'd you do? she asked, her voice shaky.

Just what we have to do, sweetie. Help a hurt thing on its way—a tiny upward shove.

Willie Pickton was about forty-five years old, born in the ninth month, ji-chou, year of the Ox. That's good news for me. An honest Ox is a good man, a dishonest Ox is trouble but not bright. Able to be outwitted by even a Rat. Although an Ox is supposed to be a hard worker, he's not very keen. The story has it that the ox had intended to be first to the New Year's party, but a rat caught a ride on his back and then slid into first place. The Ox is a big brute, but we can outwit the Ox.

LOOK! LOOK!

Back in the seventies, Willie Pickton was sixteen, old enough to drive, and he loved and feared his mother. Meg Pickton stood in the kitchen in a shift dress over pants and what he called the sameasshiteverysinglegoddamnday knit yellow sweater—a thick yarn with peek-through holes. Tight on her head was a crisp red bandana. Every day. Most folks thought she didn't have any hair. But she had a chin full and a thick bristly brown mustache. She didn't have no teeth neither.

This was a hungry time. Sometimes Willie would slice up the hide on the pig so thin and good and leave it out on a bench in back of the slaughter room to dry out like jerky. He didn't know then how to make jerky; he thought it just took some skin and sun. He didn't realize what to do with all the hairs on the skin. About as much hair as on Meg Pickton's arms.

Willie was up at New Westminster's Woodlands School for mentally and physically disabled kids. Every Thursday, he drove a van to the school to pick up the kids and took them into town to run errands. He'd sit in his van while some boy kid sat up front sucking on the seat belt, and there were sometimes kids in back making spit bubbles and swallowing them. Whenever he dropped them back at the school, a girl would almost always run in front of him and pull up her dress to her ears. She'd say, Look! Look! Look! It was the thing he saw at night. It was the thing he saw all the time. And he knew it was a forbidden thing, those nude puckered nipples staring back at him, but it was the forbidden thing that made his pulse race. It was the forbidden thing, the electric air, the secrecy that he took to bed with him at night as he stroked himself and stared at the wall.

After the girl flashed him, he'd duck around the back of the school over by the cafeteria. He'd dive into the big green dumpster with all the dressing trailed along the side. He'd pull out dinner rolls and some of the half-eaten meat and put it all in a bag to take home to his mother.

Meg was standing in the kitchen, waiting for Willie's return.

Willie ran in the house with his bag of food, and Meg stood there in that same damn outfit she always stood in. There were locks on the cupboards around her. Only she had the keys. Willie threw the bag of food on the counter, and Meg took each piece and placed it gently over the sink as she cut off all the half-bitten and dry corners. She gave him one half of a roll and a clump of partially eaten spaghetti, then placed the rest on a plate for herself, and a small bag went into one of the locked cupboards. As she cut, she'd fire off one of her sayings, *There's always a reason for everything* or *Life goes on* or *I try to help* or *Quite a spell* or *Crock of shit* or *But that's what happens.* Or *That's life.* Or *That's not here nor there* or *We're here today; we're not here tomorrow* or *That's way above my head.*

Willie tried his best to look sad. To look like there was a big loss in all of this. But inside, he was lit up with the sight of those nude nipples—the girl's screwy face, thin lips smudged with color, long messy red hair—a ginger girl, green eyes, and then on her cheek the most necessary detail, a streak of brown marker. Look look look!

she demanded, and it could have been the last thing she said that day. It could have been the thing that made the orderlies stab her with medication or cart her off to a bed somewhere equipped with straps. He imagined her in a bed with an electrical helmet. A gentle nurse dabbing her forehead with a damp sponge and then wires and her body quaking . . . but oh oh, what's that? Her gown is up. Her boobs are out. They're juggling and jittering and her nude nipples are staring up at the oval light on the ceiling. The oval of fluorescent light interrupted by dried pieces of flies, wings, tiny legs, and once-luminescent bodies all shriveled up.

Her little baby butt. Her fatless trim body. Her perverse cleft chin. Her puckered wet puss. Her excited outie of a belly button. The staircase of her spine and rib cage. Again, with her little bosom. The tiny baby hairs that curled in toward her neck. Her face. That great face. Its newness. Its youngness. Her freewheeling helicopter arms up and out and about and twirling. She must not even have her period yet, her baby powder self. The eyes that look so particularly clear of worry. She looked both delicious and not the least bit complicated. She must have the softest skull: the carefreeness, the looseness of her.

December 12, 1994, the day before my tinikling, Willie drove through Waste Redux. He told the boring hairy lady he had a drop-off. He saw the owner with his glinty necklaces and his tight jeans and his belt with the snake on it, and he thought that Polack knew something about business. He knew that people would pay good money to get rid of their shit. Hide their shit. He probably even knew that these buckets had a lot of stuff in them that people didn't want other people to find—like married guys might slip their condoms in there from when they had an affair or something. He remembered that his brother slipped a movie ticket in one of the buckets after he was out with some friends when he should have been in school. These were secrets he was burning.

He remembered once with Corrin at the movies she sort of touched his hand when getting the popcorn out of the bucket. He looked at her and kept looking at her, and she shot him back a look like Stop it enough already, and so he looked away. Still, it hurt his feelings because another time, he saw her staring at some other guy in a restaurant that same way he had always looked at her, and she couldn't even hear what Willie was saying, she was so focused.

He decided he'd stop over at the park to get some good dope, then find one of his ghost girls. He went to the corner of Maine and Hastings, that stoplight, and that's when he saw Marina.

PORK IS A SEASONING

Back at the Plastic Palace, Lola ruled the roost. She'd devised so many rules and plans for Marina.

Why? Why was she so salty and strict?

Because Lola grew up in a trash heap. Because she'd had no shoes. Because somewhere far far far down the line there was reported to be some Philippine aristocracy, she was part Spanish but part Chinese also, and the latter crosses out the former. Because she had light skin compared to the other people from her part of the island. Because she said *sige* and *tapos* all day. Sige this, sige that. Because gossip was her favorite pastime. Because she always looked displeased. Because she was a widow. Because her nails were manicured and filed into sharp points. Because every time her husband tried to make love to her, he accused, You're dry and cold down there. Only to you, she whispered to herself.

Because after the thrashing, he grabbed her arms, bore down on her, pushing his bulbous stomach into her pelvis, stared fiercely into her eyes, and as she whimpered beneath him, he declared, I love you.

Because she hadn't been strict with herself, hadn't left when she told herself to, because she said it back, partially because she felt it and partially because she was afraid.

Because she stood by as her husband beat Marina's mother, Mutya. Stood by when he locked her in a closet. Made her stand on one leg. Made her recite things. Made her stand in a corner. Made her tiny body shiver with fear and heave with the pain of disappointing her dad. Because Lolo suffered from sumpong, black mood swings that transformed him from someone sweet and gentle into someone raging and lost. Because after watching Mutya cry, Lola came by and slipped her a small chocolate and whispered she was her favorite, and when her husband came back in the room, she would recite the tail end of a lecture she had never begun—And like I said, your father is always right.

Because she knew he was a husband she loved once. Genuinely loved, and then she had a miscarriage and the next child after died from sudden infant death syndrome. Or poverty. Or crib death. Or malnutrition. Aswang. Or all of it. Because that first husband's spirit died, and he became this . . . this raging spitting man. He did not die in the war like everyone thought he would. He died of a heart attack, like Lola knew he would. She thinks the baby broke his heart.

Because the last thing she saw at night before sleep found her was that lost child's face scrunched in a colicky scream for milk.

So Lola's life had been riddled with lessons, and that gave her plenty of material from which she could make advice, mostly for Marina. When Marina was five, Lola wrote a list of how to be:

1. When you are sent to run an errand, put extra powder under your arms. You don't want to smell like a no-no girl or a poor person.

2. Use bleaching cream on your dark skin. Keep it covered in the sun and try to stay inside as much as possible to avoid getting too dark.
3. If your nose becomes flat, sleep with a clothespin attached to the bridge. (For anyone already twelve years old or older, I am afraid it is too late, but sometimes you can do this on the night before a big date. I heard it worked for Loy Loy, and now she is happily married, and only her first child came out with a flat nose, but the rest have ears that stick out too far.)
4. If, in time, you have ears that stick out, you can stick them back with Scotch tape.
5. Learn to play the piano and to sing songs. The songs you sing should be full of heart and pride, and you should not sing anything you cannot sing in front of your suitor's lola or lolo because (dead or alive) they will be watching you.
6. Never shave above your knees, or everyone will think you're a whore.
7. Never use deodorant, or everyone will think you're a puta.
8. Pray the rosary daily.
9. Always use pork when you cook. Pork is a seasoning.
10. Never make dry rice. Measure the rice by placing your index finger in the middle of the pan—the water should rise to the first creased line on your finger.
11. Never water down the peanut sauce in kare-kare and always pick a fat pig for lechon. People will think you are cheap and lazy if you take shortcuts.
12. If you wear too much makeup, people will think you are a bakla man pretending to be a woman.
13. If you are invited to eat at his house, eat everything you are offered, and compliment the cook. If they give you the head

of the fish, smile and eat around it, but know they do not like you for their son.

14. Remember not to leave any meat on any bones, or they will think you are rude or picky.
15. When you are talking to your man, try to flip your hair around when you laugh like white girls do.
16. It is best to date a man at least ten years older than you so he can take care of you. It is best to date an American man and even better if he is white.
17. Try to find an army man or a cop. Someone with a uniform.
18. Enter the room of your suitor's mother even if it smells like the toxic smoke of mosquito-repellent incense. Don't tell her it doesn't work. All her hopes are hanging on this.
19. When you are served food, watch how they eat. If they eat with their hands, eat with yours, if they eat with a fork, *still* eat with your hands, this is something we do that is like prayer. Like saying thank you for my food. Don't ever be too ashamed to eat with your hands. Unless you are in a restaurant—but true clean women hardly eat at all in public.
20. Don't be intimidated if the mother of your suitor refers to him as a *gift from God*. But if he is her only son, smile politely and find another boyfriend. He will never have enough time for you.
21. Never marry a man whose mother is a yaya. You will never be able to clean as good as her. He will be jealous of the children she raised instead of him. You will be resentful of her constant emotional presence in your marriage.
22. If you don't like something someone says, smile very big. They will understand your disapproval.
23. Never marry an Igorot; they eat dog meat.

24. Insist the man pay the check, or he will think you are a whore.
25. Be a good Catholic and practice your handwriting. There is only one magic word that matters, *maawa ka,* Reena girl: mercy.

Deep in her dressers, Lola kept Reen's grandfather's clothing, still sweet with the scent of rum and Lucky Strikes. Smoking and alcohol were things Lola detested, so these clues let Marina know how important it was to be a flexible wife.

Sixteen hours before I was hiding in the pakshet closet Marina woke up in her room at the Astoria on Hastings. Outside the Chinese restaurant next door were concrete foo dogs, the eyes of the foo dogs missing, stolen. Sold for drugs. Who would buy a set of eyes? In the Astoria, in the bar down below, where every night skinny people in stretch pants and dresses and jaundiced people sat around singing and fighting. When she left that night, she heard a junkie couple singing in the lobby. The night before they had been fighting, then crying, and now they were howling, I fuckin' love you! into each other's faces.

Marina's room, Room 210, was one single room. One room with purple carpeting. Then over by one side of the room was a closet where the carpet changed. The carpet was a shaggy red in the closet. The door was white wood and had some chunks of plywood hammered over it in places where there were holes. The carpet had a thousand burn marks and stains, and there were bugs on the floor and the walls. Microscopic beefy ones. Bedbugs. There was a sink in 210. And there was a can of Raid on the sink. Marina didn't have any calendar in her little dank room at the Astoria but she knew it was winter even if she couldn't say if it was November or December. Outside that room the Astoria is squished between Blood Alley and Pigeon Park. Pigeon Park dotted with people squatting, drinking out of puddles, the city's largest open-air drug market. Blood Alley is where all the junkies go to shoot up.

There they were, a bunch of crippled loggers, drunks, heroin junkies, crack addicts, and all of them suffering all that you could suffer from being poor.

MAN OF THE HOUSE

Mutya laid a blanket out on the beach. This time, before Marina even said hello, Mike began to speak to her in a ridiculous voice he used when talking to waiters and bus drivers. Well, don't you look exceptional today? Then he stooped, as if that would get rid of the space between them, but he was over on the edge of the blanket and she was looking off into the ocean. They all three sat there. Marina, eager to run and play and dive into the water. But Mutya seemed to be pacing herself. Steadying them in the moment. Finally, Marina, unable to contain herself, set off running.

You can't catch me, she hollered, and took off toward the ocean. It was a lie, but a successful one because they both came bounding after her. She heard their feet clapping against the sand behind her, two pairs of grown-up legs running, Mutya grunting and pinwheeling her arms as if she were swimming. Marina looked over her shoulder and saw their straining necks. The next thing she knew, they passed on her right, and then she noticed they weren't chasing her at all but one another. Once they hit the water, they arched their backs and dove in. Like synchronized dolphins. Marina was always outside of their movie.

Later that afternoon, Mike was scaling the rocks ahead of Marina; they were exploring together. He clung around one of the first boulders and stretched his long legs across to the next one down. Meanwhile, Marina was struggling to keep up. For each of Mike's big strides, Marina had to sit on her butt, extend her legs, and slide off one rock to the next. Like a six-year-old Slinky. She was hoping he would carry her down. This is what she thought a guy would do. This is what she thought was the role of a dad. To turn around and carry her from rock to rock. Better yet, to perch her atop his shoulders and carry her through the whole world. But Mike was already several boulder Slinky moves away, on a long ridge of darker rock overlooking the ocean. She slowly found her footing. The wind smacking her in her face, and her feet itchy and grated with sand. She saw a starfish plastered to the side of one of the rocks and thought this would be a good way to get his attention, she plucked it off the edge and held it up, then tried to holler out to Mike, Hey. Look. Look.

No way he could hear her from where he stood. He just kept on ahead, the waves crashing high against her feet. The gaps between the rocks were bigger where she stood now, and the waves even higher. One of the waves coming closer was well above her head. Her arms in the air like they were, she looked like a starfish waving a starfish. But as the wave got closer, she grew scared. She imagined being pulled into the ocean. Her head hitting the rocks below her. Mike jumping ahead, not knowing.

She looked back at Mutya to see what she was doing, but Mutya was just lying back on the beach far away, trying to get a tan.

Marina turned around and made her way back to Mutya. When she hit the sand, it was hot on her feet; she ran fast back to the safety of the blanket.

Ma! Ma! Did you see me? Did you see how far I got?!

I see you tore a starfish off a rock. That's not nice, Reen. How'd you like it if you got torn from your home?

I didn't tear it. It was just wanting to get some air.

What do you think that does to a starfish?

Only good things. I know it didn't die because I prayed, and when I pray, God takes care of it. Marina was quick to lie.

Marina, God is a made-up story. There is nobody watching over you or taking care of starfish. If you are a good girl or a bad girl, nobody will know but you. Bad things happen to good people, and good things happen to bad people, and there is no way to change this with prayers. Don't be dumb.

Almost an hour later, Mike came bounding back to their blanket. On the way, lunged in front of a dog mid-flight and caught a Frisbee. The redhead who threw it, she was thin. She wore a bikini. She laughed and placed her palm on one of Mike's muscles.

Marina thought then, *How the hell could Ma ever feel safe with a guy like this?* A guy who seemed to give nothing of himself to you, like how he was with her on the rocks, but then gave himself to redheads with Frisbees. The way he stared at Mutya sometimes, it was like she was some endless resource, like gazing at her gave him power. The way he looked through Marina, it was like she was an empty glass.

You like that? she asked Ma; they both knew she meant the way Mike seemed to forget about her.

Ma shrugged, her new favorite word.

When Mike finally did sit down, he opened the small cooler he'd brought with him and quickly drank a six-pack of beer. He drank them fast enough that he'd belch, crumple a can, and then start the next.

On their way back to the car, Mike was leaning hard to the left.

Marina kept on looking at Ma. She tried to send her psychic signals. *You drive. This guy is drunk.*

She thought of praying, but then remembered what Ma said about God.

They did make it back to the Plastic Palace, but Marina's fingers were sore from crossing them so tight. She crossed her fingers and her legs and shut her eyes, and even if she wasn't praying, she thought it could work if she thought good things.

Lola was waiting eagerly at the table in the dining room. How was it?

Mike got drunk, said Marina.

Mike doesn't get drunk, Ma protested.

He sure fooled me, said Marina.

Then the phone rang. Marina picked it up. The person on the other end of the line asked for the man of the house.

This is she, Marina said into the receiver.

Almost every night, Mike drove up to Lola's in his blue BMW. The small squared-off car stopped in front of the house, Mike checked himself out in the rearview mirror, maybe slicked his hair once more. Then he'd climb out and brush off his jeans. Jessie told Marina the biggest jerks drove BMWs.

This one time, Marina waited for him at the front door, let him in, and led him into the living room. They sat on the plastic-covered couch, waiting for Ma, and Marina just hated the intensity of his longing. He couldn't keep his eyes off the hallway entrance. Marina hated watching him sit there like a dumb dog. Then when Ma appeared in the doorway, he lit up. You ready? He couldn't wait to get out of there.

Mike was not the first rich guy to love Ma. And in other cases, there had been fights between Lola and Ma in which Lola tried to convince Ma of the guy's suitability, and Ma argued he was not handsome enough or young enough. Each time Ma won, or eventually, the guy heard about Marina and went packing. Because he did not want a woman tethered to a child. Either way, Lola looked heartbroken and said Ma was throwing all her chances away.

A couple of days after the séance, feelings had smoothed between Jessie and Marina. They were inseparable again. Marina tried to make Jessie feel good by asking lots of questions.

What do you think makes the sky blue?

Well, I think it has something to do with the ocean. Like the sky really isn't blue, the sky is like one big mirror, and it is just showing us what the ocean looks like.

If the sky is a mirror, then wouldn't we hit it when we're in a plane?

It's not a hard mirror, it's a soft mirror, like an invisible mirror.

A little farther north was the cannery that stank of sardines and cotton candy from the Edgewater Carousel across the street, a blend of the soaking of flesh and the cooking of flesh and the deboning and tomato-ing, the root-beer-float drinking and old-time photo taking, where round the clock in the summertime thousands of silvery fish were being sorted and scooped into cans, where family-oriented workingmen, heavily aproned, armed with hooks and staves, were driven like machines through the stink and sweat of the day that comprised all of this little sea town's pride and joy. A tourist attraction, an explosion of labor. This was where Mike was from.

Mike had to get out of his mom's house. At the same time, Lola would exclaim, No sinning under my roof! when Ma spent the night out. Sometimes Lola would try to set Ma up with other men. She'd warn that if she married a man who was not Catholic, they'd make ugly children. Dwarves! Hydrocephalics! Harelips! A legacy of bad blood and bad skin. Marina's dad was not Catholic, so this was another dig at her halo-halo half-breedness.

Meanwhile, Ma wished it were Saturday and she was in bed with Mike in some anonymous hotel room.

Mike's mother nagged, Why do you spend so much time with that woman? That woman with the child? Are you really planning on settling down? What nationality is she anyway?

The pressure to fill all the spaces for his mother, all the roles—to be son and husband and all things to this woman who had grown even more sensitive when she learned a term for the cause of all her migraines. White noise! White noise! she'd complain. He and Ma were eager to start their life together. Except looking back now, I see Ma was eager to start her life with Mike, and Mike was eager simply to start his grown-up life.

Ma was accepted to UCLA. She also started to lose her mind. One evening when Mike and Ma didn't have a date, Ma told Lola she was moving. Marina sat by Lola's bedroom door listening. Ma was trying to sound serious, but every now and again burst out into nervous gikgik. Moving with Mike, she was saying. Los Angeles, she was saying.

Marina burst down the hall and out the front door. The streetlamps were on, and the light on Jessie's front porch was lit, small moths circling around it. Marina could hear the dirty children Lola wouldn't let her say hi to playing next door. Red light! . . . Green light!

Why was she never allowed to play with them? Then a tiny boy plunged across the street as fast as he could in nothing but Underoos and a small towel for a cape.

Marina stared at the night, the hopeless, God-awful night. The street seemed so wide when she walked across it. The air filled with the chirps of crickets and the rustling of leaves. Marina looked into Jessie's living room. Jessie sat on a sofa beside her dad, watching television. His arm around her gave rise to the greatest surge of jealousy Marina ever felt. While Marina stood there looking in the window, the sensor light on their garage went off, and Jessie's dad glanced her way. She rang the doorbell and then stepped back off the porch.

Jessie hopped off the sofa behind her father; she was wearing a striped blue turtleneck and brown corduroys. Her hair was up in a high side ponytail with a lot of bumps in it.

Her dad had a thick dark black Basque mustache and matching eyebrows. He was wearing a white undershirt and tight bell-bottomed jeans.

Can Jessie come out for a little and talk?

Jessie had drifted closer to the door and put her nose up against her father's leg.

He looked at her, and she nodded her head and smiled.

As long as you two don't cross the street.

Jessie stepped outside, edging close to the handrail.

We're moving.

Where?

Los Angeles, Ma has a boyfriend, and she wants to move to Los Angeles.

Jessie looked down. Will you be gone forever?

They both stared at the ground. Jessie reached out and put her hand on Marina's shoulder. Tell me the truth—do you think we won't be friends anymore? A sudden bang swept the sky, and then raindrops pelted down on the street.

Quick, come inside! Jessie grabbed Marina's hand and pulled her onto the porch.

Jessie—Marina said, and then kissed her hard on her cheek. Marina turned toward the rain falling outside the porch, the gray darkness, and emptiness left from all the messy neighbor kids who ran inside. Marina leaned out over the railing and let her head get drenched with water.

She jumped off the porch and ran toward the Plastic Palace. Once across the street, she looked back at Jessie standing there, her ponytail a hard wet handle on the side of her head, her blue-green eyes lit up by the yellow lights on her porch. Marina waved, and she waved, and the rain slackened. It was as if a screen were slowly being lifted from between them. Marina looked at her hand. Her fingertips were rosy and cold from the rain. She swept them across her lips and kissed them.

The Downtown Eastside was no hustling bustling business district. She did not see men dressed coming from work. She did not see briefcases. There was a man scooping money out of his pockets, next to a man handing him drugs, next to a woman plucking her daughter's socks off the ground, next to a woman picking at scabs on her skin, next to a couch on the sidewalk, next to a tent with feet sticking out of it, next to a woman selling a hundred stupid necklaces.

LOS ANGELES

The next week Ma and Marina left the Plastic Palace. Lola Virgie stood at the head of her driveway to see them off and wave goodbye. The Plastic Palace wasn't just a safe haven for them; it was part of Lola, and Ma, and Marina. More than the Plastic Palace—that Time there, the Time they spent together, on the porch with the catalogs, or eating halo-halo, or watching J.R. on *Dallas*, now as they drove away that Time was left out on the street, for the Cadillac or the mercury or the trashy people, the surplus-cheese-box kids next door, and the caved-in people Lola called *smokers*.

It was a bright hot day, the height of the barbecue weather, Ma and Marina slipped into her Easter-yellow Audi. Ma drove, her wiry hair flying back, slapping against her seat. Marina could make out the smooth band where her hairline used to begin. Flakes of dandruff scattered all over. They were heading south to LA, stopping for nothing. She planned to go all night. Stopping for nothing, she repeated. Not even a restroom. The green tin MJB coffee can beneath her seat.

If nature called, she scooted out, pulled down her black stretch pants, filled the green MJB can, and threw the ihi out the window.

Mike was already in the apartment, getting settled. Smoking cigarettes. Watching television. Apartment #4 in a quadplex in Westwood.

Outside the car, billboards of scarecrows and grapes and farmers barely showed up through the fog. Marina unsure of what any of this meant, little did she know it would be the last time for her to be with Lola, or rice days, or lovebirds, or feeding horses, or Itchi Riki, or cruel plastic runners. And yes, of course, Jessie. The last of Jessie.

And Ma was becoming all jittery and luka-luka. She reached across Marina, cranked down the window, and screamed, Cocksucker! at the librarian-type driving next to them. They drove all night. This was a different mom. A jittery mom. Wired mom. Like the mom with the bird. A steering wheel tapping mom. This mom was all business. Maybe it was something about her being so tightly wound to Mike.

Marina must've fallen asleep because the next day, she awoke on the floor of an apartment she had never seen—a one-bedroom with hardwood floors, a fireplace, and a mantel. There was no furniture except for a paper kite in the shape of a fish hanging in the kitchen. It was a Japanese kite, something Mike must've bought her mother. The message: This was a new life. A life with Mike. In this new life, Ma was going to a school called UCLA, and she was going to work at night as a data entry clerk, typing and filing for a big accounting firm. As far as Marina could tell, Mike did nothing. Reen was jealous of him, but she also noticed his attentions were elsewhere. Ma would always be so anxious that everything was just so around him all the time. Mike's family was rich. Marina heard him talk about how they had a boat. His dad was dead, but he had smoked a tobacco pipe like a real fancy man—Marina had seen it, the one time she went to Mike's mother's condo, the whole time riddled with the worry of breaking something or knocking over the marble chess set or getting smudges on the carpet.

Mike and Marina dropped Ma off at her new school in Westwood. Big brick buildings. It looked like a church. It was the biggest school Marina ever saw. She thought it was beautiful. She thought it was perfect. It seemed like a place where vampires would go and hide at night. From the shows she watched, she figured this was a place of endless coffee and bands with guitars and books—tons and tons of books. Marina saw girls all with their hair swept up in I-mean-business ponytails. She saw sweaters. She saw jeans. She saw a place where people came to think and eat ice cream and go bowling. Her heart grew plump with all of it. But she missed Lola.

There were times when Ma let her stay at the school and wait for her, and she would pretend she was a student. During the day, Marina sat quietly in the library until they let Ma out of class. She'd pull a book off the shelf, a big impressive-looking one, sometimes a book bound in leather, and she'd open it to a page and stare at all the words. Then magically, she'd discover there were some that made sense to her, the three- and four-lettered words, and she'd map them throughout the page, and sometimes made up her own stories in between her words she already knew. She belonged there with the words. Years later, she'd comb the Downtown Eastside library for those same books. In those books, there was no lice, no scabies, no track marks, no whoring, no snuff films, no SROs; there was just that moment, that feeling she had when she first discovered the words on the page at Ma's school.

At night when Ma was at work, Marina spent most of her time alone, trying to find a way to make Ma and her rich. Ma nagged her to study—said that books would bring her freedom and independence. She shouldn't need a man. She shouldn't need. Ever.

Marina wanted to save lots of lives, so she thought maybe she could be a neurosurgeon. She heard they were the best paid. Ma told her that working on brains was like taking off the skin of a grape in one piece without injuring the meat of the grape and then sewing it back together. Marina sat many hours with a big pile of grapes, one by one, unpeeling them. If she made a mistake on one, she put it down and started over again. In the end she took all the skinned grapes and left them outside for squirrels and ladybugs and elves, but one time a woman walking her Pomeranian yelled at her and told her that grapes were poisonous for dogs.

Marina tried to complain about Mike to Ma, how he was sometimes late picking her up, how he didn't listen. She'd call his name a bunch of times, and he'd say nothing. He spoke to her without looking directly at her. He spoke to a spot about five inches to the right above her head. Ma didn't agree. She thought he was *the bee's knees,* she'd say, although Marina had no idea what she meant by *the bee's knees*. So she kept quiet. Ma coached her on her magic feminine wiles, swerving her hips around. Then about a month after they moved to LA, Mike left. They'd moved all the way to Los Angeles to be together. There were all those M&M packets Ma kept for Mike and Mutya, but then she'd repurpose during breakups to Mutya and Marina. It was so much togetherness. Later at night Marina'd hear her on the phone, Go on, fuckin' go. I don't give a shit—take off . . . Then later, When are you coming back? Do you think you will? Please?

Marina found Ma flung across her bed. A diagonal heap. The next morning, Marina got dressed for school. Let her sleep in. A carpool came and picked her up. Another single mom who worked a lot drove her to school some days in exchange for Ma driving them home. Ma didn't hold up her side of the bargain, so Marina would have to call the other mom and beg for a ride.

Los Angeles smelled like a military base. Canned meats. A year made up of summer temperatures. On sad nights Ma left her television on fuzz. Marina'd turn it off. Marina learned how to read Mutya's body language: when she got angry, her shoulders fell forward, her small hands made tight fists, her lips pressed together so tight they ebbed into a bright white line. Where were you? Ma'd scream before she could sneak away.

She'd yell back, School.

Actually, she was out behind the Burger King. By now, she was eight and had been placed in gifted classes. All those years of drills and traipsing behind Mutya on her college campus. The compliance of early childhood prematurely morphed into the shitty I-don't-care-but-really-care-too-much defiance of puberty.

And where will we be if something happens to you?

Getting up from her bed, Ma demanded Marina clean and stack the plates, arrange them by color, by shape. Right then. She was only as big as a thirteen-year-old boy, with a tamaraw soul, the miniature buffalo, but horns just as sharp. Marina knew better than to answer back. Eventually, Ma tired, pulled her close, and said, Don't ever leave me. Don't you dare. The anger between them like a once-fat balloon deflated and limp.

Go to sleep, Ma, Marina said.

Marina preferred this time between men. When Ma was in love she'd be only half there, a constant smug look on her face—like she was sharing an inside joke with someone else. But this time between boyfriends Marina and Ma were a team. She even hinted about going back to Lola's.

Marina met a new kid at school. He had just moved to LA from China. She was supposed to be his partner, so she sat beside him in class and introduced him to the other kids. He was always so grateful even though Marina was awkward, sometimes making up her own language mimicking what she thought was his native Cantonese. Then he was missing from school, and her tuberculosis skin test came back positive. Marina had to have chest X-rays. Ma held her hand. Ma prayed. Marina had to take a large white pill the size of a cashew. Every night. Marina did not know how to swallow them, so Ma mushed them between two spoons and tried to conceal it in a large glass of orange juice. Sometimes she promised her ice cream. It was these nights she seemed most tender to her. Desperately begging her to take the pill. Anything, anything if Marina would please take the pill.

Then later, after Marina took the pill, Ma tucked her in bed and smoothed the hair off her forehead and kissed her cheeks and then stooped low and gobbled at her arm, threatening, I'm gonna eat you up, poopee face!

Marina began wheezing at bedtime, Ma could hear it from her side of the mattress, she'd gently tickle her back and whisper stories to her. Her favorite was the story of three sisters, Little One-Eye, Little Two-Eyes, and Little Three-Eyes. Little One-Eye and Three-Eyes were viciously jealous of Little Two-Eyes' beauty and so demanded that she do all the chores and cleaning at odd hours.

Ma would later pull her out of bed in the middle of the night. Shake her awake, demand that she do the dishes. By *dishes* she meant the aluminum trays from frozen Hungry-Man dinners they kept and reused. Sometimes she'd ask if the clothes on the bathroom floor were her mess. Then before anything else. Before Marina could lie. Ma'd smack her. Marina developed asthma; she was given an inhaler. Ma showed her how to use small soft gentle puffs, how to hold her breath, how to count in her head; Marina pictured little blue fairies swooshing their way up and down her lungs, then finally she could breathe again.

While she was home sick from school, she watched a PBS special about how laundry detergent contains phosphates that create a kind of algae in fresh water that fuck up the oxygen available to the fish and can make them all polluted and messed up like a catfish that was discovered in New York with three eyes. This made her feel superior, superior for washing her clothes by hand with regular soap (she could hear her lola, *Ay! Sus! Body soap, face soap, laundry soap—too many kinds of soap, just use soap!*). And she felt powerful, like how she could, if she wanted to, fuck up aquatic life, but here she was choosing not to. At school, Marina had her enemies. It was difficult for her to make friends when she was pulled out of her regular classes to the advanced gifted classes. The worst was a girl named Tina Glazer, whose father was a dentist and who brought these small red pills to class one day. When they chewed them up, they left a residue that showed where the plaque was on their teeth. Marina's mouth was a red abyss, a plaque haven. Tina started bringing her dental hygiene samples.

Here, Marina, she said, I thought you might like this. It's pink, like your jumpsuit.

She handed her a toothbrush that had an image of dinosaurs on the handle. At least she didn't say, It's pink like your mouth. Marina took it.

Thanks.

Marina wanted to stab her with it. *Just because your fucking dad is a fucking stupid dentist doesn't mean that any of this shit really matters. My mom meets all sorts of good guys because she is pretty, and she doesn't floss either. When you have boobs, you do not need to floss.*

Ma knew Marina had trouble making friends, so she broke down and got her a puppy. But when it came time to choose the puppy, she wanted one of her own too. They found a pair of German shepherd puppies. They looked like bears the size of cereal bowls, fluffy and trusting, their eyes the color of black jewelry.

They named them Dear Abby and Ann Landers after the advice columnists in the paper. The only problem was Ma and Marina had no clue how to take care of dogs. Marina thought they were fun to wrestle with, scrambled after them sometimes with their upstairs neighbor, grabbing them by their bloated bellies and throwing them on the couch.

One day she came home and they were gone. Ma said she had to send them somewhere else. That they peed and pooped too much, and it wasn't fair they were never home enough to walk them. And that a dog really needed a proper house with a yard. The excuses came flying. The truth was that they could barely afford to feed themselves, even less two puppies.

One sad day Ma was struck with the hard choice at a cash register. Juice or milk? Milk or juice? Their food stamps could not cover both. They had to choose. She put back the milk and replaced it with a box of powdered.

Marina didn't speak to her for a week after the puppies, but that night after the grocery store, Ma crawled beside her in bed and wrapped her legs around her and said, Here we are—this is a love buckle. I'm gonna buckle you in. It was calm-making. The next day after school, when Marina came home, Ma was gone. There was no food in the fridge. For a second, Marina thought maybe she'd gone out for food, but the mess she'd left behind said different. Said she was out on a date somewhere. Her makeup case, her shoes, the two other dresses she tried on before the one she settled on wearing.

Marina went back into the kitchen and made herself a Carnation

Instant Breakfast drink. The only flavor left was strawberry. Marina hated strawberry.

With her mother out on a date, Marina had time to work on her concoction. It was a way to cure the cancer that was killing everyone. She was convinced they had all the right ingredients there at home. It was a little bit of all the oils and perfumes and lotions mixed together. Marina put them in a bowl and mix mix mix. Then she placed a small dab on her skin and saw how in those places, where her skin once looked dusty—it looked new. It's working, she thought, it's working!

Then she heard her.

Reen Reen! Come out and say hi to Mike!

He was fucking back.

Marina quickly took her little bowl of cancer cure and placed it under the sink with a small plastic spoon where no one would notice. No one ever goes under the sink in this house. Once, she'd hidden a couple of Fig Newtons there to see if Ma would notice, and she found them later with mold and a family of roaches living around them.

Marina opened the door to see Ma and Mike standing there like two dopey fools. Like they didn't live there. Like they'd come for a dinner party and they were waiting for her to take their coats. Like she was seriously in the way of the significant damage they couldn't wait to do to each other—the air gross, filled with kinky anticipation.

Yes? Marina asked. As in, what do you want?

Well, honey poo bear poo poo. Can we have the living room tonight?

Fine. She stomped off to the bedroom.

At 1:45 a.m., Marina woke up from a strange dream. She went to the kitchen for a glass of water. On the way back to the room, she peered over and saw Ma curled around Mike on the living room floor. A love buckle. Marina tiptoed over to them. She wanted to slide between them. Or maybe put her secret cure for cancer in his nose and eyes, and maybe it would kill him. Marina returned to the bathroom and got her special bowl. Ma turned away from Mike, and Marina went to her. She kneeled down close beside her and whispered, He sucks, Ma—make him go.

She whispered some more, You can't hear me now, but when you wake up, you will have a sudden urge to break up with Mike. You won't know why. You just will. And you will break up with him, and we will live happily ever after.

Marina patted Ma's head. Moved her hair away from her mouth. Curled it behind her ears. Marina walked over to Mike. She took the cancer cure, a small dollop, and mixed it in with her glass of water. She raised the glass high above his head and tilted it slightly. A small drop fell on the crown of his head. He didn't quite wake up, but his eyelids shook, and he made a small moan. She saw it hit and imagined it burrowing into his skull, then quietly tiptoed off to bed, hoping that maybe the next day, only two of them would wake up.

Why did she hate him so much? He was a symbol of Ma's deep-down aversion to her. When Ma saw her enter a room, her eyes glazed over, as if Marina were just a job.

Like a miracle, when she came home from school the next day, the shades were drawn.

Mom? Marina opened the door to their bedroom. The lights were off, and there she was again, strewn across her bed. She thought of the magic potion. She thought maybe he woke up and felt it and it irritated him, and he decided to leave. To go find a doctor, lady. Maybe she'd heard her whispers. Maybe she's magic like the mermaid in *Splash*. Only this is her magic. Grown-up love affairs. Ma said, Again. Again. Again. We're destined to be alone. We're gonna be alone forever.

It's okay, Marina said. It's okay.

She did this often. Saying things she didn't know anything about. Try to make the heart soft again.

Ma got worse. Sometimes that meant she was full of fun. Ma and Marina dancing and doing crossword puzzles. And other times, Ma was paranoid. Drilling her on things like police codes. Like Lola, she found the ways in which everything could go wrong. This was when she invented the game Chase Toast.

Ma leaned in close. A sheen of sweat on her nose. Her tight lips dry. Her face was small and round, painted with dark red blush.

Psssstttttt . . . Reenaleen . . . Reenie . . . she said.

She swatted her free hairs away. She slept in giant pointy pink curlers, her head resting a foot above the pillow. When she slept this way, it reminded Marina of a game the other girls played at slumber parties. She was eight years old and in the second grade and slumber parties were all the rage. The game was Light as a Feather, Stiff as a Board. It was a game where several children bent down around one of the others and placed just their fingertips between that person and the floor. They made like their fingertips were little planks of wood, and the idea was that if you repeated this phrase enough, it would have the effect of making the person light enough to levitate.

Marina imagined Ma's pink curlers carrying her off into the smog of LA.

Money when they had it was quick, a flash of fireworks and then sparkled up toward the moon and out into the night. Swatting at Marina's blankets, Ma said, C'mon, let's go chase toast.

Marina sat up, her hair partially stuck to her cheek, a curl trapped with her thumb and forefinger against her nose. One cheek the color of a candied apple, the other its usual tan.

Hmm? Malm? she mumbled with a thumb plunged deep in her

mouth, tongue flicking it and swooping past the back of her new teeth.

Toast, Rina! Let's chase toast!

Ohfay . . . she mumbled, then slid like oozing jelly out of bed.

There were three different Ships diners in Los Angeles at the time. One in Westwood, one thirty minutes away in Culver City, and another twenty more minutes away on Olympic and La Cienega. Ships was your typical diner with seventies décor except for one amazing facet. Toasters. There were toasters on each table, so they handed you a stack of white bread, and you could toast it yourself. This sounds like no big deal, but it was. It was huge. To have the ability to make your own toast. Everyone likes their toast different: the right golden hue, the right amount of butter.

Chase Toast meant hopping on the bus and going to all of the Ships diners and making their own toast. All three. The waitress came to them with a stack of white bread. Three pieces cut diagonally in half. Marina sat in the booth, perched on her knees, stacking her grape jelly. She wanted to be armed and ready. The perfect piece of toast came with butter and grape jelly. Not the mixed fruit. Not the strawberry. Good old-fashioned gooey fake purple grape. She was the boss at Chase Toast. She ordered herself. She made the toast herself. At some point when the sun started peeking through the blinds, she fell asleep, her head sticking against the vinyl booth or on Ma's lap. It was fine. It was more than fine to sleep there, among the white mugs that had tan rings around them. And the matching saucers and warm plates that always came with the warning, Careful, it's hot.

If anyone tried to make any racket around her and Ma, Ma would smooth the hair over her ears. Pet her head. She'd tell everyone to hold it down. The princess is sleeping, she'd say. She carried her like a little baby bean next to her chest all the way home from the last bus stop, and she never complained that she was heavy. If she startled, Ma'd whisper, Shhhh . . . Shhhhh, the princess is sleeping. It was the most tenderness she ever felt. It made those nights magic.

The next morning, Mutya moved slower than usual, running her fingers through her curls and across her forehead, resting at her temples. Sometimes she'd dig her nails into her scalp, to give herself a zap of blood rushing to her head, seemed like the memories of the previous night would slowly start marching in, like a parade motorcade. More and more color would come to her face and then she'd ask, Toast?

Some nights Mutya spent time teaching Marina how to fight. How to swing from her hip and put all her weight from her right strong side, her strong hips that held all the fury from their bad hard life and how to put that force behind her blow.

It's the Salles code, hit him before he can hit you. Always throw the first punch.

Later when Mutya and Marina were lying in the stupid ugly bed, Ma'd go over their drills.

She looked at the ceiling while Marina traced a trail up and down her arms slowly. Gliding. Up and down. She said, 10-29F.

These police codes left over from when Mutya dated a cop. She'd helped him study for patrol, and then when he made sergeant, he dumped her. But really, it was likely because she was always showing him up in his studies, always retaining the information fast and effortlessly.

Marina tensed. Subject is wanted for a felony, use caution. Advice when . . . Advice. Marina was searching.

Ma moved away from Reen's trailing finger and rolled onto her side. Not advice. Advise. Viiiiizzze. Advise what?

Advise when subject in custody and ready for information. Marina blurted it out fast, her little chest pumping with her words.

Yes. Good. 187?

Murder. That was easy.

207? She was lying on her back again.

Kidnapping. Marina reached for her. Some part of her. She wanted to feel her. Ma ignored this need of hers.

What do you do if you ever get in a fight?

Always be the first one to throw the punch.

Always. 211?

This is how she was when they were alone. Tight, overbearing, wrapping Marina in her C-grip. But when there were guys, Marina was a ghost.

Robbery, Marina said. Her hair. Reen got her hair. She patted it between her hands. Like a hamburger patty. Pat pat.

Very good, and what did I tell you to do if someone tries to kidnap you?

Kick him in the balls.

Yes. What else?

Drop a shoe.

Yes.

Marina didn't know why she thought this. Maybe Ma thought it would help her find Marina. That her shoe would be her compass. She was always devising ways they could be torn apart and brought back together again. Whenever Marina saw a shoe anywhere—a shoe on a pole, a shoe on a wire, she knew it was there for some other reason. A street sign for drugs. Heroin. H. Shabu. But she would just as much have assumed that it was there because some poor kid was stolen away. 207.

Even though she didn't have a calendar, Marina knew the next day was welfare day 'cause everyone was getting magulo throwing themselves around. Back and forth along Blood Alley, their butt cracks sticking out their pants, burnt fingertips, crusty eyes always searching for more and more and more.

That afternoon she sat up in her bedbug-infested cot, looked over at her closet, all different kinds of wood nailed over holes. She smoked rolled tobacco that she rescued from sidewalks and ashtrays. She heard some static on the television next door. In the room beside her lived an old junkie named Brewster or Bruiser, not sure, to Marina he looked like a sad dog. At some point, he fixed in his dick, and Marina wound up rescuing him by giving him a smack, calling in the paramedics, plucking the needle from his dick before they arrived with their strange gamot.

All around she saw streets overcome by people, their backs to the cars, hunched over protecting a small glass vial, cheeks puffed out holding in smoke. People with fast jerking movements, crooked gaits. She saw slumped sedated people, people in alleyways, people huddled in corners, people selling pork links stolen from the market, people hawking garbage, movies, tape cassettes, jewelry, blankets laid out on the ground, furniture. It was like a cluster of rat people. And the sounds, the yelling, she heard a woman yelling, I tried to fucking hang myself today fucking fuck this shit! Fanny packs clinging to shrunken waistlines. Children wriggling from strollers.

This is a place where people give no more pakshet.

BACK AND FORTH AND SIDE TO SIDE

It was the summer of 1989 and sports had made Los Angeles the City of Champions. The air was heavy with bug spray; sometimes Marina sprayed it as she walked and let it fall about her like mists. Their apartment was upstairs and smooshed in between lots of other units. And you could never get rid of the roaches because once you cleaned out all the cupboards and did a roach bomb and all your dishes tasted like bug poison, they just went next door and came back later. The worst feeling was when she opened a drawer or went to the bathroom and looked at the floor, and there beside her feet or in the drawer was a little brown empty cocoon. The shell of a roach egg. Tan-brown shiny, empty. Each roach can carry about sixteen roach babies in one egg. Each lady roach got pregnant about fourteen times in a lifetime so like four times fifty times four times fifty times four times fifty times fuckin' forever fucking roaches.

Beside their building was a trash bin, surrounded by a brick wall. There was a small hole in the middle of the brick wall. A possum burrowed his way into the hole. Ma and Reen hated the possum. He sat and leered. He was never afraid. Since Reen was the kid, she always got the crummy jobs. That's how it became Marina's job to throw out the trash. She ran to the brick wall, closed her eyes, threw her arm way back, hiked her right knee up in the air to meet her right fist like she was pitching the trash into Dodger Stadium, the whole while her eyes shut tight, afraid of his leering.

Below and to one side of them lived a Mexican family. Ma and Reen always got confused for being Mexican. Marina didn't really like being confused for other things because she had a dad somewhere who was Black, and it made her feel like maybe he didn't exist anymore because nobody saw him in her. She dreamt about having a different life with this dad. Ma had long thick wavy hair and little Asian eyes, and Marina liked her brown skin. When they went to bed at night, she pushed their two beds together. Marina sometimes made out that there were bugs or something crawling on Ma in her sleep, and Marina would stamp them out with her hand. And Ma let her. Night was the time Ma let her do almost anything she wanted. Ma had a lot to do on her own, and she usually missed something, a bill turned pink and urgent, or the water got shut off, or there was a mess in the sink. It embarrassed Marina sometimes, but more often than not, she was scared of her. Her mother, the daytime taskmaster.

One time Ma and Marina dressed up and went to the mall to take professional photos. They posed on carpeted squares. Ma had the big airbrushed framed results in their living room. The two of them, smiling and dressed up like a family. Ma looked straight into the camera. She had those dark eyes of infinity. Marina hated the lie of that picture. It's a fantastic power Ma possesses, to light up her face at will—shining eyes, seemingly radiant smile—forehead smooth and unlined as if she were still nineteen years old instead of thirty-one.

Beside her, Marina appeared at a disadvantage. It was as if Ma had stolen all the light. Marina had a worried look; you could see her focusing—trying not to blink, counting the seconds. Her eyes looked glassy, holding back tears. She twinkled. Look at the good-looking well-kept mother and daughter. Ma even got the picture on a payment plan that she never finished paying off. There was another one of Ma, her hair flowing over her shoulders and her eye-teeth sticking out like fangs. Marina thought she looked like a freaky vampire. One day she'd have that same faraway look on her face; she would fall into a world that smelled like sweat, spunk, armpit, and yet still the bug spray. Always the bug spray. A world of wet dark rot.

Most nights, Marina was alone. At thirteen, she was old enough to wear Ma's clothes and begin to look like a woman. She was developing little pointy susos and would soon need to wear a bra. Young enough to be afraid of the dark. She'd stand in front of the bathroom mirror with a pair of Ma's stockings over her face, trying her best to scare herself. She'd breathe hard Darth Vader breaths and stare and stare, sweating and slobbering. Her hair plastered against her skin. Her eyes big open holes of nothing, her nose squished. Marina'd stare at herself long enough to bring up a note of panic. She called this game the Predator and it helped her prepare for all bad things that could come in the night. After, she stayed awake and imagined Ma's demise. Imagined that she was unable to come home due to a car accident or a stabbing. The sense of guilt she developed outweighed the game's benefits. Ma was all she had, and she was terrified of losing her.

She loved that Ma spoke to her like she spoke to adults. She didn't have a smaller voice, or a pitched-up voice. Her mom voice was the same, except it was always full of secrets and surprises. She pulled Marina close and whispered things just for her to hear.

For extra money, Ma worked at the local park nights and weekends. Also, they let Marina go to the summer camp for free. A place where girls giggled and boys chased them, and Marina mostly saved her change to buy Tiger's Milk bars because she thought they were the types of things women ate when they were dieting, and Ma was always dieting and a large part of Marina wanted to be just like her.

Mostly, Ma supervised the DUI classes, mostly because she thought that was a great way to meet guys. But one night a woman named Fatimah came by and asked for keys to the rec room. She was all silver hoops and flowy skirts and her hair like a rich, thick veil. She was tall and curvy and beautiful in all the ways that Marina had never thought Ma to be beautiful. She took up space in the room. Her dark painted eyes, her big apple cheeks. Close up, she was younger than Ma but definitely too old to be a girl. Her underarms weren't shaved. There was hair there, a lot. Her shins and thighs and the backs of them were also not shaved. It was unbelievable. The hairs were like hundreds of little threads coming straight out of her skin: her noise and all its shimmy shimmy.

We don't have a DUI class today, Ma said.

Fatimah was carrying a ghetto blaster, a Hula-Hoop, and some coined belly chains.

Does it look like I'm here to teach a driving class?

Ma scrunched her face, then looked flustered at her. I'm sorry, I didn't realize there were any other classes at night.

Fatimah gestured for them to follow her as she walked over to a small bungalow.

Inside the bungalow, all the chairs were moved to the walls. There was no one else in the class. Fatimah moved a long thin mirror to the front of the room so they could see themselves or at least parts of themselves. Then she set down her ghetto blaster and hit play. She sat on the floor, her legs out in front of her.

The music blasted—Marina knew this song. From *Top Gun*. Her favorite movie. It was that slow song they played when they were on the motorcycle by the beach. Fatimah slowly slinked her way up off the floor. Mutya and Marina tried to copy her. The music began to pick up pace, and Fatimah extended her arms toward the ceiling. It was like she was doing the hula to the music. Making arm movements to mimic the lyrics . . . then it hit the chorus . . . TAKE MY BREATH AWAY.

At this point, Marina had completely lost her cool and done away with all the slow movements, and she just bounced around. Mutya and Fatimah were in sync with one another. Mutya quickly becoming Fatimah's shadow. Then the music really picked up a beat and was the poppy electronic theme song to *Beverly Hills Cop*. Fatimah was turning in circles and quickly shimmying her hips back and forth while keeping her torso still. Her arms moving up and down like snakes, her fingers extended and elegant. Marina thought she looked a little like she was getting electrocuted, especially in her butt.

So this was belly dancing. Not very many women showed up to Fatimah's class. Mutya often went and they spent the time talking—getting to know each other.

Later, Marina had a dream that Fatimah ducked into a church, lowered her head, and drank all the holy water. Her skin lit up by the candles, she could see all the positions of the cross strewn like twinkle lights along the tunnels of her veins.

Fatimah's father was killed in a flood. He worked on an oil rig back home in Qatar, and her mother depended on him to make all the money. They weren't the kind of parents who knew how to raise a daughter. Two nights after he was killed, in the summer of 1964, after dinner, when everyone was still hungry, Fatimah went out back to get some clean water to wash her clothes for the next day. Out behind the shed with the water pump was a boy. A boy with big eyes and round lips and a soft cotton outfit. She had never seen him before, but he looked like one of the boys who went to the upper school who she would dream about and practice kissing every night. Without a word. Without a question, he pushed Fatimah up against the wall, lifted her dress, and stuck his index finger in her. Then he handed her a coin and ran off.

This happened again and again, and eventually, the word got out, and other boys would meet Fatimah behind the wall until one day, more than one boy showed up—so instead of letting them touch her, she shimmied for them. Back and forth and side to side and teased them good until their little shriveled buto got hard, and even though they were frustrated, they were delighted in this naughty thing they got to do together—they got to enjoy together! They loved the power they thought they had in humiliating this poor girl.

She saved the money. She bought makeup and scarves. And this is the way she began belly dancing. Later, when she was a teenager, and the bachelor party filmed her dancing and then on her knees, then on her back, then bent over the sink, they said she could make a lot of money. She needed things. She needed food and rent, and maybe braces. One of the guys with the camera—he was good about bringing it up close to her face and then close to her body. He would bring up this fact again, threaten her with the small canisters of film in his hand when it came time to pay her. She thought then of the red fox of her youth. How she heard stories of how they befriended the coyote, only to drink their blood later. She would do the same, push her paws in front of her on the carpet. Keep her mind filled with stories like a movie. Listen to the sounds of the nature channel on TV. She heard the fox's catcalls.

Marina walked over to the tracks. The tracks are where the girls line up to get picked up. A line in the sidewalk separates the midtrack from the kiddy corner, then there's also the low track. The kiddy corner is for men who like little girls, the midtrack is for girls like Marina, maybe when she first got to Vancouver, and the low track is for what she'd become.

Streetlights and people with fucked-up attire. Like women in wheelchairs who didn't need wheelchairs, who wore high heels and sometimes clicked their way around town and men in dresses that are no longer pretty and little skinny cagey women with yellow veiny arms in short skirts and sequined tops and then there was Marina. Unsure of herself. She still desperately wanted to be fresh again. Her hair was a messy rat's nest on top of her head. But in her mind—in her mind, it was dazzling. In her mind she was Diana Ross or Donna Summer, she was just spectacular, but her jeans were getting a little too big for her, so she rolled over the waistband and tied a string across it, and her ropey arms had some abscesses, gaping oozing holes where bright tan flesh used to be. Still, if she squinted her eyes to the thrum and swoosh of the cars passing by, she could pretend to be another woman, someone like Ma. Full of sexual mystery—open to anything. She would be your disco queen or your ho or your foxy mama whatever. When Marina was out there, she could see herself in her mind and she didn't see the eczema, the dry skin clumps on one cheek, the messy knot of hair. She didn't see the sweater with the holes and the no bra, her titties looked all swingy and empty, the little collection of zits popping up on her forehead. She didn't smell herself, the scent of urine and desperation.

HAWTHORNE

Ma became a woman who went out and danced late at nightclubs. She'd go out to cheesy places. She never drank. Not even a drop. She'd go out dancing four, maybe five times a week. Marina saw how all the men fell in love with her. How they watched her. Her flirting, her glittery glinting self. She was small, five feet, but there on the dance floor is where her fantasy self and real self seemed to merge.

She'd practice dancing with Marina at home. She let Marina wear her shoes. She put on a Bee Gees record and stood tall and put her arms out, and Reen swooped into the empty cup of them, and she twirled her around, and they danced. She slid her through the middle of her legs. Flew her forward. Her warm chest gave off an odor of cocoa butter. She extended both of her arms like she was measuring yards of fabric and Marina stood tall on her tippy-toes so she could match her arms to Ma's and then they slowly turned together, Marina's arm gliding across the length of Ma's collarbone until they were one long extension of each other, attached only by fingertips. It was her very favorite thing to be. An extension of Ma.

Ma began wearing more racy clothing. Stuff like little red leather skirts, and one time she went to the Contempo Casuals store in the mall and bought a black velvet dress with little perfect finger-sized holes on the top. It looked like an invitation to get poked. Marina took one look at her standing there in that dress and stuck her long finger in her mouth; Barfarama, Marina said. As Ma dressed, Marina sat perched on the sink and watched her. Sometimes Ma'd reach her hand in the front of her dress and perk up her boobs like hoisting up Hawaiian rolls. Look what you did to me, she blamed. Her nipples thick little knots of flesh. Ma didn't miss a chance to let Marina know how her monthlong attempt at breastfeeding took the air out of her bubelya. Sometimes she'd look down at them and give them marching orders like a drill sergeant: Pick it up, girls!

Now that you and Mike are broken up why can't we move back with Lola? Marina'd been missing Lola and making a regular point to bring this up.

Reen, you know we can't do that. I still have school.

How much more school do you have? It seems like forever already.

I just have four more years, but if you do good in your own school you can go visit her in the summer.

Ma would see all the hope she had in her eyes if she looked up.

Promise?

Promise.

One night, Ma wound up at the Cheesecake Factory with a guy Fatimah and her friends called Sam. His given name was Yasir. Sam looked like a Middle Eastern John Travolta. Only it was the late eighties, past the time when John Travolta and VO5 and pompadours were in style, there he was in a Members Only jacket. Top buttons of his shirt undone. He looked like a disco king on the Cheesecake Factory dance floor, and that caught Ma's eye. Ma was stuck on disco. She saw this guy and twirled her way up to him. Ma, weighing in somewhere in the high double digits, a waif of a little brown woman, slid along the dance floor like his glass of whiskey shot across the wooden bar.

The strobe light flashed, Sam moved all slow with his tight pants. Mutya lip-synced the lyrics,

It's my prerogative!

She smiled big at Sam. Not sure exactly if they were dancing together or not. He didn't look at her but kept his sight above her head. He sipped his drink out of the stirrer left in his glass. This was a pet peeve of Ma's. Anytime Marina drank her hot cocoa out of the skinny red stirrers at Ma's office job, Ma would correct her.

That is not a straw, Reen. Don't be dumb.

But here, she didn't say anything. She just kept on singing along to the song. Flouncing her head forward, punching her hands down to the ground, *My prerogative.* Trying to catch Sam's eye. Sam was now swinging his arms back behind him like he was doing the backstroke, and Mutya was moving her arms forward and coming in closer like she wanted to be twirled.

Finally, Sam leaned in. Who sings this song?

Happy to be acknowledged, she said, C'mon, Bobby Brown. You don't know Bobby Brown?

Oh, Bobby Brown? he asked. Before she could answer, he continued, Keep it that way.

Humiliated, Mutya left the dance floor back to the bar to sit down. He saw he had made an impression on her. He saw it was terrible. To watch her face fall like that. Like ice cream melting off a cone. He wanted to make it up to her.

He went back to her, with a slice of cheesecake with a candle in it. He told the waitstaff it was her birthday. They sang her happy birthday, but because he didn't yet know her name, he sang, Happy birthday, habibti.

When they were finished singing, she asked him what *habibti* meant.

He smiled and said, My love.

Oh, she said. In Tagalog, it's *mahal.*

Mahal, he said, and smiled.

That night she rushed into the apartment delighted—thrilled. The way she told it, he was something to obsess about. He was the best, the most, the is-est. She came home at three in the morning. She said she met a man who looked just like John Travolta. She danced across the apartment. She made small cups of International Delight coffee. It tasted like mint chocolate. It tasted like they were having a slumber party.

It was winter in Los Angeles, and there were no sea breezes or pine-brushed winds. The air smelled like sun and fall leaves crunched under old brakes and new tires. The streets still damp from one night's rain and a stream collected in the LA River. The LA River, with its great blue heron sitting regal on a branch above the debris swooshing by.

And then came a night in December. Ma had been seeing Sam for four months. Four months of five nights a week where Ma was out and Marina was home alone. December 20, 1989, Marina begged Ma to take her with her to Sam's place. She cried and cried about it. There were already two nights earlier that same week Ma didn't come home and Marina sat staring at her stockinged face in the mirror. Marina accused Ma of not loving her. Marina told Ma she couldn't sleep—that she was frightened of all the strange noises in the apartment. Ma sighed. She said, Fine, fine, fine.

On the ride over, Marina cracked her window open. She sipped the air while Ma complained to shut it, she was cold. Marina felt hot and dizzy. All the lights whizzing by, the sound of rap music from the neighboring cars. The streets lined with palm trees, their leaves turning brown. Some Christmas lights gleaming off in the distance like from a mall or superstore. Old ladies stood at bus stops, and gangsters walked their dogs, and there was a guy shuffling across the street in slippers, or *house shoes* is how they called them.

The moment they reached the apartment, Marina regretted her begging. Now that she'd gotten what she wanted, no degree of begging would take her back home. She was stuck. What did she really want? To be alone? To be with Ma? What she wanted was to be at their apartment. Or even better to be back in Monterey with Ma and Lola. But there they were in Hawthorne—this city was the dark side, the wild boar's stomach. It flickered off and on in the distance like porn. It was the worst thing that could happen to you. If you went there for any length of time, it was like being at a discount store for too long, and suddenly that glittery disco dress wasn't so bad looking anymore. And the next day, you're at church trying to be respectable in a glittery disco dress. The apartment with the soft tan carpeting, fluffy and a virgin to shoes, the small hot kitchen, the thick incense, the tiny bathroom with tacky vinyl flooring, a stand-up shower-tub combo with a glass sliding door, the bedroom with two twin beds and a skinny long sliding window draped in black-blue towels. The living room was furnished for bachelors. Big pleather couches and a glass table. That night—this apartment was packed with Sam and his two brothers, his six male cousins, and their occasional girlfriends.

Marina felt so invisible that she could easily have slipped off and built one of her cancer cure concoctions with all the lotions and hairsprays and cologne in the apartment and no one would have noticed. She mostly just watched *Three's Company* or read. If, at any point, one of the guys wanted to watch TV, he just walked up and changed the channel. The second they arrived, Ma walked off to a back bedroom with Sam. The only thing that made sense to Marina about Sam was his smell: he smelled like olive oil and piñon wood chips. Everything else about his existence was difficult to accept or understand. Mostly his hair, his hair was very greasy. Thinking about this made her think about all the other stuff that didn't make sense to her, like how she once went to a Dodger game and learned that there were two kinds of hot dogs. There was a hot dog called the Doyer Dog, which was just like the Dodger Dog but with jalapeños and nacho cheese, and she spent the whole rest of the game thinking that it was some sort of cruel joke. *What if you just have an accent?* Recently, a kid in school explained that a happy ending massage was when the massage ended in a hand job. Marina kept on wondering why do they call it that when everyone involved would be sad in the end? Shit like that.

Then some commotion happened as Fatimah arrived, in all her thick liquid eyeliner and glittery body powder. Marina was glad to see her. Fatimah scooped Marina up in her arms and twirled her around. Fatimah made a beeline to the bathroom, and Marina followed close behind. She smelled like the Egyptian musk perfume Mutya sprayed every time she'd go out dancing. Fatimah set out all her makeup on the counter.

You want me to do your face too? Fatimah asked.

Marina nodded.

'Kay, have a seat here. Fatimah gestured toward the toilet.

There was a knock on the door, Fatimah cracked it open, and Ma peeked her head in. Is everything all right in there? She's not bothering you, is she?

Fatimah kept her gaze on herself in the mirror; she was touching up her eye makeup. She stepped back, looked at herself, pouted her lips, and then stuck a long nail on the crease below her eyelid to make sure her eyeliner was a crisp line. Without looking at Mutya, she replied, Yes, yes, she's fine. We're fine, thanks, and shut the door behind you, please.

Do me, do me.

Fatimah bent over Reen, making a tent of jangles and powder.

Shut your eyes, she said. Then leaned in and softly blew all the excess shadow off her eyelids. It felt like a wish.

The men were laughing in the other room, then arguing, there was some tussling going on, but she didn't care because there were plump loving hands on her, painting her face to resemble something gorgeous and curvy and maternal.

They left the bathroom, and Fatimah told the men something in Arabic. Right away, they shut up and turned off the TV.

Marina thought that all that flesh was beautiful, that Fatimah was decorated like a Christmas tree. She jingled and jangled; bells were everywhere . . . around her ankles, her wrists, sewn into her skirts and draped around her head. She could almost smell the men's tinny blood tingle, a sort of metal, like spiced undercooked meat.

Fatimah walked over to the indoor stereo system. It was all eyes on her. She bent slowly at the waist. Her caboose of a butt in the air. She put on music, grabbed Marina's small hand, and made mischievous darting eyes from side to side. They gyrated together. Marina smiled and bent backward, arching her back with Fatimah's. Marina's shirt was tucked up and around the neck, like Daisy in *The Dukes of Hazzard*. Marina was barefoot, and her feet were painted; she had drawn on them with a marker because there was no time for henna. Fatimah placed a quarter on Marina's belly, and Marina tucked her lower abdomen into her back like she'd been taught at the rec center. It rolled once. There was lots of whooping and hollering.

The men warmed closer. Fatimah ran around the circle they formed and shimmied her hips so fast they barely caught all the cash the men were tucking in the waistband of her skirt. Fatimah's skirts like a net around her trying to catch all the attention thrown at her. At one point, Marina looked at the corner and saw Ma crouched there, timid like a small rabbit. Marina smiled and ignored her. She didn't want Ma to ruin her good time. She bent and twirled on tiptoe. She tried to sway to the music but still possessed a child's sense of time. Move-flow-move. Twirl as much as you can. Sometimes Marina simulated Fatimah's delicate hand movements, clasping little bits of pointed air between a thumb and index finger. Waving her hips back and forth, sucking in her stomach to accentuate her bones, she was all ribs and tiny hip points. Her dark, sharply painted eyes dashed from the left to the right of the room. The men sat and drank out of small gold-gilded glasses.

The whole evening was taking on a heightened, crawling quality. For most of the dance, Ma sat in the corner. She did not want to look at Marina, and Marina was certain it was because she was jealous of her beauty. Marina was stunning. Marina was thirteen going on fourteen. Marina was like Fatimah. Marina was not like Ma. Marina had presence and rhythm and this little hidden power she had yet to know anything about. Fatimah pulled her close and then pushed her away with a force. Marina spun around in circles like a flying saucer. Then suddenly she felt deprived of Fatimah's billowy sunshine. She let out a small yelp, like a pinched sadness. Fatimah quickly folded her back into her warm musky bosom. The music eventually died down, and the guys dispersed, and Marina was still drunk off the movement, still humming and bobbing, letting little bells twinkle around her. Ma ducked out with Sam, wearing his

Members Only jacket, her face to the ground. Three men and Fatimah went back into the bedroom, leaving Marina alone with Hassan, Sam's brother.

He beckoned to Marina with his fat hairy sausage finger to come and sit on his lap. Everyone was gone. In a poof. Come 'ere, Marina. Come 'ere. That's what the boyfriend's brother said. And she looked around, but it was just her and him. She still hoped that Ma would be back soon.

She walked over and sat on his lap, and while she sat on his lap, his hairy sausage finger crawled past the knot she'd made above her belly button. He was bouncing her on his knee, she flopped forward and thought maybe this was a game they were playing, and if she laughed he would stop.

She felt a flash of discomfort but wondered if maybe this was normal? Did girls with dads feel this way from games of horsey or airplane or piggyback rides or anything that involved a general abandon of weight and worry, being tossed in the air like a pillow or football?

She jumped off his legs and ran into the bathroom. It was the last place she had felt safe, but as soon as she reached it, she felt trapped. She could hear and feel and see her heart—a grenade in her chest. He shoved his way into the tiny room. She looked at his jeans with the keenness of someone who was going to die. *These may be the last things I see. These jeans. They are dark blue with red stitching and worn looking. Levi's.* He reached with an arm that covered the length of her body, grabbed her pants, and yanked them down; she cried and fought more. She was pummeling him with one fist and holding tight to her underwear with the other.

He had her pinned against the bathroom floor, she could see under the gap of the door to the other room . . . she saw the carpeted floor, but no feet. She stared at the ceiling. It was smooth white, and the light gleamed off of it, making the paint still look wet. There was a dark stain in the center. He was holding down her arms by the wrists. She was pushing up her knees, trying to bang against his legs. But he was stronger than her. Praying for Ma to come back. She tried to bang back against his hands, twisting and turning her fists. Her little fists only made small empty sounds against the floor. She thought of the codes. 242. Battery. No, no, this was something else. 261. Rape. He shoved her underwear to one side, his hard buto out of his unbuttoned pants, his pants bunched around his ankles, his legs a forest of dark curls, and then she felt something strong and alive jamming against her thigh. It banged against her bones. She looked away over his shoulder.

He licked his palm and pressed her legs against her arms to hold them down. He rubbed himself. It felt like it was in her stomach. 261. He pumped into her. A sharp flash of pain, a psychic rupture. Her head inched closer to the stem of the sink. He didn't like her struggling. *Where is Ma?* she wondered over and over and over again. He whispered for her to stay still. His voice made her fight harder. He had her legs spread open now, and she kicked at his back. He grabbed her by her hair and hit her head against the bottom of the sink. He said, I'll kill you. She did not want to die. She thought about codes and shoes on power lines. She thought about his absolute concentration. His straining toward something.

It was as if there was a switch in him when all his rustling and rubbing was no longer about the journey but the outcome. It's there somewhere in all of us. Something primal—some isolated destination.

She didn't feel the pain in her head. She was too alive with the pain inside her. She remembered what Ma told her about sex, that it was special between two people. Good, she thought, then this must not be sex. She turned her head to the side, all her cells on fire. She stared at the ceiling, she floated around and saw Hassan from the ceiling, saw him speed up, then moved over to the tiles lining the wall of the shower. She started counting the tiles peeking out above the shower glass. 259. 260. 261. 261. 261.

He was determined, his big face avoiding her eyes. She turned toward the door and again stared at the crack between the bottom of the door and the floor, to see if anyone would come to help her. She was so stunned. She had no real sense of whether she screamed or not. Maybe she didn't because he told her to be quiet, maybe she did because of the codes, because of the kick-a-guy-where-it-counts instructions. She glared at the hollow of his neck just before his Adam's apple and imagined sticking her fingers deep into it. Because even though everyone kept on telling her she was going to be a big girl soon, she still believed in the power of bad thoughts. She looked at the dark hairs on his chest. Her face shrouded with his panting garlic breath. He took his buto out of her. She felt fluid creeping down her legs. It was warm; she felt air escape. Her thighs and hips were already bruising. He pushed her forehead back like someone getting ready to give mouth to mouth. His knees back on the points of her elbows. They felt like they were going to split against the floor. She tried to find a speck of light on the ceiling to focus on. She found a dark corner. It was precise and clean, creased dark by shadow. He put his thing in her mouth. It was smudged with the salt of her blood. In the dark corner, she could make out a silhouette of what could have been a bunny. She watched the bunny grow and leap and imagined she was somehow atop the bunny. Riding the bunny through clouds. Clouds of marshmallows. Clouds of heaven.

She tried to focus on the dream of the bunny. He shot forward, hugging her head to his pelvis. She was suffocating in his skin. She closed her eyes tight. She did not want to see this hair that stuffed her nose, her eyes, her mouth; it was wiry and gritty. She tasted salt. Back on the bathroom floor. Away from the bunny. She gagged and then vomited. He didn't stop until he was done.

He stood up. His pants still around his legs, he looked in the mirror. He was towering over her, his buto still dangling down dripping with her vomit and some of his milky fluid. He cupped handfuls of water and splashed it on himself. Droplets fell on her face. He raised his waist to the sink to soap off. He took a towel and dabbed his stomach and buto and then pulled up his pants. He handed Marina a washcloth. He looked at his pakshet face in the mirror really closely to inspect for blemishes. Marina just lay there. He left. She lay there. She looked at the ceiling. She felt tears drop behind her ear onto the tile beside her face. After that, he came back, and her body clenched. He had a small bag of white powder. He took a lime-green washcloth and wet it in the sink, then stooped over her and wiped her.

I know it hurts, habibti. This will help. He said it gently.

He sprinkled the powder on her. Her hole tingled with a sort of brightness and then went numb like your cheeks at the dentist. Just when she thought it was all over, he then pulled up her pants, scooting them under her dead weight, and zipped them up. A silver button clanged against the floor. He patted the broken pieces in place. She lay there. Her wet hair plastered against her face, snot down to her chin, her hands wrapped around her belly. He left. Don't tell. He didn't even have to say it—the loudest words in her head. The loudest thought that existed. She had a huge giant fucked-up secret. And if she told it, she would die. And if she didn't, still she could die. And the worst part about this secret was that it would need a lot of prodding to get it out of her and there was no one around interested in that sort of prodding.

She hid in the bathroom for three hours, and when Ma finally returned, Marina said she didn't feel well and went to bed. Or maybe she slept somewhere else before the bed, maybe she slept on the couch and then someone placed her in the bed. It was a twin bed that was situated parallel beside another twin bed. There was a painting of a white woman in a sheer negligee, and purple-pink nipples puckered out, staring at her.

The lady in the painting had a *woo woo* look and plump lips like a nurse saying, Pudding.

This whole while Fatimah was in the bedroom snorting lines, drinking, one guy wrapped around her back—breathing hard—grabbing her tit like he was fondling a guava, another guy rubbing himself. Both guys spitting at her how horny she made them—how her body, her flesh, her smell—like that on and on. Somewhere between being a ten-year-old girl fondled behind a shed and this moment, any thrill was all gone, and the drugs were only what it turned out to be about. It started with qat that her mom used in Fatimah's tea after her dad died. Then other stimulants. That room in her heart—left vacant by her father. Then the stuff that ended up chasing away the stuff she had to do to get it. The one guy who was much older than the other boys—his finger with a jagged nail that scraped up inside—or worse the young boy—two years younger than her, who was good friends with her cousin and came over for the holidays, how he tricked her and had rubbed a spicy pepper on his finger before he touched inside. Her pekpek hot and tingly, she tried to wash it out as he ran away, hooting with laughter without even giving her a coin. And then like a flash, she was there in Hawthorne, in that other room snorting it all away. She heard some fuss in the bathroom, but when she got up to go check—the guys threw her down on the bed and locked the door.

Take it easy, Fati.

She smelled it then. The danger. She knew what this was, these men on top, and knew there was only one way to survive it. She stood before the men and danced and swung and swayed and shimmied herself deliriously. Her hips jutted out separate from the rest of her body. Her boobs shook fast and then faster like two kittens in a sack, her arms bent at the elbow, fingers poised, and as she raised her arms higher and higher, it was like she was conducting an orchestra of horny men and they loved it. They laughed and clapped and finally many hours later she asked to go to the bathroom.

By this time, Mutya had returned from wherever she was, and Marina was curled up asleep on the couch. Later Fatimah found that little bit of evidence, those little bloodied panties, and it was all she needed to confirm what she already knew. She looked at herself in the mirror. She shook with rage. Rage at the boy with pepper fingers and rage at the bullshit men in the other room.

Marina was pretending to be sound asleep curled up in a ball, and still, no one knew about the bathroom. She heard Ma struggling in the bed beside her. Don't! Stop! she heard her say. She said it kind of like a giggle, but then Marina saw Sam and his puffy hands moving up and down Ma's clothes. She was kicking, and Marina looked over and saw him put his hand on her mouth. Her long curly hair, usually back tight and perfect in a braid or sometimes down and around and out in waves like on the Prell shampoo bottle, at that moment on that night, was everywhere. Hair was everywhere. And after Reena saw her Ma's boyfriend place his hand over Ma's mouth and heard her muffled cries, she just shut her eyes tight and tried to be still. Tears and tears and tears covering her face through her shut eyes. She understood why people burned shit, pierced stuff, broke shit. Marina understood why Joan, who sat in front of her in class, twirled string around her light yellowish finger until it turned purple and let the boogers accumulate right where they were. She understood why sometimes on the way home from school she'd see a guy get mad and haul off and kick a newspaper bin. More than anything, she knew why people got hooked on that stuff that Hassan put on her pekpek. That made you not feel anything at all.

Marina eventually cupped her hands around her ears and slept. All the lights were finally off, and the moonlight was creeping in through the living room windows. The two small windows in the room she was sleeping in overlooked a parking garage and were covered in black towels. Then a fight broke out in the living room, the men all lasing, slurring their words, getting louder, angry for nothing. Words with edges, ready to pounce or fall into a puddle of tears. One of them went for the other's throat; then a bottle was broken, it seemed they multiplied, six jumping on the others' backs, screaming to egg them on or get them to stop.

Then a solid hard knocking at the door. Hawthorne PD.

Marina heard jostling in the living room—the door opening. Ma flew over to her bed. She jumped around her and the mere act of it, her body protecting hers—like they were expecting an earthquake or a bomb—made her weak with need. But she was the bomb, and Marina was the girl. Marina cried in the way that she'd been crying all night. She finally really let it out. Moans and sobs and snot and fear. She cried in the way kids do when they know something is wrong but just don't know how to name it.

Maybe part of what was wrong was the apartment itself with its pleather couches and glass tables and the food left out in the kitchen and overflowing ashtrays and white residue on the coffee tables and big reference books with playing cards and razors on them and somewhere at the bottom of Fatimah's purse there was still a pair of underwear with red apples on them that was ripped on one of the legs and smudged with blood at its cotton mouth.

They came into the room. The light flooding in behind made them look like two black silhouettes. Like cutouts on the back of a kids' meal. A girl cop cutout and a guy cop cutout. Ma was there holding Marina tight with her long fingernails, crying, No. No. No. No. No. Her nails dug into her, and she was holding on hard. Her legs wrapped around her like maybe a mama crab would do. She was wearing a long T-shirt. And her hair was down around her face, and once Marina adjusted to the light, she was able to make out a black eye. She had a big pearly shiny blue-and-purple ring around her right eye, and that too made Marina wail for reasons she didn't know.

A 1983 Ford pickup pulled up. The truck was loud verging on embarrassment. The red neon lights of the characters on a sign cast a flashing shadow across Marina's face. It was Pickton. Marina could see that a thin pleather fanny pack rested beside his right knee, and it was clear the fanny pack was filled with her needs. Whatever she needed to get by—brown powder, black tar. Willie's eyes looked a little dull to her. Dumb and empty. He looked at her and gave a small smirk, the sound he made could've meant anything. His mouth downturned, a permanent frown. Marina glanced for one more second at the fanny pack and then grabbed a hold of the metal handle and jumped into the cab of his truck. There was something that felt weak or desperate about her. Her eye sockets had a scooped-out look with their deep shadows. She was only about ninety-five pounds—so thin, all points and bones. By then, almost every guy she went with asked her if they were hurting her. This was what let her know she'd grown meager and hollow. But mostly nothing hurt anymore.

The pleather fanny pack bigger than anything in the cab. Marina sat on the thick leather seat with holes run through it by sharp metal springs that poked against the insides of her knees. She sat in the cab and expected to go close—to one of the SROs nearby. But after they passed the two stoplights in the heart of the Downtown Eastside and he kept on driving, she asked, Where're you going?

CHILD PROTECTIVE SERVICES

The officers were responding to a noise complaint, but what they found was an apartment filled with cocaine, a woman with a black eye, and a thirteen-year-old girl scared out of her mind. Back at the station, a phone on the adjoining desk lit up and rang. A secretary's voice chirped out of the speaker on the phone atop the cop's desk, Officer Satter, you have an incoming call on line three.

Officer Satter speaking. She glanced sideways at Marina. Her mouth turned down.

Ma'am. She didn't have to tell Marina who it was, Marina could tell by her annoyed posture, by the toughness in her voice.

The cop looked up at the air above her head. Then she turned to Marina; she mouthed the words, It's your mother. Do you want to speak to her?

Do I want to talk to her? Marina crumbled at the moment she said those words. Her mother. Your mother. Mother. Where was Mutya?

She nodded and reached for the phone.

Hey, Ma.

Reena?

Her voice was pitched up. She sounded like an obedient child, an obedient child with a tiny manipulative voice.

Honey, I won't be around for a little while. There's some stuff they want me to do before we can be together again.

Marina imagined her immobile, unable to do all the tasks Marina did. Unable to take the trash out or turn off the lights at night, unable to lock the door. Mutya in a dark corner, rocking back and forth or lying on her side, doing her Saturday-morning Jane Fonda leg-lift exercises over and over and over.

Ma? They . . . They say . . . Marina was crying, hyperventilating, snot running down her face. She was shaking. Letting go of those dreams of returning to Lola's porch, sitting between Ma's legs, having her hair braided. Letting go of the thick-as-thieves feelings of the first years of her life. The cop had explained that because Lola was outside of the county, Marina could eventually be placed with her, but in the meantime she would have to stay somewhere within LA.

What? What is it, honey? What are they doing to you?

Her voice changed, turned angry. Marina heard the baritone coming in and pushing out the little disco dreamer.

Officer Satter took the phone from her and explained what was happening. Marina was going to be turned over to Child Protective Services. Mutya would have to return home without her trash thrower. Without her light turner-offer. Without her door locker. She imagined the electricity getting shut off again. The roaches taking over her bed, crawling on Ma at night. Even worse, she imagined Ma would spend all her time in that beastly apartment in Hawthorne. Men thrusting their weight on her. She could see that bathroom and that man and those hairy legs on Ma's elbows, and there would be no one there to save her, there would be no one to take Ma home, the terror from the night before would become Ma's whole life.

The pakshet driving the truck had a balding head with an oily comb-over, and even though Marina was so rank she wasn't one to talk about smells, he reeked—ripe as fuck. A guy with a truck smellin' worse than her sent her hackles up, but she rode along and listened to the radio even though it kept crapping out to fuzz. At first, something about being a passenger in this truck made her feel young again, like a small child. She watched him like she did grown-ups when she was a kid—like they had the power to make up games and take her places that were wonderful to her.

Then she remembered she was no longer young, and she tried to keep her eyes on the road, pay attention to markers where he was taking her. Where she could call out for help. There was talk at the WISH Drop-In of sketchy guys. She was trying to remember what the girls said. Did they talk about a pickup truck? Or was it a van?

But the bag was there between them. He must have known what she was thinking. He patted the fanny pack, winked. Said, It'll be fine.

Fine? Did he say fine? Or fun? It'll be fun? His tongue was thick and dawdling. He spoke like one of the slower kids from the group home, kept bloated on meds.

At that moment what she wanted to see was the fragility in the thing. The delicate parts of being delayed. A man who shares the thought process of a child can be endearing when you want his drugs. Her fingers traced the thick piping of the fanny pack between them. They drove past the city lights. By now all she could make out were trees and dark water in the distance. The highway itself beside the three rivers. Marina rolled down her window and let the breeze swim over her face. She swung her arm out and surfed the sky with the flattened palm of her hand. Willie's frown turned upright, and with a twang of giddiness, he joined along and did the same from his driver's side. Marina felt her body buoyed with a light kind of ecstasy—the hairs on her skin standing up. She felt gikgik, an urge to giggle, to open the door and roll out the side of the truck down the highway like she had with Alex over at the Pines.

Finally, they turned off the highway and onto a marshy dirt road, and there in front of a boarded fence was a sign that said BEWARE OF DOG.

The dog ran to the truck, barking, baring its teeth, seething, drooling. Marina thought that the dog must eat pigs or humans or both. Marina thought, That much hunger, it must be a girl. *She kept on rubbing the fanny pack. She was no longer giddy but seized with fear of all the things that could go wrong.*

Overshadowing the dog, trailing a few feet behind, was a six-hundred-pound boar. Marina jumped back in her seat at the sight of the boar. She imagined being eaten alive right then and there, but then she always got that way before a fix. Her thoughts became clipped and precise like she was practicing to play a detective in a movie.

Almost there. Fanny pack time. Dark leather truck cab. The ceiling covered in felt that was ripped in places and dripping down. Radio stations all buttons and dials and fuzz. Willie, a wrinkled guy with thin yellow skin and freckles. Stained teeth. The kind of man she'd been warned about.

A HUNTED THING

The social workers were overworked and underpaid, but probably all began as well-meaning people. They were, for the most part, well-meaning *white* people. People who came from the Midwest and then they studied at places like USC and Cal State Northridge, and they had big hearts, and they wanted to make change. They wanted to show the kids the pretty life they could have. They wanted to go to bed relieved of any guilt—like they had done their part and given back. They wanted to show the at-risk youth how *resilient* they were. Jenny was one of those social workers.

Jenny was on a visitation with another kid, but the parents were pretending they weren't home. She banged on the door once more. This was how it went. A choice between two kids. The apartment with one little boy, where she spied a lock high up on the closet door, and then the girl in the apartment in Hawthorne. Who wins?

Before getting her degree in social work, she studied law for a short period of time. But in each of the cases she studied the facts and saw the bad guys win, and she'd yell, But that's not fair, and her law professor would correct her, Jenny, it isn't about what's fair. The law is not always about fairness; it's about language. We have these sets of words to work with that make up rules. Can you apply your circumstances to this language and get justice? She chose social work. If she couldn't get fairness she was at least gonna do some good with her life. Help one child at a time. But now—*now* she was swimming at the center of unfair. One time she went to interview a child named Paco, and he bit her hard on the arm. When she went home and told her roommates, they teased her for years, tagged Paco Was Here all over her notebooks.

Marina sat red-faced in the police station, gulping down chocolatey coffee. Marina tried to answer all of Jenny the social worker's questions. Jenny was a thin woman with long brown hair, and even though she was skinny, she didn't have much of a neck, so it seemed like her chin rested in a couple of rolls of fat that connected to her shoulders. She seemed busy to Marina. She carried that look and sound like Ma when she was in the middle of something.

Where are you gonna take me? Marina looked at her frantically, her arms straight at her sides, she'd had to pee for a long time but was holding it to be polite. She wanted to please this woman so she would take her somewhere good.

Can I go back to my apartment, ma'am?

The social worker said to call her Jenny.

Do you have any relatives who live nearby? Jenny asked.

My lola. She's in Monterey.

Okay, well, that's out of county. We can send you someplace nice and safe while we wait for your lola to get cleared or your mom to get better.

Marina didn't really understand.

Is Ma sick?

Jenny made a kind of laugh like someone who was trying to buy time, and it made Marina feel stupid and unsafe.

I just meant better at taking care of herself and taking care of you.

Marina didn't want to go into foster care. She'd had one friend in elementary school, Jackie, who went to foster care. She lived at the motel across the street from Mutya and Marina's apartment. Her mom and dad were always drunk, and they came to the violin recital drunk and loud and laughing at all of them so much they got thrown out of the auditorium. Jackie was in foster care before the motel, and she said she hated it, she had a foster mom who put a lock on the fridge and only let them eat at certain times of the day. Jackie'd tell this story to Marina over stolen containers of Cup O' Noodles. They liked to steal gum and noodles from the 7-Eleven and then hang out in construction sites. After the violin recital, Jackie went to foster care again, and Marina never saw her since.

In the back of Jenny's car, on the way to the group home, Marina thought of all the times Ma bent over her and kissed her good night. There was that solid year of having to take a pill the size of a cashew to get through tuberculosis. It was also the time that she began using an inhaler. Ma taught her how to breathe in and hold it—smoothing away the wheeze in her chest.

Marina looked out the car window and saw all the homeless people. They looked lonely. Marina saw all the little old ladies with no one attached to them but a litter of mewling cats. Marina saw the stray dogs. Marina watched them nuzzle up against the corners of buildings as if the buildings were the bellies of moms. Marina saw cop cars, probably out picking up other kids who were being taken from their moms. Marina saw a drunk about to pass out on a bus bench. Marina saw college students. The students looked like they shared a different class of worries. Like maybe they were worried about time, or a homework assignment, or a date.

Marina saw teenagers making out too eagerly in public. Teenagers who looked like they'd done it or they were gonna do it or that this was all some big ol' fuck you to everyone else because they were halfway near doing it out in the open at the Burger King and who was gonna stop them anyway? This was the beginning of her looking at the world much more keenly. She had to keep watch, keep guard. Marina had become a hunted thing.

Jenny, her hands on the steering wheel, looking straight ahead, said: There's no reason to be scared.

There's no reason to be scared? Why did she say that? Marina felt more scared than if she hadn't said it. She pictured Ma stuck in her apartment, looking at their empty bed, banging it with her fists, crying and yelling, shaking something the way she sometimes shook Marina.

Marina looked out the window as the social worker drove through Palms, and the outdoor strip malls turned into streets with blinking college signs in Westwood Village. Jenny drove from concrete buildings to bruised red academic bricks. She drove past sprawling-front-yard Bel-Air mansions and finally onto some highway. Marina leaned her sweaty head against the glass. She closed her eyes. When she opened them again they were in the hospital parking lot.

Wait, what are we doing here?

There's a doctor here who is trained in checking our kids. Just to make sure you have no injuries. It's routine. Don't worry. There's no reason to be scared.

There's no reason to be scared . . . there it was again. The doctor would look at her, look in her eyes and ears and pekpek. The doctor would find out.

Marina's stomach hurt. The armpits of her shirt stuck to her body. Her stomach rubbed against her shirt in a way that made her uncomfortable. She wanted to reach around and cut off the tag on her neckline. She wanted to pee. She wanted to rock back and forth in a corner of darkness. The chocolate coffee from the police station, the Fritos from the vending machine, began to roll around in her stomach. Was this something like seasickness? It felt like the ocean was swelling inside her veins.

Marina opened the door, her head still out the window, and threw up small shards of Fritos and thick milky streams of chocolate. Then she noticed another sensation as she was choking herself—leaning her throat into the top of the window, trying to force something out. It came to her then. She pressed the up button on the window control. She wanted to crush her head.

The window was coming up slowly, too slowly. Marina heard a click. Jenny stopped it from her side.

I'm sorry. I know you're in a lot of pain. It will get easier.

Marina wanted to please no one. Be nowhere.

Part of her wanted to laugh, just roll over in a ball and die of laughter, let this whole sadness kill her.

Buuuuuulllllllllllsheeeeeeeiiiiiittttttttt. Marina screamed it with a force. She could not stop.

The doctor's office was like an emergency room, called Children's Village in back of the county hospital. There were plush toys, and the television sets played children's shows, and the girls at the reception desk watched their own grown-up shows on their portable television sets, and there were those *Highlights* magazines where you look at the picture and find the thing that does not belong, like a small hat on a clock or a cat in a fridge. Again, she thought of Ma. Ma teaching her to read in a doctor's office one small word at a time.

Mutya had pulled a magazine off the shelf, handed it to her, and told her to circle the *ands*, the *ofs*, the *thes*, until by the time Marina's name was called, she knew them all.

The doctor did inspect her, her stomach, her back, and pressed to see if she hurt in places. A woman doctor, who inspected her pek-pek, swabbed at her and saw bruises on the insides of her thighs. Asked her if there was anything she wanted to tell her. And Marina stared up at the big moon of fluorescent light on the ceiling, tears running down her face, shaking her head no.

The doctor told her that Officer Satter, the police officer from earlier that evening, would need to ask her a few questions about the man who hurt her. After she got dressed she went into an office in the hallway, and Officer Satter was there with her notepad and pen.

Can you tell me who hurt you?

If I tell you will I go back to my ma?

Well, honey, we are still going to have to put you somewhere safe, but if you tell us we can make sure he doesn't hurt you again. Or anyone else.

She knew that more than one person was hurt that night by more than one bad man. If there was one person she didn't want to keep on hurting people, she knew who it was.

His name is Yasir but people call him Sam.

Marina had to write out and share the story of what happened that night at least twelve more times. She remained careful to recast Sam in Hassan's place. Officer Satter already had a picture of him that Marina pointed to.

Yes, yes, that's him, she said with certainty like the women did in Mutya's whodunits. After, the doctor conferred with Jenny. Jenny buckled Marina into her seat in the car and told her they found a nice place for her to go in the Valley. A group home called the Pines, and she would be able to stay there until Lola was eligible to take her. She didn't mention Mutya this time. Mutya getting better or anything, so she figured everyone knew her secret.

What about Ma? What about our apartment?

Well, that's still a possibility, she will just have to go to some classes and a judge will help decide what is best for you.

But what if she does bad in her classes? She doesn't always like school.

This school is a special kind of school for parents. She should be fine.

Marina remembered all the drills, the codes that Ma ran her through. Marina opened her window. They were far from the salty ocean air. They were far from the apartment with the roaches. The apartment where Ma ran through all those codes at night petting her head. Marina hoped Ma's classes were less like math and more like fooling Lola that she was happy and making enough money.

Now they were in the Valley. A place for kids to live out the rest of their time as wards of the court. A place where kids darted back and forth across a lawn wearing nothing but a soft-shelled helmet. A place where, much of the time, most other people moved about in an orderly manner, walked on lines. Every minute of every day scheduled out for "programming." A word designated to mean anything. They finally arrived onto the grounds of the Pines.

There were cottages. The cottages close to the road and the main office building housed young kids, the farther away from the gated entrance, the older the residents. Each cottage bore the name of a tree or a flower. Jenny drove Marina straight to Acorn, one of the cottages set aside for the older residents.

Marina was snot. Marina was tears. Marina was hiccups. Jenny helped guide Marina off the seat and walked with her arms around her to the front door. Marina imagined hundreds of kids, gangsters, dope dealers, all leering at her. Marina became worried about sleep.

What will sleep look like? Can I close my eyes in a place full of strangers? How dirty are the beds? The idea that she would be sleeping on sheets used by thousands of homeless kids freaked her out.

Jenny opened the door, brought Marina into an airy room lined with bunk beds. The room was dark. Marina walked leaning into her and then into a vacant bed. Marina got in with all her clothes on, curled into a ball, stuffed her face into a pillow, and cried herself to sleep.

Since they'd left Lola's, Marina had become the kind of girl who needed to sleep facing the doors, to clock the exits and entrances. She wanted to see the burglar, the rapist, the murderer. Like when she covered her face in Ma's pantyhose. She wanted to prepare herself for the bad things that came in the night. Of course, now that she was here it was as if there was no way to prepare for all the bad things that could come. Here she watched the shadows dance along the wall. She tried to adjust to the darkness, she stared at the mattress above her head, the impression of another girl's body. She tried to face away from the girl on the bottom bunk beside her. Sometimes still, when she had trouble sleeping, Marina'd suck her thumb, and she did not want anyone to see her. When the girl to her right faced her, she faced the opposite direction. Then after what seemed like several hours, she heard the rustling of feet against the floor. Two girls, shoes in hand, tiptoed to the door. The only noise a small creak of the door as they slowly opened it. By now, all the other girls were snoring. She tried to see their faces, but light flashed across the cottage ceiling for only a brief moment while the door was all the way open. She could only make out their silhouettes and their gait, one was tall, and it seemed she had thin, stringy hair, and the other was slouchy and shuffled. She wondered where they were going, and what they would do there, and if they were freeing themselves forever or if they'd return.

She continued watching the door and then the mattress above

her creaked, and then her bunkmate's head dangled upside down in front of her.

Waddup? she whispered.

Marina jumped and almost screamed but the girl put her index finger on her lips. Shhhh . . . I'm Alex.

It was hard for Marina to make out what she looked like in the dark and her features upside down.

I'm Marina. Who were those girls?

They're just gonna go toke or hook up. Don't worry about them. You okay?

Now embarrassed, realizing she probably heard her crying, Marina decided to just stick with the truth. I don't know.

You don't know? Then you're okay. You'd know if you weren't okay, don't you think?

I guess so.

Cool. I hope you don't snore or nothing 'cause I am a light sleeper.

Nah, I don't snore.

Yeah, well, you moan.

She *had* heard her crying. Now Marina was embarrassed, but also sadder. She wanted to leave this stupid place. She kept on picturing Mutya alone and confused and thought back briefly to that bathroom in Hawthorne, then thought also that maybe Ma would get arrested for what they discovered in the doctor's office and this all made her cry again. She pushed her face in her pillow to try to muffle the sounds. Then where Alex's face had been she saw a hand, a small thin hand, and like one snippet of a song that recalls another, she remembered Ma's fingers. How she'd sometimes rub her back or point to things with a hooked index finger. How she laid frozen fish sticks on a cookie sheet. Fridays were for fish, Lola used to salt the fish. Marina would marvel at it as it reached the table, adorned with thin slices of lemon, a small bowl of vinegar with garlic and cut-up onion on the table. The fish's head still attached, its cloudy eye facing the window, openmouthed, like it was in the middle of saying something. Grateful for the soft warm hand dangling in front of her, Marina grabbed it and held on until she could drift off to sleep.

The next morning Marina met Sherry the Resident Advisor, a middle-aged lady with a crooked haircut. She handed Marina a thick packet with a list of rules NO PROFANITY, NO FIGHTING, NO FOOD IN THE DAY ROOM, NO MOM TALK, NO SLEEPING DURING THE DAY, QUIET AFTER LIGHTS OUT . . . Of all the rules, the sleeping during the day rule confused her the most; later her bunkmate Alex told her that they didn't want you to sleep too much because sleeping was a sign of depression. *Let us sleep already; this shit is depressing* is what Marina thought.

Then she asked Alex, What's mom talk?

She said, Yo mama so poor, when she heard about the Last Supper she thought they was running out of food stamps.

She said, Yo mama so poor, I saw her kicking a can down the street, and when I asked her what she was doing, she said, "Moving."

She said, Yo mama so poor, when I went over to her house and asked what's for dinner, she opened her legs and said fish sticks. Like that.

Marina just sighed and said, Well, at least I have a mama.

Marina felt she had a step up from the other kids since she was gonna go to Lola's soon. All these other kids had nowhere else they could live. So they agreed to almost anything. They agreed not to cuss or have sex with each other or fight or do anything that came smoothly and naturally to people who were scrapping for their lives. This was a place where boys and girls tossed a jacket over their laps so they could fuck in the cafeteria. Without noise. Without affection. Guys just stuck their dicks in you, under the jackets. Just to prove they could get away with it.

Marina was agreeing to be monitored, watched, tested, told

what to do, when to eat, sleep, clean, how to dress. She wanted to rip off her skin and hurl it into a corner. That's all you can do when you realize you're at the mercy of people who are dumber than you. That's what she thought.

Marina wanted to go to her regular school; she wanted to scream and yell at Sherry the RA lady. Then again, she wanted to emit nothing. No emotions here. She was gonna look at Sherry, and when Sherry looked back all she'd see was a blank face.

Instead, Sherry looked at her, a smile stuck on her face. A smile she thought she might see again and again in a world of awful nightmares. A smile that said, You are one giant piece of shit, aren't you?

There was a clothing bin off to the side, full of leftover clothes. Marina shyly picked through them to find something to wear. Hoping for a fresh pair of underwear but too shy to ask. Eventually, she found a large faded black T-shirt and a small slip skirt with brown turtles on it. She looked them over for fleas or lice. She smelled them. She was a scavenger. She picked at them like a mama gorilla picks at her babies.

Another memory. Was it that the girls at WISH weren't looking for a green bean kind of guy? They were looking for a more mountain kind of guy, one with a beard? Their one had a beard—maybe yes . . . this guy had a beard. One day she had said if a beard came, she'd turn her back. Another day she had said if a truck came, a van or a truck, she'd turn her back. But today they all came and all she saw was this fanny pack she was stroking. There were big sharp dog fangs, the dog looked part wolf, part Chow Chow because she thought she saw a purple mark on her tongue, and the fur was knotted and eyes fierce.

Willie pulled into the lot, and the second he parked, Marina hopped out. In her eagerness, she slammed the door, and he pouted, made a child's downturned lip, and made that grunty unhappy noise once more. Within this pig mud lot sat his small mobile home with the three concrete steps that led to the kitchen entrance. Other trailers sat scattered around the property. She assumed other people lived in them. Neighbors? Family?

Plastic planks lined the inside of his trailer, sticky contact paper meant to look like wood, peeling in the corners and toward the bottoms of each panel. She saw beneath was an eggshell color. The floor was a patchwork of brown carpeting that must have disguised a lot of spills. There was a couch, but for some reason, Willie sat on the floor, so she did the same beside him.

Out of the mystery fanny pack he pulled a bag of brown powder, poured some of that powder on a spoon, handed her a rubber tube to tie off with, and it was her lucky day. It was her lucky day because she'd been sick all morning. This had been a morning that ran straight past her—looming over her like a thin film. She saw the babies in their bright red dresses and their bows. She saw the little bald heads and the big happy balloon, and she couldn't crack a smile. That's the thing about dope. There's nothing but color and black and white, and you live in black and white until you get the color and it's possible—it's possible you'll never feel the free air again, but whaddya care? She came to like the drugs because, finally, she would stop being seen, there was no one there who could judge her and see her, or think about what she should be doing or how she should behave.

Go ahead.

THE PINES

After Sherry with the crooked bob gave Marina the list of the rules and showed her the donation bin, she walked her back to her cottage. On their way, she kept talking, pointing out all the different buildings, the daily activities, the scheduled mealtimes. Marina couldn't follow much of what she said. Instead, she noticed that Sherry's nails were painted mauve. Marina remembered this color, the name of it, because it was the same nail polish Mutya spilled all over their carpeted floor. When Mutya got mad, she'd swipe her arm across Marina's three-drawer cardboard dresser they'd bought at Pic 'N' Save. The time that mauve polish came flying down, it was the polish Marina'd bought Ma three Christmases ago. Mutya'd hand Marina her charge card and a list of things Mutya wanted. Marina hadn't yet understood how money worked, and she thought she was being generous by buying her everything on her list. Mauve. That was the color. It sounded so fancy. Mauve . . . like the Ivy League Haaahvud.

The other girls were rioting through the cottage, thin feathered hair flopping in the sunlight, their shadows dancing across the ceiling, shouting in the closed air. Beasts! Sherry said, rightly. Standing beside the bunk bed she'd slept in was a white girl, her hair cropped short, pointed nose. Wassup, Sherry, you got the new booty?

Marina recognized the voice. Alex. Marina'd never seen anyone like her before, she was handsome and pretty at the same time. She had chiseled cheekbones and light-colored eyes with flecks of yellow and a smattering of freckles on her nose and shoulders. She was skinny and her skin was taut like a mackerel, and even though she was white her skin was honey-colored, like Jessie's in the summertime. She sagged her jeans below her hips, exposing a thick band of Calvin Klein men's underwear. She looked like a boy but in a chic supermodel sort of way.

This is Alex, your bunkmate, Sherry said. She's gonna show you around—teach you the ropes.

A call for a one-on-one with the 288s came from the walkie-talkie clipped onto Sherry's belt loop. Sherry hollered into the walkie-talkie, I'm on my way . . . and then with one hand toward Marina waved goodbye and ran out, a jangle of change and keys clanging off with her.

Alex lazily shot her a reverse head nod. She looked at Marina sternly, tilted her chin to the sky.

Waddup?

Is this white girl serious? Marina thought. After last night now she was acting like she didn't know her, and worse, like she was hitting her up. This was how they became friends, two girls who'd challenge each other, testing the other—they'd continue this dance. Still, when Marina looked in her eyes she felt something inside calling her, like she was almost enough.

Nothing much.

So obviously this one's yours. Alex patted Marina's mattress.

She was wearing a tank top and Marina noticed she didn't shave her armpits, little tufts of brown hair peeked out.

Marina thought she was going to be annoying. *Is she really pissing on this shit territory?* Yeah, I got that.

Alex had the top bunk, the ceiling above it covered in CK One ads, black-and-white images of naked models, a giant bottle of perfume in the foreground.

That bunk over there belongs to Heather and Sammy, Alex continued. Oh look, speak of the devil. Alex jabbed Marina's side with her elbow and winked.

An oafy girl with thin greasy hair and large teeth walked in from the bathroom. Hey, I'm Heatha.

Her accent prompted Marina to ask, Are you from New York?

That's right, the Bronx.

Hi, I'm Marina.

Heather had a hardy workman's face and later Marina would hear she was born addicted and impulsive. Heather guffawed more than spoke. She ate her feelings, and she hated her extra weight so she would try not to eat in front of everyone, and always made a show of throwing up in the bathroom. She'd come out of the bathroom delighted, smiling from ear to ear. Alex never talked about it, just got Heather drunk off of pruno now and again so she would laugh and be free and eventually eat whatever the fuck she wanted.

And that is Sammy. Alex stuck her thumb at a silent hunched-over girl who looked like she was on too many meds. She was short and tan and had chip-chopped dirty-blond hair. She had an extra tooth, and many of the other girls called her One-Too-Many. She was emo and wore her hair oily and long in her face. Aside from shadowing Heather, she mostly chased loneliness. On the outside, she was a heavy metal girl. Turns out she came here as a last resort after her second bout in rehab. Sammy was never able to disagree, and this would later make her the perfect employee, the personality of a bobblehead.

Heather walked off, a bald spot at the crown of her head pointing back at them. She was fourteen, but she looked like she was twenty-three and had smoked a couple hundred cartons of Benson & Hedges and drank water tankers full of Mountain Dew. She wore a plaid shirt over a flower dress and work boots.

Marina watched Sammy's limbs unfold as she padded after Heather. As they walked away, she remembered the two sneaky silhouettes from the night before; it was them, they were the two who had slipped off into the night.

Alex had a rosary on her bunk.

What, are you into some sort of cult? Marina asked. Of course, Marina knew that it was a rosary, but she was still in the phase where she thought she needed to tease people about things that were precious.

You know how you can tell a cult from a religion? Alex asked.

Nah.

'Cause a cult is just a set of rules that lets certain men get laid.

I see.

C'mon, we have ILP together. I'll walk you there.

A mural of trees and fairies and lions and frogs was painted along the wall. The floors were painted with stripes. The black lines were the normal lines they walked on to get to and from class, the red line was for someone going to a medical appointment or on medical watch. The lines were intentionally painted at least arm's length apart. If adults approached while any of the kids were walking on the lines, the kids had to stand up against the wall and wait for them to pass. If Alex or Marina were coming up behind someone who was really slow because they were a janitorial worker pushing a cart or they were just old, they were supposed to say, Passing, or

Behind, so they could go against the wall and allow Alex and Marina to pass. Even though they moved so orderly around the facility, there was a manic energy around them, the place felt full of longing and violence. The courtyard bustled with birds chirping and the comings and goings, the crisscrossing of kids, and walkie-talkie white noise, and whistle blowing and code calling, Crossing lines! or Boundaries! or No nuts in butts! All orders to assure all the kids were at least arm's length apart. She'd soon learn, although she already felt it, that everything here was made more difficult for the residents. The girls fought among themselves more than the boys, they talked smack to each other and went for their hair and their boobs (if they had them). All sorts of things happened in the dark corners, at night it was worse. Marina imagined the place coming alive at night, the barren quad crawling with worms and crickets and all the lice that came burrowed into the little heads of babies, the flies, the asbestos, that harsh dust found in the ceilings—she imagined the particles frolicking together in the water and the air mingling with the maggots in the pantry, entering their food and making the girls as bitter and angry as hungry mother piglets, or as angry as Mutya was at the bank tellers. They were worse off than the boys, because the boys fought, but they almost always resolved everything in the end after a quick scrap, while the girls—the girls carried their resentments forever. They burned and burned with no end in sight.

Marina learned quickly; she was learning that this was a time of barred-up windows and plastic cutlery and hiding in closets and the locking up of cleaning supplies and smoking in game rooms.

Alex spoke like she was enjoying her authority in showing Marina the ropes—she tried to shock her or get her to admit she didn't know things. Look, here's the stuff you're gonna need to know, you're gonna need to know how to make pruno and what a Fifi is.

Marina was taking it all in. She knew kids her age drank and smoked and boys liked to touch themselves, some kids even had sex. As far as she knew the only ones she'd seen were a small gang of kids at her school that mostly hung out back behind the handball courts and kids on the after-school specials. Turned out pruno was some funky-smelling wine that folks made out of hidden fermented fruit stolen from the cafeteria, and a Fifi was a pocket pekpek guys made out of toilet paper rolls and socks and a latex glove. It seemed all the kids wanted to talk about was sex. This is how you French kiss, this is how you give a hand job, this is how you finger a girl. There were names for things. Endless ridiculous names, dirty sanchez, donkey punch, reverse knock, reverse cowgirl. Everything you could do in one way could be done in reverse.

It was not a time with guidance counselors trying to steer her in the right direction. Encouraging her to reach her full potential. Nobody was trying to help Marina get into Harvard, Yale, Brown. No, it was all ILP classes.

Wait, what's ILP?

Independent Living Program. It will prepare you to get emancipated.

What's emancipated?

You age out when you're eighteen, or if you get prepared sooner you can emancipate at seventeen and a half.

Well, I'm not gonna be here that long.

Yeah, right, you keep telling yourself that.

Their ILP class was in a bungalow, there were two small bookshelves, a guy dressed in gym clothes sat in front, the ceiling was missing little plexi squares that covered the lights, and she could see all the dead fly carcasses that had accumulated over what looked like years.

Take your seats, please, the man in the gym clothes said. His name was Mr. Hunter, and he also served as a boys basketball coach. His voice was just authoritative enough to whip a room full of teenagers into their seats.

So we take these books, and first, we take the quiz at the beginning, then we find the career we want, and then we write a paper about it. Alex pointed to a shelf lined with big colorful books, the spines read *What Color Is Your Parachute? 1977, What Color Is Your Parachute? 1979, What Color Is Your Parachute? 1984, What Color Is Your Parachute? 1986.*

Marina looked at her in amazement. You are fucking kidding me, right?

Nope. We used to host debate in this class, but they shut it down because whoever was losing would call the other one a fascist cow and they'd bust out in a fight no matter what they were arguing about.

The book didn't list careers but more jobs, like jobs in the medical profession, accounting, or retail.

Marina learned the best thing was to take up space on the paper by writing big or drawing a picture. Marina kept with her original choice: *secretary.*

Do you have a number for her yet? Alex asked Mr. Hunter.

What number? Marina asked.

You'll see.

Each of the girls got a voicemail number assigned to them so they would have a phone number they could put on résumés if they were applying for jobs or apartments as they got closer to their emancipation date.

Mr. Hunter had a telephone on his desk and an empty seat beside him. Alex sat there and used the phone to listen to her voicemails.

Marina thought it was strange she got so many voicemails in response to jobs she applied for. Marina also thought she saw Mr. Hunter put his hand on Alex's thigh.

She raised her hand. Finished!

Already, Ms. Salles? Well, let me just head over and check it. He was slowly attempting to stand, his belly pushing against his sweatpants, it seemed to take him a long time to get straightened out from sitting behind his desk, his keys a jumble the size of a melon hanging from around his neck

Alex's eyes got big and she shot Marina a warning look, then told Mr. Hunter, Actually I just got a call for an interview that is in a couple of days, do you think you can help me prepare for it?

He was already moving his hand off her leg and onto his desk, but Alex gently placed hers atop his.

Okey dokey. Looks like I'll just stay right here then.

Mr. Hunter let out a relieved sigh. For a coach, it seemed like moving wasn't his thing.

Marina knew something fucked up was going on back there. She couldn't help but feel a little bit fascinated by all the attention Alex got from Mr. Hunter. His desk was filled with graffiti and drawings Alex had done and she seemed to quickly move into sitting in the seat beside his desk. Right before class let out Mr. Hunter exclaimed, Well, young lady, you are the best.

Hey . . . hey—I might be the best but I ain't no lady.

And they both had a laugh together. Like old chums.

There was an ease about her. Marina thought she glowed from this certainty. To be so tough and soft at the same time. Marina could see she was sharp and quick. The way she swooped in between Mr. Hunter and Marina said that she was willing to sacrifice herself, that there was no way anyone could do harm to her, but there was something still precious about Marina. When Alex returned to Marina's side, she gave off the smell of something wild and gamey, her sharp cheekbones, her taut muscles, she looked pretty to Marina and for a quick moment Marina wondered if she should cut her hair short like Alex's too. If she could pull it off, or if her head would be too round and she would appear to be an ugly girl rather than a beautiful boy as Alex did now.

They had the next class together too. It was a high school proficiency prep class. This class seemed a little more focused. Before they stepped in Alex warned, The thing in this class is whoever is caught fucking around is called on.

Their teacher, Mrs. Allen, handed out the vocabulary portion of the exam, all the way down the row, while everyone sat in their seats with number two pencils poised. All the other students were staring at Marina because she was new, she heard the two boys behind them whispering.

Yo, homey, new booty look fiiiiinnne . . .

Alex sat beside Marina and turned to the guys. What are you staring at? Mind your business.

Marina figured Alex didn't get the same kind of attention because she was skinny with muscles and had a rough look about her while Marina was swollen with hormones and had the beginnings of curves. Mrs. Allen paused at Marina's desk. Well, you don't look quite old enough to take the proficiency exam.

How old do you have to be?

Sixteen.

The proficiency exam was the first step to getting emancipated, so everyone wanted to pass. Also, once you passed the proficiency exam you could work full time and you didn't need to attend these lame classes anymore.

I'm not old enough—but this is where they told me to go.

All right, Marina, well, let's start with you then. Mrs. Allen adjusted herself in opposition to Marina, as if she were challenging her to a duel. Marina didn't like the way her name sounded in Mrs. Allen's mouth, like an insult.

Number one: bildungsroman. Is it (a) a roman building, (b) a coming-of-age novel, (c) a Greek god, or (d) young adult literature?

Marina answered, B, coming-of-age.

Mrs. Allen's face lit up like she was talking to a child, which she was. That's exactly right! If it is a coming-of-age novel—here Mrs. Allen paused, looked up at the ceiling, like she would find the answer to her riddle there—that would mean *what* exactly?

Marina didn't fully understand what she was getting at, her face must've looked confused.

Mrs. Allen smiling now, wringing her hands together, content to be back in this superior position, the teacher, the bestower of knowledge. Your main character or your protagonist would be what? And here she extended the question mark in a high-pitched tone, like Californians do.

Alex tried to help and jumped in. A child?

Pleased, Mrs. Allen clapped her hands. Yes, exactly, Alex, that's correct.

A darkness closed over Marina's heart. She felt frustrated and dejected. She went from being the top of her class in her gifted programs to this teacher now in the reject school shaming her in front of everyone. And Alex already seemed to be everyone's favorite and that was beginning to grate on her.

Okay, who wants to read number two?

Actually, that's not correct, Marina interjected, her cheeks still burning from the humiliation of being berated.

I'm sorry? Mrs. Allen tilted her head to the side like a dog trying to listen.

Marina felt stuck between two pains—one, Mrs. Allen's cruelty, or two, losing Alex as an ally.

The narrator can be an adult looking back. Like in *Catcher in the Rye*.

The whole class erupted in dayummms and oohs and aahs. Mrs. Allen seemed stuck.

Alex hit her on her shoulder and teased, Show-off.

Marina was relieved Alex wasn't insulted. In fact, she seemed impressed, which was the most Marina could hope for.

What Alex lacked in vocabulary she made up for in math. What looked to Marina like a bunch of gibberish with *x*'s and *y*'s Alex formed into perfect equations, demonstrating for the rest of the class on the chalkboard.

At one point when Alex turned around self-assured with not only the correct answer laid out for everyone, but the precise movements and steps on how to get there, Marina heard Mutya's swooning chime *the bee's knees* and for the first time fully understood.

When the bell rang, Alex walked Marina to her next class.

Look, you seem nice, so I'm just gonna put you on; the new booty needs to throw down.

The who?

New booty—that's you. You gotta have a fight on your first night and they'll leave you alone. But two things.

Alex held up her index finger; Marina noticed a freckle in the center. One, you need to start it. Alex held up her middle finger. Two, you need to finish it. I'll meet you in the cafeteria for dinner, all the cottages usually eat together, so look for me there.

All right. But I never—

Shhhh . . . Alex put her index finger to Marina's lips, then turned around and sent a peace sign over her shoulder. Don't ever let 'em see you sweat, Show-off!

Marina thought she looked like a cute guy from afar. Then immediately her mind was flooded with thoughts about this fight she was supposed to have. It was as if she'd been in training for this sort of thing her whole life, with the codes and Ma's and Lola's instructions on how to kick a guy where it counts, but never had she really had to come face-to-face with another kid. Hit another kid. There would be an audience of people watching, hoping she won or hoping she lost, and she would have to empty her head of them. She would have to focus on the child in front of her. She was scared and anxious and just wanted to get it over with all at once. She thought of the fairy tale of the maganda sister and the good brother and how the brother stabbed the mean auntie's arm with a ginunting sword. Or was it a wicked stepmother? Her lola's stories were slipping from her. In the back of her mind, she thought of how soon enough she would return to Lola, and then, even further, how adorable Alex was.

All the students from Marina's last class lined up against the wall in the cafeteria. They each took a tray one at a time. She could feel all the other kids' eyes on her. She heard the whispering, Check out the new booty. There were kids with helmets and kids who wore sweatpants and sweatshirts that said LPJH for Los Padrinos Juvenile Hall and she prayed she would not have to fight with one of *those* kids. Some kids wore pajamas, some kids took their T-shirt and tucked it up and over the collar like Marina did when she was belly dancing with Fatimah. The tables all seemed pretty mixed, except the cholas and the cholos all sat together, and the kids who needed assistance sat at the two back tables with aides. It was Salisbury steak that night, and the meat was swimming in a tray of hot water, so it looked soggy halfway through. There were also green beans and powdered mashed potatoes.

The woman serving her was wearing a paper bonnet over her hair, and giant white gloves. Any particular piece?

Marina wasn't sure what it was she was looking at, so she asked, Um, uh . . . do you have anything for vegetarians? The guy standing next to her squealed, Nah, fool, just keep it pushing. It's all the same anyway.

The girl on the other side of her hollered, Ah sheeeiiiitt, new booty wants a veggie burger, yo!

She did not want to have to fight either of them, so she just smiled and took what was offered her. Looking out at the rest of the cafeteria with her tray, she spotted Alex. Marina'd already decided she wasn't going to get too attached to the other kids. She'd be leaving in a couple of weeks. She needed to set herself apart from them. She could never belong in a place like this. She looked at the pregnant girls and the cholas and the boys, all of them with their saggy pants and frozen soupy vegetables, and their same dinners and sometimes looking through the donation bin for clothes, and curfews, and chores, and lights-out. She looked at them and chanted a mantra in her head: *you are different you are different you are different.*

She walked over to the table that seemed to be all the girls from her cottage; she recognized Heather and Sammy and Alex. There was also Nikki, with a bright, unblemished face framed with straight dark hair and her shocking curves revealed in short cut-off jean shorts. Nikki was hoping to make it in television. She was the kind of girl who would have been popular on the outs. Because she had perfect teeth and a perfect body, and also 'cause she was an enigma, all religious and slutty at the same time. Danielle, a Marilyn Monroe look-alike with short platinum hair, a mole on her chin, tight white freckled skin, who wanted to become an actress. And finally, Sammy, who did not want to become an actress. Not even close.

Marina sat next to Alex, who scooted so close to her that her right thigh touched Marina's left thigh.

Nikki bowed her head and said, Bless, O Lord, this food to our use and us to thy loving service, and make us ever mindful of the needs of others, for Jesus's sake. Amen.

Marina almost choked. She still felt the heat of all the other kids' eyes on her neck. She was being tracked.

What? Nikki looked at her.

Nothing.

Now there was whispering behind her, kids saying, Aw damn, that new booty into devil worship or something?

Do you not normally say grace? asked Nikki.

Nope. Marina was getting up to put away her tray already.

Oh, well, when *I* eat dinner, *I* like to say grace.

Okay, well, if *you* want to. Marina glanced around the table to see if anyone else believed this crock of shit she was hearing. Alex's eyes smiled at Marina.

Yeah. I do.

Alex nodded her head down toward her plate, but enough to let Marina know she started something, she was gonna have to finish it.

Fuck your grace!

And it was on. Nikki got up, her svelte body and her angry eyes, and she asked, What'd you say?

The kids from the nearby tables stopped eating and leaned their heads toward the table.

You heard me, bitch. This fuckin' food sucks, and this fuckin' place sucks, and God doesn't give a shit about us.

Now all the kids jumped up, Marina could hear them behind her, Dayummm, you gonna let her talk like that?

And Nikki close to Marina's face. So close she could feel her breath on her. Marina knew if she let on now, she would be a punk. People would steal her clothes, rations of the good food, whatever shit she had. Marina kneed Nikki in her stomach. Then she pulled her head into a headlock and smashed Nikki's forehead against the table.

Oh, snap! You see that new booty, homes?

The whole while thinking, *This is it, your first fight. This is really happening.* And then, *Always be the first to throw a punch.* Ma's instructions still buried in there somewhere. Deeper than anyone, in her bones, beyond me, was Ma. The HLA and DNA thrumming inside. Sometimes it was the way she held her cup, or a strange out-of-control cackle Marina made, or if her nails ever got too long and witchy looking. Marina was caught in that prison of longing for and despising and being eternally coupled with Ma.

Nikki reached out and grabbed Marina's hair. Someone else grabbed her arms by the elbows and tried to drag Marina off of Nikki. Marina kept on hitting. Surrounding them, a blur of judgy man-faced kids, yelling, chanting to a beat, Go! Go get her!

Marina hit Nikki in the face. Marina shook off the person holding her back, really mad. Nononononononono! Marina kept screaming. Her yelling button was stuck, the screams coming from her guts. The skin over her knuckles split. Her eye swelled shut. Marina backed up and kicked Nikki in the face. Nikki bit her tongue and fell back.

This was the exact moment her eyeteeth spiked. She knew the taste of anger. There in the distance, she could hear all her prim hopes dashed and chucked into the woods. Her first big fight. She was a savage. She yelled and pulled and kicked and hit. Her sight became black with anger, and she recognized that *this* Marina came from somewhere else. This girl came from a night in a small apartment in Hawthorne. She came from years of obedience. She was no longer asking for permission—she was taking it. She was letting loose what was caught inside her.

Nikki turned toward Marina's leg and bit her thigh. Hard. Marina thought of a dogfight she once saw, how they pushed into the jaw of the dog and up in the hollow space of their chins to force them to let go. She did this to Nikki then. It worked. She coughed and let go. Marina smashed Nikki's head against her knee and dropped her to the ground. She heard staff coming to break them up. She heard, BREAK IT UP! BREAK IT UP! The staff was getting ready to restrain them. They stopped. They stepped away from each other.

Some kids liked to get restrained. It was the only time an adult touched them. That's really what got kids to go from foster care to juvie—the yearning to be touched. You'd see it in a staff's eyes. The desire to comfort you. But the liability. Everything was a liability.

Some kids grabbed at staff's boobs and body parts. Some kids felt less anxious with the weight of a staff's body on their back and their face against the cold linoleum. Nikki and Marina were not those kids.

Marina extended her legs next to Willie the pakshet pig man and relaxed. Exhaled. Tied off. The feeling of the brown rubber against her skin. Cooking the drugs. Watching them bubble. This was the only time she had razor vision—all her focus in one place. You could say anything to her then, do anything, she would not know. She got the first hit. She sunk against the couch—an explosion of euphoria. Pleasure shot through her, down to her toes, and there in that moment, she was floating, adrift, uncommitted. The only time all her worries about what she did or did not do for Alex—that small knit hat—Sabina—all melted away. Marina normally would not approve of being so high so quick, but as each day passed, she found she was making up new rules for herself.

Willie was looking at her.

Hey, what's your name anyway?

Willie. You?

Em. (She couldn't give him the full thing.)

She played with the rug. She looked away.

Let's go back to my room.

BLESSED

Those days after Marina was gone, Mutya was at home like she was stuck in a trance, sitting on their ugly bed, petting it. Each hour was its own big raw round weight. And the days were just an extension of the same torture. She wanted to stay there, in the dark, but she couldn't—there were meetings. All kinds of meetings. Work meetings and anger meetings and parenting meetings. Lots of sitting in circles. And she had to be presentable. She had to look good. Because if she didn't shower, she might stink. She might stink, and then she might also have dandruff. And if she stank and had some dandruff, they could say she was unfit. Her mom, oh, how her own mom—Lola Virgie—would think she'd become so much like that family next door. Like the Americans with their mercury. When I look at these portions of Mutya's heart, her puso, I think of Lola smashing her hands together and her teeth close to Marina's face, exclaiming, BAM! That's how fast your life can turn.

What did you expect? Are you just gonna lay here until you die? Mutya realized she was feeling sorry for herself. This was a relief, because she knew what to do with self-pity.

She got on her knees at night and prayed to O'Lord. She said, Glory to God. And she said, Hail Mary, and made a steeple out of her hands. All this so on the outside, she appeared nice and calm, but on the inside, on the inside, she was a hysterical mess. Shattering china from her head to her toes. She longed to call her mother. She knew Lola would have blamed her. She would have been right.

When the police asked, she told them right out front that she had no idea where Marina's father was. That she had called him once and he was a miserable good-for-nothing son of a bitch so no no no Marina could not go live with him. Then after lots more questioning, she sat down and wrote out his phone number and address, and it was clear that he was far away.

And the police asked how long she had been friends with Sam. And she said she had only been seeing him for a couple of months. And they wanted to know had Marina ever been left alone in the apartment. And she asked which apartment? And they said any apartment. And she explained that she worked long hours and that Marina was very independent. *Gifted*, they called her, and so she had a key. *Latchkey* is what they call it, but Mutya does not like that term. That word. *Independent* is what she prefers. Did they see how old Marina looked for her age?

The police said, How about *that* apartment in Hawthorne? And then she tapped the counter with her nails and looked embarrassed and laughed, Oh oh oh! *That* apartment. What was the question?

Ma'am? Is there something you're not telling us? Is there . . .

And then the woman cop. Officer Satter asked, Ma'am? Are you on any medication or substances that we should know about?

And her voice quivered, and she laughed some more—the crashing inside her. Oh no! Heavens, no! I just, well . . . she was just alone for a short while.

Then she got scared because she felt they could see right through her and knew that she was a liar. That she lied all the time. That she was going to be no good, and that is what this *inspection investigation interrogation* felt like right now. Proof.

In the months Mutya was apart from Marina, she completed a free class for angry people in their low-income neighborhood. Her classmates were people who had bashed heads in at work or tortured children by plucking off their toenails. Mutya did not do those things, so she could not relate and pulled her seat a little bit out of the circle, keeping herself at a distance from the others. She also attended therapy and allowed a social worker to come visit her in her apartment. The system was so overcrowded that sometimes social workers fabricated their home visits and almost always notified people in advance so otherwise messy people could appear well-kept, harmful people could act kind, gun toters and butt whuppers could lock up all their weapons and hang their crosses on the wall.

Sure, there was a split moment when Mutya thought she too could do anything—be anyone—if she didn't have the responsibility of a child. She could try hard drugs, or get a cheap easy job, or never come back to that small lonely apartment again, just dance and dance and dance. But there was something not right without Marina. Always like the stove was on, or the heater running, or a missed errand. It took her forever to go to sleep and when she woke up she always startled awake like she'd forgotten an appointment, and then it dawned on her.

She tried calling Marina at the Pines. They stumbled through a couple of phone calls—

What do you guys do over there?

Stuff.

Like what kind of stuff? Do you take any classes?

They were so awkward Marina stopped taking the calls. The woman who answered the phone always said Marina was "programming" or she couldn't find her.

What's programming? Mutya asked, but nobody was able to

really tell her, all the answers to her questions were vague and confusing, one operator said classes, the other said stuff, and then again the first one said classes and stuff.

So Mutya sent her cards.

She sent one a day and then one a week, and then finally tapered off to one large envelope with a month's worth of cards.

The social worker, Jenny, wasn't helpful at all; she never answered her phone or returned Mutya's calls. Instead of saying fuck it and running off to do what a single woman without a child could do, she did what she thought Lola might want her to do. She went to see O'Lord. Every day she went to church. The first morning she found enough energy to put on her stockings, and a dress, and she curled her hair in big neat black curls, the size and shape of soda cans. She made herself beautiful for the sake of O'Lord. She dipped her long pointy cranberry-colored nails into the holy water. She made the sign of the cross over herself, kissed her smooth tan knuckles as they passed her lips. As if to say, these are blessed fingers, *I'm a blessed blessed woman.* She walked slowly, gliding forward, stopping at the third pew from the altar. She stopped and knelt by the pew, again made the sign of the cross, again kissed herself, this time her glossy red thumbnail. Her blessed blessed thumbnail. When the organ boomed she stood up and sang with all her might, as if she were harkening some lost talent, as if maybe this is who she could be—a Woman of Grief, like those professional funeral mourners. Over time she became friendly with all the people in the social groups at the church. They'd eat at the IHOP together afterward, or host bake sales. Every night she knelt before her bed, rosary in hand, and said all the Hail Marys and Our Fathers, and begged O'Lord for her daughter back. And each morning her first thought was still that panic but then shortly after it was hope; Today is the day, she'd whisper. Part of that panic was that she had no idea what had happened to Marina. She didn't know anything about this place the social worker sent her to. The Pines. She heard some of these homes locked up the food, put an actual lock on the cabinet. But she needed something else to keep her going, something to look forward to. A change. In time the hope replaced the panic. In time hope got so big it was all around her. Signs and symbols everywhere. She found a way with these prayer rituals to eventually fall asleep at night. God would fix it. If she prayed hard enough, if she put money in the basket at church, if she lit the candles, everything would get right. And when sleep found her, she dreamt of the life she'd have with Marina. A house with a garden, a big lemon tree in the backyard, lemons the size of pig hearts, thick bright glossy rinds, plump among all the grassy green colors.

In her waking dreams she'd heed the signs—Marina's favorite TV show, or one of her favorite songs on the radio. Her room, filled with all her clothes and posters, maybe there was a sign there among all her things. Mutya came across a music box Marina used to put out for fairies in the rain. She thought maybe if she got that one fixed it would bring her home. Today is the day. And this is how she spent the rest of her days cultivating loneliness, until then she would surrender to God's will.

Marina knew it would come to this sooner or later. She was gonna have to do it, but she was glad he let her tie off first.

They went down the long hall to his room. No heat. No air. A tight, dank vacuum. Everything covered in junk-food wrappers. There was what Marina thought looked a lot like a rotting horse head. The cheeks sunken in, the bones peeking out in places. Willie must have caught her staring. She thought she saw cartilage poking out by what used to be a nose. A gaggle of flies picking and buzzing about it: a horrible stink. She wanted to back out, but maybe the horse wasn't there. Maybe none of this was real.

That's Goldie, he said.

Willie was on his bed. A mattress. No sheets. He undid his pants. There it was—yellow skin. Dark coarse hair. His skin crusted dark from dirt. His dick looked like an old plantain. Sad and greasy.

Come here, he said.

Marina undressed. Walked over to him. He grabbed her by the waist—pulled her close.

Marina jolted. Hey.

It was rough. She was used to rough. Sometimes she preferred rough. Forgo all the formality of the thing. But this with her nose against the dirty bed. With the dead horse above—with the plantain dick. She felt him sloshing between her legs.

Condom, was all she could say, and then she felt him plunging into her. Her stomach on the bed. His weight on top of her.

I'll make everything better, Em, he said.

ACORN COTTAGE

The days unfolded in a pattern that became familiar to Marina. Shower by an egg timer—

Marina awoke each morning only to find herself in that same room. The same bad dream. A moment later, she became aware of the humming of pipes and a small ticking noise.

What's that? she asked in her first week.

The shower. Alex sounded alert and intentional, as if she'd been waiting for Reen to wake up.

No. The ticking.

The timer. Fifteen minutes to take a shower. You're next.

Marina didn't want to be next. Marina wanted to sleep all day. Marina wanted to sleep until she could leave.

After showers was breakfast—always one hash brown and cereal for her, some of the other kids were more adventurous, they ate cold clumpy eggs, or sausage links, or sausage patties. Then she went to class, ILP, Proficiency Exam, all classes that were aimed toward getting them out into some kind of job.

They slept out in the open. They had to be checked on a lot. To make sure they weren't killing themselves, fucking each other, killing each other, fucking themselves. The cottage had once been a cabin for summer camp girls. The floor was a cold linoleum. Marina thought she could faintly smell the rank scent of sweat, Snappin' Apple bubble gum, and gallons of Drakkar Noir to cover up cigarette and weed smoke. There was also the smell of all-purpose cleaner, rotten fruit, nail polish, and feet. Many pubescent feet. Séances would have been held there; the hoodoo lingered, style upon style, an undercurrent of drums, a forlorn wail, garlands made of notebook-paper flowers, handwritten notes passed.

Most of all, Marina felt long jags of boredom with quick hot flashes of crisis and panic. In the beginning Mutya would try to call her, but she'd complain about all the classes and social workers, and Marina knew it would be a small matter of time before she gave it all up. She knew better than to hope for Ma to change. She stopped taking Mutya's calls, which turned into cards, and eventually the communication between them stopped altogether.

Marina and Alex would spend hours sitting cross-legged playing cards, gin rummy, bid whist, and whenever either made a good move they'd holler, Scratch! as in Scratch my dirty neck, then slowly motion with their fingernails trailing down their neck.

They were only allowed to walk to and from their classes and to play in the fields. The whole place was enclosed by a fence. The fence wore a necklace of barbed wire.

They learned to lip-read, their heads turned sideways, watching each other's mouths. In this way, they called to one another, from bed to bed. Alex. Heather. Sammy. Nikki. Danielle. Marina. Immediately after the fight Nikki offered Marina some of her lip gloss and Alex told Nikki to fuck off.

Didn't you just try to scrap with her? And now you wanna be all nice?

They told me to beat her.

Who?

Everybody. They said since she was new if she didn't get hit up, she would be too soft.

Well, when are you gonna beat her then?

Marina was touched by Alex sticking up for her. But she'd soon learn that by winning the fight with Nikki she'd become temporary head of the girl army.

There were six girls to a cottage. When Alex acted gangster, it just made Marina more lonely. But there was something else about Alex too. When Alex didn't try to act like something she wasn't. There were times when Marina lay in bed and looked up at the imprint Alex made in the bunk above her, and peace stole across her chest and covered her in warmth.

Marina would think about returning to Lola's house each night before bed. Returning to a world and way of life that was familiar. In her first weeks there, Marina called her several times.

Reena, what are you doing there?

Well, I'm talking to you while the other kids are programming.

Programming, what is this programming?

It means they are going to group, like a group meeting, or going out to do physical education, or they have a one-on-one meeting.

Then programming is anything?

Yeah, basically anything but sleeping.

Why don't they call it *anything*?

I dunno, Lola, they just don't.

You talk to your mother?

No, Lola.

Why not? She misses you.

I know but I can't talk to her right now, she has to finish some stuff before I can see her and so it makes it tough to talk to her.

She has programming too?

Kinda. I miss you, Lola, when can I come see you?

Oh, I don't know. I have to finish these paperworks. I had to go to the police department the other day and get fingerprinted—just like a real bank robber!

Lola liked all the shows with bank robber drama, she used to get a thrill out of the westerns, Stick 'em up bang bang, she said with her little index fingers pointed. When the timer went off and they had to end their call, Lola gave her a hard time.

I gotta go, Lola.

Oh! So fast?

The timer went off and other people have to use the phone.

Oh, you don't want to talk to Lola anymore?

It's not that I don't *want* to.

Marina usually returned to her cottage depressed and longing for Lola more. Explaining all the strange rules to someone else made it harder for Marina to make sense of them herself.

Lola Virgie hung up with Marina, she couldn't tell her what she thought, maybe she should. She'd started to cry while listening to her—what a smart girl. She hid it from her.

Lola, are you okay? Marina had asked.

And she replied, Of course, I just have a cold. It's so cold here since you and your mom left.

Lola! I don't know why you don't just turn on the heater.

She'd been complaining like that to Marina all these years, she said that Marina and Mutya provided body heat, warmed the house for free. She still refused to turn on the heater, afraid it'd raise the gas bill. She'd much rather invite her church friends over to pray the rosary.

Now she'd also run out of room. Room in her heart for all the feelings swirling around in there. She couldn't forget the way Marina giggled when she was a child. How she was always so happy to spend time with her, go with her to the espiritista, promise to eat her vegetables, to be good, to be clean, to care for her. Oh, how Marina wanted to please her. If Lola told her to pray she'd pray. If Lola told her to comb her hair she'd comb her hair. The doctors said Virgie had to take all those pills and stop eating the sugar and the fat. The sisig, the kare-kare, the lechon. She was tired all the time.

She couldn't bear the thought of it. So many years of not enough money and then dying alone; years of hospital visits and raising her kids, and now she was trying to get Marina. All those social worker interviews, and paperworks, all their nosy nosy. And now it was possible she couldn't even care for Marina anymore.

And now here she was, she expected every symptom—she recognized them as they appeared. But for the first time she felt something else beneath the resignation and despair. She was angry. She was also exhausted, but she didn't want to give up. She didn't want to spend all her time in bed watching J.R. on *Dallas* with her pounding heart, with her long pajamas. She sat there and tried to imagine the rest of her life, a future of pills, and applesauce, and a nurse who let her sit there in her own mess, or worse one of those homes where she would rot away. Drool on herself, her teeth in a cup, one of those gowns that let her puwit hang out.

The girls in Marina's little cottage girl army whispered gossip and giggled after lights-out. They lay down on their backs, then faced each other, then turned away, facing the walls, signaling it was time to sleep. They kept their talk quiet—a secret thing—about nothing too important, unless one of the girls was in love and then she was planning A Great Escape. And because they were teenagers, this happened often.

Perhaps O'Lord saw their late-night tears. Maybe he was present when they were last slapped by their parents, when Ma shook Marina by the shoulders and, later, Lola Virgie forgave the shaking and the screaming, swiped the crumbs of the day away, and proclaimed, Listen to your mother. She knows best. And as they lay there growing wilder, untrusting and running farther away from where they came, maybe O'Lord was there, stroking their heads at night as they dreamt of being loved. Above them were stars, the same stars for all the world, and down the block below was the highway that led anywhere, back to their mothers or away to their lovers, or farther even to the lives they wanted, and beside the highway were violent flurries of snow, unsafe and fierce and uncorrupted by the rules of this world.

The highway outside the barbed wire fence of the Pines stretched from the Valley to Portland to Vancouver to a place far north called Hope. This highway was most notorious for swallowing up the lives of Indigenous women. Some of them would hitchhike to the Downtown Eastside and stick the dream-weaving fluid gamot into their veins, and they forgot about the soldiers and their guns, and they forgot about the prunes they hate to eat, and they forgot about the blood on their achy feet, and they lived happily ever for the moment. Some of them wouldn't get that far. Instead, they'd get picked up by someone, maybe Willie Pickton.

Lola tried to warn Marina that women were hunted in this world, and it's true that along the Lougheed Highway that stretched from Seattle to Canada hundreds of women had been hunted, raped, tortured, killed. They were mostly dark-haired women, maganda like Marina. Some say 824 missing and murdered Indigenous women, others say 1,200, dating back to the 1980s. And then there are the kids who died in foster care. Hundreds and thousands in Los Angeles. When is a number high enough to care? People are strange about numbers. They will say that 109 is a small number or a big number depending on whether or not they know one of those Native women. They will say the murderer is a specific kind of predator, a sexual predator or a drug lord or a devil worshipper. Nobody misses nameless people. The Highway of Tears they call it. The highway has a name. But not many of the women have a name. Somebody missed one person. One face. One name. One daughter. One sister. One mother. People miss one person.

Aside from the CK One ads, Marina clocked that Alex's sole possession was a heavy canvas bag that, when resting by her feet as she sat on Reen's bunk, took on, with its worn and weighted life, the speckled contour of an old dog: fat and obedient. Inside the bag? A small knit hat with cat ears. And all of Alex's attempts at finding her adoptive mother, Sabina.

There is no end to the forest of missing women. They've traveled this road, some of them have the memory of their Native ancestors, some of them have toyed with these lanes, nodding out being smacked back into the cruel world only to chase a visit once again. I see them travel sometimes. A woman spread flat against the stream in the river, finding her tiny way upward. I panicked the first time I saw this. Then I heard the voice of Maria Lobo. They are human. And this is the story of humans, this litany of violence, pakshet jobs, and land grab, boom bang wars, roar roar rape. I imagined their ghost-spirits fluttering through the forest at night like sets of butterflies.

SABINA

Winter in Seattle came with red and green traffic lights slicing beams through the icy layers across the city. The sidewalks were blanketed in snow, and a coat of fog billowed halfway up the storefront windows. Coffee smells and chicory and freshly baked loaves of bread, and for Alex, this may have been the perfect time to come into the world. Sabina, in town from Canada just for the occasion, was giddy for Alex's arrival—pumping Christmas carols into her rental car, singing along (badly), stopping at shops along the way. There was always a thing (just one more thing) for her to buy. Her scalp freshly oiled, her afro picked out. A turquoise ring on her index finger, a big bright red coral pendant on her sweater. She'd read somewhere that these stones soothe the wearer, but that their colors, their textures, are stimulating for a child. Colors stimulating. Textures stimulating. The nagging question there at the back of her mind. *Will she hate me for being Black? Will she resent me for being Black? Will she hate herself for being white? Will the world look at her like a wrong thing?* Here in Seattle, she was so much more aware of herself. Her skin tone. Driving around with a white baby, would they think she was a nanny? A baby-napper?

Then with all this uncertainty swimming around in her head, she was at a stoplight and looked to her right and there in the store window was a lovely knit sweater with a matching hat, the dome of the hat adorned with the shapes of two pointed cat ears. And it was just *darling.* Just *adorable,* and it did not matter that her new baby, Alex, would not fit that outfit just yet. One day she would. It was the right size for maybe a two-year-old. Then she realized she knew nothing. Who knew what size a two-year-old wore? Maybe it was the right size for a five-year-old. Sure, she had seen both two-year-olds and five-year-olds before, but she never thought to ask them their size, and one really couldn't size things by age because children varied, didn't they? There were five-year-olds the size of eight-years-olds. She was so uncertain that morning, but then she looked at the hat with the knitted-on cat ears and it made her warm and happy. It made her feel confident. And then she went back to her rental car and put the two items in with all the other bags and the one thing that was most spectacular was that little empty baby seat. Oh no, take that back; the most *most terrific* was the plush virginal white blanket with satin edges. Organic cotton. Receiving blanket, it was called. *Oh, what a wonderful name,* she thought.

And there, as the white light from the streetlamps cast a beam across the wet pavement, she thought that maybe that whole road was like a receiving blanket. She pulled into the hospital parking lot and hesitated once more. Should she park in the emergency lot? For the emergency room? She had heard so many stories of women being in labor for ten, twelve, forty-eight hours. Maybe it'd be best if she parked in a paid spot. This was one of those many things that were not in the birthing plan. Where does the one with the *receiving blanket,* the *receiving mother,* park?

She parked in the paid lot and checked herself in the mirror once more. Smiled, put on some lipstick, coiffed her hair. Chuckled to herself. Since when was she so self-conscious? *And remember, Sabina, children are not born with racism, they learn it.* She was going to be wonderful. Any child would be lucky to go home with her. *Look at the stuff in this car, for chrissakes, and I haven't even picked her up yet.* Then for the length of a hot flash, she felt a pinching in her heart. She envisioned Lauren, Alex's birth mother, unable to give up the baby. *What if she changes her mind?* Lauren had signed the papers. Lauren was clear she needed the money. Sabina had asked her over and over and over again. *Are you sure?* But still, the panic gripped her heart.

Adoption was just this—a big gamble on heartbreak. She'd fostered before, and the child had to be returned to his birth mother, and it was maybe the best for everyone, but she was still so depressed afterward. She'd gained ten pounds and could only wear stretchy mom jeans (Ack! Mom jeans—how ironic!) and never went out, because what would she tell all those new friends she made? Parents of the kids who he'd played with? And she decided that maybe she wasn't made for this heartbreak stuff. So that's why she chose adoption rather than fostering. Something with more permanence.

A brand-new baby. In Canada, it was too complicated, too many hoops for her to foster to adopt. The lawyers and the paperwork and the background checks. So when her girlfriend called her and told her about this church program where she'd adopted her children that was based out of Seattle, just a car ride away, she jumped at it. Her girlfriend said that there were fewer hoops to jump through than traditional adoption agencies because it was from a church, and she adopted her son and after a few years it turned out his mother had another child and now she has that child too. The church was very open about keeping the relationship with the birth family. It seemed like a good program for everyone. Rather than just pay a flat fee like she was purchasing the child, she would pay for the biological mother's doctor's appointments and cost of living throughout her pregnancy. And then continue to offer a stipend one year following, as well as keep the channels of communication open. She was certain the birth mother needed the money and that the baby deserved a good home. But what if the birth mom gets too attached or wants the baby back? Sabina asked her friend. Her friend said there was a six-month window when the birth mother could choose to reunify with their child but they almost never did. She has been working with the agency for almost two decades and it had never happened.

But these feelings that came over her in the car were devastating. She didn't have to follow through. She could just keep going. She could stop wanting. But she knew that the moment this child entered her life, she would not stop wanting; she knew that this new life would etch her out, erase her as she knew herself up until this point. She'd be a different person altogether. One who lived for someone else. She'd know patience, and compromise, and a new kind of fear, the fear of losing what she had.

She remembered first seeing young Lauren at the Starbucks. Lauren had walked in slowly, a white girl with long dark hair braided back in cornrows. She was pushing a stroller with her infant. From the first moment Sabina saw her puffy cheeks and crisp green eyes and round belly and the face of the child in the stroller, *a mixed-race baby,* she sighed in relief and knew this was the one for her.

Hello! Sabina had waved vigorously, then exclaimed, Oh, I hope you're a hugger because I'm a hugger, and held Lauren close. Then she gestured for Lauren to sit down. Here, sit—sit.

Their conversation was constantly interrupted by the calls from the coffee shop barista. Double soy grande latte! Single tall mocha with whip for Karen!

Lauren did not even know who the father was and wasn't sure

whether or not the child would come out white or Black or maybe even Asian. Most of her friends were Black. She had gone to beauty school a long time ago and only knew how to do Black hairstyles because she grew up on the poor side of town. Later on, she ended up getting arrested for possession of drugs and continued to practice her braiding techniques on the other inmates. While she was in jail, she learned she was pregnant, and the other women told her about Seattle Crusade Church.

She was shy when she'd first met with the pastor. She never knew a woman pastor before. This pastor was beautiful with tan skin and dark hair and light eyes, and her eyes sparkled when they met, and when she saw Lauren for the first time, her face lit up. And Lauren felt okay confessing to her she was pregnant and she did not think she could care for the child. The pastor told her God had a plan. God had a plan for her, and that plan was for her to shine. And they held hands and cried together. But still, when she got out and went to the church for the first time, she was shy all over again. It was one of those megachurches with a big stage and ceiling lights, and the pastor who'd met her in the jail paced back and forth on the stage with a microphone and her hand in front of her mouth like she was singing. Like she was carrying her words high into heaven. Pastor Janice, she was called, met with her after and said, Well, looks like God's heard your prayers. We found someone we want you to meet. And she told her about Sabina. Now she was here in the coffee shop sitting across from her.

It was a dream of Lauren's to one day own her own salon. Sabina smiled at this and offered to maybe one day allow her to do her hair. Only she didn't put it like that; she said something more like perhaps she would be so lucky as to one day have her hair done by *her*.

The next step was for Sabina to rent a house in Seattle so she could monitor Lauren's health and drive her to medical appointments.

Lauren let her into the room during her ultrasounds, and while they looked at the screen that first time Sabina reached for Lauren's hand; her hand was limp and clammy by her side, and finally Sabina decided to just take hold of the bed rail. She massaged the cold steel of the bed rail and looked at the bright flash of white floating around on the screen. *It's not an otter; it's not an alien; it's not a seal; it's my baby.* A girl. She would be having a girl! And the echo of the baby's heartbeat rang deep in Sabina's ears like the last sound at night before sleep finds you.

Over those four months, Sabina must have asked Lauren two dozen times if she was sure that she wanted to give the baby up, and each time she seemed more and more certain.

One day after an appointment, Sabina was driving Lauren back to the Empire View Mobile Home Park. The air between them was thick, both of them contemplating the figure they'd seen on the screen. Lauren was quiet and looking out the window and then said, I wanna keep her, but I just don't have the money or a job right now. Startled, Sabina asked, Well, are you sure then you want to go through with this?

And again, she capitulated. No, no, I'm sure, it's just that I think that people might think I'm *bad* for not taking her.

Of course, you're not bad, Sabina said, then she thought about it some more. She went on, You know, sometimes people, especially men, especially men with money and *power*—they like to shame women into thinking that there is a right way and a wrong way to do things. It took me a long time to realize that's not a true story. In the end, it is the *thing* that is best for everyone involved, and right now, you are not doing a selfish *thing* but doing a generous *thing* for yourself, for me too, sure, but mostly for *the baby. What is best for the baby?*

Lauren relaxed and rubbed the inside of the rental car and looked out the window at her parked Nova, and she said, Well, *that* for sure isn't the best, and she gestured with her chin toward the patch of dust and snow she'd parked on. Sabina took this to mean they were staying in her car. As the weather grew colder she put Lauren up in a hotel room right next to one she had booked for the remainder of her stay, and she could hear Lauren and her daughter watching TV, the remnants of bad food choices strewn all about, and making noise too late at night, but she thought it was really the least she could do.

Back at the hospital, Sabina felt like maybe she'd forgotten something. She had the blanket; she had the papers to be filed; she had the baby bag. She exhaled and walked up to the hospital room, and there she saw Lauren in the bed. Worn out, sleeping, covered in sweat. Her pasty face. Sabina tiptoed toward her. Psstttt. Careful not to startle her, but still, Lauren jolted awake. Afraid. She looked at Sabina like she'd never seen her before. Like *Who is this Black woman in my room?* And then Sabina smiled and said, It's okay. It's okay, it's just me.

Lauren was hooked up to monitors. *To check her vitals,* Sabina thought. Then again resisted the urge to chuckle at herself; after all those episodes of *M*A*S*H*, she felt an authority on these things. The room was painted a warm aqua color. The ceiling flickered with the pulse of the lights from the small tree that sat on top of the nurses' station just outside Lauren's room. The hospital seemed more cheerful now than any other hospital—with mock presents in the hallways and cards propped all across the nurses' station featuring pictures of brand-new crying babies. Brand-new, almost-giggling-looking babies and older children who maybe were born here right in this room and were now standing in a yard in a matching velvet outfit with their family sheepdog, or all tall in front of a fireplace. Then all the fluids came, and there were the puffs of air that Lauren was making, huffing and hemming and pushing and hawing much like a person stuck on the toilet. And this was the part that may have been too private for the two of them to share because this was the time Lauren looked up and struck Sabina hard with an alarmed look. Sabina was sensitive enough to understand this meant *Please leave*. I'll just step outside, she said.

There was no one else there for Lauren in the waiting room. No one from the Seattle Crusade Church. Was Lauren just supposed to go home alone after this? The whole thing was heavy on Sabina's puso, the weight of Lauren alone, the bright sunshine of taking home a new baby.

And the nurses rushed in, and Lauren's feet were in stirrups, and she was going to come so soon now. It would be any moment now. Sabina waited outside in the lobby. She did not sit. She paced, and every time she turned to her book to try to read it, all the words were blurred, and every time those double doors opened, she snapped upright. She wanted to appear *worthy*. And she thought perhaps to be *worthy* you could not fall asleep or look *slack* at the television, you could maybe sit upright and ready, you could maybe read a book, or maybe be knitting. Sabina did not knit, so she just sat there astute and upright with her receiving blanket ready and waiting.

When it was time to push, the nurse called Sabina in to join them. Sabina reached down and grabbed Lauren's hand and prompted her, Breathe breathe breathe. Push push push. She did not know then that she would one day come to hate this hand; she did not know that this moment would pinch in her mind for the rest of her life. While at a checkout counter, while in line at the doctor's, while she looked at other people holding hands, lovers, mothers, daughters. She would have nightmares about this hand for many, many years, and here it was in hers—wet, sweaty, veiny, vulnerable. The sight of this hand or any hand like this hand would pull a dark curtain around her spirit.

Alex came into the world that evening, fresh into the heart of one woman, out of the belly of another. Two mothers.

Sabina was sent back out to the lobby while they washed baby Alex up (named after Lauren's grandfather), and Lauren pushed out her placenta. Then the time finally came for her to meet her daughter. And the nurse emerged with a mask on her face and gloved hands up in the air, her arms in the shape of a goalpost, and Sabina walking through those doors was thinking, *Goal! Goal!* Sabina exhaled deeply, and her eyes flared with tears before she could even make it to the room where her new Alex awaited. And the nurse, beaming, asked, So, are you ready to meet her?

And Sabina, smiling, told her, Yes yes oh yes please! and she tried her best to suppress her enthusiasm because she was afraid it would somehow tip off Lauren like in gin rummy when someone discards that exact card you want. But that's when the eerie truth was clear—Lauren was looking at the wall opposite her. Not out the windows, not at Sabina, not at the nurse, the wall. She was just staring off. And when the nurse came with the baby, bringing her to Lauren first, Lauren shook her head from left to right. No. No. No. No. She did not even want to touch the baby. And that too filled Sabina's heart with grief. Was this her first moment in the world? Was this the way the world received a human being? Rejection? Was there any amount of love or comfort that could make up for that biological diss?

I have the blanket. Here, please, this is the blanket, said Sabina. And there she stood with arms wide open. As wide as they could be and there was her daughter all new and eyes closed and mouth open, and when Sabina held her small tender body close, she heard the smacking of lips with what appeared to be a tiny blister at the point of her top lip, and she came later to know this as a seeking sound, but for that moment it was the sound of her baby.

✶

Early the next morning, Sabina and Alex left the hospital and drove home to Canada. Their house sat high on a hill where trees whistle when the wind turns with the weather, making a sound like the steam from a kettle. The giant leaves sweeping against the elms were the whisper of the iridescent fairy wings that adorned all the pages of nighttime tales Sabina read to Alex. At home, there was a Christmas tree with silver and glass bells and red velvet ribbons and gold bows. A simple, classic tree that Sabina thought would also stimulate Alex with its colors and textures. Her bassinet sat right beside Sabina's bed, and the light on her bedside table, coupled with the stars and moons that beamed around the room from Alex's mobile, created a glow that floated between them. Those first weeks were swollen with curiosity and excitement.

Sabina took the time off work and did nothing but watch Alex, coo at Alex, sing to Alex, read to Alex. And she was finally lifting out of the habit of checking Alex for signs of life every one of her first deep-sleeping moments during naps. Sabina counted off the months, making sure they could get past that six-month mark.

Sabina made spiced bread loaves and played whimsical holiday music and danced in the mirror with Alex at her chest, lip-smacking to the tunes. This is what she was doing the morning of month five, she was dancing like this when she received the call. The voice on the line said, I made a mistake. I want her back.

Dull throbbing like regret or a debt coupled with desperation tumbling out all around her. Sabina looked up at herself in the mirror, Alex at her chest, the too-large knit cap with cat ears poking up. Sabina clutched Alex closer, then the phone, her palm sweating. I suggest you get a lawyer. Her voice clear and sharp. Her hand shaking, she hung up.

Just like that, it flashed away from swoony dreams to all business.

She was on the phone and looking professional and getting her papers in order, and she scanned her documents and looked at the time stamp on all that was filed, and there right on the desk in front of her was that final document, the one that severed Lauren's parental rights. Below her signature in small writing was the disclaimer, Thank you for advancing Seattle Crusade Ministries in opening up your heart and home to this child. As stated in the Armed to Love™ classes, our main aim is to keep these children alive and able to receive the love of the Lord; should the biological parents want to reunify with their children, they have six months to revert the child back to their custody.

Sabina called the church, confused about the disclaimer, and they said they apologized, but they would happily refund her money or match her with someone else. I don't want my goddamn money back, she yelled into the phone.

Ma'am, I know you're upset, but . . .

Don't ma'am me. How could this have happened? Sabina realized she wasn't doing herself any favors. She tried to get control of her voice. Look, I know this isn't your fault. You don't deserve to be yelled at by me. I just want to know how to fix this.

Her next call was to a lawyer. The lawyer she spoke with said he couldn't help her because the child was adopted in Seattle, so Canadian laws did not apply. If she'd really wanted a legitimate adoption, she should have gone through an attorney, and yes, he understood she probably did not want to hear something like that now.

It was a fucked-up dark day in January two months after the discovery that Lauren's parental ties to Alex were not severed. Two months of Sabina loving and crying, crying and loving. She did not want to transfer her grief onto Alex. She was afraid Alex would sense her sadness. It would maybe *cause her to be depressed* and maybe *stunt her development*. And she did not want Alex to perceive this time with her as anything but a *happy time*. At night Sabina stuffed a pillow in her face and howled with such strain that she sometimes lost her voice the next day. Dousing the pillow in screams and tears and swallowing it whole. A month straight of muffled cries.

Sabina drove into the Walmart parking lot, Alex in back, in her seat, hitting the bar gleefully, playing. Tapping her little giraffe toy. Wearing her too-big cat hat. Sabina looked back at her and sang the whole way. *Hush little baby don't you cry.*

But she wasn't crying—until they parked the car, and then Alex put her hands up in the air and screamed. Like she knew. Like she sensed there was danger in the parking lot. *Mama's gonna buy you a mockingbird.* Sabina knew she was getting all the words mixed up, but she needed to keep up this singing this burbling this rambling for herself, if not for Alex.

The final letter from Lauren's attorney spoke to the fact that Sabina was a Canadian citizen and Alex was born in the United States, and there was also mention of Sabina being of mixed race of *African descent,* which was hardly relevant since she had never been to Africa did not have any relatives in Africa and then she realized that the one drawing up the papers must have been at a loss, not able to refer to her as African American, as she was from Canada, and not wanting to insult her by referring to her as *Black,* so she was now suddenly stuck in this awful debate with some politically correct, geographically challenged idiot! *I hope your house burns down in a tragic sage-burning accident! You fuck! You racist politically correct idiot fuck!* The issue of being mixed race? She was not mixed. Both of her parents were Canadian, both of them Black. Well, actually, her mother was more of a caramel. Still, the ridiculousness of this debate did not extinguish the horror that was this moment. The clouds were low and dark. She stepped out of the car and went to the back seat. Then there was the instant of Sabina unbuckling Alex from her baby seat, picking her up, the screams in her ears, the final softening of her cries as Sabina held her close, the sucking sounds in her hair, Sabina wrapped her in that first plush white receiving blanket and handed her over to Lauren, who stood outside of her old Nova, feet crossed, blank-faced. She did not smile when she saw the baby. She did not stop to listen to any of Sabina's instructions about how she *likes to do this at night* or *that in the morning* and *let me grab her bottles*. Lauren just said: I got it from here. And Sabina could not really see her face because today, every time she tries to remember, she sees the first face, the face of the woman in the bed staring at the blank wall. Looking away. Doling out the first rejection. She knew too that it was time for her to leave the parking lot, for if she did not leave, she would maybe die. She would maybe throw herself in front of the next truck that came by. But she could not. She had arranged for a therapist appointment that afternoon. She had done this on purpose. She knew that this was one of those times to ask for help.

One a.m. on December 13, 1994, Willie drove toward the Downtown Eastside, a flat palm out the window surfing the air, his other hand banging at the steering wheel, blaring the hesher music those Hells Angels played at their parties across the road. The parties were really wild. Girls walking around with their tits out and guys with hair all over their face drinking and snorting shabu, and sometimes you'd hear some squealing and revving in the back rooms. Willie always felt ill-equipped for those kinds of parties. Like he was back to being just a little boy.

Josie was standing near the corner of Hastings and Cordova. She had on jeans and a flannel shirt. She wasn't making all the feminine gestures all the other women were making. She didn't have to. She was only twenty-three. She was new to the game. She looked young—almost fresh. She still had a case of the scabs from picking for the body bugs. Other'an that you couldn't tell she was an addict. Other'an that she looked sweet. She was just leaning. Tired. She was one of those meek hoes who hid behind her smile, thinking maybe no one would murder her if she kept looking pretty.

A PLACE WITHOUT MOMS

Marina and Alex were always together. Even though Alex was only six months younger, Alex did things first, and Marina was never far behind. Alex scaled the side of one of the bungalows on the edge of campus and Marina followed her. A small rooftop where they could smoke. Alex showed her which staff to flirt with for bumming cigarettes, saying Órale or Ay Papi to Jose the janitor even though he was born in Culver City and didn't speak much Spanish. Alex taught her how to smoke, she said, No, like the ladies do on the TV when they're having a baby. A big breath in. Then hold it. Then out.

Marina felt dainty. She extended her fingers so that the cigarette rested between them, like an actress or a singer. A singer drunk on booze. This was that glamorous thing that she imagined was happening all those nights in those nightclubs Ma frequented. One day up on the roof of the bungalow, Alex pulled out a staple that she'd stolen from her counselor's office. Alex stuck the sharp points of the staple into the tip of her index finger until it bled. Marina did the same. They touched their fingertips together, closed their eyes, and made a wish. Blood sisters. This is how Alex became Marina's whole family.

Alex pointed out that the fencing behind the bungalow where their ILP class was held was not attached to the concrete at the bottom; she showed her how she could lift up the end and the gap was just wide enough to wiggle her way out. Alex also told her she and Mr. Hunter were running game.

Check this out, she said. Alex showed her a small paper, *LA X . . . PRESS*. The cover was a woman hunched down on all fours in her bra and undies, smiling at the camera. In big block letters, it read Horoscope, World News, BD&SM, Escorts.

Alex flipped to a page that had a bunch of ads, one was a close-up photo of Alex's lips, and it just said MASSAGE 555-0100.

Dayum, girl, was all Marina could think to say; she didn't know all that it meant, it was what the other kids said.

Alex explained, Mr. Hunter takes the photo and places the ad, and then I can use ILP class to check my voicemail messages, and he covers for me when I go on the outs, and he only keeps twenty percent of the profit. Sometimes I hustle the johns for more money, so really Hunter gets ten percent.

Marina knew what was coming next.

You down? Alex asked.

I dunno, let me think about it.

Sure, yeah, I get it. Alex had a disappointed look, but Marina knew she understood.

Marina'd been at the Pines over a month. Time was strange there. Their days were scheduled out, every moment there was one kind of programming task to the next, but task upon task and yet nothing ever amounted to anything. They lived in a holding pattern. A waiting room. The only reason Marina was sure it'd been a month was because she awoke one morning and it was her fourteenth birthday. She'd thought that after a couple of weeks, she would be able to go live with Lola. She had no idea that this was her new life.

Her first birthday without her mother, after breakfast she took some other girl's eyeliner, burnt the tip of it, and painted a clean black wing on her lids. It made her look sleepy and uninterested, like a cartoon girl. In the afternoons when they were bored, Alex played with Marina, her hair, her face. Now Marina did her makeup the way Alex would, outlining her lips with a dark brown pencil and then filling them in with a deep shade of red. The color of blood. The color of puta, a woman who goes out at night to sell her pekpek but is still working past sunup. So maybe it was this, the loneliness of Marina's fourteenth birthday, that drew her to the streets. Or maybe it was the audacity of being fourteen, which seemed so much more sophisticated than thirteen. She felt free of trying to live up to anyone's expectations. There was something fantastic about taking a pair of left-handed child safety scissors and cutting off half a head of hair and knowing nobody would care one bit.

Marina'd think back to when Lola warned, Your mother is a woman who craves the attention of men. Marina felt that same desire growing in her, pulsing at the backs of her eyes, not for men exactly but attention any way she could get it would be nice. The need to sparkle. She thought too of all the men who darted in and out of Mutya's life like the squirrels in Lola's front yard. Whatever it was, Marina looked at that weak fence behind the ILP class and thought, *Why shouldn't I escape?* Marina got accustomed to life without a home. Without the anchor of a biological echo. Without her compass.

It didn't take Marina long to decide to sneak out under the fence. The *outs,* Alex called it. There were some small shops on the main street—dogs, trees, children, hiking, churches, sun. Close to the center of town was a small café, and across the street, there was the Mobil station.

Inside the fence, Marina was insignificant. Inside the Pines, the walls of their classrooms that were classrooms and not bungalows were cold, anonymous gray bricks. And the people there, the staff spoke in such grammatically butchered sentences that it made Marina's head split. Outside, Marina pulled out a Camel filter, lit it, exhaled, and looked into restaurant windows. She could see herself there, in the glass, lunching with some man, wearing a new, fine, swooping dress that had been a present. She imagined that was her there with the glass of water with a skinny slice of lemon. Laughing hand on chest. Curling her hair behind her ears. Looking intent. Listening. She could do that. *That could be me,* she thought. Then she'd look over to the village green. A patch of green grass that sat in the middle of town. Bright orange poppies stacked around the edges. Each flower open for insects, for air, for little droplets from the timed sprinkler system. It was time to turn back. She went to the store. She bought a cup of coffee and walked around to a park. She sat under a tree, and she wrote and smoked as long as she could.

She stood out on the quiet sidewalks, her crisscross crooked-cut hair, her deep red lipstick, her melted-on eyeliner. She must've stood out as a Pines girl because not too long later, a guy pulled up beside her, unlocked the passenger door, and she got in. Alex told her this is how it happens. That it's this easy, but she'd never done it before. She didn't tell him she wanted to go anywhere in particular, and he didn't ask her. His car was a root-beer-brown Ford Taurus, and the seats were a soft crumbling tan velour-ish material with little white dots of embroidery. Marina looked ahead as he drove, and he sat there with his pants undone. And his fat white hand stuffed with age spots guided her young brown hand to his stupid penis that sat flopping. He had a puffy white face and a bumpy swollen alcoholic nose, and his hair was gray, cut in a military-style flattop, and his gut was pushing against the steering wheel, and Marina grabbed a hold of his dick and made a tunnel out of her fist and stroked and stroked like the girls talked about a zillion times all fucked-up pakshet day back at the Pines. He drove, his one hand on the steering wheel and his other hand reaching for her chest, but Marina shoved it away. She was thinking about whether or not she could do this—if this could be her regular job. If maybe she should join Alex's hustle. Also, she needed so badly to be touched. She wanted the fastest cheapest way to feel wanted. She wanted the fastest cheapest way to exist. Yet somehow, at the same time, if you'd asked her, she would have told you that she did not want to exist. She did not want to be touched. What she wanted more than anything, what she longed for, was Alex's attention, and this seemed a way to get back in step with her.

She shoved his hand away but took her hand that was stroking him and licked it, just like she saw Hassan do that night in the apartment in Hawthorne. Put some good spit on it to speed the process along so she could stroke faster and faster, and he made little grunty noises, and she didn't know exactly where he was going or what would happen next, but the best possible thing did. Which was, he came—his tamod lava'd out in spurts—and then he pulled the car over, handed her a twenty, and let her out on a corner. The corner was near a 7-Eleven. She had traded one thing for another. Tit for tat. This was what the girls had meant when they talked about tricks. The trick was to turn something you do into money, like magic. She ran the words over in her mind like marbles seeing if she could get used to it. But there was one thing not working out. His flesh. His hard penis. Poking up at her, staring at her with the slanted eye. His head nodded toward the thing. Like it was expected. Like that's the deal, right? And if she fought? What was she? Stupid? Lazy? A bitch? Someone who thought she deserved more than that? The small little nod of his head made it clear—to both of them—no one would miss her. No one would know she was gone.

She walked right in the store and bought herself a pack of Camel filters and a Coke and walked back to the Pines. She scuttled under the gap between the fence and the ground, went straight to her cottage, and lay on her bunk bed until it was time to do something else. Eat dinner, sleep, clean, cook, exercise, go to class. She felt suddenly that power her body had, in a way that maybe Alex knew a body had power. Like with the *LA X . . . PRESS* ads. She realized that now, like Ma, she had kind of a spell over men. *Feminine wiles,* Mutya called it, the same saucy edge to Fatimah that Marina envied, it was there burning within her.

The worst was at bedtime. Marina just lay in *the* bed, praying for sleep. Not *her* bed. Everything became The. The. The.

While she lay there, she thought about that photo that hung on the wall in the apartment she shared with Ma. They were poor but not too poor. Their relatives in the Philippines certainly wouldn't have considered them poor. Sometimes she grabbed something in the market, some cereal or a packet of cookies, and she asked, Mommy, can I have this? and Ma just smiled and said, No, but you can have this! and grabbed her arm and gobbled it up with kisses.

Marina thought of that photo they took together that was hanging in their apartment. She hated that photo the most. The lie of it all. But during nights at the Pines, she missed it so much. What she would have given to be lying in her own bed, staring at the scary picture. Marina stayed awake, trying to conjure it up, tracing the outline on her blanket. Her fingertip lightly brushing over the area that would have been her mouth. By now their contact had stopped almost completely. Mutya didn't even call her for her birthday. Some nights Marina wondered what she was doing, if she was okay, if she'd stayed out of that apartment in Hawthorne. Still, in the back of her mind she wished she'd still try to reach out—that she'd fight for her.

This was a place without moms. A couple of the kids kept photos of their mother close; she saw a wrinkled four-by-six peeking out of Heather's sock once. Sammy put her photos in one of the small cubby drawers beneath her bunk. For other kids, it wasn't their mom, it was their boyfriend, or their clique, or their best friend, or it was a photo that they stole from some other kid at some other placement that they pretended was their family. If she listened close, she could hear the small kisses pressed against them at night. It was rumored that one kid from the younger cottage had a picture frame hung by his bed with the original photo of the family that came in the frame. No one had the heart to tell him they knew he was lying. Some kids ran away from placement to the destination of the picture they carried next to their chest. They ran away to see a mom they loved so much, who worked so hard, but they couldn't stay together because maybe, like Nikki, their mom was a prostitute, or their mom was on drugs, or their mom worked in the morning, and the night, so their mom worked all the time and they never saw her, or their mom was on welfare and she was gonna let her man move in and then there'd be a man in the house and she couldn't get welfare anymore. Marina saw so many kids who wanted more than anything to be with their moms who loved them a lot, but their moms were poor so they were taken away.

When she went to bed, she thought about all the neat things about Ma. The truth was she was afraid she'd forget them. Everything else was happening so fast. She tried to make a list each night before bed.

- When she said the word *yes*, she said it fast and strong and chirped as if a team of her subordinates were staying around waiting for a decision and it was clear and sure. Yes. A boss's yes.
- She let Marina keep an unmade bed.
- She made sausage from scratch during the winter months, each night taking out the meat and kneading it (it was ground meat filled with mustard seed). For a week straight every winter, she did this.
- She taught Marina how to eat canned meat products, letting it cook on the dash of her car in the summer. Then after a day in the park, they'd run back to the car, and Marina'd pluck a warm Vienna sausage from its place in the herd and plop it in her mouth.
- She didn't make Marina wait two hours after eating before she could swim.
- She was a crappy driver, but sometimes she'd play like a race car driver—especially on road trips from LA to Monterey. She'd piss in an MJB coffee can and holler out, Stopping for nothing!
- She took Marina to dance with the Hare Krishnas that one year for the free food.
- She loved murder mysteries and whodunits, but she ruined

them all by predicting the end before they happened. She was always right.

- She taught Marina how to sharpen her pencil with a knife.

As Marina recited the list in her head, she'd stroke her inhaler—the one Ma taught her how to use when she was home sick with TB. Sometimes she'd suck on it and twist strands of hair around her fingers. The truth was she missed Ma. She missed Ma in every part of her. There was sadness tucked into every crevice of her body.

As a teenager, Josie quickly became what Jan would call "not right in her head"; she stopped living with her family in the suburbs and was known to be out on the Downtown Eastside. She'd gotten mixed up with a boyfriend who had beaten her so often the police didn't trouble to respond to complaints anymore.

It was the same motel she was found wandering in as a little girl. Her foster mother, Jan, begged her not to go down there anymore. Josie'd come home at nights when she was still in her early teens.

Who are you seeing downtown? Friends. What friends? Do your friends have names? Of course they have names. One of them is called Jennifer. Jennifer? How did you meet Jennifer? Here in school, she goes downtown to volunteer at the drop-in centre. What's the drop-in centre? Do you volunteer too? It's a place that women go when they need help. I help sometimes. Why can't you help here? In town. Our church has drop-ins. Because I like the city. There's more to do there. What do you eat? Food. I don't know, Chinese food. Chinese food? How do you get it? People make it for me. People buy it for me. I don't know—I don't like this. I don't think you can go there anymore. What do you mean you don't think I can go there anymore? I don't allow it. You don't allow it? How can you not allow it? This is a free country, right? Jan? Free country?

She said allow *all slow and exaggerated. She hated it when Josie called her Jan; she only did it to hurt her. She knew that. To remind her that she was barren.*

BLANCHE AND ARTHUR

One of Marina's best days was that day Alex played "Little Wing." A beautiful thing. Alex. Alex. Alex. There she was, the first girl to ever love Marina. Her pointy nose and blue eyes and short brown hair.

Marina and Alex sat on a bench outside, and Alex told her she had a rare skin fungus. Look, she said, pulling down the collar of her T-shirt to reveal the pale inkblots on her chest—that porcelain skin. Marina reached for it, tracing the blots with her fingertips. Alex just sat there, a sly smile forming as part of her lip curled up.

Alex looked perfect to her. She played "Little Wing" on her guitar. She wore a bracelet made of braided threads around her wrist.

She grabbed four fist-sized bottles of orange drink and drank them all in one gulp, one by one, then lay back on the bench and pulled the bottom of her shirt up and said, Listen. Marina leaned her head down on her belly and strained to hear above her own heart beating, Alex's skin was so soft. The hairs on her body were blond. Marina tried to breathe through her nose. That's when she heard it, the juice sloshing around. She pretended like she couldn't, hoping she could stay longer.

What? Marina asked, her hands sweating. She'd practiced the lie in her mind a hundred times before she said it out loud. *I can't hear.*

When Alex stood up, she was tall to Marina, and almost angelic looking. It was like there was an invisible string between them, one that controlled Marina. If Alex thought dead birds were pretty, Marina would have delivered a gaggle of dead sparrows to her in a red silk heart-shaped box of Valentine's chocolates. Thankfully, Alex liked Newports hard pack and Whatchamacallit chocolate bars instead.

They began to leave notes for each other throughout the facility. They'd play a game pretending they were someone else, an old married couple. Like once as Marina reached for her toothpaste in the medicine cabinet above the shared sink, she spied a note that said:

Dear Blanche,
Please remember to squeeze the tube from the bottom and to put the cap on.
Love,
Arthur

Then, naturally, she put a note on the lid of a toilet seat.

Dear Arthur,
Please leave the toilet seat down. We have other guests that do not appreciate sitting in your urine.
Love,
Blanche

Marina also put a note on Alex's swimsuit that read:

Dear Arthur,
I don't swim in your toilet, please don't piss in our pool.
Warmly,
Blanche

Marina had a little chuckle when she signed it *Warmly.* That became their thing. Warmly warmly. Everything warmly, they'd snicker under their breath.

They had their spats. Once Alex even laughed and said, Awww, n—h! like in a joke or something and Marina said, Don't say that.

And Alex asked why she couldn't say it and Marina could. And Marina said, Because you can't do that.

Alex asked, Do what?

And Marina said, You can't say that and still love me at the same time.

Alex replied, Who said I loved you?

And they were quiet for a minute because Marina realized Alex never did say she loved her and she felt embarrassed and then Alex did something unexpected, she laughed and said, Nah, homey, I'm just fucking with you. You know I love your goofy ass.

Marina, stunned by how nice those words sounded coming from Alex, had to stop and hold her breath. Marina held out her hand to steady herself and Alex grabbed it. This changed everything between them forever.

It was after Mr. Hunter's class one day, Alex pulled out a pink brochure he'd given her. Check this out. It was a bright pink pamphlet that said Know Your Rights across the top. Alex pointed to the Right to Practice Your Religion.

Marina always wanted to be in league with Alex, she liked to act like they were so close words didn't matter, so at first, she faked like she got what she was saying. Sooo . . . we can ask for money?

This always seemed to be what they were after, money or freedom.

Nah, fool—we can go to church. Like we can actually leave and go to any church we want. Well, except they offer Christian services here so it has to be a church that doesn't have services here. This would be easy to convince the administration of because Alex subscribed to *Freedom* magazine. The Scientologists had hit her up one day when she was waiting for the van to pick her up outside of a doctor's appointment on Sunset Boulevard. She could tell the staff she was a practicing Scientologist.

They dressed up and made like they were going to the church. The first time they left, Marina and Alex waited out along the main boulevard for the bus, shrubs lining their backs, the night was cold and dark and surprisingly quiet. When the bus finally arrived, they looked back to the cottages, the purring hum of the engine below their feet, inside their hearts a rising thrill. They'd try not to think of the trail of parentless children they'd left in their wake. The plain truth of it all, that they were the loneliest unhappiest-looking cottages they had ever seen. When they got closer to the city, they took off their sweaters, and Marina put on more makeup. She added wing tips to her eyeliner and refreshed her dark lipstick. Alex pulled the cord on the bus and they raced off and down the steps and flew excitedly onto the sidewalk. They held hands and walked along the bright lights of street signs, people walking their dogs, and cars honking. Dazed and delighted, they kept going, Alex pulled out a cigarette from her backpack, lit it, and then shouted, Holler at your girls, LA!

Immediately Marina shouted and laughed with her, Holla holla! Hands clasped together, their free hands little fists in the air, the pleasure of their voices, their fear diminished. It was a special night, just the two of them. They stayed holding hands or linked arm in arm and relished the feelings of being attached. Sometimes when they returned back at the cottage, they'd keep the link going and Alex would slip beside Marina in the cot, their bodies touching sometimes back-to-back or side by side, their dreams wandering to different neverlands, neither one in the lead, but still they were joined together.

They had an easy way together flipping through the pages of teeny-bopper magazines into the quiet of the night wondering how to make their money stretch to buy all the acid-wash denim, and bangles, and shoes with pockets, and Wet 'n' Wild makeup. They both knew the sharp edges of want. They'd daydream about the lives they'd build together on the outs, from roommates to neighbors to matching homes and matching yards and matching husbands. They even mapped out that their husbands would die matching natural deaths at the same time so they would be widows together and come back around to being roommates once more.

Alex kept her seat across the aisle from Marina in the high school proficiency class. Even though Alex was also too young for that class, she'd been transferred there from another one because of behavioral issues, so Marina thought that gave Alex an edge.

Marina Marina, the brown-haired Queena, Alex taunted.

She laughed, like a real sincere, delighted, happy laugh.

Marina was having a hard time sitting still in class. She'd taken some Robitussin earlier that morning. She was trying to pay attention. But Alex kept on writing notes on the edge of her notebook paper and then tipping them toward the edge of the desk.

Marina made big graffiti X's and O's on a note and sent it to Alex. Marina smiled to herself. Thinking how she was acting cool, doing graffiti but something sweet and cute. She liked to be both sweet and tough at the same time.

Out of the corner of her eye, she watched Alex. Alex slowly unfolded the note and stretched out her legs, her dark brown bangs falling in her eyes. Just then, she saw the graffiti because she smiled and then started to write something back, but Mrs. Allen began to walk through the aisles, inspecting for notes. The thing that Mrs. Allen did when she caught you with a note is that she took it and read it in front of the class. Alex folded the note and stuffed it deep in her pocket.

Marina was sure Alex would be confused about what that note meant. Like X's and O's could mean something like *Let's hook up.* Like *Let's go fuck,* or it could mean something small like *You're my homegirl.* To Alex, everything was just a joke. And for them, everything started as a bunch of jokes until it wasn't anymore, and then you never really talked about it.

Just to seal the deal, make sure all possibilities were out there, Marina sat up straight and jutted her big tits out. Like *Look at me now, Alex. Look at me now.* She was still only fourteen, but no one ever thought she was so young with those tits.

Mrs. Allen was at the door to the classroom. Someone was knocking on a window—*clink clink clink.* Marina was a little tired. The knocking, and Mrs. Allen turned her back to the class, and then it happened. Alex reached across the aisle of seats and grabbed her face.

Marina was shocked. She thought Alex was such a nice girl. Alex was kind of dirty. Alex grabbed her and kissed her. Kiss kiss kiss. It was so fast. Did she kiss her? Was that real? What was going on? Did Marina like it? Alex kissed her with such familiarity she lost herself for a moment, she went swinging on a little swing set in her mind—then hopped off into the liquid sky.

Yes, of course. Yes, she liked that kiss.

Mrs. Allen turned around. Everyone in the class alert now. Marina, they need to see you in the counselor's office. Marina fumbled with her books. The Robitussin and the kiss all swirling together. This was unexpected.

Sherry the RA with the big jangle of keys walked Marina to the counselor's office.

Ms. Jennifer Mitchell, MFT, ATR-P, the counselor, was a woman with white frizzy hair who smoked cigarettes and seemed to have worked there for a hundred years.

She asked Marina to sit down.

Uh-oh.

I got bad news. How would you like it?

Straight.

Your grandmother had a stroke.

Shit.

Marina was trying to act cool, but she lost all auditory, she couldn't hear what the counselor was saying, she tried to focus on all the little stickers and magnets on her file cabinet. Her eyesight blurred from tears. Then the real truth of it all slowly rose to the surface.

Can I call her?

From what we've been told she's not capable of speaking right now.

Marina remembered a kind of stern tenderness, the thing that has been gone, along with Lola.

Can I go see her at least?

We can't have you go on any unsupervised overnights.

This is fucking bullshit. Wait. What does this mean?

As far as what?

As far as where I'm gonna live.

Well, you'll stay here until we can see if the court decides to reunify you with your mother or you get emancipated. The good news is you've been doing well in your ILP classes; you could be on track to emancipate early if you keep it up.

Early? Like when—how early?

Marina tried to keep focused, look at the objects in the room, there was a red picture frame, six yellow pencils in a black cup, there were four family photos on a blue bookshelf.

Well, generally you age out at eighteen or seventeen and a half, but if we find you a placement you can age out at sixteen.

Marina slowly nodded. Now she was getting it. She would be here in this kind of sad life, this world where children disappeared. They came and went so often. One day a kid goes to court, another day a kid goes to juvie. But never are they returned to their biological family. Anna's mother went to jail for welfare fraud. JoJo's mother had no address and moved into the homeless shelter. That's just how it went. She thought of all the things she'd been dreaming for and would probably never know again, like an allowance, and Lola's recipes, and her cold funeral kisses.

Jan forbade it, and Josie went anyway. The first time it was one day, and then it was three, and then it was a month at a time. Josie quit school at sixteen. It got to be that Jan was so happy Josie was alive that she forgave her every time she came home. She made her a lot of food—potato salad and schnitzel and sauerkraut—and she placed the plate in front of Josie's vacant-eyed worn-out face. Josie, who was found sometimes outside their house sleeping in a car or wrapped in a blanket under their tree or in their garage. Once, she found Josie in the backyard. Almost always, when Jan tiptoed over to wake her, the first thing she'd do, her thumb still propped in her mouth, is open her completely unstartled eyes and ask, Mom? Jan would say, Yes, Josie, oh yes.

Then she stayed home that time for over nine months. She had a beautiful baby girl. A girl named Sasha. A girl she was goofy in love with, but it wasn't even a full month after she gave birth that she ran back to the streets again. By then, it'd been two years back and forth, back and forth. Jan just thought she had a better chance with her not asking anything of her anymore. Josie'd leave the baby with her. Sometimes when she looked at Josie's baby girl Sasha, she saw little Josie, puffed-out cheeks and glassy black eyes.

STRIDE RITE IN HEAVEN

Marina slowly pretended to accept the way things were, cut out a path for her dreams from the reality. She behaved in class at the Pines; she said, Yes, ma'am. She said, May I please? She acted out of respect for authority, even though it was exhausting. She tucked her truth deep inside.

Navigating what was allowed versus what was not allowed was like navigating public transportation in Los Angeles. Random and absurd. Cussing was okay. Sleeping during the day was not okay. If you were sixteen or older, you were allowed to smoke. However, no one who worked at the Pines was allowed to give you a cigarette. But you could most definitely pick up a cigarette that was dropped on the ground or left in an ashtray and smoke it.

It was later the night she'd heard of Lola's stroke, on her bunk in the Pines, where Marina learned of Lola's death in a dream. She was in a deep sleep, and Lola appeared on the corner of her bunk. Lola wore a muumuu, her skin brighter and clearer than Marina remembered it, her hair thicker and longer than Marina had ever seen it. She had the fresh look of a movie star who had never been hungry.

I have a story to tell, and if you were younger, I couldn't tell it, this story so dangerous that tomorrow you must forget it entirely and make up another. She went on and told the story of the brother and sister and the aswang again, of how the boy mangled his auntie with a ginunting sword.

She twirled her hair there on the edge of Marina's bed, looking young like she'd never seen her. Lola, Marina said. Lola pulled Marina close. Reen's head on her chest. But there were no smells, no warmth, no home in her.

Listen, Reen . . . I have something important to tell you—the most important thing. Remember when we talked about the different ways we can come back? When men are turned into animals, it's hard for them to find their way back to themselves. When children are turned into animals, there's no self to find. Please listen to your mother. You must be good. You must use hot curlers. You must never eat in bed. Don't be a wild girl. Life is too hard for a wild girl. Reena, there were plenty of times I wanted to give you an easy life. But if I did, the world would eat you up. We only have now for me to be soft with you. I can tell you all my secrets. I have a secret to tell about a bad priest. A priest who came and touched me on my pekpek. A priest who made us all speak English, which is how I learned. When I was alive with you, I forgot so many things to tell your mother. I forgot to be gentle with her, so she didn't sleep with her hands clutched tight, so that you didn't dream of a fantasy life out there in the rain with fairies. Now there are things I'm forgetting in death, how it felt to run free against the wind, or how it was to swear Ay! Susmaryosep! at a truck driver who came too close to my feet. I remember the morning you were born. You were like a weight dropping on the ankle of your ma's life, holding her down, but holding us together. She was eager to go out and see the world. Always looking for bad fun. Your eyes opened and they were my eyes. Black, not like your ma's. Too much fight in you. One day I may forget everything, and you may forget me. You might remember it was your ma who taught you how to hit a person, but I taught you how to fight, how to pull all the weight of your bad life up from your pekpek into the pit of your stomach into the center of you and put that all behind your punch. I might vanish from your memories, but maybe on those days when you have stormy weather and the wind is big you will brace yourself against the harshness and think of the times I held you when you were a baby, rocked you and put the fight in you, a killa and a thrilla and a chilla.

The next morning when Marina woke up, she knew that Lola was dead.

Now, on the other side, Lola is sitting at some kitchen table eating a piece of toast topped with sweetened condensed milk. This is her favorite thing. The sweet goopiness reminds her of coming to the States from the Philippines. Of all the vulgar extravagant things to discover. There are shiny cars; there are various types of domestic animals. There is clothing for the pets. There is bottled water. There is a gymnasium, sometimes more than one, within two blocks of another. Just a place that people go to and pay money to sweat in. There is food from every country. There is clothing that is more expensive if it looks well-worn. But this. This toast. This sweet cream. This is the sweetest cream. The gluttony of it. She can, if she wants, eat the entire loaf. Toast each piece of bread and pour a generous amount of sweetened condensed milk on it. Yet what makes this even more extravagant, what makes her feel the *most* rich about this, is she does not. She saves it for later. She partakes only a little at a time—the dog. Somebody else's German shepherd is sitting beside her, staring at her with sad, longing eyes. She breaks off the crust and shares it with the dog.

This, to her, is a luxurious thing. To practice self-restraint. *Self-restraint.* Two words not available to her in life.

In my day, Reen, everybody knew how to act. How to curtsy when they met you. How to keep your elbows off the table. How to ask to please be excused. Then like my little baby, we girls, we knew how to disappear. And if some boy came to pick you up. To go on a date, or to eat ice cream—you knew he was there—for your hiya. I tell all the girls, make him come knock. Make him come ring the bell, at least. When a man cannot be bothered to leave his car—he is not a man of honor. Nowadays you are all in a hurry, to try to be seen. You move so fast. You think if you move fast, you will not disappear. You think if you move a lot, you will not die. But running to a man, not a man, a tamad, slouching in his sirang-sira loud car. He'll never rise. He'll never carry you. You will be there on the sidelines of his life, cheering so loud, and then you will forget to live your own life. To grow new life. To make a difference. There are many days that I was still, and my heart felt alone. But when you came, my heart rose up, on all her tiny little feet, and she cheered ¡Viva! He will never know, no matter how much bulbol you flick at him. The tiny curly hairs could get confused for a dog's. Don't forget to bundle up for winter. Don't forget to eat your breakfast. Spam and eggs. Rice is good too. Remember when I used to work at the Stride Rite? Sometimes I spent long days staring out the window. And I would put all that murang crap on the conveyer belt one by one. Then sometimes you'd come visit. Or pass by the window. And my heart would start dancing again. Sometimes I would catch you with your thumb in your mouth. I asked, What are you doing? You said, Nothing. That is okay. It is okay to lie to your lola sometimes. That is respect. Especially when it is a clumsy lie. I look into your dark world now, and I wonder, *Where has all the love gone?* I notice you don't have anything. That's okay too. You come from a people who feel good when we lose everything. When you lose everything, the only thing left is winning. In my day, you prayed for that kind of loss. And sometimes it would come. And when it came, you would laugh. You laughed so hard, in that car, Reen, and it was because the joke was on you. Today, Reen, I'm a ghost. And someday soon, you will be a ghost-spirit. This is good. We know how to be ghosts. When you were a little girl, you crawled into the cupboards, and crouched low, and sat in the darkness, and whispered, Cupcake, cuppa caka—popping your P's loud like you were in a lip gloss commercial. You did that for hours. You knew just how to be still. Just how to savor one word inside your mouth. Back then, you knew how to disappear. We'd all sit at the same table, and Mutya would come scuttering and moving around. Like a feather duster. She did not see you. Maybe life is different in America. Maybe you need to jingle-jangle more. If I am wrong, I am sorry. If this is not enough, we can jingle-jangle here, in the Stride Rite in heaven. We can dance and burn down the house and eat all the ashes.

Willie pulled up in his white van. Josie looked him up and down: skinny, balding, but he kept the hair on the top of his head long. He liked to play with it, brush it out of his eyes like he had a ponytail. Hey there, you working?

For some. Whatcha need?

I was thinking about taking you over to my place.

She was up off the wall now talking close to the window, still not leaning in like the other girls, just trying to be smooth. She'd been picked up on a possession charge the other night, so she needed to act cool. Whereabout?

Port Coquitlam. It's about thirty kilometers out thataway. Willie pointed east.

That's far.

Yeah, but I'll give you a couple hundred bucks, and I got all this junk too.

He pulled some baggies out of his pants pocket. Josie looked around and then hopped in.

Happy Groundhog Day. Willie was humming and tapping along on his steering wheel.

Groundhog Day, is it?

She was getting jittery. As they drove farther into the woods away from the lights, away from the city, it all didn't seem right. He looked straight ahead but put his hand on her leg.

PUT ON

They took the high school proficiency exam the first Friday of every month. You needed at least a 350 in each section in order to pass and the highest score was 450. Both Marina and Alex were determined to pass the exam, but also they had entered silent competition with one another. One month Alex got a 325 on the math and Marina got 323, then in language and reading Marina got 345 and Alex got 325. They were just fourteen and thirteen, too young to take the actual exam but there they were preparing for the life that awaited them.

Alex liked to curl Marina's hair into elaborate dos. She said she always loved to play with hair. Marina liked the way her fingers felt on her scalp, and the easy way they sat together. She liked how Alex fussed with her, the gentle softness of her fingers, how she pushed the hair back from her eyes and face. Marina sometimes felt so pretty when Alex was finished that she wanted to show the world, she felt envy from the other girls, and she wanted them all to take a long, good look. After, Alex would do her own hair, line her edges and slick it back, and they'd strut around like two warriors across the busted painted asphalt. They walked along the campus, amid the other kids, and the service workers, and the RA staff, the do-gooders with their donations, like two young college students taking the measure of their future endeavors. The way Marina remembered the young women on Mutya's campus of brick buildings at UCLA. Marina and Alex clung to each other. No one understood them, they thought. No one could feel their dreams pulsing as strongly and fiercely as they could. They were walking toward the unknown. Forward or backward, it seemed they were going toward something terrible that existed long before them yet was waiting for them, like a trap. Just for them.

During the holidays the staff at the Pines played on a large projector in the cafeteria movies with children singing and dancing. Marina and Alex sat close enough to each other their legs touched. They'd try to whisper to one another without getting caught. It seemed all they could do was talk and touch all day long.

At night they perfected the art of sneaking out, Marina would fold back her blanket and carefully tiptoe to the door on bare feet. Outside the air smelled peaceful, like chimneys from nearby homes. The sky was clear, lit up by the moon and stars. Once outside their cottage Marina and Alex quickly grabbed hands and made verbs of themselves, ran across the open lawn. Sometimes they'd sneak into the teachers' break room.

There was a small light that lined the main hallway, it glowed a warm yellow across their bare feet. Inside the building, they'd again step carefully, setting one foot down in front of the other. Sneaking, their hearts quick and loud. Then in the break room they'd raid the fridge. There was usually at least half of a leftover sandwich. Once they scored a jar of pickles that they kept to make pruno in.

One night Marina and Alex planned to meet, Alex and the rest of their cottage had to stay late in some kind of group. Marina got up, she thought maybe at first this whole thing was a hoax, some bad dream. She was moving so freely from place to place but then she knew it was real because of the small alarms beeping beside the forbidden doors, the clothes she wore to bed, regular street clothes, not a long T-shirt or the kinds of pajamas she had when she lived with Ma. She remembered again being sick as a child and Ma bringing her small cakes or a fried apple pie from the McDonald's and how nothing tasted right when she was sick and how she cried. Often in this place, the Pines, Marina felt drugged. Time felt strange, every day the same as the last. She felt like she was living in dream time.

Then once she reached the break room, first she smelled it, the rank teenage scent of girls, their skin, that seasoned smell of blood, something animal, and then she smelled Alex, the harsh Brut deodorant she sprayed, and finally something sweet and bright, lemons and crème. They'd surprised her with a cake. It was all of them, the girl army. Alex. Heather. Sammy. Nikki. Danielle. Another birthday. They remembered. Marina felt thankful, they all beamed there in the center of the break room and ate cake, and for that night they soothed the ache. She knew then this was the thing to be thankful for. It was the small mercies.

By now, it'd been two years and Marina was fifteen, she'd developed big boobs and Alex was still flat chested. And all the other girls in Acorn Cottage had their periods except Alex. Some of the other girls teased her by putting Band-Aids in her underwear cubby where bras should be. Alex didn't give a shit, she liked not wearing a bra or having to fuss with tampons or maxi pads, and she was taller than Marina by several inches. But it wasn't just that she was taller, it was how she was proportioned, the length of her legs, and the length of her neck. Marina could make out a small curl that curved in at the nape of her neck, and she was sometimes jealous of that curl, that it got to nestle there so close to Alex's skin. The length of her fingers. She had long thin fingers and unlike most of the kids their age who were tall, she was graceful and coordinated. Sidestepping obstacles.

One of the weeks they went out to "church" they came across a bunch of other teenagers. They were hanging around the pay phones, smoking clove cigarettes, bumming change from people and begging them to buy them beer.

They fronted like they needed change for the bus. Excuse me, sir, can you spare a quarter for the bus home?

Then after they got the money, they begged people to buy the beer, they'd look for someone cool and young, someone who could be in college. Hey there, can you do us a favor, I left my ID at home.

Eventually a guy would look them over, especially Marina with her big boobs, she was the best at it, and he'd be sucker enough. Yeah, sure, lemme guess, you forgot your ID. No sweat.

Sometimes the guy would buy it on account that he could keep a dollar for himself or he could drink it with them. When they got enough beer, usually a couple of forties, they'd head over to a park around the corner to drink it. Like most teenagers they got thick together real soon. They called themselves a crew, like a gang but without guns. They gave themselves a name, Nothing But Criminals, NBC, and darted around the town as if they owned the place. Most of them were rich kids whose parents were never home, and then there were the occasional group home kids like Marina and Alex, there were also rehab kids who were kind of like both rich kids and group home kids because they were on the run and if any of them got caught, they'd end up in juvie, their parents having given up on them long ago.

At the park they'd put people on. Which meant they had to get jumped into their crew.

On the day that Alex was gonna get put on, there was so much buzz they sat around just waiting for night to come. If a guy wanted to get put on, he'd just get jumped in, but if a girl wanted to get put on it was a different story—the guys would run a train on her. Except for Marina. She didn't have to get put on. Because she always got the beer, so she got a pass. All she had to do was watch and be the counter.

Before it was Alex's turn, a guy called Shallow got jumped in. Marina sat in the vacant skull of a slide shaped like an elephant. Her Doc Martens propped against the slope of the trunk while the guys circled each other on the ground down below.

Shallow, a thin blond boy, stood in the middle of the circle posturing, back hunched, elbows up. His eyes darted around the circle. He hopped around. Fists up by his cheeks. The guys forming the circle looked like boys imitating gorillas imitating vultures.

Then, suddenly, the first blow came from behind. Trax did it. Trax was a stout kid, short, with muscles. Trax had a lisp that gave him a tinge of innocence. That innocence was shifted by his deep vodka rasp. Once the hitting started, Marina began counting out loud: One two three. Smoking and counting, feigning disinterest.

Shallow had no chance. The guys, at least ten, were all running in close, socking him at once. He looked at Marina, his eyes asking for mercy. Marina started to speed up her counting: Five-six-seven. He lifted his arms to his face and curved his body into the shape of a C.

When Marina got to thirty, they stopped. The swarm died down. The punches turned into hugs. Shallow lay slumped on the ground, his nose and eyes the mushiest parts of him. Wet gobs of blood. One eye already swollen half shut.

Ahhh, man, I think you broke my nose. They always said that. Most often it wasn't broken.

That's how the guys got into whatever silly thing they were calling themselves that day.

The rabid bundle of guys who were jumping Shallow in were ready to celebrate, to be bros. They poured beers on each other and hugged. Then Alex came forward and walked toward the slide. She was drunk. She stumbled on a rock.

Marina searched her face for a sign she wanted to change her mind. Marina wanted her to want to change her mind. But when Alex looked up, she only seemed more determined. She straightened her dress. She'd dressed femme—a dress and fishnets. Just like when she did bids in the *X . . . PRESS,* she tried to keep it separate from her regular life, her *real* self, she said, where she sagged her jeans and wore tank tops. She smoothed over her short dark hair.

The clot of guys that were a circle of fury just moments ago started to act modest. They passed around a bottle, drank, poured a little on the ground for a friend who was in jail. Some of them formed a line. Marina walked over to a bench.

Marina sat on the bench, facing the swings. Once Alex reached the elephant she turned around, facing Marina. She put her hands on the slide behind her and propped herself up backward like a kid hopping onto a kitchen counter. Only her feet slipped, and she fell off-balance. She looked drunk. She fell on the ground and the back of her head banged against the sculpture. A couple guys rushed to help her. Prop her up. *Yeah, sure, they're gonna help her and then they're gonna fuck her,* Marina thought.

Marina hated her then. Something about her big eyes and her

clumsiness made Marina hate her. The truth was the clear opposite, she loved her and desperately wanted to stop her, to tell all the boys to fuck off. But Alex had a way about her, she'd let go of those parts of her long ago, and even though she was on the bottom of all this she made this her power, giving herself away. There was nothing anyone could take from her.

Marina left her bench and went to the swings. Marina didn't wear socks and she could feel the sand pass through the eyelets in her shoes. Marina looked over occasionally and saw the line form. The sand was sifting between her toes. From where she was sitting, she could make out little things and fill in the blanks.

Shallow went first. When he left the elephant, Viper unbuckled his belt. He didn't have to bother because his pants were so big, they fell off his flat hips. Some guys walked forward with their cocks hanging out the slit in front. Trax was next in line. He warmed himself up. Spit on his hand, stroked himself. He wanted to appear big. He joked awkwardly while he was waiting in line with the other guys.

From Marina's spot on the swing, she'd imagine them pulling Alex closer. Alex, the paper girl, tiny bones. They'd tear a hole in the crotch of her fishnets and take her from there. Alex probably looked at the ceiling of the hollowed-out skull of the elephant. Maybe she was counting with Marina at that moment. One two three. It didn't stop at thirty seconds like the guys who got jumped in. For the girls, the train didn't stop until all the guys had their turn.

Marina looked at the moon. Marina tried to swing toward it, curling her feet underneath her and then shooting her legs forward, keeping her toes pointed. She wanted to launch herself higher and higher. She thought of how Alex always jumped from the swing to the ground when they got to the highest point. That was her. Fearless. Marina got so high she was afraid the chains from the swing would wrap around the pole. That's when she brought her feet back to the ground. She stopped the swing and broke the dream.

Josie couldn't wait. Hey there, can we pull over and have a little? I'm getting dope sick, I think.

Sure. But we're almost there. Can you hang on a couple of minutes?

She nodded and began counting in her head like she did whenever she was waiting for anything to pass. She did that when she had to sleep with them too.

We're here.

They pulled up to a big lot with a fence on the outside that said ***BEWARE OF DOG.***

What kinda place is this?

A farm.

Whatchu farmin'?

He looked at her—smiled. He was missing teeth. Pigs. Just when he said that a big boar came to the gate, grunting back and forth. There were dogs too. German shepherds barking up a storm. And a large Chow Chow mix.

She jumped back in her seat while that six-hundred-pound baboy Machine brambled toward her.

He looks tough, all right.

Her? She won't do nuthin', she's just the greetin' committee, he said.

Josie, still afraid of the boar, tried to keep her eyes forward.

He parked in the back of the property by a mobile home.

It looked like it was falling apart. It was held up on cinder blocks. Three steps. There were windows. The lights were on.

THE OUTS

After that night, Alex said she was too busy to go to church the next week. The next time they took the proficiency exam Marina got a 351 in math and a 425 in language and reading comprehension. She ran to tell Alex, but Alex said it didn't matter anyway because they couldn't take the exam for a couple of years no matter how well they did on it. Then Alex was transferred out of the proficiency exam class and into woodshop with Nikki. She'd come back after dinner with all the different things she'd made, the letter A, a small box with a trick secret compartment.

Every now and again Marina saw Nikki and Alex walking together to class from ILP and she felt like maybe Alex liked Nikki better and didn't want to be friends with her anymore.

The loneliness of this kind of rejection was too much for Marina, to see Alex there laughing, capable of friendship and kindness, just not toward her. Marina tried desperately to fill her time—she read, she snuck out and ran into town, she smoked cigarettes—but still she wanted someone to talk to. She tried to call

Mutya but she almost always got an answering machine. Strange thing, Ma's outgoing message was different. It used to be a fun play on words:

Leave a massage!

Now it was all Lordy—Marina knew she was listening to them because she changed her outgoing messages daily. The first time she called her, the message began with a blessing—Bless those who love Jesus and bless us with understanding—and bless *you* for . . . leaving a message.

The next time she called, Mutya had quoted some scripture—one of those about self-control. Marina couldn't believe what she was hearing, initially she thought it was a joke. When she finally did get through it was clear Mutya had turned some kind of corner. As usual she spoke to Marina like she was older than she was, like they were friends of the same age, but then there was something else—Marina felt like there was an impenetrable wall around Ma's words. Marina wished Ma'd at least pretend like she was some kind of doting mother who missed her, this new way she felt distant like a talking doll Jessie had. Marina remembered the way it felt when they figured out what she would say based on what direction you tipped her. It wasn't fun anymore.

Oh, Reen, you should have heard today's mass, the father read from this scripture, Galatians 5:22–23. Do you know it?

For Marina it felt again like she was on the beach with her and Mike outside of their movie, but instead of Mike it was all this Lordy stuff.

Look, Ma, how are things going with your classes?

Well, poopsy, poopsikins, I've been praying about that, and I want to do whatever really is God's will.

Marina was getting impatient, tapping her feet to the rhythm of the egg timer. Uh-huh—look, I'm on a timer here.

Ignoring Marina, Mutya continued, I prayed and prayed about

it and I was having a hard time understanding what he wanted, and then you'll never believe it.

Here Mutya's voice got all big and dreamy and at least she started sounding more familiar to Marina.

I went to one of those parenting classes, you know the ones I didn't like? I'm sure I complained about it to you before. The teacher and half the class always drank out of those hot drink stirrers, ugh, you know how I hate that, she giggled.

Ma, seriously I'm on a timer.

Okay, okay, anyway, I went to the class and it was—CANCELED. Can you believe it?

Umm, yeah, sure, that's—that's one hundred percent believable.

They are gonna move it to the other clinic in Venice. Which I don't like that clinic because it's the clinic where they give birth control and abortions to the young girls. So then I thought, oh wait, for sure—it's a sign! MY PRAYERS WERE ANSWERED.

What? Wait, Ma, are you saying you're not going to go to the classes anymore because the classes were moved?

No, not just that, Reen, it's not that simple—here is what I know. I know God loves me. I also know that it'll be okay. Whatever is meant to happen will happen. We're gonna be okay.

Just when Marina thought she couldn't feel more lonely. Marina laughed, just as she did when she was in the car with the social worker, she laughed because she had to. Laughed, tears streaming down her face, she was trying her best to fit herself into this new idea of a life. A life where Ma was claiming some faith-based reason to not participate in motherhood. Of all the horrors Lola had warned her about, this was not one of them, but this shit seemed to be the worst.

Marina stopped calling Mutya after that. She spent most of her afternoons by herself. The other kids noticed. Especially the boys, they took the opportunity to try to get in close and holler at her.

One day a boy named Jory, who was two years younger than her, offered her twenty bucks to see her tits, she told him to meet her up by the bungalow that she and Alex used to hide away and smoke cigarettes on. She walked with the defiance and grace she thought Alex had in her walk, long steady confident steps. When she reached the bungalow, Jory was there waiting for her.

Do you have the money?

He showed her the edge of a twenty-dollar bill. I'll give it to you after.

She thought again what Alex would do. No. I want it now. Give me the twenty bucks and then climb up the ladder.

Jory gave her the money and then slowly climbed up the ladder. She climbed up right behind him.

She was afraid someone could sneak up behind her, so she told him to sit with his back facing the ladder. Quickly she lifted up her shirt and put it down.

Can I touch them?

That's not what we agreed on.

Yeah, but I can give you more money if you let me touch them.

Right then Alex's head appeared behind Jory. She had her index finger to her lips indicating that Marina be quiet.

Marina tried to maintain eye contact with Jory so it wouldn't tip him off. Uh, close your eyes. Okay, now follow my voice and come sit closer to me. Just two steps closer.

Alex snuck up carefully behind him.

What's that noise?

I'm just getting closer so you can feel them.

Alex was holding something in her hand.

Okay, now put out your hand. Jory put his arms out like a mummy.

No, not like that. Put your hands out flat, palms up.

But how am I gonna feel them?

Just do as I say.

He did, and Alex put something in his right hand.

Marina looked closer and realized it was a bloody tampon.

Alex screamed, Look, ho, I'm a woman now!

Jory opened his eyes and freaked, threw the bloody tampon, and ran down the ladder.

Marina and Alex laughed all over each other.

Alex kept her dreams. Alex said she was gonna one day have her own business. Maybe a hair salon like she'd heard her mom wanted to do. Marina sat still for hours while Alex practiced on her, pulling and yanking and combing. Her braids tight against her head.

Girrrrrllll, you're gonna look so fly.

The pointy comb like fire against her scalp.

You should let me take some pictures of you after this, Alex said.

Alex meant for the *LA X . . . PRESS*. Alex just used them *to give massages*, she said. It was more. It always started that way—sexy pictures—and then a massage and then maybe head and then sex. Alex didn't really care about her body. Alex could accidentally not get dressed or have big bruises on her thighs that she didn't feel. She never saw the bottom half of her body. She never looked—never touched.

When she first came to the Pines, Alex was three, she was still in diapers, the pull-up kind for toddlers. She had to get potty trained, and still sometimes when she was having a mental break, or she was upset, she'd swipe a stream of shit across the bathroom wall. For this reason, it was hard at first for Alex to make friends with the other girls. This fact only made Marina love her even more.

Alex told her she'd start with some small bids.

This became a regular thing for her, going to town and riding in a car through the Valley. She never went far. Kept it local. The little warning card in the basket in the dayroom: A Tisket A Tasket A

Condom or A Casket. Swooping black lanes, lines of cars, big oak trees embracing the highway, orange signs saying DETOUR. Yellow signs saying SLOW CHILDREN, sitting in a car beside a man, not a teacher, not a caseworker, not a foster father. He is a stranger. He is saying, Well . . . what about here? His hand covers her hand. His hand moves onto her thigh. She moves toward him, her skirt sliding up, without haste. Now they are somewhere else, a darkened hotel room. The kind that as a kid her friend Jackie lived in, Extended Stay, that had turned itself over to long-term renters—folks who paid by the week, for ever and ever. Laid-off people, and hustlers, and folks who cooked smelly stuff and stole laundry from the dryers in the communal space.

He is on top of her. With his legs he spreads her legs . . . anything can happen, any sharp, swift surprise. She waits, counts the pockmarks on the ceiling, counts in her mind the money she hasn't yet earned, counts to one hundred. He enters her and everything stands still, fixed by him, by what he is doing, her body works itself to helplessness, to numbers, to numbness. This pain, the great equalizer everything inside her, a beam of light merged to a single point.

The room adjacent to theirs, the one that shares a wall, the television set is on. She imagines a mother and daughter staying in that room, she had stayed in a motel with Ma once, but it was an adventure, when they were driving back to Seaside from LA. Marina didn't mind at all because it was better than traveling to live with one pakshet man or another. The motel they stayed in had a kind of princess wonderland theme, there was another hotel with a pea soup theme. Ma liked themes. Across the street from this hotel was a graveyard, and if she got up and opened the blackout curtains, she'd see tombstones trailing the horizon. After he gets up to wash off, she lies alone. The tamod scares her. It can seep up into her. It can carry diseases. The little ooze of it can destroy her. Sometimes she imagines it there between her thighs, sliding in, killing her.

This is how it begins. The *other* Marina, the other her, is out on the street, leaning on a pole, sitting in a donut shop. Slits for eyes, a pretty mouth, everything soft. Before she leaves, she pauses in the mirror, fixes her lipstick, checks her teeth for black things, shimmies her hair. Every now and again, she has a regular. He comes up to her before she goes. He sees her there leaning before the mirror, her perfect small body. Giving him something to remember during lonely nights: his arms out and up toward the sky like one of those animated characters in a Disney movie. Offering up and gently cradling each cheek of her perfect bouncy puwit. With his hands, he clutches her throat. He stares into her face. He pulls her close and kisses her passionately like he waited up for her from work. Like what's for dinner? Fuck dinner! I want you now. He kisses her the way she wants to be kissed—like the end of time. Like the end of them.

No. Wait. Before the hotel they stopped at a diner, she got a burger and fries, and then in the parking lot, he leaned over to her in her seat belt and kissed her, and if someone had seen, just judging by the back of their heads, they would not see a little girl and a pakshet pervert, they would have thought they saw two people kissing each other gently, and then maybe they would've longed for someone to kiss them like that.

No. Wait. Before the diner, when he first picked her up, he saw her standing there on the corner and he asked did she wanna ride, and she winced for just a second, she felt at that moment that all her days were just like this moment, tiny cuts, one upon the next, and she needed just a minute, to tuck away her heart. She heard something in his voice, something sad and needy, and she waited a few more beats and then said, Sure, which, to him, was the most perfect word there was.

Now. Here, in the motel, as he kissed her one final time, she heard that needy sadness in his small moan, and she made a gentle tracing motion on his back, the kind of gesture Mutya used to calm her at night. One day earlier that week, she was on the highest level and was able to get out of class and help on the grounds at the Pines. They called her in to work in the baby cottage. The newborns needed to be held throughout the day, she picked up the newest young thing, her eyes shut, that little blistered dimple where her top lip met the bottom, Marina made this same gentle patting motion on the baby's back. Of all the pakshet johns, she tried to remember this one, to try to keep a safe soft space where she could pretend there was still something about any of them to love.

Ay! Susmaryosep! Here I am. Aswang, in the body that was Marina's, in the closet, in this pakshet dump. The hunger for his masamang soul, to cut off his buto and fling it in the woods, to end my time here. I heard two pairs of footsteps walk into the living room. I heard that pakshet Willie sit down and slump on the floor. I heard him unbutton the sleeves of his shirt—roll them up. He had thin arms. Blond hairs. Some freckles. Some cuts and bruises. Still some big veins.

I could picture them from Marina's memories. I sensed that animal desire to use growing in Josie. That's what she looked for now—the veins. He tied himself off first. Shot up. She sat there, jittery. Watching. Watching the dope cook on the spoon. I could hear everything. How she tried to tap her fingers on her knees. Make it seem cool, smooth, nonchalant.

Josie wasn't chill. He could tell she was jonesing. He took his time. She wanted to go. She kept on looking at the door like it wasn't too late to go. She got up like she was gonna leave.

Where you goin', groundhog? he asked.

Huh? She stopped and looked at him.

It's your turn; he made that grimace that, for him, was a smile.

He handed her the needle. She smacked the inside of her arm. Nothing. She turned her hand over—made a fist. There they were—old faith-

ful. Top of the hand. All those years of reading and writing in school paid off. Made her hands strong. Made her veins come out. Made her get that first sip so nice. So nice. So nice. Her body tingled. Her edges blurred. She was fuzzy. She decided to stay awhile.

CASE FILES

Over that next year, Marina worked her way up the ranks. The girls started to like her. She worked out with Nikki in the morning. Took pictures of Alex in the afternoon. Nikki and Marina noticed each other smoking cigarettes and didn't tell. Nikki was always telling stories of the fancy rehab programs her parents sent her to. Outward Bound, a program where she went white-water kayaking, and some cooking classes with Mennonites in Iowa, and a kibbutz in Israel. It all sounded so beautiful to Marina, the idea of all that nature or the privacy or baking loaves of bread made her wild with want.

Did it work? she asked Nikki.

Don't be ridiculous. Girls can't be protected from themselves. There's no saving a girl like me; this is the mistake everyone makes. You can't give to a taker; you can take from a taker, now that would be interesting. My parents will spend all their money trying to figure that out.

So what's your story? they asked. Sometimes Nikki, sometimes Heather, all the time Alex.

No story, my mom just wasn't cut out to be a mom.

Uh . . . no story. That sounds like a story to me. But whatever, you don't have to say if you don't want to. Alex rolled her eyes and finished doing Marina's lipstick. She puckered her lips together and then made a *pop* noise to demonstrate what she wanted Marina to do with her lips. It reminded Marina of a cartoon ad with a sexy personified hot dog—glassy luscious lips, eyes with long-ass lashes, plopped into a bun, ready for you to bite into her. Giggle giggle.

So, what do you think, you like it here? Alex asked.

Does it matter? I mean, like it or not, I'm gonna have to be here.

Yeah, true that.

The truth was Marina would rather be back in that apartment with all the roaches with Ma, but she couldn't say that because most of the girls here didn't have anywhere else to go, and she didn't want to hurt anyone's feelings. There was some solidarity in the shared longing of it all.

Marina had developed real feelings for Alex. She'd seen women together like Tracy Chapman and whoever. And Marina didn't know what she found more enticing, the freedom of love without men, or the actual sexual act of it. She looked at girls differently, almost too long when they were changing clothes. Marina glanced at the way the other girls' hips moved or their posture or their fingertips and wondered exactly what counted as sex between women. One day on her way to ILP she could see some of the girls from another cottage, the girls with their Los Padrinos sweats, leaning against each other in the space between two cottages and it made her flush in a way that she hadn't felt before.

There were some girls who'd hump the corner of their bed or sleep on their stomachs, their hands down their panties. They'd try to fuck doorknobs or table edges. Marina wanted something different. Marina wanted books and Mexican food and cigarette smoking and stroking of hair and someplace safe.

In Mrs. Allen's, they were reading a series on babysitters. Books Marina read when she was eight. Marina read the pages angry, but also jealous. The girls in the books wore stylish jeans and their hair in high ponytails and had two parents. But even worse, everything they complained about—she wanted. She wanted to babysit, or learn to drive, or beg for an allowance. Marina wanted to complain about no one inviting her to prom, or the drag of wearing braces or glasses. She wanted to talk on the phone all night. She wanted to be class president. She wanted to be a cheerleader. A chance at all that stuff. And Alex was the one part of her life that made her feel like a regular teenager.

Alex and Marina whispered until they fell asleep. They lay bunk upon bunk in the dark, Alex talking about her favorite foster mother and Marina, her wild, crazy mom. Both of them mouthing out words with barely any sounds, tears quietly rolling down their cheeks. One night it began to rain outside, and Alex said, It's raining, I'm not sleepy, please let's talk all night.

Marina was happy for the request, the sound of rain on the roof and against the window, she'd never felt so open to affection. Alex let her arm fall off her bunk, and they held hands. The rain pitter-patter on the window. Marina wanted more of her; her skin trembled each time Alex stroked her fingertips up and down Marina's arm.

As Marina neared her sixteenth birthday, the fact she could get emancipated early lingered heavy between her and the other girls. Alex grew distant. Marina'd try to play a game of cards with her, and she'd tell her to kick rocks. Alex stopped looking at her. At first, Marina acted fine about it all. I don't give a mad fuck, Marina'd say under her breath every time Alex ignored her.

One night, Marina lay in bed, straining to hear Alex breathing. She was reminded of that feeling of being in a room full of people but being alone. She tried to hold the feeling in, but her small cries seeped out. Alex could hear her whimpering and sniffling, then she dropped her arm off her side of the bunk. Marina felt for her fingers. They lay there, both of them crying and holding hands. Alex quietly came down from her bunk, crawled in beside Marina, and rested her head on her shoulder.

At the same time Marina was preparing for emancipation, Alex got her case files from the Department of Children and Family Services. She'd been requesting them from the court clerk's office for several months, and they kept pushing back, saying that the information was confidential, but Alex told them these were her case files and she was entitled to them. Then the court clerk said she was going to charge her twenty-five cents per page for photocopying, and when Alex asked how many pages it was, the court clerk could not tell her but told her it could end up costing her hundreds of dollars. Alex thought that was ridiculous, considering they were *her* files. She contacted the public defender in the children's court, and finally, finally after all this time, received her complete file. Most of the pages redacted any logistical information, like addresses. There were black boxes where street names and phone numbers would appear.

CHILD(REN) NAME

Referral Number:

Referral Date 01/28/1982

Summaryof Incident: female 3 years old (at the t me of report)is an alleged victim of Physical Abuse by step father and mother, Reporting party contacted the Child Protection Hotline report abuse of

Children Information:

/1982,- was left in the care of stepfather while the mother was at work.

- reported had an upset stomach and stepfather gave her a " small amount of Cisco" in an oral syringe. coughed a little but seemed ok. Shortly after, stepfather was reportedly giving a bath when she b e.

Stepfather reported that stomach distended and turned blue. Stepfather began push in her stomach and breathing for possibly an hour.

StepFather then took a manicure tool and poked in the vagina to help her breathe, water was noted coming from mouth and anus Stepfather put his finger in her anus to help water escape.

He then took the manicure tool and poked a hole in vagina to help water escape.

Began to open and shut her eyes and stepfather wrapped her in a towel and put her in the closet.

At this time, the stepfather is in custod

Both minors placed in foster care

LASD is invest gat ng Police report# **SCREENERINFORMATION** COIM«'491 m

ELSEWHERE

In the short time Alex was with Sabina, Lauren had married an old friend, Ken Aronson. They moved to LA so Lauren could do hair. But they wound up in a mobile home park in Palmdale, a city desert in the far northern part of LA County known as Antelope Valley—named for the pronghorn antelopes that used to roam the area—home to the aerospace industry, Edwards Air Force Base, and the largest borax open pit mine. Palmdale, a city within Antelope Valley, is vast and hot and slow. When the sun comes up, birds chirp overhead; people walk to bus stops carrying lunches in plastic bags from Walmart. It's the kind of neighborhood where kids travel in packs to school and back, the suburbs sixty-three miles outside of Los Angeles. Initially tract house territory, a bedroom community for Angelenos to nab that affordable dream.

This time of Alex's life is big splotches of darkness, bits and pieces. She was thrust into a place where she stopped getting food. She started to look different than Lauren's other daughter. A girl who Lauren always said was good. She was a good girl because she had a different father than Alex, a loving father, and because she stayed with Lauren—and didn't know that life could be different. This little girl did not remind Lauren of all her failures. When Lauren looked at Alex all she could see was handing her over to That Lady, and sometimes when Lauren looked at Alex in her bright eyes, in the center of them, the dark pupils, she saw judgment. Anger, resentment, despair. Meanwhile Alex's sister looked more and more like Lauren every day. They called her LJ for Lauren, Jr. They brought her home Big Macs and french fries while Alex's stomach growled. She started to shove anything in her mouth, carpet, her fingernails, the hair from her head. Sometimes LJ would save a couple of french fries and sneak them to her.

Alex is alone in the dark.

She's naked, sitting cross-legged in her own piss and shit, the carpet below her damp with it. They began locking her there when she was one, and then two, and then three. Now she was three.

Eyes focused on a sliver of light.

It's all she has, that light.

It glows from underneath a locked closet door, and Alex discovered that if she stares at it long enough, her mind will open a portal.

To another place. Elsewhere.

It went on like this day after day, but much more helter-skelter than in this summary. Disassociation—the psyche's ability to float away from pain. That is what the doctors called it when Alex was finally rescued from her tiny closet in the back of the mobile home. The way she was able to separate her mind from her body, how she was able to think of the cards she saw once, in her sister's room, cards with suns and moons and crystals and fairies on them. The drawings looked delicate and sparkly, and she held them all there below the surface of her mind.

Three years of torture and starvation. Three years of cigarette burns. Three years of listening to all the other kids playing, laughing, singing. Three years of being brought a small bucket of butter for food.

Three years of rape. Three years of drowning.

In that mobile home, death sounded like running water, and the heavy metal music Ken played while they abused her. The pulses of electronics and guitars. She wanted to run so fast she could run on the ceiling. The music that made you want to bang your head and jump and spin, your hair wild and free, your teeth showing, your body pushed into the laminate floors.

Three years of being teased, *You can chew this, but don't you swallow it.*

It was a neighbor who reported Lauren. She had suspicions of something off. She saw when they first moved in there was a little girl, younger than LJ, but she never saw her anymore. She thought maybe she was only there part time, had another parent somewhere else. Sometimes, she thought she heard crying, like baby crying, and sometimes she heard loud music to cover up crying. She came over one night with pizza and beer. Lauren and Ken let her in. Told her come in and sat her down. When she had the chance, after it seemed Ken and Lauren were buzzed, she slipped off to the bathroom. LJ's eyes were big when she stood up, like *Where is she going?* LJ looked maybe scared, maybe relieved. The neighbor tiptoed off toward the bedroom and saw a closet with a lock high on the door.

When she opened the closet there was . . . The neighbor, who—due to the publicity of the case—chose to remain anonymous, said, *What* is that? upon seeing the girl.

Unable to comprehend what she was looking at. Was it actually a child? A child the weight of a small dog? A thirty-pound child? A big belly, and sunken eyes, like the child on the TV commercial with the fly in the corner of his eye?

But she was white, and no flies and there in the mobile home in Palmdale? And not Ethiopia, or was it India? And with lice and ratty hair and stomach filled with air and fluid and bones jutting out at her hips and shoulders and sunken eyes and What is that? was all the neighbor could say until she finally focused her sight and understood and clasped hard onto the door handle, because it was the saddest sight she ever saw and because up until this moment she could not comprehend that there was this kind of monster in the world that could do this. Penny-sized burns polka-dotted up and down her arms and in the hollow of her armpits and the top of her neck. Her hands were tied together with a pink jump rope.

And then she stood—the true horror of her life revealed. She was abnormal *down there*. She was inflamed down there. Her genitalia disfigured, her asshole and vagina ripped and fused—a gaping pulp of a girl.

And yet when she saw the neighbor, her big blue eyes flickered, and she smiled. Help. She tried to say, to whisper, but didn't know how. It came out as air, her vocal cords rusty. Ep. Ep, she said.

I remember when I was a kid on Groundhog Day, yeah. They had a big festival, and you had to speak German. Josie got chatty.

You speak German, eh? asked Willie.

My German's not so good, but if I didn' I had to put a nickel in the bucket, and I didn' have a nickel, so I just said ya and nein. Those were the two I knew.

Yeah, I know those two.

She thought he seemed kinda slow, this guy.

(She thought about her daughter and before she could stop herself, she was thinking about her out loud. But before she went too far, she called her girl a boy, to keep that little truth to herself.)

I wonder if my ma is gonna take my lil' boy out to the Groundhog Day parade, and if she does, I hope she remembers his coat.

You got a lil' boy?

Yeah, one year old. I know I used to fuss all the time with a coat, but now it's all I do is wonder if he's out there with a coat.

Ha. It's funny that way, being a ma. Willie sort of snickered, but it sounded forced. He got up, put out his hand. C'mon.

Oh. Can't we just do it in here? Josie was feeling her high.

A memory buried deep down flashed across her mind, Ken bathing her, heavy metal music blaring loud thrumming and banging, and water on her face on her eyes, the harsh pinch and probe of something small and pointed. MANICURE TOOL, the report said, warmth in her throat, CISCO, the report said. There were other flashes that mixed and blended with those. Ken bringing everyone McDonald's and him demanding that she chew the fries and spit them back out. Then later, the darkness of the closet. Always the closet.

The later pages were from the hospital, a diagram of a child, her, and marks wherever there were injuries, blunt force trauma, laceration, circles on her head, and toes, and ankles, and anus, and vagina. Alex trembled when she read those hospital records.

Alex read the reports, crying, tracing the outline of this girl, hoping to heal over the wounds that still scarred her, she could match her own skin to this hospital sketch, raised scar tissue wherever there were X's. Grieving for this childhood that belonged to no one.

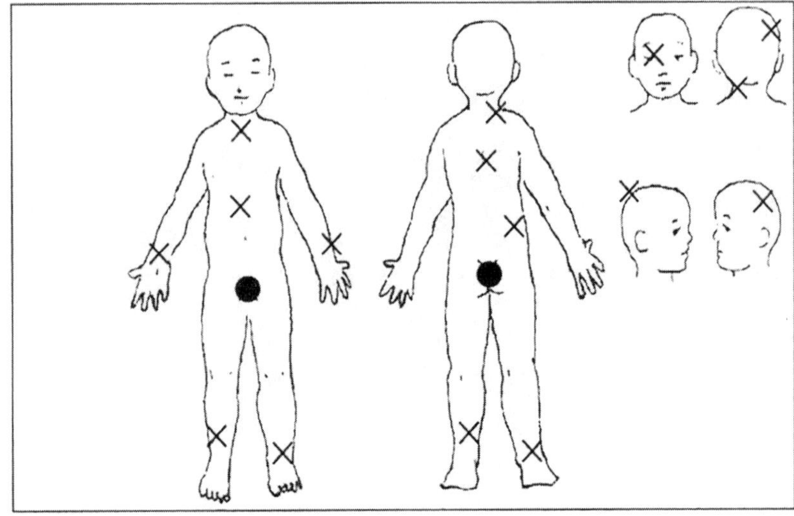

Indicate site of injury with an "x"

Then, buried toward the beginning of the file, there was one form that wasn't redacted, there under Referral History it said:

2 PREVIOUS REFERRALS, CLOSED ADOPTION CASE IN CANADA

> Previous placement: Sabina Hartman, 3310 Ash St Vancouver BC V5Z 3E3 (Vancouver, British Columbia)

And there in her hands were Sabina's full name and address. Alex held the form close to her face, smelled it as if it was the actual original document and not a photocopy.

Marina looked at her with all her hope and her heart growing big and juicy, her eyes tearing up.

I can't believe you went through all that, was all she could say. Do you remember it?

Not really, just parts of it.

Flashes of that night Alex got put on ran in Marina's head, she felt more protective of her than ever, how could she have let her go through with that? She put her arm around Alex, who just kept staring down at the papers. Finally, Alex looked at Marina. Marina, I got something I got to ask you.

Sure, anything.

Would you help me look for her? If they let you emancipate early like they say?

Well, yeah, I mean, of course. I don't really know anything about Canada, but I'll try my best—do whatever.

Marina. I have a person. Look, she has to love me. Look.

Alex grabbed out of her duffle bag that she slept on like a sack of diamonds a knit cap, with two pointed ears knit into the top, a cap with cat ears.

They say that I threw such a horrible fit if anyone tried to touch it or take it away from me. I refused to leave that shitty place without it. It's all I have from her. I kept it all this time.

It was true. Only a woman who loved you was capable of purchasing such an item. What a goofy, gentle gift.

There was only one thing Marina knew how to tell her. Yes. Yes. Of course, yes.

So this was it—the lightness where grace shall pass.

I stayed quiet in the closet, tried to calm the banging of Marina's heart. I hoped they would stay there in the living room . . . so I could rush out and kill 'im right then.

Then the pakshet hollered, It's more comfortable on the bed.

I heard their feet pad their way past me down the hallway.

I could picture them there in the bedroom, with that rotting horse head.

His bedroom was just a bed. No dresser. Clothes on the floor. A couple of T-shirts, boxer shorts, jeans. There were no sheets on the bed. And that smell, that unmistakable smell, of death. I stay focused in the closet. Pictured them there. Made a scene of it in Marina's mind.

LOVE BUCKLE

On the morning of Marina's sixteenth birthday, it was possible she was going to be emancipated. It's a big word. *Emancipate.* To be free. They swoon when they say: What was it like to get emancipated? They think there are tricks. They push: What did you do? But the truth is, all anyone has to do to get emancipated is age out and not go to juvie.

Once Marina was no longer a ward of the court, she'd be eligible to apply for GR, general relief, which was the equivalent of about two hundred dollars a month and some hundred dollars in food stamps. In addition to GR, she could either receive supportive housing, which was an affordable housing program, or she could get a monthly check of $776. For all the kids in foster care in Los Angeles, there were only eighty beds available in supportive housing units for eighteen- to twenty-one-year-olds. They mostly got the check. It was cheaper and easier for the county. Trying to survive off of $776 a month in Los Angeles was like trying to survive off of $56 a month in Los Angeles. To qualify for a check, your social worker or probation officer must administer a readiness assessment. Marina passed.

The night before her hearing, she looked around the cottage: Alex's ceiling wallpapered with her Calvin Klein ads, Marina's side bare except for photos she'd taken of Alex. Alex sitting on a pile of branches, a long stick pointing toward her open mouth, ready to simulate fellatio. Aside from this sexual act, she looked like a very plain girl. She wore jean shorts and a white V-neck T-shirt. She had the thin build of a boy, and her hair was freed from its gel all wispy and feathered. She had freckles, and Marina could make out Alex's braces. In this photo, Marina could not hear Alex talking like a gangster or smell her obnoxious perfume. She couldn't make out Alex's needy-needy epal ways to materialistic items. In this picture, Alex was a perfect ordinary beauty. She could be anyone. She could be a ballerina, or a nerd, or a painter, or just a girl who sat around a lot. Marina looked at the photo and thought how when she sat still for a while, Alex was so maganda.

Marina sat and looked at Alex's picture. It was nighttime. Time for bed and Alex hadn't come to the cottage. It was lights-out, and Alex still wasn't there. Marina got up and walked to the main building. The grass was still wet from the sprinkler system. There were leaves crackling everywhere. This was not such a bad place at all. In the main building were the classes and the cafeteria and upstairs there was a line of RA offices. Lights on all the time. Twenty-four hours. The door to one of the RA's rooms was slightly ajar, and there on the floor huddled in a ball was Alex. A blanket shrouded over her head and shoulders.

Coming and going wasn't something girls there talked about much. But what else was there to talk about? It was the wound of their lives.

Knock knock.

Go away! Alex yelled from her ball of blanket on the floor.

Marina opened the door. What's going on?

Sherry the RA, with her strange hair, stood up. Well, Marina, Alex here was just talking about how she was going to miss you.

Without her makeup Sherry's face looked like a helium balloon left behind to deflate over the weekend after the office birthday party. Marina smiled. She got in closer. Alex's hair was popping out from the blanket. The flesh of her neck exposed and red like it was hot. A small freckle at the nape. She was only fifteen and would be emancipated soon enough. A year and a half. Everyone had to emancipate by eighteen at the latest, but most of them, if they could pass the readiness assessment, emancipated early, just not as early as Marina.

We'll see each other again soon.

How do you know? the curled-up mass of blanket on the floor screamed.

I can come back and visit. Marina made a concerned face, held out her arms.

They never come back! They always say that.

Eventually they returned to their cottage. Can I come into bed with you? Alex asked.

Marina pulled back the covers, then when Alex turned her back toward her, she snuggled in behind her and wrapped her arms around Alex, the same way Ma had cuddled her. Alex was being belted in the love buckle. First came the arms, then her legs, and she whispered over and over again, *Please don't be sad. Please, no more sad.*

Alex flipped, faced her. They hugged each other tight. They stayed like that, trying to edge closer and closer. Marina put her arms around Alex's neck, and Alex put her arms around Marina's hips. Slowly Marina could smell Alex, her sweet breath, her warm skin. Closer, Alex whispered, and they held each other closer. They were too eager to make love to be afraid of getting caught.

Marina let Alex trail her fingers along her body, stopped at her tits, Marina took off her shirt, Alex crawled on top of her, kissed her neck, her breasts. Marina moved with her, against her.

Alex took off her shirt and sweatpants. Alex slipped Marina's fingers into the cotton mouth of her underwear. Alex repeated, Closer.

And they kissed each other, long and soft. Alex kept on begging her for things, begging Marina to touch her, to lick her. Marina. Alex. Alex. Marina. They stayed up all night, slippery with sweat. Scattered in all the right ways. The most beautiful gift they could give one another was to find a way to find pleasure in this thing that'd done so much damage to them.

Their two bodies clasped together, the moon and stars above, it did feel like a love buckle. Alex's body ached with the low bad hum of that death metal music when she was a girl, and Marina's puso beat steady and warm against Alex's. They stayed that way until yesterday finally felt of another time, and they lay there wrapped in all the love and comfort they remembered from before rape and before beatings. Before closets. And when they slept, it was for once and finally the real sleep of people in love. This is what sealed Marina's promise. She would find Sabina.

The mattress was the silky blue kind with white flowers. The pakshet sat down. Patted the mattress. Josie hesitated. She looked at him. For a moment, she looked sixteen. Her short hair. Her big eyes. She looked lost. She had those heart-shaped lips. The kind you can imagine a perfect heart painted on like those geisha dolls. Maybe if she just stood there like that forever.

But she didn't. She slowly unbuttoned her shirt. Counting the buttons. One. She undid the top button, her skin soft pink with freckles.

Two. She had such small tits, she didn't need a bra—still some scabs from picking there.

He looked on. He had his hand on his crotch. The power had shifted. Just then, the air thick with it. And it was very nice for her, moving like this to no music. The power passing over, knowing that he'd do almost anything at that moment. As long as she kept on. As long as she didn't stop. But don't look at her like she's good for anything else. Don't plan a future with her. Don't dream of getting married. Josie could dance and dance, but don't kill the moment and get ahead of yourself.

EMANCIPATION

Marina sat in the lobby early that morning, waiting for a van. It was a quiet jittery thing, waiting for a van that was going to take her to Edelman Children's Court in LA County's Monterey Park, where she was gonna ask to be emancipated.

The only other kid in the van was a little boy, brown with big curly hair. He reminded her of a gerbil in his overalls and striped shirt. He looked about four years old.

Hi! He waved like Marina was far away, across the street or something, rather than coming to sit right next to him.

Hey.

I'm gonna see my mama today.

He sounded delighted, kids always thought that all sorts of good things could happen on this day. That's how the group homes got them to act right and straighten up. Court was the baby Jesus or Santa Claus or aswang of foster care. Still the same thought ran steady in Marina's mind, that maybe today she'd see Mutya.

The seats were sturdy leather, crumbs stuck in the piping. Marina noticed a razor blade stashed deep in the well that held her seat belt clicker.

They drove past the high school with the dolphins on the sign, along the 405, past the beach, back onto the freeway. They stopped in two other places on the Westside, where three more kids piled into the van. A fat eight-year-old-looking girl, a skinny white boy who looked about twelve, and an Asian teenage girl who did not look at Reen. Each time someone boarded the van, the little boy next to her hollered out, I'm gonna see my mom today! And Marina'd feel a synchronized flinch in her heart.

The driver of the van was an older Latino guy who ignored them. He listened to oldies music and tapped his steering wheel: whistle and tap, whistle and tap. Would she see Mutya? What would she look like? A dandruffy mess? All business? A church lady? Would she have pulled herself together like Marina did? Marina had a binder that held every single one of her accomplishments up until this point. She was going to show it to the judge. It had sports ribbons from Mr. Hunter and her passing proficiency exam scores from Mrs. Allen and the write-up of just exactly how she would become a secretary.

The moment they hit the parking lot, the atmosphere changed. It was thick with agitated drivers, homeless parents, drug addicts, people afraid of losing the one person they cared about, and people afraid of being disappointed. Marina had always thought that if given the chance, she could do a much better job taking care of herself on her own. This was her chance.

Inside, a woman walked in front of them. She was short and round and wore a brown dress with a skirt that scooped up into her butt. Gobble butt, one of the kids in line said.

Gobble gobble, her cute little gerbil friend repeated.

After the metal detector, they were taken to the children's side—a room with six round tables and a carpeted area where the kids sat and watched a movie. *Home Alone*. Marina snuck off, hoping to find a light and smoke a cigarette. She eyed the other teenagers.

The janitor. He was white and wore a blue cleaning uniform. He looked older, maybe sixty, but he was strong, with little muscles on the small parts of his arm. Marina asked him, Hey, do you know where I can smoke?

He laughed.

Marina saw him checking her out like she was hot. Like she was the hottest, saddest thing in there.

Marina wasn't dopey in front of a television like the other kids. Nah, she was stuck sitting on one of those tiny plastic chairs designed for toddlers, at sixteen, her knees up by her ears. The chair a bright yellow. The tiny wooden table had graffiti etchings in it. She looked at the tray of cafeteria food: a carton of milk, a hamburger patty, a dry bun, little condiment packets, and an apple. The boy from the van sat across from her. Her little gerbil friend.

He took one look at the cafeteria tray and with a gleeful voice bellowed, County foooood!

Yeah, you know this is the same stuff they eat in jail? The boy was already half done when she finished telling him. He nodded like a seesaw. He just liked to stuff his mouth and scratch and burp and hiccup. When he swallowed, he said, County foooood.

The janitor nodded toward the bathroom and whispered, I'll cover for you.

You got a light? He slipped her a book of matches.

She sat in the bathroom. There was a small window up top, not big enough for a kid, but a long skinny window that went to the outside basketball courts. She stood on the toilet, opened the window, and lit the cigarette. She took a drag and blew the smoke out. And even though there was only one toilet, there was a bathroom stall adding another door between the bathroom door. None of the kids were outside playing basketball. She thought how silly it was to be standing there smoking, risking it all. She wasn't even enjoying the cigarette. She took five quick drags, dropped the cigarette in the toilet, flushed, washed her hands, scrubbed her face with soap and water, and batted at the air above her head.

After, she sat down at a table away from everyone so she wouldn't feel strange watching some kids' movie, but it had the opposite effect. She felt strange as hell. She inspected her shoes. She tried to look busy. She flipped through her binder. She looked at all the ribbons, the blue ones for sports, the yellow ones for academics. She decided by now that it would be nice to see Mutya, that she'd visit with her afterward and ask her how she was doing and show her all the work in her binder. Mutya always pushed her to do well in school, maybe she'd be proud. Everything she had tried to accomplish in that small space of time on her own. Maybe Mutya would give her stuff for her first apartment, towels and a broom.

The halls and rooms outside buzzed with chaos. People waited to be reunited or to be separated. Most of the cases continued unresolved. People waited around in their Sunday best to be continued. To be continued, that's what the judge said when all of the parties didn't show up or she didn't make a final ruling. Finally, they called her name.

She thought she saw Ma there in the courtroom. Marina caught a glimpse of a woman, kind of small, with big frizzy hair. Sitting there she was all dressed in a sad feeling. Her face reminded Marina that she once saw Mutya crying, that one time when her mercy prayers didn't work. A whole two days without any food, Marina took her fat markers that smelled like grapes and strawberries and tried to color her hunger away. First, she drew long thin stripes along her tongue until it turned a mottled brown color. They did not taste as good as they smelled but they smelled so yummy she took turns sucking on each marker like a lollipop, first one, then two, then three, she walked around the apartment like a rainbow-toothed walrus. When the ink ran out, she took one of Mutya's raspberry-colored lipsticks and tried to eat that too. It tasted blank to her, so she tried to cover it up by putting the cap back on. Later when Mutya went to use the lipstick, she saw little Reena's teeth marks. Mutya so defeated. Her disco body, once upon a time a sought-after thing, bragging about desire, now empty and filled with fear and grief. Marina, when she saw her slumped on the edge of their bed, afraid if she touched her, their lives would end from any kind of tenderness, her childish needs drowning out Ma's dreams. She did it anyway, rubbed Ma's back, and destroy them it did. Up until then Ma had wrangled something of a life for them, a life of books, and tightly braided hair, and clean clothes. Ma used to care so much about what other people saw. Since that day, something in each of them shook loose. And in truth, Mutya died when they took Marina away. Mutya's world had narrowed to the inside of their small apartment, and Marina's world had expanded to the space outside and across to Canada, and eventually to the contents of cloudy liquid trapped in cotton on a spoon.

Then Marina looked closer and realized it wasn't her at all. Mutya hadn't shown up. She realized then she had felt as much enthusiasm fill her heart as the little gerbil boy in the county van, only to deflate.

Whatever was left of their relationship was now severed.

Marina had heard from the social worker that she'd stopped going to her parenting classes and her counseling and so none of that stuff mattered to her. Mutya had given up on them. She'd taught her to kick guys where it counts and kept her close, at times too close, and then neglected her altogether, and still, neither of them would ever get back what they needed. Neither of them could be made whole from here.

Marina tried to shift her hopes and attention to something else. Instead of wallowing in the disappointment of Ma's absence, she thought, okay, now the thing was to get emancipated. If Marina was lucky, the most she would get was a certificate, a cake, and a check for two hundred dollars. Mutya had stopped fighting. She had some chances, anger management, parenting classes. It wasn't her style. She wasn't interested in fighting, at least not over the course of three years, three months maybe, but three years was a long time to fight a system that worked against you. Marina still made excuses for her. Maybe she stopped because she was grieving. That losing her was too hard, and to try and fail would have been worse.

The judge heard her case and said that Marina could now consider herself emancipated. Marina stayed sitting on her wooden bench, staring forward at the county seal. Those long county benches—right then she let herself feel the saddest she ever felt about Ma, she felt tears puddle around the neck of her shirt, she bent and tore at the edges of her stupid fucking binder. For all this time, she thought maybe she felt Mutya there hovering. She remembered a day when she was pattering close behind her in their apartment and sheepishly she admitted, Yeah, I'm following you. Mutya turned quickly on her heels and exclaimed, Baby doll, you can't escape me—poopsikins, I am *in* you. Something about that gave Marina comfort. Now it felt cheap and unreal.

When she was at the Pines she thought the distance between her and Ma was all that was left to hold all the bits and pieces of their life together. The frozen meals, and the haircuts, and the bruises, and the joy, and the boredom, and the overdrawn bank statements, and the disconnection notices, and the chasing toast.

Mutya remembers: Marina blowing spit bubbles and running

her small wet fingers, with their tiny paper-thin nails, clanging across her cheeks, baby powder smells. Marina remembers: pretending to sleep, releasing the full weight of her head against Ma's neck, inhaling the scent of her, her dark curls fluttering against her nose, wrapping a leg tighter around her waist to get a better grasp on her safe escape from the cruel world.

The contradiction of Mutya, her obsession, her doting, yet the fact of her absence there in the courtroom, a cross etched into Marina's heart and soul. Then just before Marina stepped out of the courtroom, she fixed her gaze on something in the distance, she seemed to be peering at something just beyond the judge's shoulder, she let the freedom of it all wash over her, and she smiled, and for the first time Marina realized she and Mutya had the exact same smile, and she asked herself how she had gone on that long without noticing.

Marina chose to meet her social worker outside. She pushed open the double doors, looked out toward the beating core of her new life, and walked through.

Her social worker came walking fast, the sound of heels on concrete coming toward her. She extended her hand. Introduced herself. She was white, Latina, Iranian. She had white hair.

Was it Margaret? Mary? Madeline? Something proper.

She walked Marina back to her car. Gestured for her to get in.

We are on the way to your SILP housing. Did anyone explain to you what that is?

Marina looked out the windows at the trees, the kids shuffling back into vans. She thought she could make out in the distance her little gerbil friend.

Is it like an apartment?

Yes, kind of, they are apartments for emancipated foster youth. They're Section 8, so the rent has to stay within market.

Where is it?

South LA.

And what if I want to leave?

You're gonna have to get a job, of course. And earn enough for your own apartment eventually. You understand now that you are considered an adult in the eyes of the law, which means after this, you'll only be eligible for all the things the county gives all the other adults. You have no kids, no disabilities, so beyond GR there's not much else the county can do for you.

What she was trying to say was if Marina failed, the only stop left was homeless shelters. A bunk in a room full of bunk beds. In by six p.m., out by six a.m. Those county-issued blankets made of wool that can't be cleaned, their dark gray masking the stains. Lice, everywhere, all the time. A shower if she's lucky. She heard jail might be easier. Jail, you get a shower. Jail is not a daily hustle—a daily grind. Jail, you know where you will be between six a.m. and six p.m. when the emergency shelter opens again. But jail is jail. And there was a time Marina wanted to go to college. It felt interstellar that on this arbitrary date, she was suddenly An Adult.

The supportive housing was a room in the back of an alley in what appeared to be a converted old motel. It was painted lime green and surrounded by a low white stucco wall. The bathroom was in the hallway, and everyone had to share it.

This is your place here, the social worker said, and strolled around a room that was ten by thirteen feet and contained one window.

Marina tried the lock on the window. The small metal crank was dangling loose. It didn't work.

Is this for real?

This here is your dresser. The social worker motioned to a small dresser, the drawer open with an empty bag of Cheetos inside. And over here is a refrigerator; it says here that you should not store any food outside of the fridge and you should purchase a lock for it, and that management is not responsible for any lost or stolen items.

The fridge sat just beside the door, with red syrupy fruit-punch stains on the inside. The room itself smelled a little as if the previous tenant had a baby, which would become more evident later when Marina found a used diaper in the corner beneath her mattress.

How much are they charging me to stay here?

Five hundred a month.

And how much is my voucher for again?

Seven fifty.

Is there any way we can look at other places?

There's already a waiting list for this place. And if you don't have any kids or mental health disorders, you aren't eligible for a Section 8 voucher.

How do you know I don't have a mental health disorder?

I don't have any record of it.

Okay, well, let's say I do, then what can I get?

You would have to get me some documentation and get on a waiting list for a Section 8 voucher and then find a landlord who will accept Section 8.

Can you help me with that?

I'm afraid not, now that you're emancipated, you're an adult in the eyes of the state. I work with kids. Department of Public Social Services works with adults. As far as I know all you're eligible for is GR. Unless you're pregnant. Are you pregnant?

Not that I know of.

The social worker gave Marina her keys and the lease, which was month to month, and left. That was it. She was alone. Aside from the radio blaring down the hallway, and someone else's television set, and people screaming at one another. She was alone. She had no blankets. She put away her few possessions, clothes, and put her hair stuff in the drawer. The social worker had given her bus tokens and food stamps and a towel. She lay on the uncovered mattress, imagined that the loud whirring from a swamp cooler that sat in the window was the sound of the ocean. A surge of swells, the open stillness ahead, the beach, soon a far-off hazy mass in the distance, under a mesa of clouds. She fell asleep and woke up hours later, in pure darkness. There seemed in that moment to be quiet. Stillness. She removed the swamp cooler from her window, and the air was still and cool, she looked up to the sky. It was filled with stars. She thought to herself how she was in that moment alone, alive, free. But also, she was missing the girls back at Acorn Cottage and of course mostly Alex, she tried to imagine that indentation in the mattress above her, that hand dropping down in front of her, those long sleek fingers, and then the feel and smell and touch of her. She grabbed Alex's knit hat and held it close to her nose, trying to find comfort in it, so sleep could eventually find her.

The next morning, she met a single mom down the hall named Trish. Trish was tall and thin, and she had an adorable son named Maddox. Trish was Black and wore her hair in cute afro-puffs; her son had long hair he wore in braids that went all the way down to his shoulders.

Here's what's up. I'ma tell you right now, this bathroom door don't lock, and there's all kinds of perverts around here. So let's do like I did with the girl who used to stay in your unit and keep the buddy system.

Marina agreed to stay watch while Trish showered, and Trish did the same.

Marina learned later there were several registered sex offenders in the building. Trish also taught Marina how to do her laundry in the sink and hang her clothes on pipes in the ceiling. She also learned to put a sheet over her door to cover an opening that men used to look into her room.

There in her drawer was that sweet knit cap Alex had given her to bring when she met Sabina. She was trying to get adjusted to being on the outs every day, and this promise was nagging at her, but also, she wanted to know what life was like without rules, without staff. There was so much to explore, but also there was a lot for her to be afraid of. And Alex. Without her to wake up to every day, without her smell, her touch, the sound of her laugh, she was trying and failing to ignore her loneliness.

Despite sitting in ILP class and passing the county's readiness assessment, the only thing Marina'd learned about getting a job was from the movies. She walked to the corner store in the morning to grab a cup of coffee and a newspaper. A quick glance at the cover of the paper reported: A serial killer is sentenced to life in prison. Apartheid is over. There's an earthquake in Turkey. Things were happening with the stock market—but none of it affected Marina. In the other paper without the want ads there were more sensational headlines about extraterrestrials having babies and celebrities aging faster than their time. Back at the SILP Marina grabbed a pen and combed the want ads. She circled all the jobs for secretary, clerk, or administrative assistant.

She used a pay phone out in the hall to call the places that were hiring and not too far to reach by bus. A couple of them asked her to fax over a résumé. Which she didn't have. She planned on going over to the Kinko's to use their computer and write a résumé, but she was waiting for her monthly stipend.

It'd already been a month and she still hadn't gotten her check so when Trish asked Marina to watch Maddox while she showered, she asked, Hey, do you know when we're supposed to get these checks?

The mail comes to the front office and sometimes people gaffle it and sometimes it takes a couple of months for them to get you started.

Shit, are you for real? I gotta get my money so I can go type up a résumé.

It turned out mail got lost all the time at the SILP housing unit. Part of Marina felt maybe she deserved these hard times; she walked around hating herself because deep down she always felt Mutya gave up on her. That in the end Ma rejected her, and maybe, maybe, what happened to her in that bathroom in Hawthorne made her worthless in the end. At night the moment before she fell asleep, she saw herself there, sitting in the courtroom, wearing a nice dress, waiting and hoping for Mutya to show up, then alone looking at the empty bench across from her and crying at the floor in front of her. Lola's demand, *Listen to your mother,* haunting her.

Trish put her on to a new hustle. She dressed up as a bottle of Excedrin tablets and passed out samples on the street. She worked for this company that sent her to various corners to hold a sign and hand out flyers, sell things, give out samples. Once, she was supposed to give out chocolate samples. But the pay was awful, like three bucks an hour, so she just took all the chocolate samples back to the SILP, and she and Trish lived off of chocolates for a week. She sold newspaper ads, Herbalife, telemarketed timeshares. Basically, she spent a good chunk of time doing legitimate little things that never got her anywhere; she had to compete with all the other kids on the street, running up to cars and buses, slanging their stuff. She hated every minute of it but in many ways, it was easier than the plan she'd made up for the judge. She saved some of the money she earned and managed to fax over a couple of résumés to the jobs listed in the paper, but they always asked for documents and information she didn't have or even begin to understand how to get. Social security number, driver's license, or a California ID. In order to get an ID she needed a birth certificate and she didn't even know which hospital she was born in.

Then there were the times when she saw Trish walk up to tourists in a pair of old sunglasses and pretend she was blind. Marina led Trish up to them on streets where rich people shopped, trying hard to ignore her outstretched hand. But eventually, Marina ran out of patience for all that begging. She wanted the life that she dreamed of. The life with all the clothes and makeup from those teenybopper magazines she fawned over with Alex.

Back in her room, she did everything she could to escape that little knit hat. Trish would come in when Maddox was sleeping, and they'd get fucked up together, drink forties, smoke weed, Trish told her all sorts of stories. Like the way Maddox got his name. She said she was five months pregnant when she stumbled upon a nest of starlings. She thought for sure her baby was gonna be a girl and she was gonna name her Star, and then when she went to the store, the mama starling'd follow her all the way to the corner and back. When she got back to her place, they were all there with their little pudgy faces huddled up inside the nest together. The day Maddox was born, he came three weeks early, and the mama starling had followed her to the corner again. And she and her baby daddy took the bus all the way to County. When they got there, she didn't realize how long labor was, so she lay there for a long time, and he went off to a waiting room and watched TV. There was a wrestling show on, WWF, and one of the guys who won was this big white dude named Brad Maddox, so when the baby was a boy, her baby daddy told the doctor his name was Maddox 'cause he wanted his son to be a winner and meanwhile Trish was trying to think of what's a boy version of Star. And she looked him in the eyes when she held him close, and she said, Hi there, Star, even though the birth certificate said Maddox.

Ain't that some shit? Trish said at the end of her story, and by now, the weed was wearing off and they needed more.

Marina learned how to steal. She was wiry, fast, and fearless. A natural talent. She slid a pair of Gap jeans across a shop floor beneath her feet, walked outside to the glorious sun, then went to a different Gap store and returned the jeans for cash. This evolved to pickpocketing and stealing credit card numbers from trash receipts. Marina enjoyed stealing, the heady rush that hit her as she disappeared into a crowd, stolen goods burning in her hand. A ring, a watch, a chain around someone's neck. The money sometimes still warm from someone's back pocket. A pleasure so private, delicious, and powerful. She never once got caught—that's how good she was.

Josie kept counting, Three.

More skin. If she had bigger boobs, he would see them now. But he didn't. Just skin. Her shirt sat there—heavy.

I waited a few beats then slowly made my way out of the closet, I shifted the jacket hanging over my shoulder, slowly creaked open the door, quietly stepped out, I didn't pause to shut the door but worried that it made a small shadow in the hallway, the lights were still on in the living room and off in most of the other parts of the house, I tiptoed down the hallway where I saw more light coming from Willie's room.

UPRISING

Ten o'clock on a rainy evening in April, Alex was picked up by a guy she knew as Taylor. He was a regular trick, he always just wanted a quickie from her. For her to suck him off while he drove around town. That was his fetish. He almost always bust a nut at the stoplight in the center of town, especially if there were people at the crosswalk, old ladies or teenagers. She knew if he was taking too long she'd just have to moan or make noises like she was into it.

She also liked that he wasn't much of a dribbler, meaning he didn't dribble the back of her head onto his junk as much as he pushed his pelvis up into her mouth. On the seat between him and Alex was the remainder of a sack lunch his wife had prepared for him, a half of a PB&J sandwich, wrapped thoughtfully in wax paper, a couple veggie chips, and a Coke.

Alex reached for the bag. Can I have some of this?

Sure, yeah, you can have the whole thing, but why don't you suck me off first?

His pants were already undone, his buto lying limp.

Okay, fine, whatever.

Like usual he rubbed the back of her head while she went down on him, he was pushing into her mouth while he was driving.

Unfortunately, this time of night the streets were empty, so when they got to the stoplight no one was there. He made his way to the part of the town that turned into a two-lane highway. The Crest. His truck bed creaked, two sacks of soil he kept in the back to steady it.

His windshield wipers, worn and thinned, sometimes did more harm than good. Like slugs, they left smudged trails across his view. The night sky above the city, smattered with stars and the neon lights of big-box stores, Walmart and Juice It Up! and Office Depot. This was taking longer than usual; Alex moaned, made it sound like she was into it. He grabbed her ass and squeezed his dick hard up into her mouth, felt the tip of her tongue against his burat. Flick flick, just on the tip. The guys from Home Depot he picked up to do a quick job, some cleaning out of an old empty shed, he'd paid them at the end of the day, and then in good cheer he offered them some beer too. He wasn't drunk. He'd always been able to hold his liquor. All those golf tournaments when he was younger.

Ohhh fuck . . . fuck fuck ooooohhhh yeah fuck yeah. He was cumming now, he reached in his pocket for a tissue. The Kleenex in his pocket had turned to cotton pills. In his glove compartment he kept a bandana, he moved to get it and took his eyes off the road for a split moment. He was driving at about sixty on the almost deserted Crest. The Angeles Crest Highway had narrowed into two lanes without a passing lane, even though oftentimes speed racers tried to pass into oncoming traffic. He'd consider doing the same himself when there was a slow truck in front of him, but the stuff in the cab of his truck reminded him of what he had to live for, a small plastic Binky in the back seat that belonged to his daughter.

His eyes winced shut for half a moment, and when he looked again, he was blinded by the lights in his rearview mirror. Another truck, a newer model, the kind with the really bright headlights, was no more than ten feet from his rear bumper. It seemed like it'd been lifted—it had bigger tires than usual. The lights flooding the cab of his truck. Fucking asshole. Taylor pressed on his gas. He turned on the defroster to see if that could increase his visibility.

Alex looked up at him now. Jesus. Pull over and let me out.

The truck sped up behind him. Taylor hit the accelerator again. A yellow sign read PASSING LANE FIVE MILES. He ignored Alex but kept talking to the truck behind him. Take it easy, you can pass in five miles, asshole. He thought for a brief moment of hitting his brakes, teaching the truck a lesson. But he couldn't risk it. He was driving seventy miles an hour now, dangerous on this highway, under these conditions. He gripped the steering wheel tight with both hands.

Did you hear me? I said let me out of this fucking truck!

Beside the highway on his left was a cliff that fell into the mouth of the Angeles National Forest. It always shocked him to see the steep drop so close to the side of the road. How many times had he envisioned himself losing control, falling asleep or something stupid, and flying off the side of the mountain? Taylor managed to put a little distance between him and the truck, then the truck was on his ass again just eight feet behind. Get off my fucking ass! Pissed off, Taylor flicked him off in his rearview mirror, then the truck swooped beside him to pass him in the lane of oncoming traffic. Just around the bend another set of headlights were coming toward them, this time a huge cube truck, one of those with a production studio name on it.

Alex's hands grew clammy, she didn't know what to do, if she opened the door she'd probably get run over by the truck behind them. Boxed in now by the two trucks playing chicken, Alex reached across Taylor and pushed on his horn. Her body gushed full of adrenaline. She saw that they were speeding toward the guardrail, so she opened her passenger door and jumped out. Taylor hit his brakes and skidded, continued skidding straight through the guardrail. Alex was tumbling down the highway until she saw nothing but the eerie thick fog, black sky above, that truck fly off the cliff, it hit some rocks then stumbled, flipping over ridges, once, twice, three times, then up in flames.

April 29, 1992, a jury acquitted four police officers of using excessive force in the arrest and beating of Rodney King. The news was plastered with videos of the officers pulling him out of his vehicle, clubbing him. Thousands of people were swarming the streets. Marina could hear folks running outside, their anger, their need. Marina smoked weed laced with all kinds of shit with Trish. Mostly heroin, until they finally just moved on to using straight heroin. What's up, you wanna get high? Trish asked, and Marina decided she was game, the city was on fire outside their motel, and she was just gonna be up all paranoid the rest of the time anyway. Before Trish, she'd never done these kinds of drugs. Now she was used to it, so used to it she couldn't keep track of time, how long had she been staying here? First, she knew she needed money for rent, then money for a train ticket to go to Canada. Then food, then Trish and her needed more dope. Trish was with a friend she'd never seen before, another girl who looked like maybe she was a little younger than them.

Yo, this is Sunny, Sunny meet Marina.

Trish came out with a needle and put some powder in a janky flat spoon and cooked it a bit.

Oh hey, Marina, you all have something in common, you both stayed at that place, that tree place.

The Pines? Marina looked surprised. Trish tied Marina off and gave her a taste. The drug made her feel like a ghost girl. Like she could go out into the streets and loot with all the others and no one would pay much attention to her.

No shit, yo. Yeah. Me too. Sunny put out her hand like Marina should shake it but then grabbed Marina's hand and pulled her into a hug, tapping her back. They laughed like family at a picnic.

But you look kind of young, did you emancipate or what?

Nah, dude, I'm AWOL.

No shit. Marina felt a surge of energy.

Let's go cop some shit! she told Trish and Sunny, all sweaty and wide-eyed, her heart pumping. This felt different than the other times she did dope. It must've been cut with something. One of those new jittery drugs.

Trish said, Nah, fool, I gotta look after my boy but cop me some diapers and formula if you go.

Yeah, man, I'm good, Sunny said.

Then it occurred to her. Hey, did you see a girl at the Pines named Alex?

As high as she was starting to feel, her heart was racing now, like she was excited.

Oh man, it's fucked up what happened to her, yo.

Wait, what happened? She's my homegirl.

Oh shit, you know her! Trish interrupted. Now, don't go ruining my girl's high, Sunny.

Marina's heart was really racing now. Serious, what the fuck happened to Alex? You have to tell me.

I heard she got in some kind of accident. She was out riding with some john and ended up in the ICU.

Are you fucking for real?

One hundred percent.

And you're sure it's Alex?

Yeah, butch girl, skinny, tries to act gangster. Last I heard they were trying to find a next of kin or some shit.

Marina jumped up now. Oh shit! I gotta go.

Moments later, Marina was running through the streets, gaggles, throngs of people running toward her. Confused by her racial ambiguity. Men jumping on white women's cars, rocking the cars back and forth. People falling out of cars. Marina ran into a Pep Boys; her heart was thudding. She was frightened. She searched for a back door. Television cameras were everywhere. Microphones and news anchors and helicopters. A box fell over. Marina ran outside, and there were Korean men with rifles on the tops of liquor stores, and some buildings were being lit on fire. Or were they? She was fucked up. Hard to tell what was real and what wasn't. The air was stinging. Sparks and pieces of blackened paper floated everywhere. People's hands grazed her thighs as they clambered back in the direction she'd come from. Some came out with tires and oil for their cars, and there was a solid mass of flame across the street. Gunfire shot up into the sky. There were other shots. A dog ran past her, in a hurry and knowing where it wanted to go. Dogs. What about all the dogs? The noise, the banging, must have freaked them out as it freaked her out. Marina tried to think of where she would not die.

In a burnt-out block, she got some food left behind on smashed shelves—sticky buns. A helicopter passed overhead, at some distance. She began to feel a little sick. *What can I get here that I could trade for cash to get to Canada?* she thought.

Steak? Do people like steak? It would go bad. She couldn't get her mind right. Surely everything in here could go bad. She went to the alcohol aisle. She snuck emerald bottles of booze up her sleeves. But there was no need to be slick then. It was an uprising. People were taking all that they needed and all that they wanted everywhere.

She crossed to an alley, very much alone in all this noise. A police cruiser spotted her but did not pause. *What* is *she?* she felt the police officer wonder. *Is she white? Is she Black? Mulatto?* Best not to bother her. And here in this mass of people, she felt free. She felt invisible. The freest she ever was. The roofless buildings opened and outstretched to the heavens.

She passed a Safeway still being looted. Women were using shopping carts and taking their time. Marina paused to watch the ladies shopping, stomping back and forth through the big broken windows. They took baby formula. They took diapers. They took bread. They took milk.

Marina was standing there when she saw a boy running toward her. A white boy. A pretty boy. Or was it a girl? A butchy kind of girl. She imagined he was a girl. Like Alex. Alex! Her Alex. The butchy girl held a crossbow in her arms. The air jangled with cries and laughter. Sirens. Electricity. This imaginary Alex grabbed her arm and pulled her into an alleyway. Crossbow? Why a crossbow? He shoved Marina against a wall. Was he going to shoot her? Was he going to save her? He kissed her. Like that time in class. She was so dirty. Alex pushed her body up against Marina's. Her boy's face no longer the face of a boy. Her hair was trimmed close to her scalp. But her arms. Her arms were muscular rocks around Marina. Alex clutched at her waist, breathing hard. Marina wanted to get it all out. She wanted to say everything. Gunshots fired in the distance.

I couldn't sleep or eat. I kept crying all the time, Marina said impatiently. All I could think about was you guys at the Pines. Alex? I tried to starve myself. I felt sorry for myself, and I wanted to be punished. I kept thinking about you. Only you.

Shhh . . . Shhh . . . Alex said as she stroked Marina's face, her neck, her breasts.

I wrote long letters to you, crazy things. Oh wait. So you're good. You're okay. You're not in the ICU.

The person she imagined was Alex paused their stroking when they found the place where Marina injected drugs. Marina went on talking as if this guy was Alex. I'd jump the fence and go into town and hook up with men. Sometimes I'd look at these men and listen to them, but I didn't see them or hear them, I kept waiting for them to change into you. I couldn't think of a man who wasn't you, they all seemed to be you.

Alex stared at her. Alex shook her head, *no no no no,* her finger on her lips. Shushing her. Marina looked closer. Of course it wasn't Alex. He was a guy. A guy with a crossbow. His hair was short—a buzz cut. He was a skinhead. Marina was his prey.

Some Black guys were running into the alley, they had car parts and stereos and VCRs. The guy who was not Alex covered Marina's mouth and asked, What are you? Some kind of crazy Oreo? He spit a hot wad of phlegm in her face and ran off down the alley. Marina fell on her knees. The stench of his spit on her cheeks.

On her knees, in an alley within a world on fire with rage and race wars, an alley between streets where women were being dragged from their cars, where people were hiding in church basements, where children were left home alone wondering, watching their streets go up in flames and yet wanting new sneakers and watches and radios and more and more stuff, in an alley with a hot wad of hate-filled spit on her cheeks, she had never in her life been more in need of a change.

Sabina. In Canada. *I will find her before it's too late,* she thought. She'd been fucking around too long. How long had she been fucking around? Two months. Two months of hustling and doing dope. She ran back to the SILP unit and grabbed the two things she needed, her backpack with the address Alex gave her, and that little hat.

She took the bus to Union Station and bought a one-way ticket to Vancouver, British Columbia. It was only $144. She couldn't believe it. It was called the Coast Starlight, and it went first to Seattle then on to Canada. Afraid of missing her train, she walked straight to the terminal even though she had forty minutes to wait. Standing out on the platform, the trains rushing by, the air, the people, their kids, she saw teenagers get off trains coming from San Diego and New York. She thought of Heather from the Bronx. Finally, she saw the Coast Starlight; it was a double-decker train and looked sleeker than the rest.

She boarded with an eerie feeling. She had no idea of what was to come and there was this tiny ache inside that maybe it would all go terribly wrong. And then came the timeless silence of the mountains they passed, the distance that stretched between downtown Los Angeles and Canada. Once on the train, she rode through dark tunneled mouths of mountains and held her breath and made a wish, like she did with Ma. As the train picked up speed, the tracks sounded louder, a fast ticking and clacking, metal on metal, and she lay her head back holding on to her backpack like Alex guarded her big duffle. She looked out at the sky—the night was blank—there was just the breeze and the twinkling of stars. She thought of Alex, and the other girls, Nikki and Heather and Sammy, and that small cottage. She thought of that longing she'd held her whole life, her hand outside the window surfing the air when Ma drove them in the exact opposite direction from Seaside to Los Angeles. Nobody had ever described to her how freeing this would be. Just then right there, the night was so full of promise. She knew all these mountains by name, the San Gabriel Valley, San Bernardino, San Fernando. She'd ridden the RTD, and the Santa Monica Blue Bus, and the green Culver City line. She thought of summer nights with Alex drinking Olde E eight-ball, sometimes looking out the window in her motel, surrounded by stars. Then there were those nights she rode the bus with Ma to a Ships diner and they'd play Chase Toast and, finally, at the end of it all, she'd fall asleep, her rosy cheeks plastered to the pleather bench. Now it began to seem as though she would never go back, that her feet might never touch Los Angeles land again. The hills vast and yet embracing tightly around her. Getting on the train felt like both an escape and a betrayal.

A woman sitting across the aisle asked her if she was hungry. She had a small boy asleep on her lap; it looked like she had packed a sack lunch with two apples and a bologna sandwich.

I'm fine. Thank you, Marina said out of politeness, but by now, her stomach was growling. She'd been taught to refuse at least two times.

You sure? We have plenty . . . the woman asked, opening her purse wider to reveal two more brown paper sacks.

Actually, yes, please. Marina shook off Lola's warnings and grabbed the brown bag.

She bit into the sandwich, the mayonnaise and yellow mustard and American cheese stuck to the roof of her mouth. Nothing had ever tasted so wonderful.

Josie got to four. This was her navel. Her belly was soft and round like she had a kid. Which she did.

Five. There was only one more button. One more. This showed more of her belly, but as she moved now, he could make out a little bit of her nipples, they were lightly colored, not fully nude. Not like the kind that look almost invisible. And they were thick like licorice—another piece of her showing off that she had a baby.

Too bad he was going to do this from behind. He wanted to see them now. With all the counting. Still, his heart wasn't quite in it. This was just going to be a final ghost girl. She'd be fifty. He wanted to make them an even fifty.

THE ASTORIA

Marina landed in Pacific Central Station in Vancouver. Pigeons dove and flipped as the sky turned periwinkle. She realized then she had no idea where anything was or how to get to places. All around her people were either being greeted by their beloveds or stepping into cabs. She jumped into a cab. Still unsure of how she looked or what she should do next, she thought she would get her bearings first, check into a motel and take a shower. She told the driver to take her to where the cheap motels were. He took one look at her and headed straight to the Downtown Eastside. Her plan was to unpack, maybe rest, then shower, then go to the address on the slip of paper. This was her master plan. She planned like a girl on the run. The cabbie kept on promising, You're gonna love it here.

He was taking her to the Astoria Hotel. It sounded great. It sounded nice. *Astoria,* the word swirled in her mouth like a curly fry. The cabbie chatted the whole way. He chatted about free health-care and good schools and all the fantastic people. Everyone being so wonderful, why, just the other night he and people at the hotel were talking about what a talented dancer and singer that Michael Jackson was. As if that meant something about how open-minded he was.

Downtown is freezing, the lanes between streets lined with graffiti calling out Jesus, and pentagrams, and for help, and the words *stop using* and a dozen or more times you see in white, red, black drippy spray paint *Hell. Drip. Drop.* Gliding down the red brick. Beside dumpsters, in alcoves behind buildings were tiny, wasted people on the needle. People the constable sometimes had to coax back from the dead. People walk the lanes and see the cold blue-green fish-like people sway back and forth—eyes closed, mouth open to the sky—and then slump to their momentary death as the lights go out. The constable calls for an ambulance and cuts open their shirt and breathes air into them through a tube, using the small mouth shield he keeps on him for this reason. The EMTs come and try to shock-treat the overdosed person. People run up and down the lane to watch, and other people, people who have had the same thing happen to them before and expect that they may have to have it again one day, want desperately to preserve the overdoser's dignity, so they holler, Get away, rat! Get away!

When that person returns from the dead, another woman is deep into a cocaine psychosis crawling through a crowded street, rolling, warbling, Rape! Rape! Rape! It's a trill tune she sings as she imagines that there in the center of Downtown she is getting raped or snuff films are being made of her. Because that's how the rooms get paid; that's how the fix gets got. Ten bucks an hour for twelve hours a day is at least one hundred and twenty bucks. No one wants to do the drugs. They do them because they're in pain. They do them because they want to be numb. Outside and across from the Astoria is the Woodbine Hotel and the WISH Drop-In Centre below that, a dozen Chinese restaurants, six more SROs. If you're lucky you get admitted to the VGH, Vancouver General Hospital, because of something else, a domestic dispute, a slap in the face, a shot in the foot, and while you're there they can treat the abscess on your arm the size of a grown rabbit, a big hole, you thought it was bugs on your arm from the drugs, so you pick at it and then pick some more, and then you shoot up in it, and it's a mouth, and it's bugs, and it's a big hole, and in the end, your flesh just starts eating itself and while you're at the VGH they give you skin grafts, skin from somewhere else to help you heal there. You begin to think, *Where do I not need skin so much? Where can they take the skin from?* Most people think their ass, but then others want to preserve their ass, it's something they feel they got going for them, but chances are if you're at a general hospital, you don't get much choice in these matters.

Marina walked up the stairs through halls crowded with people to the second floor. Televisions blaring, people talking, high women draped on the stairs, there was a shared toilet and stand-up shower in the hallway: one toilet and one shower for the whole floor. A hotel stuffed with jaundiced pest people.

She felt a tiny bite on her arm and immediately the area turned puffy and irritated. Bedbugs. She tried searching out the mattress for the bugs and smushing them with her fingers, plucking them between her thumb and index and dropping them in the toilet. She tried flipping the mattress but found way more on the bottom side. She tried scrubbing the mattress with soap and water. She eventually gave in and lay on it, stared at a water stain on the cottage cheese ceiling.

Her plan was to rest, shower in the morning, and then go looking for Sabina when she was fresh. Marina went down to the bar to get a drink. And there they were staring at her—a dozen of them. Junkies. High. Drinking. They smiled missing-teeth smiles. They had a cackle laugh. She asked for a soda or something nonalcoholic. She could hear sirens outside—yelling, cars, prices, radios, the most desperate sounds. The bartender went in back and returned with a Moosehead. She drank it and went up to her room. She felt strange. She lay on the bed. And she felt heavy. Like she had no control over her limbs. Like she was wading in concrete. She was slow. All the sounds of voices and horns bled into one another. She was drugged. She knew she was drugged, but she couldn't do anything. Speech caught in her throat. Thoughts milky. Everything turning in on itself. She thought she saw Fati, Fatimah, draped in bright yellow with gold trim, her shawl drawn to her lips, coy with the dignity of a queen, her spun skirts, her back, her belly undulating, her pointed fingers, her mystery eyes. Her glamour. Marina began a meticulous gratitude list thanking God for her toes and her feet and her ankles, and then went on to thank God for the things they could do. The miles they could walk. How she was able to be a slick-ass pickpocket. She was a connoisseur of herself. She smelled and tasted her own breath, her skin, inspected her pores, licked her teeth, placed her hands above her face to inspect their babyishness. Their absolute childlike rendering, no matter if there was nail polish or not, these were the hands of a child, and then there were the veins, her big veins and little veins, and the tangle of her pubic hair and then again it hit her—she was high. How did this happen? They must've roofied her in the bar.

The door opened, a man came in. Two men came in. They blurred together. One disappeared. It's Alex. He comes closer. He's not Alex. He's Filipino. With lips that are slack and wet and taste of onions. His tongue is digging into her mouth. She was stuck under the weight of him. She could not see or move or breathe. He took off his pants. He moved the body that was hers. Her legs. The concrete poles that she had no command over. He pushed himself between her thighs. A scream, the worst kind of chilling scream, is stuck far back in her mouth. She tries to squirm or move. He's biting and licking and grunting—the sound of an oink-oink baboy.

The moment had come to do what she'd been training to do, to put her body on the line. It was a moment to submit. It was not a moment to fight, to have pride. To be self-righteous. It was certainly not a moment to remember Lola preaching about Seven Fingers, Seven Fingers dito, she'd say, she was talking about Larry Itliong. How nobody ever talked about the real leader of the farmworkers. What did they teach you today? she'd ask Mutya every day she walked in from school. Did they teach you about Seven Fingers yet? It'd been years since she'd seen Lola, and even though she was dead, her spirit seemed to follow Marina wherever she went, even into her mind and thoughts. She'd think she was alone and then the room filled with her, her grandma, her lola. She could see her calling out to her, then she'd be off, Salamat! Off to Otherworld!

Sure, she shouldn't have been thinking about that, but her mind was working on so many different levels. She thought about this guy on top of her, how he looked like that other guy Lola was going on about, she thought about how she felt like she was moving through a slow thick cloud, and how when she used to feel like this at the Pines, she'd always challenge Alex to a game of speed. SPEED, she thought. THAT MICHAEL JACKSON CAN DANCE. She felt a longing then, a strong one, for the afternoons she and Ma would dance to the Bee Gees and there were memories of toast. Eating toast—chasing it. Bus after bus and brown-ringed plates, and how she sometimes pretended to be asleep when she was not so Ma would carry her, even though she was getting too heavy for that. And then a frightened image of Ma alone in their apartment staring at the wall. YOU ARE BEING RAPED, she is reminded, she closes her eyes and begins to count, hoping he's almost done. This is where all the levels go in the end, the codes 242 BATTERY, 261 RAPE. Just like she learned with Hassan, she stared at the ceiling, until her spirit could float up and out and skim the surface, she could count the stains above and imagine they curved and twisted into shapes. A watermark in the corner looked like a bunny rabbit, she was born in the year of the rabbit, the rabbit is sly, the rabbit is slick.

As she regained consciousness, she pounded on the door. She had been locked in. She howled. She prayed. She paced the room. She kicked the walls. Her screams were like all the other screams. She cried. She cried and cried and cried. In between, men came. They crushed her with their weight. They split her open. Then they disappeared.

Josie got to six. The last button. She slowly eased her arms out of her sleeves and stood there some more, half naked. She sighed.

Okay, that's enough now. He grabbed her pants and pulled her close. He undid the button. She felt his fingers on her skin. They were clammy and rough. He had dirt packed into his nails. All of his pores looked big to her. This was when her private counting started.

JANE DOE

Constable Sherman knows these people who are fixing in the lanes. Sherman knows these people because he asks them questions, and sometimes he buys them food, and they all say the same thing. They all say they come from a good home—they say they got folks who still treat them like they left home yesterday. They try their best to give Sherman presents, I was digging in the trash, and I saw this nice army jacket that I think would be perfect for you! Also, I saw some books, and I don't like books being thrown away.

In the rain, the people in the lanes make forts out of overturned shopping carts and sleep under them. There are gadgets for sale in most of the storefronts, used gadgets that were pawned or hocked or used to pay the rent, alarm clocks and microwaves and useful things that lost their meaning. For most of these girls, it's the same thing: fix, date, fix, date, all day. Except some days, they ask for help. Sherman says, Sure, I'll help. You wanna go now?

And they say, I have a couple of things to do first.

Most of the time, Sherman's job is to listen to liars. They're strung out and dopey and look him in the eye and say, Nah, I'm not using. I'm through with that stuff. Then the next week, you see them there with their hands clenched in fists, dehydrated, their body begins to eat itself, shooting vomit and diarrhea everywhere. That's what happens when they try to kick. Sherman knew that they wanted more than anything to get out and couldn't do it.

Some people in the force thought of Sherman as a social worker. His office—the streets of Downtown. When Sherman inquired about the rising number of missing women, the other cops said it was no big deal. That's what hoes did. They went missing. But there were a number of welfare checks left unclaimed—tips left by the women to one another at the WISH Drop-In Centre for *bad dates*. None of them led to any good suspects.

The cops knew of one serial killer still active, Gilbert Paul Jordan, an alcoholic barber with a criminal record of sexual assaults. Jordan picked up Native prostitutes, forced them to drink a lethal amount of alcohol. Anytime a body came up with a high alcohol level, the other cops said, We got another Jordanesque.

Jordan's style was to say, Down the hatch, baby, I'll give you ten, twenty, fifty bucks. Whatever you want. Come on. I want to see you get it all down.

But these ladies coming up missing Sherman didn't feel were Jordan's work. They weren't all Native. Every time he pushed—he couldn't get any resources. The other provinces didn't even track missing prostitutes, let alone search for them.

Steve Sherman got a list from the First Nations people, a list of missing women. He took that list and added his own, figured more like fourteen rather than two or three remained unsolved.

His task room was a dim eggshell color, no windows, five desks clustered at the center, whiteboards on every wall. Scribbled notes in dry-erase marker, in the corner blown-up photos of the missing women. Steve Sherman walked to his board of faces. He looked in their eyes. Jane Doe eyes. Searching. Searching.

Josie wasn't wearing any underwear. Her legs and vagina were hairy.

You're a real hippie, aren't yah?

Yeah, I guess.

He lowered her pants. He was having trouble getting them over her shoes. She kept on thinking how slow he seemed to her. She sat down and untied her shoes. Took them off one by one. Put them on the floor beside each other. They looked big and sad. She left her socks on.

It's cold in here. Can I leave 'em?

All she's thinking about these days is if her daughter has a coat on. Well, actually she's got one other thing on her mind all the time. It started small at first, just a taste, but after that, she wanted to get some all of the time, and then there was all the stuff she had to do to get the stuff. It got so she didn't know what was worse, the stuff or the doing, and they go hand in hand.

Suit yourself. He pulled her onto the bed. Turned her over on her knees, so her ass was up in the air in his face. It had no marks on it. Soft, doughy. The youngest part of her.

Nothing's going that way, she said, pointing in back.

WISH

Time slipped by. The days mirrored one another so much, Marina barely noticed when they turned into months. Spring into summer, the air thinning out, the garbage stench strengthening, new blossoms on the trees. By this time she was allowed to come and go, but she was already hooked on dope so she never went too far. The landlord of the Astoria bugged her about rent. When was she gonna pay, how was she gonna pay? She paid by turning tricks with the guys who came in her room. She turned tricks with the guys by getting high.

When it began, she thought, what does this guy want from me? This beast? Does he want to eat me, or rape me, or kill me? There were some of those pakshet Hells Angels who liked to make snuff films. Was she gonna be in a snuff film? Then she realized she was worth much more alive. They all just wanted her pekpek. It would be too easy to kill her. Sometimes she wished they would. They would end it all. Everything so long and hard and painful now. Yet, there in the back of her mind was the night that Alex got put on in the park. She realized now how exceptionally brutal that was for her. Alex had edges but a much more tender spirit and here in this place she saw also how sometimes when she had panic in her eyes, their dingle dangle buto got hard, and she learned that the more scared she acted and the more scared she sounded the quicker it would be. She knew now all the men, she could see it in their eyes, their eyes said they wanted all of her, they wanted the worst thing. When they unbutton their shirts and their tummy skin shows, all that mottled skin, those eyes flash down in shame at their own nudity, and then quickly all of them, the tall ones the short ones the dark ones the light ones the fat ones, they all look quickly back to her, their eyes go dark and when they are inside of her, in the center of her, they have the eyes of Hassan. They have the dark distant look of someone looking at a speck on the wall, they plow into her trying to fix their broken parts.

She was able to come and go now, just long enough to get a fix. Her room had a window, a barred window, but she could look out onto the street and see the lights across the way. The plan was to get cleaned up, to just maybe fix once more before she got cleaned up, and then to get ready and get dressed and go find Sabina. Directly across the street was the Woodbine Hotel. It looked just as bad as the Astoria, maybe even a little worse, but instead of a pub downstairs, it had a giant blue cross. She stared into the rooms at night, trying to make out the silhouettes of girls like her. She'd heard that the racket going on in the Astoria was going on all up and down Hastings.

She watched one door in particular, it was connected to a drop-in center called WISH, it was a place some of the women went to go and get cleaned up. She'd try to track one of the case managers who was always coming and going, a thin Black woman. Marina sometimes made believe she was Sabina. Night after night, Marina sat on her creaky tiny bed and watched out the pane of her window at the Black woman's silhouette across the way. She watched the door down below, the people and their comings and goings, but she was always drawn back to the lady, she left every night at around six p.m. She smoked cigarettes.

Marina saw her sometimes at the corner store buying cigarettes, and she wanted to talk to her, but she was so self-conscious about her shuffling in with her eye boogers and crud at the corners of her mouth and she wasn't wearing any socks or shoes.

You got something, the guy behind the counter said, gesturing to her face; she'd pick at her eye crud and then when she got to her room, she'd see she had a streak of dried blood down her face from a nosebleed. She spent most days up in her room and hadn't had a conversation with any of the other girls. She got to know one of her neighbors, a junkie who lived next door to her. He'd come by and sometimes they'd shoot dope together but mostly she walked around spaced out. Her life before all this felt as if she had dreamt it—it seemed so far away, and now maybe she could just stay sleeping until it was all fucking done with.

Time was strange and fucked up for her, depending on how high she could get. She barely ate, and when she did nothing tasted right to her. Sweets were not sweet enough, salt was not salty enough. It seemed the only thing she could taste was her own bad breath or the rank guys and their dingle dangle buto. Her favorite days were the ones where she seemed to be nodded out the whole time. She'd eventually wake up and remember that she was alive, that she was a girl and once she mattered very much to someone. Once upon a time she was in love, then everything would fade to black again, and she'd pass the fuck out.

As the seasons changed, her tolerance grew and she was gonna need much stronger drugs or more drugs to keep the dream going to get her sleep thick again. Throughout this time her soul had detached from her, had become thinner and more distant. She dreamt that eventually she could disappear.

She knew she'd have to start tricking outside of the Astoria. She began venturing outside of the hotel room. Watching where the girls got picked up on the ho-track. She still saw the case manager from the WISH center every now and again. Marina wanted to become her friend. She wished she was more like her. One night she got up, drank a glass of water from the sink, and then stood at the window and looked into the electric night, she noticed that woman was also standing by the window in the drop-in center and looking into the lights too. She felt she looked sad or seeking. She saw herself reflected in the window, and the woman was also reflected in her window, two sleepless women, and for a moment, their mirrored images fused.

She thought of Alex often, of how she was failing her, of how she wished she could tell Alex what happened, but she was never sure where to begin, so instead she wrote cheeky letters to Arthur from Blanche, like at the Pines. She kept a small stack of these unsent letters on a shelf in the closet. She still wondered from time to time if Alex ever recovered from her accident, but she couldn't bring herself to confront how much time she'd let pass. How with each passing day she was further and further from being able to keep her promise. She noticed the woman across the way never looked like she was drinking or doing drugs. Once she went to adjust her curtains, and she thought the lady caught her looking. *Can she see me?* She wondered what it would be like to have control over your body and your life like that. She thought these things with the lights blinking outside and the sounds and the yelling and all the goings-on in her motel building. Marina began to keep track of the woman's schedule. Occasionally when the woman left, she seemed to be dressed nicer, like she was going to see someone special. She seemed so animated and happy. Marina could feel it on her lonely dim side of the street. She needed to see her in person. She decided that woman was going to help her.

It was a lucky week for her. She'd scored some dope, so she held off as long as she could and made every hour seem like a thousand hours, and she did the dope at night, and she nodded out, and when she got up, it was 11:00. That was early for her, and she got up and checked to make sure it was 11:00 a.m. and not p.m., and it was light out, and she checked on the lady. The lady was there, headed out for her lunch break. Marina quickly shimmied on some pants and some slippers, threw water on her face, gargled water, and ran outside. Marina ran downstairs in the bright sunlight. She'd forgotten how bright it was, and she could see the woman walking toward her. She was wearing a small white dress with tiny blue flowers and yellow roses, and she had on a coral lipstick. Marina tried to hang back so the woman could get in front of her and Marina could follow her, and when she got close Marina smelled her, and she smelled like cocoa butter, which is a smell that reminded her so much of Alex and the life she had before this that suddenly everything hurt.

Marina couldn't help herself; she said, Ma'am? Miss? Pardon me, and the woman kept on walking like she didn't hear her, only she walked faster, and Marina tried to keep up with her. Marina saw her turn into a twenty-four-hour Chinese restaurant. Marina opened the door, and bells rang, and there behind the counter was a buffet with white rice, fried rice, and an array of fried meats and fish in thick sticky red sauces and this was not the type of food Marina imagined her eating, but maybe she would get a soup, and just as Marina thought that, she heard her say, Yes, I'll have the egg drop soup. And to her, that was a sign. She stood there, her knees bent against the counter, her feet crossed, the tips of her toes on her right foot touching the floor, her arms out to her sides, palms with long fingers on the counter, she had a small bright yellow purse wrapped across her body.

Marina ran up to her and began again, Hey—

I'm sorry, you're gonna have to see me at the drop-in.

And then the Chinese lady behind the counter, You get out! Get outta my store! and she *shoo shoo shoo*ed her away with her hands, and there along the wall opposite Marina was a big mirror. She could see what she'd become, all scabs and thin skin and messy hair, no bath, and no money and no job, no morals, no esteem, and no integrity. And the pretty silhouette woman looked at her with a little bit of fear.

But you don't understand; I'm, I'm trying.

The woman raised her hand around her mouth and nose to protect her from what Marina must've smelled like.

By now I'd made it to the entrance of the room, he was so focused on her he didn't see me, I just saw her socked feet and his back. He had on a flannel shirt; I could see his covered back and hairy legs.

Dontcha worry about that, he said.

I know what her view was; it was the wall, stained dark from smoke. And the horse head.

He was in her now pounding away. I could see his backside bopping back and forth.

No use asking for a condom since they already shared needles, and she probably had the hep.

One, two, three, four. She just wanted to get this stuff all out of her system so she could go back and see her daughter and make sure she's got a good coat on her. Five, six. It was all going too slow. Or too fast. She needed to add one thousand. One one thousand. Two one thousand. Her forehead was lightly tapping the wall in front of her. She was really dry from all the drugs.

The dryness was making it hurt. He put some spit on his hand and rubbed her. He grunted. Then he reached under the bed. She couldn't see him reaching under the bed; she was too busy trying to protect her forehead. This is how he does it; he grabs a needle with the antifreeze, he grabs the zip-tie handcuffs from under his mattress.

MINAMAHAL

The only person who knew Willie's story, I mean his full story, was Corrin Young. Corrin was being cared for by her grandparents; her own parents had abandoned her when she was just born. Sometimes her grandfather would take her out fishing on the Stave, a mucky river layered in gnats. On the way home, he'd stop at the Pickton store for meat. Willie, at about nine or ten, handed Corrin a pack of hot dogs.

In 1996, when Corrin finally talked, she told Constable Sherman everything. She started with the good stuff. I wasn't used to people being so nice to me. I was already so struck by his blond hair, but then he handed me those hot dogs like a present—well, I never forgot him, she said.

Willie tells people Mother made him quit school, but the way I remember it is that he had a pen he bought at the Cracker Jack, it was a pen with a lady, and if you flipped it upside down it was rude underneath. The principal saw that and said he'd beat him, and Willie said if he did that, he was gonna quit. The principal went for Willie, and Willie stood up and quit right there.

Thirty years later, Corrin'd seen that fire in him again. In the meantime, she'd fallen into what she called *the bad years*. After her grandparents died, she was sent to foster homes where she was messed with, molested, and beat. That's where I got this sorority pin, Corrin says as she points to a tattoo of three dots right beside her right eye.

The bad years I was into drugs, and that led to prostitution. Then I got messed up with a bad guy and got married and lived over in the Downtown Eastside, then rehab, and finally, after cleaning up, I landed a place on Dominion Avenue in Port Coquitlam. My son, Greg, he was just a teenager. He was out with this new friend, Bert. I liked this kid Bert a lot. But it was New Year's, and I didn't want him out there driving around and getting in trouble, so I went ahead and called the number my son left me for Bert.

A man answered the phone, and I asked him was it Bert's place, and sure enough, it was Bert's uncle. He went out and found my kid and his nephew and brought my kid home safe, and I'll be darned if that wasn't Willie Pickton, the same little blond boy who gave me that pack of hot dogs! Turns out, we were right around the corner from one another.

We soon became best friends. Nothing sexual. I didn't like him like that. Sometimes he'd even spend the night. I remember his skinny legs the most. They were so pale. That and his long toenails. He never cut them, so they were long sharp things. He never touched me. Other people don't really touch me either though. I don't let them near me. I don't want to get them mixed up with myself. Once one of his long nails accidentally scratched me and I flinched, and he said, I hope I didn't hurt you, sluggish and sweaty, all pale body. He was so timid and sorry; it is hard for me to picture him hurting anyone. I don't think it's like what other people say about him not being able to perform like a man though, because sometimes he woke up with a hard-on and I'd see it when I passed him on the couch in the morning, but he just tried to hide it, he'd roll on his stomach and sleep on it.

Well, that is sinungaling—what you call a lie. What she's said here isn't completely true. There was a time when both Willie and Corrin spent every pakshet moment of every pakshet day together. Let's look at them on one of those summer days. The light of Corrin's television cast a lonely shadow across their faces when it felt as if they were together, but they were both still utterly alone. Corrin fighting with her boyfriend. Willie working on the farm all day. When he looked at Corrin, he thought, *Now, there is a woman who can appreciate hard work.* Willie would come by and talk for hours and hours about work. However long it took to break down a pig. Corrin just sat and listened. Never hurried him along. Willie felt a twang of impatience in anyone else when he spoke. A sort of *hurry it along.* Not with Corrin. They were both drunk on the sweat of hard labor. The relief of having two weeks' worth of groceries in the kitchen and the rent paid off. Now they just had to face the urgings of their inner life. To take away what they already had with what they wanted. A minamahal, a partner, someone to love. This day was like so many others except Willie turned to face Corrin and asked, Kiss me like you kiss your boyfriend.

Surprised, Corrin said no. But Willie came closer to her on the couch, and she started to think of what it might be like. And at just that moment she understood that they had been skirting around this type of thing if not for much of their lives then at least in that week. Their friendship had felt like harmless playacting. Corrin making pancakes for Willie and her son in the morning. Willie offering to do the dishes and take out the trash in return. It seemed as if they had begun the unwritten contract and ritual of courting. Yet she felt no attraction for the man, just a wave of relief from loneliness. But here it was, an instant of dangerous curiosity. Corrin grabbed Willie's shirt collar, pulled him close, and kissed him. Once their lips touched, the dream of playacting ended, and her mind was flooded with the reality. This was not a cure for loneliness. This kissing was, in fact, the source of ultimate loneliness. He tasted gooey and sour. He tasted of rot. Willie began to push himself forward. Corrin was falling back, and Willie pushed to position himself on top of her. Corrin felt his clammy stench coming closer and closer. Inside, Corrin felt disgusted, and scared, his warm mouth on hers, his scratchy hands, she could not turn her mind off of his breath. The whole thing felt disgusting; she revulsed at the idea of his skin on her skin, there was something foul about him, he began to thrust into her, and his searching hands were traveling all up and over her sweater. He was so sloppy and inexperienced she felt, she did the only thing she could think to do—she laughed uncontrollably.

I'm sorry. I'm sorry, nothing's funny, she said.

Willie sat up, and they never mentioned it again.

Corrin'd go over to his trailer sometimes, and she'd always end up cleaning the place because it was such a mess. Soon he hired her on. She'd do some cleaning, and she'd also help with the butchering and over at the auctions. Corrin loved to talk about the auctions to anyone who'd listen. She'd say that he'd buy the good stuff and also take home what you call the culls, the leftover game that could not sell because they were sick or dying.

Willie was her best friend. She'd have him and his brother over for movies. They liked scary movies, both of them always got sucked in—even when they watched the same one a dozen times, they'd be scared like new. Willie believed in all the fairy tales. Once, he took Corrin to a magic show and afterward could not for the life of him understand how a woman who was sawed in half could come out whole.

There came a time that reminded Corrin of the firecracker he was at school. Willie's brother, Elder, didn't like her too much. He'd call her a loser and whatnot. Every morning Willie and Elder'd meet at this strip joint in town and have breakfast, and Elder would lay out for Willie all the things Willie had to do that day. So basically, Elder would just boss Willie around all the time. Willie took it most times. But once, Elder was over at Corrin's place, and Corrin was walking past them coming back from cleaning Willie's trailer, and who knows why he wanted to do this—most likely Elder was jealous Corrin did these kinds of things for Willie—he stuck his foot out like he was gonna trip Corrin. In a fit of something so unlike Willie, he caught this little tick of Elder's foot and ran over and charged at Elder, knocked the wind out of him. Elder fell flat on his back, and Willie hooted with laughter at him. That's the only time she thinks she saw Willie get the best of Elder.

Willie did some dealings in cars. He was a mechanic, and he had all these junked-up cars on the property, and he fixed them up. Corrin likes fast things, so one day, Willie called her from auction and said they had a Trans Am there that he knew she'd like. What was the most she was willing to bid on it, he wanted to know. He got her that red Trans Am for $1,300, and that thing was fast. The only thing that could get Corrin off a Harley was a nice fast car.

THE FINAL GIRL

I hear Josie's thoughts now, a loud jumble and buzz.

I got two parents who love me. Three one thousand. I'm not like these other girls. Four one thousand. I know there's a place I could go back to. Five one thousand. I also gotta show my parents I'm capable on my own. Six one thousand. In a way, it's true. Not really by the looks of me, but I managed to get a room at the hotel and keep myself good on drugs for a four-hundred-dollar-a-day habit.

He clasped her wrist behind her back; she bucked onto her right side, she couldn't hold herself up. She felt the zip tie.

WHAT?!

Shhhh . . . don't worry.

He zip-tied her other wrist to the first one. She was lying on her stomach, her ass in the air. Her hands strapped together behind her. Her nose on the mattress sniffing it in. Up close where it was itchy, her head bouncing up and down on the old sweat-filled material, the buttons of the mattress filled with small crumbs, she tried to erase her thoughts, her fears, she continued counting. Then an idea . . .

The girls. The missing girls. He was them. Panic took over; she took a breath and knew the world had devoured her—a bundle of good intentions. *I'm going to die.*

He pulled a belt from under the mattress and brought it around her neck. He pulled her head back. I tiptoed closer into the room. She was choking. She could feel the leather making indentations in her neck. She could feel her air getting cut off. Seven one thousand. She was in darkness. Like swimming underwater, not breathing. Holding her breath. Drowning. She was drowning. Eight one thousand. She shat herself. Nine one thousand. She didn't scream. She thought of her daughter. Of her little coat. It was green and puffy, but that wasn't her daughter's coat, it was hers. It was her puffy green coat that her mom used to fuss at her about all the time. She was standing alone on a carousel—beads of sweat around her face. Everyone was leaving. Everyone was gone, and she was left by herself. She was by herself, and the man was pulling and pulling, her throat filled with her tongue. She was going to go back with her daughter. Her body. Her body is First Nations. Her body is female. Her body was recently penetrated. Her body gave birth. Her body held a fetus once. Her body scarred with the following marks: track marks on the arms, a C-section scar, another long scar on her right side near her hip from when her appendix was removed. No tattoos. A history of abscesses, O-positive blood, high cholesterol, high blood pressure, 20/20 vision.

I lunged for his neck from where I stood in the doorway; he lost hold of the belt, she hunched up her back like a spooked cat, gasping for air. He tried to turn toward me, then he looked stunned to see a person he thought was Marina. The woman whose body he remembered lighting on fire in a heap. I was just a clot of dark hair upon his back. Go! Go! I hollered at Josie. She squiggled from under him. He was still naked from the waist down, he tried to throw me off his back, but Josie kneed him in his pakshet droopy droopy buto. He had gotten a look at me. His eyes bugging out.

Remember when I said eyes on a girl make a big difference? When Willie saw me this way, in Marina's body—as someone who knew Marina, he looked confused, agitated. I looked familiar but different; something so familiar but critical about her had shifted. It was the eyes. I went for him with my teeth, hearing the women and their schoolyard chant *Get'im in his sleep, get'im with a needle.* But like the day when he kissed Corrin, his skin was maysakit, disgusting, clammy, yellow, and as I began to tinikling back, I could see deep inside his pakshet soul. There was something so flat and dead about him. Had there always been something evil brewing inside his blood? His pipi pakshet face. His buto that ruled his bad mind. I was swimming in the repulsive feelings of him. I felt Willie's longing for the girls—for their lives, how it began with Want and turned into Envy, a desire for their desire, that Attention, that love that somebody somewhere must have for them, that ultimately turned into a sickening kind of Rage. A Rage that could take over. I needed to focus. I had one duty—to find Sabina.

The only way I could keep from drowning in the gravity of his Rage was to think of Alex, Marina's love, to hold on to those memories, the lightness, visions of their past, her soft hand dropping right beside Marina's face at night, those fingers strumming sad songs on her guitar, the love buckles from Ma, from Alex, Lola's chant *a thrilla and a killa,* the small pulse of determination. It'd be too easy to get distracted by my desire to kill this pakshet, I needed to keep my attention on Marina's quest—to unite Alex with Sabina. Maawa ka.

I tore a piece of his flesh and then released my grip on his arm, feelings of relief, then shock, and all the while pain bounced up and down his arm. He looked at the bite mark. There was lots of blood. It dripped from his arm, from our mouth. I ran outside where the sky was endless and mostly dark, a smattering of bright glinting stars, the air filled with farm smells, the sweaty grunty baboys, the winds and swooping trees. Everything fresh and wild.

Josie made her way out of the gate past that six-hundred-pound boar and onto the dark Lougheed Highway; she was bloody and naked, and yet she was determined to get back to her baby girl and back to that small coat. She ran half a mile until she came upon a car, a sedan driven by a nice older couple, she ran right in front of the headlights, a silhouette of an innocent girl. The couple looked at one another, shocked.

Help. Please help.

It was there atop that pakshet man swimming in his sour soup that I realized this would not bring justice for the forest of missing women. If I ended it here, no one would ever know the extent of his crimes—he wouldn't have to account for ALL the women. There would be no coroner's report. There would be no hospital records. There would be no rape kit for any of the girls. Those bodies buried and burned in with the heap of other bodies. Anita killed by Willie's bare hands; Jordan strangled with a belt around her neck; and Elaine, her final breath on a slaughtering hook. If I ended it here, ended him, their names would not be known. When I first entered Marina's body, I felt two forces jerking at her soul—gravity and light—always the way with the Salles women. And which was greater? Which was stronger? Marina's desire to kill this pakshet man or to finish her quest?

These eyes that blinked in the sun, and this mind that sheltered a vision of Alex each moment of her days. This body that wanted more than anything at this moment to sleep curled up tight around her beloved. If I left this pakshet dead right here, his life would be too easy, and hers would go unfinished. In order to complete my duties here with the Salles women, in order to move on, I have to finish the quest that lies heaviest on Marina's heart. The light—that fairy dust dancing in the shadows—is her love for Alex, her desire to bring her joy—her promise to find Sabina.

The couple on the highway took Josie to the hospital on the Eastside. The road went from the thick forest to the abandoned-looking low buildings, gray and dark and blue at night, the people warbling in the streets, she opened her window to inhale the smell of rain-slicked streets and gas. At the hospital, she was able to talk to Constable Sherman; she was able to get healing fluids. Jan burst in the room, Josie's daughter in tow bundled in a coat. Her daughter climbed onto the hospital bed, and Josie held her close.

ASH ST.

Where do brokenhearted mothers go?

Where would I find Sabina? I entered her life, the wheel of routines she performed each day like Lola's prayers. Open her eyes, walk to the gym, sit on the stationary bike, walk home, eat a yogurt, shower. Get dressed, take a work call on the way into the office. Sometimes, manage to see some friends. Mostly she let the days blend in, lean into one another, bland day after bland day.

The days like rows of tan stockings.

It's how she maintains.

On the top shelf of Room 210 was a slip of paper with Sabina's address scribbled in Alex's handwriting. 3310 Ash St. I grabbed the hat with the ears, ran downstairs, hopped in a cab, and told the driver the address.

What's the best way to get there?

Ay! Susmaryosep! You need directions?

Yes. I just drive.

Well, I don't. You figure it out.

Then I don't know dito if he took me the direct route or the long route, to charge me extra because I don't know Vancouver, but then twenty minutes later, we were there. A quiet residential street. I was flooded with Marina's memories of wandering around in the town by the Pines. There was a pharmacy and a diner, and each residential block ended in a cul-de-sac, and the sidewalks were not painted with numbers, so we had to peer past gates to arched doorways looking for an address. The cabbie stopped women with dogs four times. The fact that there were so many women walking dogs in this neighborhood made me hopeful, alert, almost giddy. One of the women wore a pair of overalls, one of the arms unhooked, dragging behind her. She was hip-hop stylish with big poofed-out hair and electric-blue eyeliner. Her dog was a vicious Maltese barking and growling while she pointed this way and that. Eventually, we arrived in front of a small Craftsman with big windows facing the street, a bright lawn, an iron gate. The type of home Marina dreamt of living in with Ma when she'd weave tales of rich-girl dreams. A house with a chimney, which meant a fireplace; through the window I was able to make out a wall of shelving filled with books. And on the empty couch, I pictured Alex there, legs tucked into herself, reading.

I stood for a moment. The street was empty; the sky seemed especially still up above. Standing there felt familiar, felt like the ghost of Marina, of how often she looked in at other people's lives in other people's homes and imagined what it would feel like if it were *her* life.

I slowly made my way down the walkway and finally to the door; on the door was a knocker, and beside the door was a small black button for the bell. *Knock? Ring? Should I ring? Should I knock? If I knock, do a noise, a beat, a rhythm?* Before I could think about it any longer, I pushed the button. I heard motion, a shadow gliding near, I stepped back, the door opened, and there she was. Average height, glorious dark hair, a peach dress with a smile—with wet eyes—there was Sabina. She reminded me of one of the women caricatures that appeared on the cards at the Stride Rite Lola worked at. A perfect drawing of a mother. She looked curious, patient.

Pardon me . . . I . . . I . . . Suddenly aware of my appearance—of my smell—of what I might look like to her. I saw her looking past me a couple of times. Searching the sidewalk. Maybe she was afraid someone would come out of the bushes or in a car. I couldn't find the words, and then I remembered . . . I fumbled in Marina's backpack. Just a second . . . and held out the small knit hat with the cat ears.

Where did you get this? she asked.

She gave it to me. I promised I'd find you.

And the little knit hat stunned and terrorized her because in that very instant, the wreckage of all her pitiless regret and desire for Alex was replaced with bliss.

Come in, please, please, come in. Sabina gestured me into the house.

Can I make you some tea, or . . .

No, no, I'm fine. I don't have much time.

Oh, yes, of course, I'm sorry, you have other things . . .

Nothing more important than this.

And I told her about Alex, how she got to the Pines, and how she had been struggling to get her files, and how she finally got them and Sabina's address, but then there was the accident. And I gave her Alex's information so she could connect with her, and the whole time I looked around the house, I noticed the shiny floors, and the marble kitchen countertops, and the fireplace. I was right, there was a fireplace, and the soft face of the woman. I knew I'd made the right choice.

NAILED TO THE CROSS

Robert Willie Pickton was arrested Wednesday, December 21, 1994, at 9:00 a.m. just inside the wooden gate. A warning sign and the Machine, a six-hundred-pound boar, and dogs protected the farm. He was working on a junked-out vehicle as Constable Sherman approached with a search warrant.

Pickton apologized for his disheveled appearance. He said he'd overslept and that the place itself was under a lot of renovations. The lot was covered in junked-up car parts, so Sherman smiled and said, Looks like it. Then he whistled and made a sweeping gesture with his face. Pickton smiled, let out half a laugh.

The other officers went and searched the property, and Pickton walked with Sherman back to the squad car. Do you mind if I go in and pull myself together here?

Well, yeah, go ahead, but I gotta send some of my guys with you to make sure nothing is tampered with.

Pickton reappeared in under ten minutes, looking far more presentable than the guy who was slouching there ten minutes ago. Some agents came out of his trailer with trinkets that belonged to some of the victims in Ziploc bags—earrings, a belt, a tube of lipstick, and finally an inhaler with Marina's name on it.

Constable Sherman took a pair of handcuffs, he pulled back Willie's right arm, and Willie felt the weight of a handcuff on his right wrist then the clink of his left wrist.

Here he is in a holding tank after a grueling five-hour interrogation. Constable Sherman showed Pickton pictures of all of the women whose spirits were dancing in the forest behind Pickton's farm.

Have you seen this woman? Constable Sherman asked.

Nah, I never seen that one.

What about this one? Sherman with another photo.

Never seen that one.

Like that for hours.

Pickton's in a white T-shirt and orange pants in a concrete cell. The walls flattened out to a bench that doubles as a bed. Pickton sits eating his meal. Sitting opposite Pickton is Steve Sherman's partner, Constable Robert Suave. He's working undercover to try to get a confession out of Pickton.

Willie slurps at his plate, hungry, tired, done in. They got me. They got me on this one.

Suave leans in. No way . . . No. Shit. Fuck, what have they got? he asks.

Pickton scoops the food around his plate, shovels the green and brown slop in his mouth. Fuck all . . . Carcasses, he says.

Carcasses, that can be anything—really, what have they got? Suave continues to egg him on.

DNA.

Suave speaks in a loud whisper—tries to gain Pickton's confidence. He wants to nail Pickton so bad.

How long does DNA even last? When'd you start?

They've got DNA, Willie said, mouth full, still eating.

Suave knows this is his chance. He's gonna do what he's good at. He's gonna do what got him this job in the first place. When he was a kid, Suave won recognition for being in a school play. This was a gift of his, and if he were better looking, he might've tried out for television.

Why didn't you get rid of it? Me, I find the best way to dispose of something is to fucking take it to the ocean, Suave says.

This gets Willie's attention. He finally looks up from his plate. Oh, really? Willie smiles.

You know what the fucking ocean does to things? Suave asks.

Willie gets up and sits over next to Suave. Side by side. Pals. Bros. I did better than that, he said.

Who? Suave asks.

Me. Willie's gonna show him. He's no dummy. No dum-dum.

Better than an ocean? Ocean will make shit go away and no prints . . . says Suave.

Willie smiles, looks smooth. Rendering plant, he says.

Ha ha, no shit.

Yeah.

Can't be much fucking left, Suave says.

No, only I was kinda sloppy at the end of this too, got too sloppy.

Willie said *this*, but he meant Marina. He was sloppy with Marina.

Really? Suave asks.

They got me, oh fuck too sloppy, there was a girl, Em. Made me get sloppy on myself, Willie says.

You gotta be fucking meticulous. But rendering plant . . . that's pretty fucking pretty good. You must be doing something right—fucking beautiful.

But they haven't fingerprinted me yet, Willie says.

No shit, eh—they probably haven't got the prints to prove anything.

But prints don't prove anything. They said they're not going to let me go. I won't even get bail, Willie says, then he walks back to his corner. Finishes the plate of food and sets it down. I was gonna do one more—make it an even fifty. But I was a little sloppy at the end on account of that last girl.

Make it the big five zero. Fuck, that's fucked. Fucking five zero, fucking half a hundred, Suave says.

In the room, the detective asked me how many of those? Like how many of 'em I seen or how many I killed. I dunno. He was pointing to the pictures of the girls. Wouldn't tell 'im. I wouldn't tell 'im. Willie rambles on.

Suave knows he has him now. Willie keeps on talking, he can't help himself. (*That's how these guys are,* Suave thinks.)

They asked how many of these girls you seen before? When they showed me the pictures. I said I seen none of 'em. You know the list of all those pictures and names has only got like, only got half the girls in there I did, Willie says.

Willie takes off his pants and gets under a gray wool blanket. Based on that fucking stuff they found on me, I think I'm nailed to the cross. But you know what else, something real strange, eh—

Between you and me, man—you have to fucking look after yourself, Suave says. Yeah, where's the world—

Willie interrupts, That's just part of it; they got a lot of stuff on me. But the thing I don't get is one of 'em was there in the room with me. One of the ones I did before. Number forty-nine. She jumped on top of me. I know she wasn't alive. They're going to nail me big time. They're going to nail me to the cross. I made my own; I made my own grave by being sloppy.

He lies back down.

WHEREVER YOU GO—THERE YOU ARE

Reen.

My princess. My poo, my poopee face. My little girl. From when I had her, she was always so happy when she was little, with her moon face, with her questions. *Mama, why is the sky blue? Ma, why? Why? Why? Why?*

She stayed in that stage her whole childhood. Then it was like all of a sudden when she was around ten, she always wanted to be alone to play by herself with her dolls. Play with a box. I remember walking into the room and seeing her sitting there talking to herself. I warned her then about strangers but never thought I had to worry about her going with strangers because she really loved the most to be alone.

Actually, let me correct that. To be alone and with me. To be alone in the apartment with me there. When I stayed the night out, she would cry, she would beg me to stay at home with her, but you know I had a boyfriend, and I didn't always think it was appropriate to do what he wanted to do with a child in the house, so I spent the night at his. But that last night. Well, it just broke my heart the way she cried and begged to come with me. I had to let her. She was very skilled at getting what she wanted. I don't think she got that from me. I know I asked a lot of her in return, but please understand that I was always being told, *Challenge her, challenge her. A girl like Marina needs to always be challenged.* I guess the message was if she was bored, she was this hotbed of danger. Able to get into all kinds of difficulties. I was trying to do the right thing. Always—isn't that how it is? You are trying to do the right thing, but that ends up being the exact wrong thing?

I was so young when I had her. I didn't know any better. I had her when I was nineteen and her father, her father, who loved me. I mean, he loved me a lot. He wanted to take care of us and for me to raise his sons and to have a house and be a military wife. To live out there on the air force base and send her to a school with all those matching outfits and shop at the PX and to be friends with the other military wives, and I think it was one winter when I was wrapping gifts for people during the holidays when I thought how I was exactly like my mother, the way my hands looked. The way my index finger looked pressed down against the gift with the ribbon wrapping around it, making a bow. I wondered if this was an inherited trait, gift wrapping, bow making. I looked around at the gifts on the wall. The ones I'd done for display with the bows all curled into themselves using the sharp edge of the scissors. The *zip zip* sound it made. And it looked just like the way my mom did it. And then I thought of Marina sitting there in our boring house that was like all the others. How maybe she was being bored and not challenged, and that would lead to a hotbed of problems for her, and also, to tell the truth, I wanted to be somebody else, anybody else than my mom. Because she was smart and she was beautiful, but she was only ever a wife and a mom and an aider and abettor, she used to tell me to do whatever my father said, that my father was always right, and really he wasn't, he was not always right, and sometimes he was downright wrong and mean. Like he would put me in a closet and have me recite things on one leg and use me as an example.

So I left.

And what I think happened with Marina is that maybe it wasn't as bad as all the news says. Because like I say, she was a smart girl, a really, really smart girl. I'm not just saying all this—they took her IQ once, and it turned out she was too smart for her class, and they wanted her to skip a grade, but I thought that would be too hard with all the other girls and boys going on dates and being cool and her being behind, not in class but in her body—and socially—so I said no but I continued to test her at home when she came home from school. I continued to have her learn about other things. Outside things. Like memorize those police codes. And I would drill her every night. Yes, she was quick, so what I think is, I think she knew that this guy was a killer and I think she knew how to trap him, and I think she was tired of running. From me. She loved me so much, and she was so much like me that maybe she looked at herself in the mirror or felt that feeling I sometimes get when I can feel my ma inside. It's a scary thing when you try to run from something that is inside you. But I don't blame her. I don't blame her one bit. I know what that is like. But then she maybe found out what I found out. That you cannot outrun yourself. Like those people say in those meetings I was ordered to go to: wherever you go—there you are. And maybe that's when she decided she was gonna find and expose this Willie pig farmer killer guy. She knew it was him, and she knew she was special enough to get him to confess. Because that's my Reen, she is special. For a long time after she was taken from me, I let my broken heart be all that I was. I just lay in bed and cried, and I couldn't do anything. But then, it was like I told her, God has a plan. Recently I had a dream, I swear to you she came to me, she came to me and she took a lock of my hair and she patted it between her two hands like a hamburger patty, like she used to do when she was little. She told me, Ma, this sadness is weighing you down . . . it's in your eyes, you need to let it go. Then when I moved to wake up to reach for her, she shook her head no and said, Shhh . . . the princess is sleeping.

Mercy.

DEPARTURE

It's winter in Canada. Sabina and Alex are drinking warm cups of cocoa with marshmallows—the whipped cream kissing their noses. They have a Christmas tree and, perched on top, a bright silver star. They're wearing plush plaid robes, and Sabina pulls a freshly baked sheet of sugar cookies out of the oven. Alex meets her at the island in the kitchen, and they bump butts back and forth as they dance to some music using wooden spoons and mixer whisks as microphones. They are singing and jiggling and holding hands like this is every Christmas they never had. Their hearts are swollen with everything. Alex liked how Sabina treated her as an equal. She was an attentive listener and would share with her about the gardening she'd done or some recipe she'd attempted. She let Alex braid her hair and vulnerably leaned her head into Alex's stomach and hands, closed her eyes, and released any of the day's tension while Alex told her about some canary she rescued that morning or a particularly stunning actor on television, she gossiped and braided with the precision of a practiced stylist. Sabina talked about her girlhood and her mother's gentle but stern voice and cruel hair-heating instruments, and there was a mature ease about them. They had loved each other a long time.

And at night, Sabina held her close, and Alex sometimes whimpered, and they slept with the lights on the tree blinking across the ceiling, flashing love across their faces, and with the quiet mechanical noise of the ice-skating figurine sliding through Santa's village they had set up on the mantel. Two red plush stockings below it. One of them held a small knit hat—the dome of the hat adorned with pointed cat's ears.

Screeching cries of gulls—gulls with wide gunmetal-gray wings bobbed frantically above the Pickton farm on Dominion Avenue in Coquitlam. The property was cautioned off with yellow tape, the animals gone; the Machine, Willie's six-hundred-pound boar, held in a metal warehouse owned and operated by the Hells Angels, grunted and wheezed, harmless and confused, while tractors sifted through the forty acres. A collective sigh as body parts and bones were lifted out of the dirt, sometimes a finger or arm would snag on something and fall back into the ground. Not all the bodies made it to the rendering plant; some were left to the pigs. Half-decomposed thighs like soured hams, the bottom half of a leering smile. Smiling into the befouled earth.

And finally, my time. A line comes to me. I shimmy down, along the surface of this world. I try to focus on the moon in the dark sky. The world swells up around me, and once again the moon makes a diamond-shaped pattern across the floor, I ask the good Lord to help me shrink the world again, pat the farm with baboys and the shabu shabu and the sad girls back together; while I return to my safe dark place, there's howling along the way. I tinikling between the poles of light. They tap the ground twice and clap together once—*tap tap clap tap tap clap.* I see those beautiful bright lights beyond death's doorstep. They tinkle glitzy at the end of the tunnel. I'm pulled toward the light, I float toward it, this is ligaya, joy, happiness, everything around me bursts into a festival of colors. So maganda, there are no words for how pretty. Then finally I'm united with the chants of little girls with wings made of pillowcases and jasmine in their hair bam be bi bo bu.

Something had united Willie and Marina. It wasn't merely in where they came from but in where they were going and how they would get there.

Perhaps it came when Mutya Salles and Mary Margaret Pickton became careless mothers. Perhaps it came when Willie Pickton could not get it up with ladies he liked—ladies he thought of loving forever. Maybe it came in that small bathroom in Hawthorne, when Hassan tore into the tender parts of Marina and then after. After. Maybe it came when Corrin Young laughed at little Willie's willy. Maybe Marina did try to run from the parts of herself she didn't like, the parts she associated with Mutya, but in the end, those parts were the strongest parts. The parts made of lolas. And me. Because really, the reason was simple. That night I bit into him it was clear: I could see how closely their lives intertwined, how they were both shaped by the same kinds of hurts and disappointments. Even as children they thought their God allowed bad shit to happen.

That's true, that is absolutely true. God let bad shit happen. But the Goddess granted Marina and Willie a miracle of sorts. Because somehow what they all got, in the end, was what they'd hoped for all along—a kind of mercy.

CODA

According to the National Crime Information Center, to date, more than 5,800* Indigenous womxn, girls, and two-spirit persons throughout the United States and Canada have been reported as missing or murdered. This novel asks that we recognize those who have died, those who are still missing, those who have survived, and their beloved grievers.

We do not know the names of all those who have been taken or killed, but I would like to take this opportunity to bring attention to the #AmINext movement and the ongoing inequities by honoring the women whose lives were taken or likely taken by Willie Pickton:

Sereena Abotsway
Yvonne Marie Boen
Andrea Fay Borhaven
Heather Kathleen Bottomley
Heather Chinnook
Mary Ann Clark

* I hesitate to offer a number here because due to lack of research and resources, these numbers vary widely and there is a large data gap. Also, it's hard to determine what would constitute a substantial enough number, a right number of deaths, or a grievable number.

Wendy Crawford
Dawn Teresa Crey
Jane Doe
Tiffany Drew
Cara Louise Ellis aka Nicky Trimble
Cynthia Feliks
Marnie Lee Frey
Jennifer Lynn Furminger
Inga Monique Hall
Helen Mae Hallmark
Tanya Holyk
Sherry Irving
Angela Rebecca Jardine
Andrea Joesbury
Patricia Rose Johnson
Debra Lynne Jones
Kerry Koski
Jacqueline Michelle McDonell
Diana Melnick
Georgina Faith Papin
Dianne Rosemary Rock
Sarah de Vries
Mona Lee Wilson
Brenda Ann Wolfe

AUTHOR'S NOTE

This book is a work of fiction that contains economic and sexual violence that is inspired by all-too-real events.

While the specific characters and events are creations of my imagination, I have based the serial killer on a real person, Willie Pickton, and given my character his name. I have drawn from real events in Pickton's life to ground my narrative. For background about Pickton, I am indebted to the wonderfully thorough reporting of Stevie Cameron in her nonfiction book *On the Farm: Robert William Pickton and the Tragic Story of Vancouver's Missing Women*. Other works that were instrumental to my research were Malcolm Clarke's film *The Pig Farm*, Christine Welsh's film *Finding Dawn*, and Veronica Mannix's film *Through a Blue Lens*.

The language used in the holding cell between Pickton and the undercover cop, for example, is largely fictional, but the real-life scene upon which I drew can be viewed on YouTube.

I have also drawn from real events in creating my victims. Over the last several years, as part of my journalism and work on this book, I've increasingly focused on the stories and redacted case files of children who died while in Los Angeles County's child welfare system. I have unearthed names of children and the circumstances of their lives from behind darkened black blocks of state redaction. The redaction—a final inadequate attempt to protect the children who've already been failed by our foster care system. I have unwrinkled time in their files, unreversed the chronology. But the chaos remains—a loud, bright, brokenhearted hum slashing through the text—and this effort, and its limitations, have informed my narrative. Despite a majority of these children receiving multiple visits from Department of Children and Family Services social workers, the complaints in their cases were never escalated to a higher level of scrutiny. Conservative estimates indicate that almost two thousand infants and young children in the United States die from abuse or neglect by their parents or caretakers each year.* While my novel does not tell any of their specific stories, I believe it all too accurately reflects many of them.

* The Children's Bureau received data from fifty-one states (including Puerto Rico), from 2015 to 2019. Of those states, forty-five reported case-level data on 1,515 fatalities, and thirty-four reported aggregate data on 294 fatalities. https://www.childwelfare.gov/pubPDFs/fatality.pdf.

ACKNOWLEDGMENTS

To my agent, Ellen Levine, who flags when I've been gratuitous with "all the penises and secretions." I get a kick out of hearing you talk that way. For reals though, thank you so much for taking a chance on this spunky rascal. To my editor, Jenna Johnson, for all your patient feedback and giving *A Tiny Upward Shove* . . . well a ~~tiny upward~~ shove. All the editorial assistants who have offered valuable fresh eyeballs: Pilar Garcia-Brown, Sara Birmingham, and Lianna Culp. The late Dr. Ivan Strausz, for being such a neat secret ally. Susan VanHecke and Christine Paik, for seeing the commas when I did not. To Alexa Stark and Martha Wydysh, for all your grace in handling my calls and emails. Elisa Rivlin, for keeping my words legit.

All my early writing instructors at Antioch University, in particular Dana Johnson, my very first writing mentor. Thank you for believing in me, Antioch—and I hope you won't take it personally when I come to unionize your faculty. To my graduating class, the Citrons, whose weekly check-ins keep me keepin' on. In particular, Antonia Crane—thanks for making the mountains possible (all of them)—and Seth Fischer for all of it, publishing my first story ever and helping my words shine.

All the lovely people of Tin House—my incredibly attractive, slightly dysfunctional literary family. Especially Tony Le Tigre Perez, for saying the kindest shit and making my heart pitter-patter when I found myself, and my ego, pancake flat on the floor of an Extended Stay America after a devastating bout of rejections. Dana Spiotta, who said most generously that I was an accomplished writer. Reframing my world so it was the *words* on the paper and the sensations that arise in the reader that was the accomplishment and not the notoriety of the writer. Matthew Specktor, whose spirit and sheer talent and humility make me sometimes feel like the good people are winning. Speaking of good people winning, Cheryl Strayed for offering sugar even before there was a Sugar. Isaac Fitzgerald, Julie Greicius, Roxane Gay, for shifting the literary landscape with *The Rumpus*, and for giving me a community and a place where I could unload when the revolution raging inside of me was too much to handle.

To the graduate summer Iowa Writers' Workshop, my instructor, Amber Dermont, and my buddy supreme, Kyle Minor, and my oatmeal roommate, Dini Parayitam, both of whom I think witnessed and inspired this essayist's transformation into a novelist. All the beautiful generous novelists before me, who made the possible possible.

Lauren Groff, when I think of you, I think of that scene in *The Breakfast Club* when Molly Ringwald is giving Ally Sheedy a makeover and Ally Sheedy asks Molly Ringwald, "Why are you being so nice to me?" and Molly Ringwald says, "Because you're letting me." And fuck—you are so fucking nice to me and you're such a star in my eyes. Half my dreams came true when I met you. The other half came true when I met my honeybee tocayo Melissa Febos . . . thank you for keeping the lights on. My Pilipinx literary fam . . . Gina Apostol, Laurel Fantauzzo, Melissa Sipin, Lara Stapleton, M. Evelina Galang, Nita Noveno, Daryll Delgado. Ate Josefina Quiambao, thank you for helping me translate all these dirty words. Faith Santilla—girlfriend, I can't even start with you hukilau.

To the Aspen Summer Words Writers Conference, especially the late George Hodgman, thank you for creating a space safe enough to cry in. Who knew I'd been holding it in all that time? My fellow workshoppers at Bread Loaf, for your insight and feedback. My instructor Danzy Senna, I felt so much like I already knew you, my fellow Jim Gavin, and my neat roommate Kira Procter, thanks for getting me inspired to launch the next thing while I was waiting for this book to get out into the world.

My Hedgebrook sisters, Joshunda Sanders, Anna Vodicka, Ruby Hansen, Ladee Hubbard, Dr. Kimberlé Crenshaw—the yummy food, building fires, the laughter.

Writing Workshops Los Angeles, and Edan Lepucki, for forcing me to answer those haunting first-draft questions. Steve Almond, I cannot believe I am finally writing this sentence. This whole section belongs to you. In real life when I'm in pain, a pain that is larger than the actual circumstances, I ask myself what the original wound is. You have such a talent for finding the original wound of my characters. Because you're honest, or more importantly you are interested in the truth. I don't think I can find any greater quality in a writer than that. Time and time again you've done me the great service of calling bullshit on me, and I know that this truth on the page is a compulsion of yours so I don't take it personally and really that's the most one can ever ask for.

My ragtag writing group, J. Ryan Stradal, Cecil Castellucci, Chris Terry, Sacha Howells, thanks so much for pulling together such a rapid-response team when I was so anxious about these words. Speaking of rapid response, Tisha Reichle-Aguilera, I'm so lucky to have had you step before me in these spaces, what a great literary citizen and smart generous colleague you are. You've read so many versions. And my other Trojan readers, thank you so much, Cameron Lange, Brian Lin, Leesa Fenderson, Khaliah Reed, your feedback came at just the right time.

To all the literary stewards at PEN America, thanks for creating a space that I'd only dreamt of as a child. The Service Employees International Union, for your tireless efforts and allowing me to participate in fighting for the rights of working families everywhere. The janitorial workers, hospital workers, and security officers I've had the great honor of representing—forever thank you for keeping us all safe.

Women Who Submit, for motivating me and inspiring women everywhere to continue to submit to journals—the world needs women's words. Amelia Gray, neighbor, lifesaver, social arsonist, friend friend—who but you is thoughtful enough to offer a silk pillowcase . . . I mean really—I miss you too much.

To the generous faculty at USC, Dana Johnson (yes twice!), Danzy Senna, David Treuer, Karen Tongson, Percival Everett, Aimee Bender, Geoff Dyer, Viet Nguyen, and my brilliant advisor, Maggie Nelson—thank you also, David St. John, for believing in me, and please don't take it personally when I come and unionize all the graduate student workers. Graduate Student Workers Organizing Committee—let's turn se puede into Podemos.

My Serenity Team, Danny Mulia, Linda Santiman, Stephen Roseberry, Moore Rhys, Celine Alvarez, Christina Soletti, Mataji Booker, Anna Joy Springer, thanks for making my world big. My Saturday night team who got us through a pandemic of Saturday nights, I love the shit out of you and thanks for loving me when I couldn't love myself. Speaking pandemic survival, Debbie Weingarten, for politicking and Pelotoning, and MAFSing, you are the best.

To my birth mother, Maria, who gave me whimsy and a love for language, taught me how to kick guys where it counts, and how to sharpen a pencil with a knife.

To all the people I have been blessed to call my family. Thank you for generously opening your hearts and home to me when I was scared and had nowhere to go. That's the Clintons, Kathy, Stephanie, Chris, I love you for all eternity. The Crispi family, David, Diana, Elisa, Illana (little Henry and Lev), thank you for your encouragement, for safety and love and acceptance. The Stranger, Vlieger, Camilleri clan, Sue, John, Gino, Cory, Danielle, Sam, Marissa, Cameron (did I forget anyone?)—what a long strange journey it's been. God, Sue, do you remember when I showed up at your home with my jeans sagging on my hips and big sweatshirts and my smoking, and yet you let me in, you gave me a family and all those empty journals, year after year after year.

And of course, The One, my first reader, Jaimie Sarra, whenever you're around, I'm the luckiest girl in the world. Thank you for loving me so good.

A Note About the Author

Melissa Chadburn's writing has appeared in the *Los Angeles Times, The New York Times Book Review, The New York Review of Books, The Paris Review Daily, The Best American Food Writing,* and many other publications. Her extensive reporting on the child welfare system appears in the Netflix docuseries *The Trials of Gabriel Fernandez.* Chadburn is a worker lover and through her own labor and literary citizenship strives to upend economic violence. Her mother taught her how to sharpen a pencil with a knife and she's basically been doing that ever since. She is a PhD candidate in creative writing at the University of Southern California and lives in greater Los Angeles.